JILLIAN HART
Heaven Sent
&
His Hometown Girl

Steeple Hill®

Published by Steeple Hill Books™

STEEPLE HILL BOOKS

Steeple Hill®

ISBN-13: 978-0-373-65119-1
ISBN-10:   0-373-65119-8

HEAVEN SENT AND HIS HOMETOWN GIRL

HEAVEN SENT
Copyright © 2001 by Jillian Strickler

HIS HOMETOWN GIRL
Copyright © 2002 by Jillian Strickler

www.SteepleHill.com

Printed in U.S.A.

CONTENTS

Books by Jillian Hart

Love Inspired

Love Inspired Historical

Heaven Sent #143
*His Hometown Girl #180
*A Love Worth
   Waiting For* #203
Heaven Knows #212
*The Sweetest Gift #243
*Heart and Soul #251
*Almost Heaven #260
*Holiday Homecoming #272
*Sweet Blessings #295
For the Twins' Sake #308
*Heaven's Touch #315
*Blessed Vows #327
*A Handful of Heaven #335
*A Soldier for Christmas #367
*Precious Blessings #383
*Every Kind of Heaven #387
*Everyday Blessings #400
*A McKaslin Homecoming #403
**A Holiday to Remember #425

Homespun Bride #2

*The McKaslin Clan
**A Tiny Blessings Tale

JILLIAN HART

makes her home in Washington State, where she has lived most of her life. When Jillian is not hard at work on her next story, she loves to read, go to lunch with her friends and spend quiet evenings with her family.

HEAVEN SENT

You can make many plans,
but the Lord's purpose will prevail.

—Proverbs 19:21

Chapter One

Hope Ashton leaned her forehead against the wet edge of the lifted hood and tried not to give in to a growing sense of defeat. Her brand-new rental Jeep was dead, and she was stranded miles from nowhere in the middle of a mean Montana storm. Strong north winds drove cold spikes of rain through her T-shirt and jeans and she shivered, wet to the skin.

How was she going to get to her grandmother now?

Just get back inside the Jeep and think this through. There was nothing else she could do. Hope took a step in the dark and felt her left foot sink into water. Cold sticky mud seeped through the thin canvas mesh all the way up to her top lace. She jumped back, only to sink up to her right ankle in a different puddle.

Great. Just great. But hadn't her life been one obstacle after another since she'd received the call about her grandmother's fall? It was emotion, that's all. Frantic worry had consumed her as she'd tried to book a flight across the Atlantic.

She'd come too far to lose heart now—Nanna was only a few miles away. God had granted Hope two good legs. She would simply walk. A little rain and wind wouldn't hurt her.

Lightning cut through the night, so bright it seared her eyes. Thunder pealed with an earsplitting ring. Directly overhead.

Okay, maybe she wouldn't start out just yet. She ached to be near Nanna's side, to comfort her, to see with her own eyes how the dear old woman was doing, but getting struck by lightning wasn't on her to-do list for the night. Hope eased around the side of the Jeep, resigning herself to the cold puddles, and into her vehicle.

Warmth from the heater still lingered, and it drove away some of the chill from her bones. As lightning arced across the black sky and rain pelted like falling rocks against her windshield, she tried the cell phone one more time on the chance it was working. It wasn't.

The electrical storm wouldn't last long, right? She tried to comfort herself with that thought as the wind hit the Jeep broadside and shook it like an angry bull on the rampage. Shadowed by the flashes of lightning, a tall grove of trees rocked like furious giants in the dark.

Okay, she was getting a little scared. She was safe in the Jeep. The Lord would keep her safe. She'd just lived too long in cities and had only spent a year of high school here in Montana, on these high lonely plains.

Round lights flashed through the dark behind her,

and she dropped the phone. Rain drummed hard against the windshield so she couldn't see anything more of the approaching vehicle. Twin headlights floated closer on the unlit two-lane road, and she felt a little too alone and vulnerable.

Maybe whoever it was would just keep going, she prayed, but of course, the lights slowed and, through the rain sluicing down her side window, she could see the vehicle ease to a stop on the road beside her. Her heart dropped as his passenger window slid downward, revealing a man's face through the dark sheets of rain.

She eased her window down a crack.

"Got trouble?" he asked. "I'd be happy to give you a lift into town."

"No, thanks. Really, I'm fine."

"Sure about that?" His door opened.

Years of living on her own in big cities had fine-tuned her sense of self-preservation. Habit called out to her to roll up her window and lock her doors. But instinct kept her from it. For some reason she didn't feel in danger.

"Don't be afraid, I don't bite." He hopped out into the road, stopping right there in the only westbound lane. "If you don't mind, let me take a look at your engine first. Maybe I can get you going again."

Relief spilled through her. "Thanks."

Through the slant of the headlights, she could see the lower half of his jeans and the leather boots he wore, comfortable and scuffed. He approached with an easy stride, not a predatory one, but she couldn't see more of him in the darkness, and he disappeared behind the Jeep's raised hood.

Maybe it was something easily fixed. Maybe this man with a voice as warm as melted chocolate was a guardian angel in disguise.

Then his boots sloshed to a stop right beside her. "Hope Ashton, is that you? I can't believe you'd step foot in this part of Montana again."

And then she recognized something in his voice, something from a life that felt long past. When she was a millionaire's daughter from the city lost in a high school full of modest Montana bred kids. She searched her memory. "Matthew Sheridan?"

"You remember me." His voice caressed the words, as rich and resonant as a hymn. "Good, then maybe you'll stop looking as if you expect me to rob you. You've got a busted fan belt. C'mon, I'll give you a lift."

"I'm not sure—"

"This time of night you'll be lucky to see another car. Lower your pride a notch. Unless you think being seen with me will ruin your reputation."

She winced, remembering with a pang of shame the prideful schoolgirl she'd once been. "My reputation has survived worse than accepting help from an old friend."

"We were never old friends, Hope."

"You're not one to sugarcoat the past, is that it?"

"Something like that." Lightning broke through the dark, flashing bright enough for her to see. He appeared taller, his shoulders had broadened, and his chest and arms looked iron strong.

"That was too close for comfort," he said above the

crash of thunder. "Let me grab your bags and we'll get you to your grandmother's."

"I can manage on my own." She hopped out, and wind and rain slammed into her. She wrestled with the back door, but a strong arm brushed hers.

"All three bags?" he asked as if he hadn't heard her, his breath warm against the back of her neck.

She trembled and nodded. Words seemed to stick in her throat. It was the cold weather, that was all. That had to be the reason her heart sputtered in her chest.

"You're shivering. I'll come back for the bags. Let's get you inside the truck where it's good and warm." One strong, warm hand curled around her elbow, seeing her safely through the slick mud at her feet.

His behavior and his kindness surprised her so much, she didn't even argue. "You're a gentleman, Matthew Sheridan. I won't forget it."

He chuckled, warm and deep. "I do what I can. Hop up."

The warm interior of his pickup wrapped around her like a hug. She settled onto the seat, dripping rain all over his interior. The dome light overhead cast just enough of a glow to see the rolled up bag of cookies at her feet.

Matthew reached past her and flicked the fan on high. "There should be a blanket behind your seat. Just sit back and take it easy. I'll be right in."

He shut her door, and the cab light winked off. Rain pummeled the roof overhead, and she saw the faint shadows of tall trees waving angrily in the gusty wind. Lightning blazed, thunder answered. She found the blanket behind the seat, just as Matthew said, and noticed three empty car seats in the back seat of the extended cab.

Funny, how life changed. It seemed everyone she knew was married with children and, while she wished them happiness, she certainly didn't believe that marriage could bring happiness. She felt colder and snuggled into the soft thermal cotton blanket that smelled of fabric softener and chocolate chip cookies.

The driver's door snapped open and the dome light illuminated Matthew's profile. Strong, straight, handsome. He'd grown into a fine-looking man. He stowed her luggage, then joined her in the cab and slammed the door against the bitter storm.

"I'll give Zach at the garage a call first thing in the morning." Matthew didn't look at her as he slid the gearshift into second.

Her teeth clacked in answer, and she snuggled deeper into the blanket. The blast of the truck's heat fanned hot air against her, but she couldn't stop shaking.

"I heard about your grandmother's fall. I bet seeing you will cheer her up some."

"I hope so." Her fingers curled around her purse strap. "I plan to stay as long as she needs me."

"Is that so?" He quirked one brow. "I heard you've never been back to visit her."

"How do you know?" His question set her on edge, as if she didn't love her grandmother. As if all the times she'd flown Nanna out to California for every holiday didn't count. Or the vacation they went on every year.

"You didn't show up for the ten-year reunion. Everybody talked about it."

"They did?" Except for a few close friends she'd made, she hadn't even thought of the small town where she'd spent one year of her teenage life. But it had been a pivotal year for her, emotionally and spiritually. "I got an invitation, but I was—"

"In Venice," he finished with a lopsided grin. "I heard that, too."

"I was working."

"On a new book. I know." He slowed down as a pronghorn antelope leaped across the road.

"Look at that." Hope's chest caught. The fragile animal flew through the air with grace and speed. The light sheened on the antelope's white flanks and tan markings. In a flash, it was gone, leaving only the dark road behind.

"I've seen thousands of them, but it takes my breath away every time." Matthew's grin was genuine, and for a moment it felt as if they'd touched.

As if they were no longer practically strangers and all the differences in their lives and in their experiences had vanished. She saw his loneliness and shadows.

Then she tore her gaze from his. She was being foolish, really. She and Matthew Sheridan had nothing in common—the three car seats in the back were proof of that.

Silence settled between them as he drove, and she welcomed it. The loneliness she'd witnessed in Matthew's eyes troubled her. Maybe because she didn't want to be reminded of the loneliness in her life, a loneliness that had no solution. She didn't want love, she didn't want marriage. She didn't even want to feel her heart flicker once in the presence of a handsome man.

She was surviving just fine on her own. God was in her corner, and that was enough. Even on the loneliest of nights.

"Thanks for the ride, Matthew." Her fingers fumbled for the door handle in the near dark. "I know you had to go out of your way."

"Not too far. And it's always my pleasure to help out one of Manhattan, Montana's most esteemed citizens. Or ex-citizens." His gaze didn't meet hers as he hopped out of the truck.

Maybe he'd felt the same way as she did, that when their gazes had met, she'd seen something far too personal. Her feet hit the muddy ground. "Matthew?"

He didn't look up as he tugged out her carry-on, heavy with her computer and camera equipment, and two suitcases. "Go on ahead, get out of this rain. I'll bring your things."

"That's not right." She eased around to take her baggage, but Matthew's grip remained firm on the leather handles. "You've done enough. I'm more than capable of carrying my own bags."

"I'll let you know when I've had enough." As if insulted, he shouldered past her. "I was raised to look after stranded women in distress."

"I've been taking care of myself for a long time."

"I'm sure you have." Matthew set the bags down on

the front porch next to the neatly painted swing and pulled back the squeaky screen door.

She'd forgotten how macho and strong men were in Montana. Plus, she figured she was right. She'd seen loneliness in his eyes, a loneliness they might have in common, and that bothered her.

His wide knuckles rapped on the wood frame. "I'll get a hold of Zach at first light."

"Matthew, you've done more than enough. You haven't seen me since high school and—"

"It's just the way I'm made, Hope. Or should I say Miss Ashton?" He tipped his Stetson and backed down the steps and into the darkness, distant but kind. "Give my best to your grandmother."

She opened her mouth, but the words fumbled on her tongue. She didn't know what to say to make things right between them. He'd gone out of his way to help her, as one good neighbor helps another, and instead of recognizing that, she'd put up the same old defenses.

Some lessons in life were hard to let go of, no matter how much she prayed.

She heard Matthew's truck pull away. Red taillights glowed in the black sheets of rain plummeting from sky to earth. She would have to find a way to make things right, to thank him for helping her when he didn't have to.

The door squeaked open, and a woman in a teal tunic and slacks smiled at her. "You must be Nora's granddaughter. Goodness, she's been talking of nothing else all day. Come in, dear. Heavens, but you're soaked clear through to the skin."

"My Jeep broke down and stranded me."

"No!" The nurse looked stricken. "And on a night like this. Haven't seen a storm as bad as this in some time. Was that Matthew Sheridan's truck I saw driving away?"

"He took pity on me and gave me a ride."

"Matthew's a good man. Shame about his wife, though. Let's get you inside and out of those wet clothes, shall we? My name's Roberta—" She made a move to grab the carry-on bag.

Hope managed to get there first, hauling all three pieces into the living room. The nurse had enough work to do without waiting on Hope, too.

"Dear, you're soaked clear through to the skin," Roberta fussed. "Let me draw a bath for you—"

"Thank you, but no." Only one thing—one person—mattered. "How's Nanna?"

"She's been having trouble sleeping."

"Because she was waiting up for me? I called her after supper and told her not to—"

"Why, she can't wait to see you. You and your brother are the only real family she has left." Roberta bustled into the kitchen, flipping on lights as she went. "As I see it, she's got the right to worry about you traveling all the way from Italy on your own. And besides, it's given her something else to think about besides the pain."

Hope's stomach fluttered. She hated the thought of her sweet Nanna suffering. "Is she awake?"

"I'm sure she is. Go on up. Do you want to take this to her?"

Hope took the prepared tea tray, thanking the nurse

who'd gone to the trouble, and headed upstairs. She knew each step and knew which stair creaked. Memories flooded back, filling her heart, warming her from the inside out.

Some memories weren't filled with hurt. Like the year she'd spent with Nanna when her parents were divorcing.

As she climbed into the second story, the smell of dried roses, lavender and honeysuckle tickled her nose, just as it had so many years ago.

"Hope? Is that you?" Nanna's voice trilled like a morning lark, joyful and filled with melody. "Heavens, I've worried about you, child. Do you know what time it is?"

"I told you not to expect me until morning." Hope breezed into the room, unchanged from memory with the lace curtains shimmering like new ivory at the windows, the antiques polished to a shine and the wedding ring quilt draped across the carved, four-poster bed. Just like always.

But the woman beneath the covers was fragile and old, changed from the sprightly grandmother Hope remembered.

Deep affection welled in her heart, and she set the silver tray on the cedar chest at the foot of the bed. "Nanna, it's good to see you."

"Come give me a hug."

Hope bent at the waist, lightly folding her arms around the frail woman. Nanna felt delicate and not tough and robust like she'd been at Christmas, less than four months ago. "You smell like honeysuckle."

"One of my favorites. You should have seen last summer's garden! Goodness, the sachets and things Helen and I made. We were busy bees. Why, we had the entire basement filled from floor to rafter with drying flowers." Nanna's eyes warmed with the happy memory, and she patted the bed beside her. "Dear heart, it's good to see you, but you're thinner."

"Been busy." Hope sat on the edge of the mattress.

"Too busy to eat? You work too much. What is it with young girls these days? You should eat, enjoy life, indulge a little."

"Is that what you do, Nanna?"

"Why, it's one of the secrets to a happy life." Trouble twinkled in dark eyes. "I saw your last book. It's absolutely beautiful. Not everyone has the God given talent to take pictures the way you do."

"I'm glad you like it." Hope watched her grandmother's weathered hands lift the hardcover book from the nightstand. "I worked hard on it."

"Love always shows." Nanna's fingers traced her name on the cover, in gold. "It's good work that you do, using your pictures to remind us all the beauty God gives us in each and every day. But work isn't everything in life, remember that."

"You've told me that about a billion times." Trying to avoid a well-worn subject, Hope pressed a kiss to her grandmother's cheek. "You get your rest. We have all tomorrow to talk."

"And what a fine day it will be because you've come home." Nanna returned the kiss. Her fingers held tight and would not let go. "I've missed my Hope."

"Not half as much as I've missed you." A love so sharp it hurt edged into her heart. Hope didn't move away, not until after Grandmother sipped her chamomile tea, whispered her prayers and closed her eyes. Not until sleep claimed Nanna and she was lost in dreams of happier times.

Hope sat in the dark for a long while and watched Nanna sleep. The lightning returned. Rain beat against the window and drummed on the roof, but they were safe from the storm and never alone.

Chapter Two

Hope Ashton. Matthew couldn't get her out of his mind. Not when he'd gone to sleep and not now that the first pink light of morning was teasing the darkness from the sky.

He hadn't recognized her at first glance. She'd softened, grown taller, changed from girl to woman. But that graceful elegance was still there in the fall of her dark hair, in the rich timbre of her alto voice and in every lithe, careful movement she made.

The phone rang, and he turned from the kitchen sink, nearly tripping over a little boy who wasn't quite as tall as his knee. "Whoa, there, Josh. Look where you're going."

The little boy tilted his head all the way back. "Goin' to Gramma's?"

"Almost." He wove around an identical little boy. "Ian, stop eyeing the cookie jar."

"I still hungry, Daddy."

"Hungry? You ate four whole pancakes." He ruffled

the boy's dark hair and intentionally turned him away from the counter as the phone continued to ring.

He dodged another identical little boy and snatched up the receiver.

"Matthew? I got your message." It was Zach from the garage. "Got the belt you asked for right here. What happened? That truck of yours leave you stranded?"

"You wish."

"Hey, I'm thinking of my profits," the only mechanic in town teased.

"Nothing like that. I came across Hope Ashton last night, broke down in the middle of that storm. You remember her, don't you?"

There was a moment of silence, then Zach gasped. "Tall, slender, pretty. Nora's granddaughter. Sure, I remember. Is she back in town? Why don't I run the belt out to the Greenley place—"

"Her Jeep's broken down on the highway south of town."

"Then I'll warm up the tow truck and bring it in."

"You can't miss it. Bright red, brand-new model about four miles out." Matthew felt his stomach tighten, as if he didn't like the idea of Zach giving Hope a hand and he couldn't explain why. Maybe it was his conscience.

Sure, the woman troubled him, stirred up all sorts of emotions. He knew he was out of her league— which wasn't why he wanted to help. It didn't sit right backing away now. He liked to see things to the end.

Matthew heard silence and peeked around the

doorway into the kitchen. "Ian, stay away from the counter. Go put on your shoes like your brothers."

The little urchin hesitated, tossed him an innocent grin, then dashed away to join his brothers at the table. Matthew headed down the center hallway and to the front door, careful to keep an eye and an ear on his sons.

"Hope Ashton, huh?" Zach laughed at that. "It'll be something to see her again. I bet she's still a knockout."

"Yep." She was pretty, all right. Model-good looks but there was a girl-next-door freshness to her. A freshness he didn't remember seeing in the unhappy rich girl he'd gone to school with.

Matthew ended the call, checked on the three boys busily pulling on shoes in the corner of the kitchen and went in search of his work boots. He sat down on the bottom step to tug them on.

Morning was his favorite time as the sun rose, so bold and bright. The world was waking up, the birds' songs brand-new and the breeze as soft as a whisper. Peace filled him for a moment, and then he heard a loud crash coming from directly behind him—the kitchen.

That was his two seconds of peace for the day. He took off at a dead run. Six strides took him into the kitchen where he saw his three sons standing in a half circle.

"Josh did it, Daddy!" Kale pointed. "He climbed up on the chair and dropped the cookies."

"They smashed all over the floor!" Ian looked pleased.

Josh's head was bowed, his hands clasped together as he whispered a prayer.

Matthew saw the shattered cookies and stoneware littered all over the clean floor and the pitcher of grape juice at Ian's feet. The refrigerator door stood open and a chair from the table was butted up against the cabinets. He remembered to count to ten.

"We got real hungry." Ian rubbed at a juice stain on his crisp white T-shirt.

"Real hungry," Kale added.

Josh took one look at the floor and bowed his head again. "The cookie jar's still broken, God."

Since he was short on time, Matthew decided to ignore for now the purple stains splattered on his kitchen floor, nudged the refrigerator door shut and grabbed the broom from the corner. "You boys step back. Careful of those sharp pieces."

"Daddy, it's all Josh's fault." Ian tugged on Matthew's jeans, transferring the grape juice from those little fingers onto the clean denim above Matthew's knee.

"Somehow I doubt Josh did this all by himself." He laid his hand against the flat of Ian's back and eased him away from the broken stoneware shards. "Any owies I should know about?"

"There ain't no blood nowhere," Ian announced.

But there *was* grape juice spattered all over the little boy who'd obviously been the one to try to heft the full pitcher from the refrigerator shelf and failed.

One thing was clear. He couldn't go on like this. He needed a new housekeeper or he'd never get off to work on time. "Into the truck. C'mon. Step around the mess, Ian."

"Sorry, Daddy." The oldest triplet looked angelic as he stopped his sneaker in midair, about to crunch right through the cookies and shattered pottery.

He caught Ian by the shoulder, Kale by the arm and was grateful for Josh who clambered after them, muttering an amen to end his prayer. The mess would wait. The boys would have to change at Mom's.

Lord knew, this was all a balancing act. Every morning wasn't as bad as this, but then he was used to having a housekeeper. With three three-year-olds, it made a big difference having another adult to run interference.

Matthew locked the door and herded the boys toward the black pickup in the gravel drive. He opened the door, and the scent of Hope Ashton's perfume—light and pretty—lingered, a faint reminder that she'd sat beside him on the ride to town. Longing swept through him. Not for Hope, but for a woman gone from his life forever.

It had been over two long years since he'd smelled the pleasing gentleness of a woman's perfume in his truck. Two years had passed since he'd buried Kathy, and he still wasn't over his grief.

And how could he? There would never be another woman who would make his heart brighter, his life better.

Kathy had been his once-in-a-lifetime, a gift of love that a man was lucky to know at all. Something that miraculous didn't happen twice.

It just didn't.

Chest tight, he buckled Josh into the remaining car seat and hopped into the cab.

"I'm so glad I have the committee meeting today," Nanna announced as the new day's sun tossed a cheerful pattern across the quilt. "I'll take any excuse I can to get out of this house."

"I thought you were supposed to be on bed rest. How are we going to get you to town if your doctor's orders are to keep you right here?" Hope slid open the closet door.

"We could always drive. It's easier than hobbling. I'm still not used to those crutches."

"Very funny." Hope pulled out a blue summer dress. "This would look nice. Before I take you anywhere, I'm checking with your doctor."

"You worry too much, and I want the yellow dress. The flirty one."

"Flirty? You're in your sixties. You shouldn't be flirting."

"That's what you think." Nanna's chuckle was a merry one. "Howard Renton joined the planning committee last month. Both Sadie and Helen made fools of themselves fighting to sit next to him. But I think I won him with my charm."

"Wear the yellow but don't flirt. Too much." Hope laid the cheerful sundress on the foot of the bed. "Isn't that what you used to tell me?"

"Hope, you're twenty-nine years old. You're *supposed* to be flirting."

"I'm supposed to, huh? Is there some unwritten law or something?"

"Go ahead and pretend you don't know what I'm talking about. You're going to let the best years of your life slip away alone without a man to love you."

"I didn't fly all the way from Rome and drive down from the closest airport through a terrible storm to hear that kind of advice."

"Well, then what kind do you want to hear?"

"The kind that doesn't have anything to do with getting me married off." Hope unzipped the dress and lifted it from the hanger. "'God gives to some the gift of marriage, and to others he gives the gift of singleness.'"

"'And the Lord God said, "It is not good for the man to be alone. I will make a companion who will help him.""' Nanna lifted her arms as Hope slipped the dress over her head. "It's not good for a woman to be alone, either."

"So, the person who marries does well, and the person who doesn't marry does even better." Hope smoothed the dress over her grandmother's back. "I think I've proven my point."

"You've proven nothing. Love is one of God's greatest gifts. Don't let your life pass you by without knowing it." Nanna's hand brushed hers with warmth. "Goodness, this dress makes me feel young. Fix my hair for me."

"Do you want it up or down?"

Nanna squinted into the mirror against the far wall. "Down."

Hope reached for the brush and started working. "Tell me more about this man you and your friends are fighting over."

"He's moved back to town after being away for what, nearly twenty years. He wanted to be close to what remains of his family. Sad, it is. You didn't hear about the tragedy, did you? Lost his son, daughter-in-law and two of his grandchildren in a small plane crash a few years back. In fact, one of the grandchildren was Matthew Sheridan's wife."

The brush slipped from her fingers. "I didn't know."

"Lucky thing, one of the boys got sick right before the plane took off, so she left the children with Matthew. He was devastated. It shook all of us to the core, I tell you. We lost a lot of friends that day."

Matthew lost his wife and the mother of his children. Her chest tightened. She remembered how he'd seen her safely home last night. And remembered the loneliness in his eyes. "It's strange to be here after being gone for so many years. All the people I know are much older now. So much has happened to them."

"And your classmates grown up and married." Nanna's eyes sparkled. "Everyone except you."

"Surely not *everyone's* married. There has to be a few people in this town as smart as I am." She winked at Nanna's reflection in the big, beveled mirror.

"You mean as *misguided.* I think your old friend Karen McKaslin isn't married yet. Now, don't get your hopes up. Her wedding is scheduled for sometime this fall."

"A mistake." Hope shook her head. "I'll have to give her a call and see if I can't wisen her up."

Nanna laughed. "Tease all you want. You never know when the lovebug will bite."

"Lovebug?" Hope reached for a headband on the edge of the nightstand. "If love is a bug, then all I need is a good can of pesticide."

"Really, Hope. You're impossible." Nanna's hand caught hers, warm and accepting, as always. "And no, I won't change your mind. I'll let God do that."

"What's He gonna do? Send a lovebug?"

"You never know. There are a few handsome men in this town looking for the right woman to share their lives with."

"Oh, there are men, all right, but I don't think marriage is what they're looking for."

"Then you've been living in all the wrong places." Nanna winked, then caught her reflection in the mirror. "Oh, Hope. Why, this is wonderful. I hardly recognize myself."

"You look beautiful, Nanna." Hope brushed her hand gently over a few stray wisps, guiding them into place. "What do you want for breakfast?"

"My day nurse Kirby is taking care of that."

"Well, she has enough to do taking care of you."

"Yes, but the real question is, can you cook?" Nanna looked terribly skeptical. "I know how you live, always traveling—"

"That's because I'm always working."

"If you had a husband and a family, you would have more to do with your time than work." Nanna pressed a kiss to Hope's cheek, one of comfort and love. "Go ahead, make breakfast. I'm a brave woman with good digestion."

"I'm not going to poison you."

"And be careful of the sink handle. It's been leaking something fierce. And that right front stove burner is wobbly. I mean to talk to someone in town about it today."

"Have a little faith, Nanna. I'm all grown up. I think I can figure out a faucet handle and an ancient stove."

"'Pride goes before destruction, and haughtiness before a fall.'"

"Relax." Hope helped Nanna lean back into her pillows, then reached for the quilt to cover her. "I'm not going to burn down the kitchen."

"You almost did once, you know."

"I was seventeen years old." Hope pressed a kiss to Nanna's brow. How fast time passed. And it was passing faster every day. "You get some rest, and I'll be right back with some scrambled eggs."

"Now this I have to see," Nanna mused.

Hope pulled the door closed and hurried downstairs, her heart heavy. Nanna was wrong, she didn't need the pain of marriage. She'd watched her parents up close and personal, and she'd sworn never to live like that. Ever.

Even now, remembering, her stomach tensed and she laid her hand there. The ulcer still bothered her from time to time. Usually whenever she thought about her family.

Yes, singleness was one gift from the Lord she intended to cherish for the rest of her life.

* * *

"Matthew, you *have* to take my place on the Founder's Days planning committee. I can't do everything." Matthew's mother herded three little boys into her living room. Building blocks clattered and sounds of glee filled the air. "I don't mind keeping the triplets over the summer, you know that. But these three are a lot to keep up to. You're going to have to do some things for me."

"The committee meetings are during the day, and you know I can't take off work. I've got a roof to put on the McKaslins' hay barn—"

"You can work it out. You're self-employed." Mom pressed a kiss to his cheek. "Tell you what, I'll sweeten the deal. I'll keep the boys past supper every night if you'll take over this one tiny, little obligation for me."

"I'm a carpenter. I don't know the first thing about committees."

"Nonsense, a smart man like you. The meeting is this morning, from ten-thirty to eleven-thirty at Karen's little coffee shop. Oh, those boys are a busy bunch, aren't they?" Mom took off at a run. "Ian, don't climb up the fireplace. No, not even if you're a fireman."

There was a twinkle in her eye. The planning committee, as far as he knew, consisted of the town's oldest citizens.

If Mom wasn't playing matchmaker, she was still up to something. If only he knew what.

Manhattan, Montana crept into sight around the last bend. Hope hadn't seen this place since she was seventeen. Last night, when she'd driven through with Matthew, it had been dark and late, the streets deserted.

In the light of day, she saw that much was different from what she remembered. Businesses had changed hands, new stores had come in, but the character and the small-town feel remained.

It was the closest thing to home she'd known in her entire life.

"It's good to be back, isn't it?" Why did Nanna sound triumphant? "I always knew you belonged here, Hope, and not in your parents' world."

"What does that mean, exactly?" Hope braked as an elderly man jaywalked leisurely across the wide, two-lane street.

"It means you're the kind of person who needs roots, like me. To plant them deep and watch your life grow." Nanna tapped her fingers against the dash. "Turn here. Right there in front of the blue shop."

Hope eased Nanna's old sedan into a parking spot. The hand-painted sign on the row of shops read Field of Beans. "I'm not a tree. I don't have roots."

"You know darn well what I mean, you're being stubborn." Nanna opened her door. "Kirby, dear, bring those crutches. I can handle the steps by myself."

Hope saw the nurse's exasperated look in the rearview. "Don't tell me she's always like this?"

"Usually she's worse." The young nurse hopped out of the car, hurrying to help.

Hope listened to her grandmother issue orders to Kirby as she situated the crutches beneath her arms. Nanna might be injured, but her spirit remained unscathed. Hope stepped out into the fresh spring morning to lend Kirby a hand.

Already the sun was hot, and dust mixed in the air. She smelled freshly ground coffee and baking muffins. "Nanna, is there anything you want from the store?"

"Oh, no, you don't." Nanna wobbled to a stop. "You're coming to the meeting with me. You can do your errands-running later."

"But you have Kirby—"

"Kirby has to go fill some prescriptions for me."

"I have to run over to Zach's garage and rescue my Jeep. Then I have to grocery shop." Hope took hold of her grandmother's fragile elbow. "Don't worry, I'll help Kirby get you inside—"

"Look, there's Matthew Sheridan crossing the street." Nanna took a stronger step. "It looks like he's heading for Karen's coffee place, too. Good. I've been needing to speak with him."

"What you need to do is concentrate or you're going to fall off those things. Maybe we should get the wheelchair from the trunk—"

"Don't you dare. There's only three stairs, and I'm starting to get the hang of these crutches." Nanna hobbled forward, then stopped in the middle of the first board step. "Why, Matthew. The man I've been looking for."

"Me?" He strolled to a stop on the sidewalk above, his face shaded by the brim of his Stetson. "Nora Greenley. I can't believe you're up and around."

"It's hard to keep an old warhorse down," Nanna quipped as her fingers caught Hope's sleeve.

"Matthew, I have a terrible problem up at the house. Now, I could have called the McKaslin boy, but I hear you're a better carpenter. I need some work done on my kitchen."

"I'd be happy to come take a look." He held out his hand, palm up. It was a strong hand with calluses thick on his sun-browned skin. "Do you need help up these stairs?"

"I can handle the stairs. You talk a minute with my granddaughter and find a time she can show you the kitchen." Nanna was suddenly busy crutching up the steps and avoiding Matthew's gaze. "Hope, be a dear and handle this for me."

"You know I can't say no to you, Nanna." But Hope *did* feel suspicion burn in her heart. What was her grandmother up to?

"Kirby will see me in, dear. Just make sure you come and join me. If I need help, I'd hate to interrupt the meeting. You understand."

"I understand." Was that a twinkle in the older woman's eye? Nanna knew better than to try to fix her up with poor Matthew Sheridan, didn't she? "Try to behave until I get in there, Nanna."

"You know me." Her crutches creaked against the board walkway.

"That's what I'm afraid of." Hope's chest felt tight watching the frail lady ease her way over the threshold and into the café, as determined as an Olympic athlete.

Matthew leaned against the wooden rail. "Looks like Nora's keeping you busy."

"Busy? I'm running like a madwoman. It's not even lunchtime and she's exhausted me." Hope couldn't quite meet his gaze. She remembered what Nanna had said about his wife's death. She remembered the loneliness in his eyes. "I guess she wants some work done on her stove and sink."

"Well, I don't pretend to be the best in town when it comes to appliances, but I can take a look at that sink." Matthew splayed both hands on the weathered rail. "I'm roofing the McKaslins' barn this week. I can drop by, say, Monday morning, if that's no problem."

"That will be soon enough, I'm sure. I didn't notice any leak when I washed the dishes this morning. I have this funny feeling there's no real hurry. I think Nanna wanted to try to get the two of us together."

"I had that feeling, too." He shrugged one shoulder uneasily, looking off down the street. "Did Zach get your Jeep fixed?"

"It's repaired and waiting for me. Thanks again for helping me out. It would have been a long miserable walk."

"No problem." He tipped his hat, a polite gesture. "Well, I better get going. Don't want to be late for my first committee meeting."

"*You're* on the planning committee?"

"My mom talked me into it this morning. She extorted me, is more like it." A wry grin touched his mouth as he took a step toward the open door. "She's taking care of my sons, so I'm in a bind and she knows it. It's a shame when you can't trust your own mother."

"Or grandmother." Hope hated that she had to

follow him toward the gaping door. A bad feeling settled hard in her stomach, the kind that foretold disaster.

"What does that mean?" he asked. Sunlight brushed him with a golden glow, highlighting the wary slant to his eyes. The wry grin faded from his mouth. "You don't think my mom and your grandmother—"

"I sure hope not, but at this point do we give them the benefit of the doubt?"

"I don't know, my mom's been kind of sneaky lately." Matthew shook his head. "And obviously off her rocker. She knows you're only visiting. Maybe it's co-incidence."

"Let's hope so, or my grandmother is in big trouble, and I don't care how fragile she is."

"Somehow, I doubt she's in much danger." Matthew caught the edge of the open door and gestured for Hope to go first.

"You haven't seen my temper." Laughing, she breezed by him.

The wind caught her long curls and brushed the silken tips against the inside of his wrist. His grip on the door faltered, but she didn't seem to notice that the bell overhead jingled furiously. She smelled like spring, like new sunshine and fresh flowers.

"Isn't it marvelous that Hope has agreed to take my place on the committee?" Nora Greenley's voice rang like a merry bell above the clash of conversation in the homey little café. "Matthew, that means the two of you will be working side by side. Doesn't that sound terrific?"

"Nanna!" Shock paled Hope's face. "But—"

"You know I'm not well, dear, and the doctor wants me to get as much rest as possible."

"Yeah, but—" A fall of black hair cascaded across Hope's face, hiding her profile as she leaned her grandmother's crutches against the wall. Embarrassment stained her creamy complexion. She looked at him helplessly.

"It's all right, Hope. I'm getting used to the manipulative behavior of old women with nothing else to do but interfere in my business." He gave Nora a wink so she'd know he wasn't mad. Well, not too mad.

"Watch who you're calling old, young man." But Nora's eyes were laughing at him, as if she were enjoying this far too much. "Helen is calling the meeting to order. She's about to announce Hope is taking over my position. I can't tell you what a relief it is. Hope, dear, come sit down here between me and Matthew—"

It was too late to escape. Helen's voice rose above the sound of the coffee grinder at the counter. And only two unoccupied chairs remained close by. If he wanted to escape, he would have to excuse himself through half of the crowded café.

Hope shot him an apologetic look as she took one of the two remaining chairs. Her hair, unbound and rich, tumbled across her shoulders, catching the sprinkle of sunlight through the curtained window. Her curls shone like polished ebony.

"Now, if Nora is settled," Helen said as the room silenced. "I'll let her tell about how her wonderful granddaughter, whom we haven't seen in quite a few years, has agreed to take her position on our committee. Nora—"

"I didn't agree to anything," Hope leaned close to whisper. "Just so you know."

"Oh, I know." He did. He knew how his mother thought. Mom figured that enough time had passed since losing Kathy and that he ought to get on with his life. The boys needed more than a housekeeper—they needed a mother to love them. And he needed a wife.

But what she didn't know, what she couldn't accept, was that Kathy had been his whole heart.

Regret tightened in his chest until Nora's words and the sounds of the café faded. His parents' marriage had been based on respect, but not true love. Not like his and Kathy's. Mom couldn't understand.

Pain cut like a newly sharpened knife straight through the center of his chest. Mom didn't realize she was hurting him, but she was. Her matchmaking attempts stirred up old memories and grief.

Applause ripped through the café, tearing into his thoughts. The meeting continued, and the sun flirting with the curtains grew warm on his back. Karen McKaslin arrived with coffee and tea for everyone.

Matthew leaned across the table, stretching for the packets of sugar. Hope scooted the little ceramic holder closer, so it was within his reach. She avoided his gaze and maybe it was because she was a woman, soft and pretty, but it made him feel keenly alone.

He remembered a verse from John, one he'd relied on heavily these last difficult years. "Here on this earth you will have many trials and sorrows. But take heart, because I have overcome the world."

Matthew stirred sugar into his tea and clung to those treasured words.

Chapter Three

Hope snapped open the kitchen cupboards. "You embarrassed the poor man."

"I don't know what you're talking about."

"Go ahead, play innocent. But I'm not fooled and neither is Matthew." She slammed the cans of food onto the shelves. "It wasn't fair to volunteer me like that. You could have asked me. I would have been happy to do anything for you. Don't you know that? But this—"

"Don't you see? It's for your own good, Hope." Nanna didn't sound quite as confident. "Time is slipping away from me, and I want to know my beloved granddaughter is happy and cared for."

"I can take care of myself." Hope slammed two more cans onto the wooden shelf. "Besides, I'm perfectly happy."

"Sure, but you could be happier." Nanna sighed. "Don't be mad at me, Hope. With this injury I can't serve on the committee, and your spending time with poor widowed Matthew Sheridan can't hurt."

"It's your intentions that bother me. You know how I feel about marriage. And you know why." Hope kept out a box of crackers and folded up the paper grocery sack. "I'm not going to marry anyone. Ever. I'm never going to go through what my parents did."

"Just because your mom and dad couldn't get along doesn't mean that you can't have a fulfilling marriage."

"That's exactly what it means." Hope grabbed the bright yellow box and set it on the table in front of her grandmother. Her chest ached. Old wounds beat within her heart, and she didn't want to be angry with Nanna. "Stop trying to change my life, okay? I like it just the way it is. And no, I don't want a husband. I don't miss having a family."

"But, Hope—"

"Please, just drop it, Nanna. I can't talk about this anymore. *I'm* the result of a bad marriage, remember?" The memories of her parents always fighting, always hurting each other tore through her. Memories she wanted to forget. The wind teased the chimes outside the open window, and Hope spun away, determined to keep control of her emotions.

The past was gone. There was no sense letting it hurt her now. She watched the light in Nanna's eyes fade and she hated that, but she couldn't back down. Marriage was not—and never would be—for her. No matter what. And if she felt lonely in the evenings cooking for one, well, that was a small price to pay for a life without hurt, blame and endless battles.

"What you haven't seen," Nanna continued above the musical jingle of the chimes, "is that some marriages can be a great blessing. Filled with joy and enduring love."

"Sure, I've seen the movies. I've read the books. Notice how they're all fiction?" Hope grabbed the tea-kettle from the stove and carried it to the sink. "I don't want to hear any more about this, Nanna. Isn't there a passage somewhere in the Bible about minding your own business?"

"Well, Thessalonians. 'This should be your ambition: to live a quiet life, minding your own business—'" Nanna broke into a chuckle. "All right, fine, you've won. I'll stop trying to match you up with handsome, kind, marriageable men even if it *is* for your own good."

"Finally! You've come to your senses." Hope grabbed hold of the cold water faucet.

"I'll have you know there are many young women in this town who would appreciate my efforts."

"Then maybe you should try matchmaking for *them.*" Hope gave the faucet a twist and felt the old metal handle give.

A blast of cold water slammed against her right cheekbone and across the front of her neck. She jumped back. Water sluiced down her face and dripped off her chin. Her shirt was wet through and plastered to her skin.

She could only stare at the geyser shooting water everywhere—straight up at the ceiling and sideways in every direction.

When Nanna had asked her to talk to Matthew, there really was a problem with the plumbing. She set the broken cold water handle on the counter and swiped more drops from her eyes.

"Kirby, quick, call Matthew." Nanna's voice rang high with distress above the sounds of the cascading waterfall. "Ever since Ethan Brisbane left town, we don't have a decent plumber. Hope, quick, can you make it stop?"

"I'm trying." Her sneakers slid on the wet surface as she tugged open the cabinet doors. She scrunched down and peered under the sink.

The old pipes groaned. Droplets plinked against her forehead. She knew next to nothing about plumbing, but she did own a small condo. She'd had her share of homeowner disasters. "I don't see any shutoff valves. Nanna, how old are these pipes?"

"Who knows? Seventy years or more?"

"Maybe it's time to replace 'em." There was no way to stop the water, not here at the sink. "There must be a shutoff in the basement. I'll see what I can do."

"Hurry, dear, my knickknacks—"

Hope spun toward the sink. The pretty porcelain figurines on the corner shelves above the sink were taking a direct hit.

She stepped into the force of cold water, wincing as it struck like a thousand icy pinpricks. "Kirby, could you help me out here?"

"Sure thing." The young nurse abandoned the phone and hurried across the growing puddle on the floor to carry the rescued figurines to the table. "Mr. Sheridan wasn't in. I got his pager."

"We're going to need someone right away." Hope

curled her fingers around the last wet porcelain child. "And it would be better—" she fixed a warning gaze on her grandmother "—if it *wasn't* Matthew Sheridan."

"Don't worry, Hope." Nanna spoke up. "I'm a defeated old woman resigned to live without a single great grandchild."

"Sure. Make me feel guilty." Hope handed Kirby the last figurine and stood, dripping wet, in the middle of the kitchen. Water crept in an ever-widening puddle across the ancient flooring. As far as she could tell, puddles and crutches didn't look like they would mix. "C'mon, Nanna, let's get you to safer ground."

"I'll take her into the living room," Kirby volunteered, the crutches already in hand. "And I'll try to find someone—anyone—to come right away."

"Thanks, Kirby." Hope caught Nanna's elbow as she wobbled, a little unsteady on her feet. "I'm going to see what I can do downstairs."

"Now be careful of those narrow steps," Nanna warned.

Hope resisted the urge to remind her grandmother that she was no longer a child. The warmth in her chest doubled knowing someone worried over her—that someone still cared.

The water was still spewing like Old Faithful, so Hope ran for the basement door.

No light greeted her when she hit the switch. She guessed Nanna hadn't been down here in a while. She found a flashlight on a hook by the door and searched the lengths of wrapped pipes visible overhead. They ended by the hot water tank in the back corner, where huge cobwebs warned of even bigger spiders.

"No way am I going in there." She shivered, her skin crawling just at the sight of those thick, dust-coated gossamer strands.

Then a dark object slinked across the cement floor toward her sneaker. She screamed in midair, already jumping back. The flashlight slipped from her grip. It hit the ground with a crash and rolled, the light eerily aimed at the ceiling. The shadowy spider skidded to a stop, waiting—like he was preparing to launch an all-out assault on her ankle.

"Chances are it's more scared of you." A rich masculine voice rumbled like low valley thunder through the dark. Then boots clipped on the concrete. "He's looking up at you and thinking, boy, that giant sure looks dangerous. I hope she doesn't attack me."

"Matthew Sheridan." She took another cautious step back, her pulse fast, her limbs shaky. "You scared me to death."

"Didn't hear me come down the stairs, huh? I guess you were too busy screaming at this poor defenseless spider." He strode closer, his presence like a fire in the darkness, radiating heat without light. A heat she felt.

"How did you get here so fast?"

"Kirby left a desperate message so I came over. I was next door at the Joneses'." He flashed her a grin in the eerie mix of shadows and knelt down, unafraid. "If you shoo him off, he'll go hide and leave you alone."

"Sure. I feel so much safer knowing he's in the shadows watching and waiting for the right moment to take a bite." Hope tripped back, away from the narrow hallway, not sure which was affecting her more—the spider or the man. "I was trying to find the shutoff."

"Let me take it from here. After all, I'm the professional." He held up a big wrench and stepped into the light. Lemony rays brushed across his face, accenting the fine cut of his profile and the curve of his lopsided grin. "Tell Nora not to worry. I'm on the job."

"Oh, that's a comfort." Why was she feeling like this? The last thing she wanted was to feel attracted to a man. Especially Matthew Sheridan.

She remembered how he'd looked in the coffee shop with sadness so huge in his eyes. How he'd leaned slightly away from her in his chair, placed right beside hers, so that their shoulders wouldn't brush. As if he wanted to make it clear just how much distance he wanted.

Well, he was in luck. She wanted distance, too. And yet, she felt sorry for him. Sorry because beneath his easy grin lurked a great grief, one so obvious how could Nanna even think he'd want to remarry?

Not knowing what to say, Hope backed away, leaving the flashlight on the floor in case Matthew needed it, finding her way through the dark by touch and by memory.

Matthew listened to her light step against the stairs, tapping away into silence. Hope had looked at him like a deer blinded by headlights. Maybe it was the spider or the way he refused to look at her at the meeting today.

Either way, he knew he had to make things right. Since he couldn't back out of his obligation to the committee, it looked like he'd be seeing Hope a lot during the preparations for the Founder's Days dance. He didn't want any strain or bruised feelings confusing things. As soon as he turned off the water and fixed Nora's sink, he'd pull Hope aside and talk with her.

Unfortunately, the old valve was rusted wide open, and he had to use every bit of his strength to turn it. The old metal groaned, and he whispered a prayer for the ancient pipes to hold. They did, and the rush of water faded into silence.

Overhead he heard the soft tap of shoes—probably Hope's. He tried not to think about that as he brushed the cobwebs off his shirt and retrieved the fallen flashlight. He hadn't looked at a woman since he'd fallen in love with Kathy, and it bothered him. He didn't know what to make of it as he headed upstairs.

Hope was in the kitchen, guiding a mop across the floor. Sunlight spilled through the back door, highlighting the sheen of her dark hair and the agile grace in her slender arms.

She knelt, wrung water from the mop into a bucket, then straightened. "You came to the rescue. Again."

"That I did. I even survived the spider." He couldn't get over the sight of Hope Ashton handling a mop. He couldn't seem to tear his gaze away.

"You're a braver person than I am." She bent to work, swiping with practice. "Sharing dark cramped spaces with arachnids isn't high on my list."

He knew she was from a wealthy family—she

probably had her own housekeeper and cook, a chauffeur and gardener—but here she was in simple blue jeans and a light yellow T-shirt cleaning her grandmother's floor with a steady competence. As if she mopped floors all the time.

Not that Hope's lifestyle was any of his business, he reminded himself and he forced his gaze away. But as he crossed the kitchen with water slick against his work boots, he could hear the stroke of Hope's mop back and forth.

"I'm going to have to replace this entire setup." He checked under the sink to make sure. "Either that, or chances are this kitchen will end up flooded again."

"Then we'll just have you fix it right." Hope swiped her forearm across her brow. "Kirby took Nanna outside for some fresh air. I think she's more upset than she's letting on."

"She's lived here, what, fifty years? It's hard to see something you love damaged." He eased onto his back and adjusted his pipe wrench, determined to concentrate on his job and not on Hope mopping the floor. "I'm going to take out the sink and all these pipes. Put in proper shutoff valves. She'll even get a new faucet out of the deal. Lucky for you, I have a faucet in the carpenter boxes in the back of my truck—I get these emergencies often enough. It's a nice white European one."

"Oh, boy. I can't remember the last time a handsome man gave me a new faucet."

She was kidding—he knew that. But why did his pulse perk up? Did she really think he was handsome?

He couldn't see it—he doubted anyone else did, either. That was the thing that made him wary about women like Hope—easy flattery, a drop of kindness, it was superficial and not always innocent. He ought to remember that the next time he couldn't stop looking at her.

Disgusted with himself, he gave his wrench a hard twist, and the old pipe came loose from the wall. "So, you'll be staying in town through Founder's Days?"

"If Nanna needs me that long." Hope knelt to wring the mop. Water splashed into the bucket. "I'm sorry about the committee meeting. She's just trying to throw us together. I hope you know I had nothing to do with that."

"I figured it out easy enough." He slid out from beneath the sink and caught sight of Hope hefting the full bucket toward the back door, so at odds with what he expected from her. Maybe that's why his gaze kept finding her in the room. "I believe you. Remember, my mom blackmailed me."

"Your own mother? That's hard to believe. I remember how sweet she was." Hope disappeared in the shimmer of the midday sun.

"Sweet? Sure, she once was, I suppose. Then she became a grandmother and started meddling."

Hope breezed back inside, swinging the empty bucket, and her smile looked genuine enough to make his heart flip. She lifted one delicate brow. "Meddling?"

"Yep. Mom decided she wanted more grandchildren so I needed another wife to provide her with some."

He concentrated on coaxing the broken faucet out from the tiled wall. "It's a desperate situation."

"I understand that completely. Poor Nanna won't be happy until she thinks I'm taken care of." The mop smacked against the floor. "She isn't satisfied when I say I can take care of myself. As if any man will do."

Any man. A common, middle-class working man. Matthew knew it wasn't a fair way to think, but even though Hope Ashton looked kind and casual and good-hearted and even though she was mopping a floor, she was a millionaire's daughter. She was a renowned photographer. She wasn't looking for just any man.

The pipe stuck, and he gave it a hard tug. It split into pieces and tumbled into the sink. "These pipes look as old as the house."

"I'm sure they are." Hope swept past him, leaving a lingering trail of sweet, light perfume. "Grandfather was notoriously frugal. Do you think you can get the water at least running today?"

"Sure can." He shook his head at the rot where the pipes had been leaking for some time. Better to concentrate on his work. "This wall is going to have to be replaced. And this set of cupboards."

"Nanna is going to be heartbroken. Grandfather made those cabinets for her. They're custom—"

"I'm not a bad carpenter. I bet I can match them." He couldn't help teasing her, she looked so serious, so concerned. "Have a little faith, Hope."

"I'm trying." She smiled, soft and sweet, and he noticed the way her dark curls caught the light, shimmering like rare silk.

Heaven help him.

A bell rang, spinning her toward the front door. Long locks flicked over her shoulder, glimmering with such beauty he couldn't look away. She hustled from his sight, padding across the damp floor and into the dim recesses of the entry hall.

He recognized Helen's voice and then heard only silence. Hope must have taken her out to see Nora in the flower garden. Matthew headed out the back door to grab what he needed from his truck. He'd put in new pipe, valves and a faucet.

An older lady with a broken leg needed running water. He figured the McKaslin family wouldn't mind if he was a day late finishing their barn.

"How are you and Matthew getting along?" Nanna asked after she'd greeted, Helen, her lifetime friend. "Did you notice how wide his shoulders are? I just love a man with broad shoulders."

"Then *you* flirt with him," Hope teased as she tucked a cushion in the black metal chair for Helen. "Let me fetch some iced tea. I'll be right back."

"She's hurrying back to him." Nanna's loud whisper carried on the sweet breezes.

"To look at his shoulders," Helen teased.

Okay, so his shoulders *were* broad. Hope hopped up the back steps and she couldn't help it—her gaze found and traced the strong line of Matthew's muscled arms, corded as he worked to set the new pipe in the wall.

"Would you like some iced tea?" She reached into

the cupboards for three glasses, determined not to notice his well-honed physique.

"Sounds good." He didn't look up from his work. As if he were afraid to make eye contact with her.

Why now? Then she noticed the windows were open, and Nanna's voice lifted on the breeze through the window. He couldn't have accidentally overheard what they were talking about, right?

The curtains fluttered with a gust of wind. "Goodness, Hope is so alone. Matthew's mom and I thought since they were both so lonely, we'd try to toss them together—"

The curtain snapped closed, cutting off the rest of Nanna's words.

A cold feeling gripped Hope's stomach. She felt her heart stop as she met Matthew's gaze.

"I guess that's as close to a confession as we're going to get." He stretched a kink in his neck, flexing the muscles in his left shoulder and arm. "Our own families are working against us."

"Nanna just promised to stop—" Hope's knees felt weak. "No, she didn't exactly say that. She sort of skirted the issue and changed the subject. You heard her. She doesn't sound one bit sorry."

"It sure didn't sound that way."

Hope set the pitcher on the counter. She remembered how he'd looked in the coffee shop, lost and sad and brokenhearted. "I'm sorry, Matthew. This must be painful for you."

"I'm used to it." His words were as warm as spring rain. "*This* is what I've been up against ever since the boys wanted a mother for their third birthday. My mom has been on a nonstop campaign to find me a wife, and now she's involving her friends in the search."

"Like any woman will do, right?" It hurt to see the shadows in his eyes, so deep hazel and mingled with pain. She didn't know what to say. How to comfort him.

He laid a packaged faucet, shiny knobs wrapped in plastic, on the counter. "It sounds to me like these women are pretty determined. Just how do you think we can stop them?"

"It's going to be a long awkward summer unless we find a way."

Matthew rubbed the heel of his hand against his brow. He looked tired. He looked as if a world of burden rested on those wide shoulders. Her heart ached for him.

She poured iced tea into the three tumblers, and then inspiration gripped her. "I know! Proverbs. 'If you set a trap for others, you will get caught in it yourself.'"

"You mean…"

"Have you noticed how your mother and my grandmother have all this time on their hands? Notice how they both live alone."

"I noticed." Light began to twinkle in Matthew's eyes.

"Poor lonely widows. With no one to take care of them." Hope tugged the curtain aside and caught sight of Nanna in the garden shaded by the tall maple. "Nanna mentioned a certain older gentleman she thought was very attractive. Maybe there's someone your mother might like…."

"Hope, you're a genius." Matthew laughed, relief chasing away the shadows in his eyes and the furrows from his brow. "We turn the tables on them. And why not?"

"That's right. Why not?" She topped off the last tumbler and handed it to Matthew. "Your mother and my grandmother had no qualms about torturing us."

"That's right. We find the two of them husbands, and they'll be so happy they'll forget all about us." Matthew leaned against the counter and sipped his tea. "It's not deceptive. After all, we're bid to let love be our highest goal…."

"Like Nanna said, it's not good to be alone." Hope felt the sunlight on her face, warm and sustaining. She knew Nanna wasn't alone, not truly, but she also remembered how years had slipped from Nanna's face at the thought of Matthew's handsome grandfather-in-law.

Nanna had spent too many years in this empty house watching for the mailman to slip letters into her box or waiting for the phone to ring. That was about to change. Hope could feel it down deep in her soul.

Maybe that's why the Lord had brought Matthew to her in the middle of that dangerous storm. And why Matthew stood here now.

If God kept watch over the smallest sparrow, then surely He cared about the loneliness in an old woman's heart.

Chapter Four

The new morning's sun had already burned the dew off the ground as Hope made her way through the neighbor's fields. Dark green, knee-high alfalfa swayed in the warm breezes and brushed her knees as she spotted the Joneses' barn and the man kneeling on its steep peak, tacking down new gray shingles with a nail gun.

She only had to look at him for her heart to flip in her chest. For one brief moment she noticed the wind tangling his collar-length hair and let her gaze wander over the lean hard height of him. In a white T-shirt and wash-worn jeans, he was a good-looking man. As if he felt her gaze, he glanced up from his work and shaded his eyes with one gloved hand. Then he waved in welcome.

A prairie dog gave a chirp of alarm and scampered out of sight as Hope hurried through the field, alfalfa shoots brushing against her bare skin. Matthew disappeared from the roof only to reappear circling from behind the weathered barn, stripping off his work gloves.

"Hey, I began to think you stood me up."

"I know, and I'm sorry. Nanna was in a lot of pain this morning and we couldn't get her to eat. I finally tempted her with fresh cinnamon rolls, but it took more time than I figured." She held up a paper sack. "I brought a peace offering, though. Figured you couldn't be too mad with me if I brought sweets."

"A wise woman."

"No, a grateful one. You've helped me twice now, and I'm indebted. The cinnamon rolls are only a start."

"You don't owe me a thing." Matthew flicked his gaze away toward the west side of the barn where shade stretched over soft grasses in an empty corral. "I've got a cooler with juice over here. Let's get down to business."

"Sure." She followed him past the wooden posts, worn gray from time and the elements, and when she saw the blanket spread out on the small patch of wild grasses, she realized that Matthew had gone to some trouble. She regretted being late.

"Tell me how the new kitchen plumbing is working out," he said over his shoulder as he knelt down in front of a battered blue cooler.

"Nanna's happy with your work, but she's fretting over the ruined cabinet."

"It shouldn't be long until I have the replacement for her. I planned on tooling it in my workshop at home this weekend. Tell her I won't forget to come by and make the cabinet as good as new."

"Oh, I think she can't wait to get us in the same house together." Drawing closer, Hope knelt on one edge of the fleece blanket. "After you left last night, she kept going on and on about all your wonderful attributes."

"She had to resort to lying, huh?" His eyes twinkled with merriment.

And she felt that twinkle in her heart. "I can see a few good things about you, Matthew, not that either of us is interested in the way Nanna thinks. I tried to tell her that you were more interested in fixing her ancient pipes than in making small talk with me, but she wanted to know every single word we exchanged when we were alone in her kitchen."

"She couldn't hear us well enough from the garden, huh?"

"That's what I thought, too." Hope unfolded the neat crease at the top of her sack, and the fresh scent of frosting and cinnamon made her stomach rumble.

Matthew handed her an unopened juice box and knelt down a fair distance from her. "My mom was singing your praises last night when I went to pick up my boys. She had that same look in her eyes that Nora had."

"You're right, they are shameless meddlers and they need to be taught a lesson." She held out the bag to him.

He reached inside and withdrew a gooey pastry. "Now I'm doubly grateful you came by. These cinnamon rolls are the best things I've seen in a long time. Nora's baking is famous county-wide."

"Nora's recipe, but I baked them."

"You?" Did he have to look so surprised?

"Hey, I have my uses. I packed enough for you to take home to your boys." She took one sticky roll and plopped the bag on the blanket between them. "Now, wipe that shocked look off your face and tell me. Do you have any idea who your mom might be interested in?"

"Not one. I'll have to pry into her life a little, like she's been doing to mine lately." He sank his teeth into the roll and moaned. "I took a long hard look at Mom last night, and I figure she's got to be lonely. I've got my boys, but when the day is done, she's alone."

"Nanna's the same way. It's got to be sad. All the work they did and the sacrifices they made to raise their families, and now, when they should be enjoying their lives, they have no one to share with."

"Do you know how we can fix that?"

"Not really. I was hoping you'd have a brilliant idea and get me off the hook."

"Give me another cinnamon roll and we'll see what I can come up with."

He's deeply lonely, too. Again, Hope felt it with the same certainty as the gentle breezes on her face. She wondered if he sat up at night, watching the late shows or reading to the end of a book just to keep from going to bed alone, as she did. She wondered if he, too, had a hard time sleeping with the dark and the silence of the night, when prayer could only ease the empty space....

"Nanna let it slip that she has a crush on Harold."

"Kathy's grand dad?" Matthew nodded slowly as he

helped himself to another roll. "I noticed Helen fought to sit next to him at the Founder's Days committee meeting, but I didn't know Nora was interested in him, too."

"He wouldn't be lonely, would he?"

"He's been a widower as long as I have." Matthew stared down at the pastry and didn't take a bite, the sadness in his eyes stark and unmistakable.

Maybe Nanna was right, Hope considered. Maybe, every now and then, true love was possible. Every now and then.

"I'm taking the boys to see him at his ranch this weekend. Between chasing after my sons, I'll try to figure out if Harold is interested in Nora."

"And if he is, we could casually set them up so they wouldn't know it was us. Something not as obvious as what they did to us on the Founder's Days committee."

"Sounds like a good plan." Matthew took a bite of the roll, but the sadness remained in his eyes. The breeze tangled his hair, tossing a dark hank over his brow, and she fought the urge to brush it away, fought the urge to reach out and try to comfort him.

"How's the roof coming along?" she asked, not knowing what else to say to change the direction of their conversation. She stood, drawn toward the ladder stretching twenty feet in the air, and studied the roof's steeply pitched slope. "Do you mind if I climb up?"

"Yeah, I mind." He leaped to his feet, all business, square jaw set and hands fisted. "You could fall, and then what would I say to your grandmother?"

"I won't fall." She spun around, taking in the

expanse of the river valley bright with the colors of spring, and ached for her camera. "Okay, I'm not interested in your roofing job, but on the walk over here my mind clicked back to work and I could get a great view from up there."

"You can get a great view of the valley from the road."

"Yeah, but I'm already here." She grabbed hold of the ladder and fit her sneaker onto the weathered rung.

"Hope, I'm not kidding. You're going to break your neck." But he didn't sound too upset with her.

When she looked over her shoulder, she saw that he was holding the ladder steady for her and shaking his head as if to say women didn't belong on ladders. Well, she wouldn't be on for long. "I appreciate this, Matthew."

"If you weren't helping me out with my mom, I'd let go of this ladder."

"Sure you would. You're too nice of a guy."

"That's only according to rumor. You can't trust everything you hear."

"Nanna says a man who can raise three small boys at the same time has to have the patience of Job and the temperament of an angel."

"Either that or he's on psychiatric medication."

Hope stumbled onto the roof, laughing, but Matthew hadn't fooled her. Sure, he was joking, but there was no way he could disguise the patience and good humor lighting him up from within, not quite chasing away his sadness. It touched her somewhere deep inside her well-defended heart. How was it that *this* man could affect her so much and so quickly?

"Be careful up there." The ladder rubbed against the weathered eaves with each step Matthew took as he climbed higher. "I don't want to have to explain to Nora how I let her only granddaughter tumble off a barn roof. I'd never get work from her again."

"Repeat business is all that matters, is it?"

"Sure." He hopped onto the roof with an athletic prowess that drew Hope's gaze, and a slow smile tugged at the left corner of his mouth. "Now before you start running around up here, some of the shingles aren't tacked down yet."

"I noticed that. Really." Wisps had escaped from her ponytail, and she swept them back with one hand. "Between you and Nanna, I feel like an awkward kid again. Stop worrying about me, okay? I'm not going to take a nosedive off the barn. I've been on a roof before."

"Not as often as I have, I bet." He curved his hand around her elbow, holding her secure. "Just in case."

"I'm not afraid of heights."

"I am."

"You? Manhattan's best carpenter?"

"My roof jobs would dry up if word like that got around. You'll keep my secret, right?" His grip on her arm remained, sure and steady, keeping her safe.

"I don't know," she teased in turn, heading toward the roof's peak. "Seems to me keeping a secret like that could be worth some money."

He chuckled, rich and deep, and it somehow moved through her even though they hardly touched. Like a vibration of warmth and sunlight, she felt it, and when her sneaker hit a loose shingle, his grip on her arm held her steady even before she could stumble.

His touch remained, branding her with his skin's heat, and she almost stumbled again. Why was her heart beating as if she'd run a mile? With every step she took, she was aware of the way he moved beside her—the easy, athletic movements as he escorted her safely to the peak of the sloped roof.

No, she *wasn't* attracted to him. He was simply being a gentleman, as he'd been when he'd carried her luggage and driven her home on the night of the storm. A gentleman, nothing more and nothing less, and even if that was attractive to her, she didn't need to panic. He was no threat to her heart. No threat at all.

She faced the wind, and the sweet country breezes lifted the hair from her brow and whirred in her ears. Sunlight slanted in ragged, luminous fingers from the wide blue sky to the rich green earth.

"I should have brought my camera. Look at the cloud shadow on those hills."

"The Tobacco Roots." He nodded toward the wrinkled hills in the distance, rugged and rocky, in contrast to the regal Rockies to the West. "Kathy and I used to hike there before the boys were born. We tried it once afterward, carting the three of them in backpacks, but they were hot and miserable and, unfortunately, teething. We decided not to make that mistake again."

"Scared away the wildlife, did they?"

"I still think half the deer never did return to their natural habitat. The park ranger threatened to ticket us." He shrugged one capable shoulder but his grin didn't reach all the way to his eyes.

"I remember Kathy. She was two years behind us in school, wasn't she?"

"Yes." A muscle worked in his jaw as he towered over her, his back to the sun, his face shadowed.

Hope sat on the hot shingles, emotions tangled into a knot in her stomach. She didn't want to say anything more that would make sadness shade his eyes. "How old are your boys?"

"Three, almost four. Their birthday is in July."

"Triplets. That must be a handful."

"When Kathy was alive, it was *almost* manageable. When we finally got them on the same sleeping schedule, that is." The sadness crept into his eyes anyway as he sat down beside her, leaving a deliberate space between them. "Right now I'm between housekeepers. It's hard to find someone with the right temperament."

"I bet it isn't easy keeping up with triplets."

"It's not impossible. They are something, I'll tell you that, always going in different directions at once, but I wouldn't trade 'em for the world."

The wind tossed dark shocks of hair over his brow as he looked everywhere but at her. "I haven't seen the world like you have, heck, I haven't even been out of Montana, but I have everything I want right now. I have my boys and that's all I need."

"Then you're a lucky man."

"I'm not going to argue with you about that."

His voice dipped and he turned away from her to study the valley spread out before them. As the silence lengthened, Hope tried to pretend she wasn't touched by what she'd seen in Matthew's eyes and heard unspoken in his words, but she failed. She *was* touched. Anyone could see a father's steadfast love in him as certain as the warm sun overhead.

Not that what lived in Matthew's heart was any of her business.

Maybe this jumpy, skittery feeling wasn't an attraction to Matthew at all. Maybe she was itching to start working again. That's it. "I'd better get back before Nanna misses me."

Matthew stood, not meeting her gaze, and offered his hand.

She straightened on her own, not certain if she could touch him one more time. She *wasn't* attracted to him…and she didn't want her physical reaction to him proving her wrong.

"Looks like we're in trouble." Without looking at her, he nodded across the field toward the dirt road, where a dust plume rose behind a sedate burgundy sedan. "It's my mom. No, there's no time to run. There she is. We're busted."

The look of dismay on Hope's face told Matthew she didn't like the prospect of being caught alone with him, and he couldn't blame her. Mom would jump to conclusions and only take seeing them together as encouragement. He held the ladder for Hope so she could climb down safely.

She knelt and carefully placed her designer sneakers on the top rung. "Sure, send me down first into enemy territory."

"Better you than me. Mom will show you mercy."

"Not if she's anything like Nanna."

Her attempt at humor touched him because she couldn't like this situation. It was absurd that anyone would think that a small-town carpenter belonged anywhere near a millionaire's daughter.

"Daddy! Daddy! Daddy!" The words rang on the air the instant the passenger door of Mom's car swung open. As Hope finished descending, Matthew watched his sons race full out toward the fence until Mom shouted at them to wait and not touch the barbed wire.

Hope lighted on the ground and tilted her head back to look at him. "I didn't know they were identical."

"Keeps things interesting."

"I bet it does." She covered her eyes with her free hand and squinted through the glaring sun to watch the triplets tumble into the field.

He started down the ladder, descending quickly. Already Mom was helping the boys through the fence and there was no mistaking the look of delight in that grin of hers, which he could see plainly from across the field. This wasn't what he needed. Mom would think she was on the right track and start really pushing.

"Daddy, Daddy, Daddy!" The triplets plowed through the sweet-smelling alfalfa and scrambled to him, arms flung open.

Matthew barely had time to brace himself before the boys threw their arms around his knees and held on tight, bouncing and shouting. "Did you three give your gramma so much trouble she decided to give you back?"

"It was tempting," Mom teased over the racket of the boys talking at once. He heard the words "fire," "fireman" and "big truck." "Agnes had a small kitchen fire and wanted you to give her an estimate on the damage."

"You could have called, Mom." Matthew lifted Josh onto his hip.

"Yes, but you know I hate talking to that beeper thing of yours. Hope, what a pleasure to see you again." Mom practically beamed as she approached the slim woman who stood off by herself, as if not sure what to think of them all. "I heard from Nora you were in town."

"She finally figured out a way to get me back here." Hope took Mom's hand, her manner warm, as if she wasn't upset in the slightest. "It's good to see you again, Patsy."

The boys demanded Matthew's attention, telling him everything about the sirens and the big red truck, but his gaze kept straying to the woman talking with his mother, whose girl-next-door freshness was at odds with everything he remembered about Hope Ashton from high school.

"Is that lady gonna take us?" Josh asked, both fists tight in Matthew's T-shirt.

The other boys turned to frown at Hope, and before Matthew could answer, she did.

"No, but I did bring you boys something." Hope swirled away from his mother and snatched the paper bag from the blanket.

Of course, his mother took one look at the blanket, not an item he usually took to work with him, and lifted one curious—or was that accusing?—eyebrow.

Ian took one step forward, interested in Hope's paper bag. "Cookies?"

"Candy?" Kale looked tempted.

Josh buried his face in Matthew's shoulder and held on tight.

Matthew watched as Hope shook her head, dark wisps tangling in the wind, and knelt down, opening the sack. "If you boys don't like cinnamon rolls, I could eat them all by myself—"

"Cinnamon rolls?" Kale shot forward, not caring if this woman was a stranger. "Like the kind Gramma makes? With frosting?"

"With frosting."

Ian scrambled closer. "Does it got raisins? Don't like raisins."

"No raisins, but they do have icing. Go ahead and try one." Hope shook the bag, as if she were trying to coax them closer.

Huge mistake. Matthew set out to rescue her as both boys plunged their hands into the sack, fighting for the biggest roll. But Hope only laughed, a warm gentle sound that made him stop and really look at her, at this outsider who had never quite belonged in their small Montana town.

She didn't look like an outsider now. Her faded denims hugged her slender legs with an easy casualness, and her T-shirt was probably a big-label brand, but the cherry-red color brought out the bronzed hue of her skin and the gleam of laughter in her eyes. She didn't look like a millionaire's daughter and an established photographer.

She looked like a beautiful woman who liked children. His children.

"No, only take one." She merely shrugged when Kale got away with two plump rolls, and Matthew was about to make Kale put the pastry back when Hope shook her head, her cheeks pink with laughter, her eyes bright and merry. "Good thing I brought enough for second helpings."

Josh buried his face harder into Matthew's shoulder and held on tighter.

"He's sensitive." Matthew leaned his cheek against the top of the boy's head. "We've gone through a lot of baby-sitters and it's been hard on him."

"I know exactly what that feels like. I had a lot of different nannies when I was little. All that change can be hard." She pressed the bag into Matthew's free hand. "He might be interested once I'm gone."

Why did he feel disappointed that she was leaving? "So, you're leaving me alone with my mom?"

Hope glanced over her shoulder to watch his mother sit Ian and Kale down on the blanket, admonishing them to eat with their mouths closed. "I bet a grown man like you can handle anything and besides, I don't want to be in the way."

"You're welcome to stay." And it surprised him because he meant it.

"This will be the perfect opportunity to talk with your mother and try to figure out who we should fix her up with." She backed away, lifting a hand to wave at Mom and the boys.

"I hope to see you again soon," Mom called. "Say thank-you, Ian, Kale."

Two thank-yous chimed in unison.

Matthew watched helplessly as she breezed away from him, the big blue sky at her back, the green field at her feet. He wanted to stop her, to keep her here with him. It didn't make a bit of sense, but that's how he felt. He couldn't help it.

He watched as she turned around to glance at his boys eating unfurled sections of their cinnamon rolls, sticky and happy, and the look in her eyes, the softness on her face made his knees weak. He had to lean against the corner of the old barn for support.

Was that longing he saw on Hope Ashton's face? Before he could be sure, it was gone. She shouted across the widening distance. "I'll tell Nanna you haven't forgotten about repairing her cabinets."

"Sure." He felt tongue-tied, not sure what to say as she spun around and headed off through the fields, leaving him with a strange, yearning feeling.

A feeling he decided he wouldn't look at too closely.

"Those boys are the cutest things I ever did see," Nanna crooned as Matthew's triplets tripped down the church aisle, their father towering over them. "And Matthew is cute in an entirely different way. Why, if I were you, Hope, I'd cut a path for that man, I tell you. He's as dependable as the day is long, and you already know he'll make a wonderful father. Look how he handles those boys."

"I'm immune to the lovebug, Nanna. Don't get your hopes up because I'm not planning on marrying anyone."

"Still, Matthew is a very handsome man."

"He's still grieving his wife, Nanna. Have you and Patsy given one thought about how much your match-making is hurting him?"

"Well, if that's true, then I'm sorry about that, but honestly, grief does fade, maybe not completely, but there comes a time when you're ready to start accept-ing what life has to give." Nanna's hand covered Hope's and squeezed gently, lovingly. "In time a heart is ready to love again."

"You've been a widow for over ten years."

"That I have." Her sigh was sad, and the old lady looked hard at the stained glass windows bursting with color beneath the sun's touch. "But I'm more con-cerned about you. You should be thinking about starting a family of your own. Patsy told me you went to see Matthew for a little picnic the other day."

"No, I went to remind him about your cabinets."

"With cinnamon rolls?"

Hope glanced around, desperate for a change of subject. She spotted an elderly man, his back straight and his shoulders strong as if he'd done battle with age and won, his gray hair distinguished as he strode pow-erfully down the aisle toward Matthew and the triplets. "Look, there's Harold. I can see why you have a crush on him."

"It's probably foolish, but I—" Nanna stopped, the brightness in her eyes fading. "I'm just having a little fun, and it makes me feel young again."

Hope wondered at the change in her grandmother, and when she saw Helen hurrying down the aisle to speak with Harold, she knew why. Helen might not have any idea how Nanna felt about the handsome older gentleman, and Hope knew that Nanna wasn't about to say anything differently now.

Organ music broke through the din of the congregation settling onto the old wooden pews, and disappointment wrapped around Hope's heart as Helen took Harold by the arm and led him to Matthew's pew.

"It's not like I'm crazy over the man or anything," Nanna said staunchly, but her voice sounded too tight and strained to be telling the truth. "But a handsome man is always a joy to behold."

Six rows ahead of them, Matthew stood to greet his grandfather-in-law. Patsy was there and ordered the boys to squeeze closer together to make room, and there was enough space on the bench for Helen to settle down beside Harold.

As if he felt her gaze, Matthew turned and found her in the crowd. He wore a dark suit and a white shirt that emphasized his sun-browned, wholesome good looks, the kind a man had when he worked outside for a living.

Her heart gave a strange little flip-flop.

"I'm sorry," he seemed to say as he shrugged.

She shrugged back. Matchmaking wasn't as easy as it looked.

Sad for Nanna, Hope wrapped her arm around the old woman's shoulders and held her tight. They were in God's house. Surely here of all places He could gaze into the old woman's heart and see the loneliness—and now the hurt.

Please help her feel young again, Hope prayed. *With the days she has left, let her know love one more time.*

Chapter Five

Matthew knew what his mother was up to the minute that he saw Hope through the Sunshine Café's front window.

"Look, there's Nora and her granddaughter." Mom flashed him a not-so-innocent smile. "I told Nora to get a table big enough for all of us. I thought brunch sounded like just the thing. I told Harold to meet us there, but it looks like Helen might be coming, too."

"Mom, tell me you didn't invite Hope and Nora to join us." Matthew kept tight hold on Ian and Kale as he stopped in his tracks in the middle of the sidewalk crowded with after-church traffic. "Tell me you wouldn't meddle in my life like that."

"It's just brunch. Nora's been so housebound I thought—"

"You didn't think. You just decided what you wanted to do and lied about it to me."

"Lied?" Her jaw sagged and her free hand lighted

on the back of his. "I did no such thing. I just didn't tell you—"

"The truth?"

"No, that Hope would be joining us." Mom looked so proud of herself, as if she truly believed she was doing what was best for him. "Well, look, Nora's waving at us through the window. It's too late to back out now, but if you want to—"

Matthew's jaw snapped tight. He hated it when his mother did this. She meant well, and he figured she didn't want him to be as lonely as she was, but that didn't mean she could break open his heart like this and make him remember everything he was missing.

"Daddy!" Ian complained loudly, tugging hard against Matthew's grip. "I wanna hamburger."

"Hamburger, Daddy," Kale demanded. "I'm hungry."

They went inside, but he didn't like it. The boys were already counting on devouring one of their favorite meals and he wouldn't disappoint them. Not that he could stomach his mother thinking that her plan was working.

"Look at those darling boys," Nora crooned, welcoming them all with a bright hello.

Hope sat at her grandmother's side, somehow elegant and country-fresh at the same time in a lavender cotton dress, the kind that swirled around her woman's form, making her look as tempting as spring. She met his gaze and shrugged, letting him know she'd been as tricked into this as he was.

"It's the lady!" Ian raced straight to Hope and climbed onto the empty chair beside her with a clatter.

Hope held the chair steady as the boy settled down next to her. "I like your shirt."

"Trucks." Ian looked down at his shirt and slapped his little hand across a red truck imprinted there. "This is a fire truck—" he moved his fingers "—and a ladder truck and a tanker truck."

Matthew hefted Kale onto a chair at the end of the table, leaving his mother to deal with the booster seats the waitress was lugging toward them, and went to rescue Hope.

"He's into trucks," Matthew explained as he bent to haul Ian out of the chair next to Hope, where he clearly didn't belong.

"So am I, as a matter of fact." She laid her warm fingers on his forearm to stop him from lifting the boy away, and her touch and words surprised him. "Ian, guess what? I saw a dump truck yesterday."

"I seed a fire truck and…and it had water and everything." Ian looked proud of himself.

Mom, at the end of the table, shot a happy look at Nora and beamed as if she'd discovered a big pot of gold.

"Okay, that's enough." Matthew grabbed Ian around the middle. Hope might be a good sport about his mother's meddling and she was being kind to his son, but she clearly wasn't into children. It wasn't as if, at her age, she was married with kids of her own. "Little fireman, let's get you over here with Gramma so you can't bother Hope."

"He can stay, Matthew." Her words were velvet steel. "If you want to move him, fine, but he's not bothering me."

"He'll be like this through the whole meal."

"I like Ian. He's a fellow truck lover." The truth shone in her eyes—she seemed to really want Ian beside her. "Look, if you don't trust me with him, sit right here with us and make sure I don't start a food fight."

"Are you kidding? Look at those two old meddling women." He looked up to find both Mom and Nora watching him.

"Watch who you're calling old, young man," Nora admonished but looked undaunted as she winked at him. "Look at how your little boy takes to Hope."

Help. That's what he needed. Big-time help. Before he could protest, Hope spoke up.

"Nanna, you know I like children, so stop torturing Matthew or I'll burn your supper tonight." Hope flashed her grandmother a warning look, but her words held no real threat.

The door behind him snapped open and Helen walked through, escorting Harold. As the older women turned to greet the newcomers, Matthew knelt beside Hope and lowered his voice. "If we don't protest this with a united front, they'll think their matchmaking tricks are working."

"So? Let them." There were shadows in Hope's eyes, too, and he watched her press a hand to her stomach, as if she were in pain. "Sooner or later they'll figure out the truth and they'll be happily married by then."

She looked confident and somehow unhappy, too, and that troubled him. He wasn't the only one hurt by this. As Helen and Harold made their way to the table, settling down on the far side of Nora, Matthew couldn't help leaning close to whisper in Hope's ear. "What about Helen?"

"Good question." She swept a lock of hair from her face, an unconscious gesture that drew his gaze, and he couldn't look away from her beauty. Her skin looked silken-soft, and she smelled like sun-kissed wildflowers.

Why couldn't he stop noticing?

Hope caught Matthew alone in front of the egg trays at the buffet server. Grabbing a plate, she slid into line behind him. "Those women are incorrigible, using little children to further their matchmaking plans. Look at them."

Matthew peered over his shoulder toward their table situated near the front of the café, where Patsy straightened up from pouring ketchup on Josh's plate. His mom flashed him a triumphant smile that might mean, "See, I was right." Seated next to Helen, Nanna laughed, caught in the act of spying.

"I see." He reached for a serving spoon, trying to control a building anger. "They look pleased with themselves."

"Too darn pleased."

"You're encouraging them." Matthew spooned a heap of scrambled eggs onto his plate. "And I don't like it. It's not like I want Mom to think there's a chance I would want—"

He paused. No, those words hadn't sounded right. That wasn't what he meant.

"Oh." Hope heard his words and her fingers knocked against a serving spoon with a clatter. "That's fine, Matthew. I'll straighten things out once we get back to the table."

He'd spoken without thinking, out of anger and hurt and frustration. "I'm sorry. I didn't mean I wouldn't want to be seen with you."

"It's okay. You have every right to your opinion." She scooped up a poached egg and plopped it on her plate, concentrating very hard so she didn't have to look at him. "I wasn't the nicest person in high school, I'll grant you that. But I was young and with the way my family behaved, I didn't know any better. That must be what you see when you look at me."

"That's not what I see." His gaze shot behind her to where customers were grabbing plates from the stack, and moved forward to the heated trays of crisp bacon and spicy sausages. "I meant, why would a beautiful woman who has everything want to hang out with me."

"Really, it's okay." Hope grabbed blindly for the tongs and dropped a bunch of sausages on her plate, then circled around Matthew, leaving him alone.

It wasn't okay, and she didn't know why, but a horrible tightness was squeezing into her chest. When she reached the table piled high with fruit and breads, she set her plate down and took a deep breath.

This was irrational. Completely insane. She should get a grip before someone noticed how upset she was. Taking a deep breath, she ladled melon slices onto her plate and tried not to take flight when Matthew eased beside her, reaching for a few sweet breads.

"Cinnamon rolls, for the boys." His shoulder brushed her arm as he arranged the sweet-smelling pastries onto his crowded plate. "Hope, I'm sorry. I just meant that it's not like either one of us wants half the town thinking we're together. Rumors spread fast in a small town."

"I see your point." Trying to hide her hurt, she released the spoon too quickly, and metal clattered against the glass bowl. "For your information, I'm not all that bad to be around, at least, I've had other people think so. I might not be the best person in the world but I'm not the worst, thank you very much."

Without looking at him, even as he was opening his mouth to say whatever it was that would just make her angrier, she grabbed her plate and stormed toward the table, no longer caring who noticed.

"Have a nice chat with Matthew?"

Hope set the plate on the table in front of Nanna and glared at her grandmother. She caught Patsy with a withering look and willed her voice to be quiet but firm. "No more matchmaking. I've had enough of it, and so has Matthew. Believe me, there's no chance in a blue moon that we'll ever have anything in common, so not another word. Not one more word."

"She's right." Matthew towered behind her, square jaw clenched, broad shoulders set and a look of fury in his eyes. But his anger was controlled as he looked from his mother to Nanna, and then it seemed to fade away. "You heard Hope. We're from different worlds and whatever you two have in mind is never going to work."

"Don't they say that opposites attract?" Patsy looked ready to launch into a full-out, charming defense but seemed to change her mind when she saw the look on her son's face. "I only wanted to help, that's all. Look at these little tykes. They need a mother's care."

"Yes, that's right, and we love you both. We want you to be happy." Nanna didn't look one bit sorry. "Now, enough with this nonsense. Matthew, sit down and tend to your boys. Look what they've done with the ketchup."

Matthew caught Kale before he wiped ketchup on his brother, distracted from the issue at hand, but Hope wasn't fooled. She knew that Nanna had survived a life filled with losses and loneliness with an indomitable heart, and nothing would derail her, especially not something she felt was this important.

Frustrated, she kissed her grandmother's cheek and headed for the buffet table to fill a plate for herself. Her stomach burned and even if she wasn't hungry, she had to eat.

It wouldn't be easy, sitting next to Matthew's son and feeling Matthew's solid presence all through the meal…and maybe feeling his dislike of her.

There was no way he would ever make Mom understand. Matthew fought frustration as he opened the refrigerator and hauled out a yellow pitcher. He slammed the door and rummaged in the cupboard for a plastic glass.

Sure, Mom was sorry but she didn't understand.

She thought he was lonely and that he was holding onto Kathy's memory so that he could keep his heart safe from the risk of loving again. Well, she couldn't be more wrong.

After pouring, he left the pitcher on the counter, snatched the glass and headed through the house. His footsteps echoed in the too-quiet rooms, and the dark shadows made him all too aware that he was alone. A wife would have turned on the lamps and maybe put on some soothing music. That's what Kathy always did. His heart warmed, remembering.

He switched on the lamps and shuffled through the CDs, but couldn't find anything that felt right. Silence was okay; he didn't need to cover up the sound of the empty hours between the triplets' bedtime and his own.

Matthew sat down in the recliner, put his feet up, drank some juice and grabbed the paperback book lying facedown on the end table. But when he flipped to where he'd left off reading last, the printed words stared back at him and he couldn't concentrate.

He kept seeing Hope storming away from him in the café, hiding her hurt feelings behind cool anger, and he slammed the book shut. Frustration and conscience tugged at him. He wanted to head outside and keep going until the darkness and the cool night air breezed away this horrible knot of emotion and confusion tightening around his heart.

As he launched out of the chair, his feet hit the ground with a thud and he flew across the room. The silence felt thunderous and the emptiness inside felt as endless as the night. The doorknob was in his hand and the next thing he knew he was pounding down the front steps and into the cool darkness.

The crisp winds lashed across him, tangling his hair and driving through his shirt and jeans. He shivered, but at least he was feeling something besides heartache. Besides loneliness.

The wind rustled through the maple leaves near the house, and the rattling whisper of the aspens along the property line chased away the silence still ringing in his ears. He breathed in the scents of night earth, grass and ripening alfalfa from the nearby fields at the edge of town as a distant coyote called out and was answered. An owl swooped close on broad, silent wings and cut across the path of light spilling through the open door. He missed Kathy so much.

Father, help me to put an end to this.

There was no answer from the night, no sense of calm, no solution whispering on the wind.

"Daddy?"

Matthew heard a sniff and spun around. Josh huddled on the doorstep, rubbing at his eyes with both fists, his spaceship printed pajamas trembling around his small form. "What are you doing out of bed, hotshot?"

"I'm thirsty."

"Then come have some water with me." Matthew scooped his youngest son into his arms and held him close. He headed back into the house, shut the door with his foot and carried Josh into the kitchen.

The boy didn't want to let go, so Matthew balanced him on one hip while he searched for a second glass and found a clean one in the top rack of the dishwasher. He filled the glass while Josh clung to him.

The small boy was too sleepy to talk. He drank, smacked his lips and closed his eyes. Matthew's heart tightened with love for his child. For Kathy's child.

With Josh's head bobbing against Matthew's shoulder, he carried his son down the hall to the dark bedroom where a Pooh Bear night-light cast a faint glow across the two other boys sound asleep in their beds, teddy bears clutched in small hands.

"Sweet dreams," Matthew whispered as he laid Josh down on the spaceship sheets and covered him with the matching comforter.

Josh murmured, reaching out. Matthew spotted the bear lying forgotten against the wall and pressed it against his son's chest. The boy yawned, eyes closed, and sleep claimed him. He didn't stir when Matthew kissed his brow.

Kathy would have loved this, tucking in the boys, basking in the peace and quiet. She would have treasured the sense of rightness, of a day well spent and the blessing of three healthy sons asleep in their beds. With every beat of his heart, he missed her.

She was no more than a blurred face in his mind, the distant memory of a kind voice, and maybe that's what troubled him most of all. The real reason he was on edge with his mother and had hurt Hope's feelings. Because his beloved Kathy was fading from his memory, a little bit at a time, leaving a void in his heart. He could no longer recall the exact tone of her voice or the exact shade of her blond hair. And her smile, her touch, her presence...

She'd been the love of his life, and she was fading away from him slowly, piece by piece, memory by memory.

Clenching his fists, Matthew stood, crossed the room and pulled the door closed behind him. The empty feeling of the house seemed to vibrate around him, and he knew what he had to do. He'd behaved badly today, and it tugged at his conscience like a fifty-pound weight.

After looking up the number in the white pages, Matthew punched the lighted buttons on the pad, glowing a faint yellow, and glanced at the kitchen clock. Not ten yet. Maybe she'd still be awake.

"Hello?" Hope's voice answered after the second ring, gentle as an evening breeze.

"It's Matthew. You have every right to hang up on me, but I wanted to talk with you. I need to apologize."

"It isn't important." A reserve crept into her words, now that she knew he was the caller.

"What could be more important than your feelings?" He waited while the seconds ticked by.

"Fine, apology accepted."

"Wait, give me a chance to actually apologize. And there's something I wanted to talk about with you—"

"Good night, Matthew." There was a click and the line went dead.

It was worse than he'd thought. Hope was truly angry with him. You sure handled that just fine. Did he call her back and tell her what Harold had told him today?

The static on the line seemed to answer him, and he dropped the receiver into the cradle. The night, the shadows and the loneliness remained, and now he could add being a horse's rear to the list.

Troubled, he paced through the house, locking the doors, checking the windows, turning out the lights, feeling empty inside. A verse came to him, quiet as the night. *So if you are suffering according to God's will, keep on doing what is right, and trust yourself to the God who made you, for He will never fail you.*

The frustration and pain raging inside him eased, and he no longer felt alone in the dark night. *Father, I'm struggling. Please show me the way.*

Nanna looked old, older than Hope had ever seen her. Bright, fresh morning light teased at the window and tossed lemony rays across the foot of the old four-poster bed. Heart heavy, Hope lifted the breakfast tray laden with untouched food as Nanna curled on her side, pale with pain and still from the effects of the medication.

"She overdid it yesterday." Kirby tried to reassure Hope in the kitchen, where she sat at the table bent over her paperwork. "Nora isn't young anymore, and an injury like this is hard on a woman her age. Try not to worry so much. The new dose of painkiller seems to be working, so let's hope she sleeps through the morning."

Hope prayed that Kirby was right as she filled the coffee carafe at the sink, the spray of water into the empty container ringing in her ears. She shut off the faucet and looked down at the smooth, shiny handles Matthew had installed, and the worry eased away, which made no sense because she was still angry at the way he'd treated her in the restaurant. His behavior toward her had been so different from when he'd helped her to the top of the McKaslin's barn roof, when he'd held her safe and kept her from stumbling.

He didn't want his sons near her, and he didn't want to be seen in the same café as her. Well, that was perfectly fine. She wasn't looking for a man, especially not a settling-down widower with three kids in tow. Really, that's not what she was looking for. And it didn't matter how cute those little boys were. Not one bit.

She didn't need a family. She didn't need love. She didn't need to start seeing a fairy tale where none could ever exist. At least, fairy tales didn't happen to her and she was wise enough and old enough to know it.

After spooning ground gourmet coffee into the filter and turning the coffeemaker on, she grabbed an old knife and headed outside. The sweet gentle warmth of morning breezed against her as she hopped down the steps. She then knelt alongside the flower bed that ran the length of the house.

Untended since Nanna's injury, weeds were taking a firm hold in the rich soil. Tulips vied with dandelions and thistles, and Hope vowed to do some weeding, maybe later today when Nanna was doing better. The thought strengthened her, but even as she cut flowers, her mind kept drifting back to Matthew Sheridan and her heart clenched.

Yesterday, as he worked to keep his little boys from playing with their food, he'd handled them with tenderness and patience. Something she wouldn't have thought a man, even one as good as Matthew, could have possessed. And this was the man who hadn't wanted her befriending his boys, and the man who didn't want half the town thinking he was with her.

Good, fine, get over it, she told herself. But part of her felt hurt and angry. Hurt because she wished he didn't look at her and see her mother's daughter. Angry because it was easier than admitting the truth.

She gathered the cut flowers, arranged them in a vase and carried them upstairs. Nanna slept on her side, one hand curled on her pillow, her gray hair swept back from her eyes making her look as vulnerable as a child.

Yesterday had been tough on Nanna, although she would never admit it. Hope had seen the look on her grandmother's face when Helen had walked into the café with her hand on Harold's arm. There had been a brief flicker of sadness and regret, and then she'd invited Helen to sit down next to her. Nanna had let go of her hopes, just like that, for the sake of her lifelong friend.

There had to be a way to make her happy. But what? Feeling lost, Hope scooted the vase onto the edge of the nightstand and nudged it into place, bumping into a gold-framed photograph.

Hope's heart melted when she saw her grandfather's picture, a man she'd met only twice as a child, and Nanna's love. They'd met in grade school, Nanna told her, and they played together in the creek that bordered their family's properties.

He'd been her true love, one that didn't fade even after his death. Nanna had been newly widowed when Hope had visited the year she'd turned seventeen—it felt so long ago now, but the memories filled her with emotion. She remembered how two females, one old and one young and both hurting, forged a bond of love that summer.

She looked at the kind man in the photograph, taken at a summer picnic, maybe the town's annual Founder's Days celebration. It was easy to recognize the love in Granddad's eyes as he danced with a younger Nanna beneath an endless azure sky.

For the first time, Hope let herself consider that maybe Nanna meant what she said about love. That sometimes, it was honest and true. It didn't hurt or belittle but made the whole world right.

Sometimes.

With Kirby's words of warning, Matthew negotiated the narrow staircase as quietly as he could in his work boots. A few boards squeaked as he reached the top, and he felt odd prowling down the hall, drawn by the splash of light through an open doorway.

No sounds of conversation came from the room at the end of the corridor. No soothing music or low drone of a television broke the stillness. There was only Hope perched on a chair at her grandmother's bedside, head bowed as she read from the Bible held open on her lap, the light from the window pouring over her shoulder to illuminate the pages.

In the span of a breath, he saw the depths of her heart as she turned the page, searching for passages. Every opinion he'd formed of Hope Ashton faded like fog in sun.

"Matthew," she whispered, startled, and closed her Bible with quiet reverence. "What are you doing here?"

He gestured toward the bed, where Nora barely disturbed the quilt. "I have the cabinets."

"Now isn't the best time." Hope laid her Bible on the crowded nightstand and padded across the wood floor as quietly as she could manage. "Where's Kirby?"

"Downstairs on the phone speaking with the doctor," he explained once they were in the hallway. "She said her call might take a while and that you might be up here all morning, so if I wanted you, I'd better fetch you myself."

"She's right." Hope led the way down the hallway. "I wouldn't be able to bribe you into coming back another day, could I?"

"If it's a good enough bribe," he teased, wishing he could mend how he'd hurt her.

She almost smiled, but it was enough to chase the lines of exhaustion from her soft face. When they reached the bottom of the stairs, the bright morning light accentuated the bruises of exhaustion beneath her eyes and surprised him.

He followed her through the front door and onto the

wide old-fashioned porch where flowering vines clutched at the railing. The morning's breeze tossed back the dark curls escaping from Hope's ponytail and ruffled the hem of her T-shirt.

It was only then he realized what she was wearing—an old T-shirt with the imprint faded away and a stretched-out neck, and a pair of old gray sweatpants with a hole in the knee. She ambled to the old porch swing on stocking feet and sighed as she eased onto the board seat.

"Rough night?" he asked.

She nodded, this woman who could have hired a legion of nurses to take care of her grandmother. But she had come herself without nurses or help from the rest of her family. By the looks of it, she'd spent most of the night at Nora's side.

"I know what that's like. I didn't get a whole lot of sleep during the triplets' first two years." He headed toward the steps. "I better leave so you can get some rest. We'll worry about the cabinets some other time."

"I hope this doesn't mess up your work schedule."

"Don't you worry about my work. Since I finished the McKaslins' barn, I've got a few roofing jobs to do, but I'm always waiting on deliveries. I'll just give a call when I've got time and head on over. When Nora is feeling better, that is."

"I'm determined to feel optimistic—she's going to be fine." Hope offered him a weary smile. "You don't have to run off, you know. At least not before I get a chance to apologize."

"I'm the one who owes you an apology. I practiced

it on the drive over here." He leaned against the rail, arms folded over his chest. "I gave you the wrong impression at the café."

"No, I understand. You've told me how you feel about your mom's matchmaking schemes, and I shouldn't have expected you to just shrug them off. You're right, we shouldn't encourage them."

"Now wait a minute. I was going to say that you were right. That those two stubborn opinionated wonderful women can matchmake all they want, but it won't do a bit of good. They can't influence us. And if you can have enough grace and class not to be obviously insulted that my mom would try to marry you off to a working man like me, then I can do the same."

"Yep, spending time with you has been torture. And those boys." Hope managed a weary smile, but emotion glinted like a new dawn in her eyes and told him what her words didn't. "Those sons of yours are the cutest kids I've ever seen in my life."

"You won Ian over. He loves a woman with truck knowledge."

"I'm a working-class woman, so I've seen a lot of trucks in my day." She glanced at him, chin up and gauntlet thrown.

"You're not a working-class woman, Hope. Not with your family's income bracket."

"I was never a part of that family." Her chin inched a notch higher. "I make my own way in this world."

"So, that explains the outfit."

"What?" Then she looked down at the battered pair of gray sweats with a gaping hole in the right knee and the white, so-old-it-was-graying T-shirt. "A true gentleman wouldn't have said a word, but you had to, didn't ya?"

"I'm tarnished around the edges."

"No kidding." Half-laughing, she swiped the stray curls that had escaped from her ponytail with one hand. "Who needs makeup, presentable clothes and combed hair, right?"

"It's like seeing you in a whole new light." The old impressions of the remote, pampered girl he'd known in high school and the expectations he'd had of a rich woman fell away, shattered forever. "It's not bad from where I'm standing."

"Sure, try to make me feel better. Yikes, I need a shower and, wow, I can't believe I look like this." Embarrassed, laughing at herself, she hopped to her stocking feet, leaving the swing rocking. "I have to go and…and…do something, anything."

"You look the best I've ever seen you." Maybe he shouldn't have spoken his heart, but it was too late, and Hope stopped her rapid departure.

She turned, and he saw again the woman seated at her grandmother's bedside, head bowed over the Bible in her lap. The exhaustion bruising Hope's eyes and the comfortable clothes she wore to care for an old woman through the night made her all the more beautiful to him.

"Tell anyone about this, and I'll deny it," she said.

"So, you *are* worried about your reputation, after all."

"You bet, buddy. Guess what your mother will

assume if you tell her that you got a good glance at my bare knee?"

"It's not a bad knee," he confessed, but before she could answer Kirby stepped into sight and whispered something to Hope.

Alarm spread across Hope's face, chasing away the smile until only worry remained. "I have to go, Matthew."

"Is there anything I can do?"

Hope's gaze latched onto his, filling with tears. "She's in a lot of pain, and the doctor isn't certain that the fracture is healing. Prayer would be a help."

"You've got it." Chest tight, Matthew watched her spin with a flick of her ponytail, and she was gone. Leaving him feeling both lonelier and more alive than he'd been in what felt like a lifetime.

At sixteen minutes before noon, Hope heard a car rumble down the long gravel drive. Patsy Sheridan climbed out into the brisk spring sunshine and, leaving the triplets belted into their car seats, carried a steaming casserole to the front door.

She'd handed the meal over to Kirby before Hope could make it downstairs, but the gratefulness washing over her didn't diminish after Patsy's car drove out of sight.

Later, flowers arrived and cakes and Helen brought supper by, a potluck favorite that was always the first to go at the church's picnics, according to Kirby.

As the dusk came, bringing shadows and evening light, Hope knew that in all her travels, all the places she'd been and photographed, home was here in Montana, in this small town where neighbors took care of one another.

She knew who to thank. Matthew Sheridan had spread the word of Nanna's relapse. And she owed him the world.

Chapter Six

"Is that Matthew's truck?" Nanna leaned toward the
edge of the bed, fighting to see out the window.

"Hey, careful." Hope gently caught Nanna's elbow.
"All we need for you is to fall and break another bone."

"I may have broken my leg, but I'm not fragile."
Nanna nodded with satisfaction as Matthew's dark red
pickup gleamed in the sun in the driveway below. "At
least, not anymore. This bone will heal, or else. I've lost
nearly a week in this room, and it's time to get a move
on."

"Just remember what your doctor said, Nanna."
Hope reached for the hairbrush and knelt on the floor,
gently swiping the smooth-bristled brush through
Nanna's soft cloud of gray hair. "Want me to braid this
for you?"

"I'd love it, dear heart. I'm in a festive mood, as long
as young Matthew Sheridan can get my cabinets right."

Hope bit her lip so she wouldn't smile. Fretting
over the cabinetry work might give Nanna something

to think about other than her injury. "I don't know if I'd trust Matthew. He's one of the only carpenters in town. Without much competition, how good can he be?"

Nanna's eyes sparkled. "So, you like him, do you?"

"Keep dreaming."

"A girl's got to try." Nanna fell silent, allowing Hope to part and braid her hair, then finish the thick French braid with a cheerful pink bow.

As Hope pulled a comfortable pair of clean pajamas from the bottom bureau drawer, the sound of a second vehicle coming up the driveway drew their attention.

Nanna tipped sideways again. "Goodness, that looks like—"

"Harold." Hope couldn't believe her eyes as she watched the distinguished-looking older man climb from a restored 1950s forest-green pickup. A carpenter's belt hung at his waist as he headed for the back door, his deep voice carrying as he greeted Matthew.

Was this what Matthew had tried to tell her on the phone the night she'd been so abrupt with him? Hope leaned against the window frame and felt the sun warm her face. In the yard below, Matthew and Harold appeared, talking jovially as they unloaded the heavy wood pieces from the back of Matthew's truck.

The sun gilded Matthew's powerful frame and heaven knew, she shouldn't be noticing. A tingle zinged down her spine, and a yearning she'd never felt before opened wide in her heart.

"There's no way I'm going downstairs in these."

Nanna's two-piece cotton pajamas landed with a thunk on the end of the bed.

Hope turned from the window. "Nanna, have you ever thought about falling in love again?"

"Goodness, child, a woman my age doesn't waste what's left of her days wishing for romance. You have the greatest happiness life has to offer ahead of you. Marriage and children. Now don't lie to me, you have to want children."

Hope felt the warmth inside her wither and fade at the word *marriage*. Her stomach burned at the memory of exactly what that word meant to her, the old ulcer always remembering. Endless battles, bitter unhappiness and her parents' habitual neglect of her.

She tried to put the memory aside of the unhappy child hiding in the dark hallway, listening to the hurtful words her parents hurled at each other as if they were grenades. Fearful that this argument would be the one to drive Dad away.

And it reminded her of her own attempt at marriage, ended before it began. And her stomach felt as if it had caught fire. No, she wouldn't think about the time she was foolish enough to think that love could be real for her.

Determined to distract herself, Hope paced the sunny room. "Where's the shorts set I bought for you when we took that cruise last summer?"

"Try the drawer chest, second to the bottom."

Sure enough, the soft blue-and-pink print knit shorts and top were folded amid Nanna's summer wear, surrounded by sachets of sweet honeysuckle. As she helped her grandmother into the clothes, she wished Matthew had told her he'd invited Harold over.

Kirby tapped down the hall and into the room and together they carried Nanna downstairs. "No, the garden," she insisted when they tried to situate her in the living room. "I need to feel the warmth of the sun on these old bones."

"Let me help." Matthew strode into the room like a myth—all power, steel and hero. He lifted Nanna into his strong arms, cradling her against his chest. "Nora, it's been a long time since I've held such a beautiful woman in my arms."

"That's a line you ought to use on my granddaughter, not on an old woman like me."

"I'm partial to older women."

Now I'm going to have to like him. Really, really like him, Hope thought as she held open the wooden framed screen door for Matthew. I've run completely out of excuses.

There was no turning back her feelings, especially when he set Nanna onto the shaded, wrought-iron bench with the same care he showed his sons. Tender, gentle, kind, he grabbed one of the matching chairs and drew it close. Watching him made that tingle zing down Hope's spine again.

No doubt about it, she was in trouble now. As she accepted the pillows Kirby had thought to fetch, she tried not to look at him, but he drew her attention like dawn to the sun.

"Are you going to give me that last pillow?" His mouth curved into a one-sided grin as she handed it over. "I'll have you ladies know that this service is entirely free. It won't show up on the bill."

"You're a real bargain." Hope tried to sound light but failed as he laid the pillow on the seat of a chair and lifted Nanna's leg into place.

Their gazes met and Hope heard the morning breezes loud in her ears. Awareness shot down her spine again.

His slow grin broadened. "I've been told that before. I never overcharge." He stood, towering over her, casting her in shadow. "But I do accept tips. Cash or baked goods."

He was kidding, but Hope couldn't smile. Kirby arrived with Nanna's Bible, reading glasses and the cordless phone.

They were shooed away by the old woman who thought she was matchmaking by sending them off to be together. "Take your time, Matthew. I don't need the cabinets today."

Hope shook her head, taking the lead down the garden path. "Sure, she's been fretting over the cabinets all week."

"That's all right, we'll fix her." Matthew's feet tapped on the flagstones behind her. "I brought Harold."

"I noticed. I thought he was interested in Helen."

"Helen is interested in him." Matthew caught her arm, stopping her before she could reach the back porch. "He avoided the subject when I asked him how he felt. All he would say is that he hardly knew Helen, that's all. I figure, until it's decided for sure, we might as well put him and Nora together and see what happens."

"Great idea, but you could have warned me."

"Harold didn't make up his mind until the last minute." Matthew's hand flew to his jeans pocket and withdrew a black pager, vibrating in his open palm. "It's Mom. Can I use your phone?"

"For a fee."

His grin was slow and stunning, and he darted past her, taking the porch steps in one stride, leaving her breathless.

She wasn't interested in Matthew Sheridan and he wasn't looking for marriage, but she couldn't help but wonder for the first time in her life what it would feel like to spend time with a man like him. To know the shelter of his arms and the tenderness of his kiss.

Gentle warmth spilled through her at the thought. What was wrong with her? Why on earth was she feeling this way? Hadn't she failed miserably at her one attempt to open her heart and hadn't she learned her lesson? That it was better to live alone and safe than give a man control of her heart?

Matthew reappeared, frowning, his hair disheveled as if he'd been raking one hand through it. "The job's off for this morning. Harold can't do the heavy work alone because of his bad back, and I've got to go. I can rearrange things for tomorrow afternoon. How about it?"

"What happened? Is something wrong with your boys?"

"No, not with the triplets." Matthew's frown

deepened. "My mom's sick. She didn't look so good this morning, but she insisted she was fine enough to baby-sit."

"Of course, you need to check on her." Hope followed him down the path. "Is there anything I can do?"

"Yeah, find me a real good baby-sitter. One who isn't afraid of three little boys."

"That shouldn't be hard." Nanna spoke up from her serene bench in the shade. "Is something wrong, Matthew?"

"Mom's allergies are acting up and she isn't up to handling the boys." Matthew's brow frowned with concern.

Hope's heart twisted. He was a good man, one who cared for his family genuinely and selflessly. She tried to imagine her own father setting aside work for any reason, especially his family. "I hired extra nurses. If your mom needs any care—"

"No." Matthew dug in his pocket for his keys, loping down the path and onto the gravel. "It's nothing like that. Appreciate it, though. Her new medication is making her drowsy, and she's just not up to chasing after the boys."

Hope stepped after him, wanting to soothe away the worry on his face and the lines of hardship bracketing his eyes. "If you need someone to look after your sons for the day, I could do it. You could bring them here. Nora now has two nurses to take care of her and hardly needs me. I wouldn't mind keeping an eye on them."

"Nora needs peace and quiet."

"Let me go ask her. I—"

"Don't mind a bit," Nanna's voice called clear as a bell through the foliage that separated the driveway from the garden. "Doesn't Proverbs say that a cheerful heart is good medicine? Watching those boys of yours play will be all the cheer I need."

"No. Absolutely not." Matthew yanked open his truck door. "Hope, it's a nice offer, but you don't want to look after my sons."

"Why not? Ian and I struck up a friendship in the café, and I'm sure I can charm the other two."

"No. You're a…" He looked at her from head to toe and blushed. "You're a beautiful woman, and I can't see you getting down and dirty with three energetic little boys. You don't know what you'd be getting yourself into."

"I saw them in action at Sunday brunch. They move fast, but I'm faster. Besides, Nanna needs some joy in her life, and something tells me your sons will keep her laughing."

"You don't want to take care of these kids, trust me."

But he was weakening, she could see it, and so she went in for the kill. "Nanna really wants her cabinets finished."

"Nora's been ailing. She wouldn't be able to get any rest."

"She's listening to every word we're saying, so she'd speak up if that were true. Besides, I owe you a favor for all the wonderful things you've done for my grandmother and me. So consider this payback, got it? After this we're even."

"It's a bad idea, Hope." Matthew raked one hand through his hair, leaving more dark strands standing up on end to ruffle in the breeze.

Hope fought the urge to reach out and smooth down those strands. Her hand tingled at the thought of touching him that way.

"You're not used to one kid, let alone three."

"We have certified registered nurses on the premises. What could go wrong?"

Laugh lines crinkled around his eyes. "You'll be sorry you said that, just wait and see."

"Then it's decided."

"Well…it would help me out. If you're sure."

"Absolutely."

Doubt lingered in his eyes, but his grin came easily. "Fine. We'll just see how the morning goes first, then we'll see if you've changed your mind."

Long after he'd driven off, Hope still felt the tingle in her spine and warmth in her heart.

Kneeling in dirt in what would soon be Nanna's vegetable garden, Hope looked up as Matthew strolled onto the back porch looking as though he'd been working hard. His T-shirt and jeans were smudged with sawdust, and the carpenter's belt cinched at his hips was missing a few tools.

He squinted in her direction, his amusement as bright as spring. "You look exhausted. Are you sorry yet?"

"Give me ten more minutes, then I might be." Laughing, Hope ducked as a handful of dirt came flying her way. "Hey, Kale, I saw that. Lower that hand right now. *Right now.*"

As the boy reluctantly complied, tossing a look of warning to his older brother, whom he was aiming for, Matthew's chuckle rang out, effecting her from her head to her toes. "Boys, I told you no fighting."

"It's Josh's fault." Kale spoke up, always ready to pass the blame. "He's throwing."

"Nope, I'm talking to you, buddy." Matthew loped down the steps and moved a potted tomato plant out of the way. Then he crouched down, his gaze meeting Hope's across the span of freshly turned dirt. "I didn't know dump trucks and graders were useful in a garden."

"Of vital importance. Look how busy it's keeping them. For now." Hope laughed as Josh made a truck engine sound, content on leveling out the far end of Nanna's unplanted garden. "How's the work coming?"

"The cabinet's in. I talked Harold into fetching Nora. Figured she'd want to see what I'd done before he starts the finishing work."

"I thought you two were going to do that work together."

"We were, until I lost Mom as a baby-sitter. I just called her and she's feeling better, but not well enough to take the boys."

"They can stay the rest of the afternoon, don't worry. You're not putting me out, and Nanna's getting a kick out of watching them. Ian took a worm he found over for her to praise, and she's still glowing. Over a worm."

"She's pining for great grandchildren."

"Count on it. She figures I'm her only hope." Longing speared her sharp as a new blade. Really, she didn't need a family. She didn't need a man in her life trying to dominate her and belittle her. Isn't that what most marriages were?

Ian dashed through the fragile rows of newly planted vegetables, carrying a bright yellow tractor. "Daddy, come see right now."

"Over here, Daddy." Kale hollered as he scooted a bright yellow dump truck into a rock with a clang. "Come see the big hole we dug."

"It's a huge one, Matthew, so be careful not to fall into it." Hope winked as she grabbed a six-pack of tomato plants.

Matthew watched her hands gently break apart the dirt and ease the first sprout into the rich earth. Her touch was gentle as she patted the dirt around the roots, and for one brief second he wondered what it would feel like to take her hand in his. Not in a quick touch to steady her on the barn roof or help her from the ladder, but to hold her hand, her palm to his, their fingers entwined.

He felt ashamed for even thinking of it. He was a man, he was human, and the Good Lord knew he was lonely, but this was the first time since Kathy's death he thought about another woman. Guilt cinched hard around his heart, leaving him confused.

Then Hope reached past him, brushing his knee with the edge of her glove as she grabbed one of the last tomato plants.

"You look at home here in the garden." Matthew couldn't seem to take his eyes from her. "There's dirt smudges on your face."

"Probably." She swiped her forearm across her brow and left another. "I'm a mess. Why is it that whenever you come over, I look like I've rolled out of a drainage ditch?"

"Lucky for you, it's a look I like. Especially the leaf in your hair."

"Oh, dear." She tore off one glove, revealing slender fingers stained with dirt.

"Here, let me." It was a simple thing, reaching forward and lifting the green half of a tomato leaf from her hair, but it felt as natural as if he'd been this close to Hope all his life. Already the floral scents of her skin and shampoo felt like a memory, and he knew, if he lowered his hand just a few inches to brush the side of her face, her skin would feel like warm silk against his callused fingers.

Guilt pounded through him with renewed force, and he let the leaf blow away in the wind.

"Daddy!" Ian stomped his foot, his voice hard with indignation. "Listen."

Oh, boy, how long had the kid been trying to get his attention? And how could he not hear his own son? "I'm coming, buddy."

He climbed to his feet, and Ian's small gritty fingers curled around his and held on with viselike force. He watched as Ian shot a jealous look at Hope. A lot of women who'd sacrificed their morning to watch over someone else's children might have taken offense, but

Hope merely shrugged, her mouth soft with amusement.

It was there on her face, radiant and sincere, and he couldn't get it out of his head as he knelt in front of a small pit to praise the boys' busywork. She liked his boys, and he couldn't fault her for that.

"Matthew, look." Her whispered words as gentle as a spring breeze tingled over him and, at the look of hope in her eyes, his heart skipped a beat.

Harold was carrying Nora in his arms from the garden to the back porch. It was one of the sweetest things he'd ever seen.

"Daddy." Josh let go of his grader, and the truck tumbled to the ground with a clang. "I'm *real* hungry."

"Me, too!" the other boys chimed.

"You've got to be kidding. It's ten-thirty in the morning. Nope, no food. I'm starving you three from here on out."

The triplets started demanding hamburgers, and Matthew watched Hope climb to her feet, brushing the dirt off her clothes.

"It will be after eleven by the time we get to town." She lifted her chin in challenge. "We can get take-out hamburgers and they'll be fueled up for the rest of the afternoon."

"No way. I'm not imposing on you like that. You have Nora to look after."

"She's a soft spot in my heart, and I let her stay up too long this morning. She's going to be napping all afternoon, believe me, so I'll have plenty of free time." Hope rubbed a smudge of dirt from her cheek with her hands, leaving another bigger smudge. "Besides, I have it on good authority that Nanna loves cheeseburgers. Even older women need their protein."

"Hamburgers, hamburgers," the triplets chanted.

"All right, boys, you win. Let's get you in the truck. And you. Stop encouraging them." He shot a gaze at Hope, who was carefully treading through the rows of vulnerable new plants.

"Hey, I wanted hamburgers, too." The wind tousled the dark strands that framed her face.

His chest cinched tight, and he wished he could stop noticing how the sunlight sheened on her velvet hair and caressed the silken curve of her cheek.

But most of all, it was her hands that caught his attention, slim but capable-looking, sensitive but strong. Hands that had helped care for her ailing grandmother, hands that could coax beauty from a camera and hands that he wanted to take in his own.

But that was because he missed Kathy. That was the only explanation. The longing in his heart for a woman's touch was really the longing for Kathy's touch, forever lost to him. It wasn't an attraction to Hope.

"I'll help get the boys buckled in," she offered, following the triplets to the truck.

His heart cinched. A part of him knew that it wasn't Kathy he wanted to touch right now, and as Hope trotted away, offering to race the boys, he wondered what his feelings meant.

He'd asked the Lord to show him the way. Surely these feelings for Hope weren't God's answer to his prayers.

* * *

"I tried to seat them together," Matthew whispered as he climbed onto the picnic bench beside her, his breath warm against the outer shell of her ear. "Harold was stubborn."

"And look at Nanna, she's talking to Josh and completely ignoring Harold." Hope snatched an onion ring from one of the waxed paper boxes in the middle of the old weatherworn table. "We're dismal failures as matchmakers."

"Good thing we're not done yet."

"I'm glad you're not easily defeated, because neither am I." Not now that she realized how much her grandmother needed someone in her life, someone to love. And that's what she would concentrate on. "I know Nanna's interested in him, but you wouldn't know it to look at them."

"Kale, throw that fry and you won't get more," Matthew interrupted as one dark-haired little boy held a ketchup-tipped curly French fry in midair, contemplating the merits of lobbing it at Ian and losing his fry privilege completely.

Ian solved the dilemma by flinging a fry at Kale instead and splattering ketchup across the table.

"That's it, you boys have sat long enough." Matthew leaped up to prevent any more throwing. "Get up and run off that energy. And stay where I can see you."

Two identical little boys hopped off the bench, legs pumping, sneakers pounding, tearing through the grass field behind the house. A small plane cut through the wispy white clouds in the blue sky above, and the boys spread their arms like wings, making plane engine noises.

"My, I'd forgotten what fun they are at that age. And so much energy!" Nanna beamed with delight as she watched them. "My son was just like that, always on the go, always thinking. About ran me ragged, he did. How you manage with three of them, I'll never know. It would take a special woman to be a stepmother to three three-year-olds."

"Nanna, I think it's time for you to go upstairs." Hope snatched another onion ring from the basket and shared a conspiratorial smile with Matthew. He looked ready to set Nanna straight, ready to come to Hope's aid if she needed him.

Not that she needed him.

Matthew stood alongside her, scooped Josh from the bench and set him on the ground. The little boy raced off to join his brothers, arms spread, soaring through the fresh young grass waving in the wind. "Harold, if you keep an eye on my sons, I'll carry Nora upstairs."

"Sure thing." The older man nodded, pride at his great grandsons alight on his handsome face, before nodding politely to Nanna. "You take care, Nora."

"Oh, my granddaughter will see to that." There was no want, no coveting in Nanna's clear eyes as she smiled.

Hope ached for her grandmother. Harold seemed as if he liked Nanna, and Hope fought disappointment as she took Nanna's hand.

"She looks too tired." Matthew appeared at Hope's

side, his strong warm presence unmistakable. "Nora, come lean on me."

So it was with gratitude that she followed Matthew up the stairs as he cradled Nanna in his arms. The bedroom windows were open to the sun, and the lace curtains fluttered in cadence with the wind. The distant sounds of small boys' laughter and the hum of engines sounded merry and seemed to fill the lonely old house with a welcome joy.

Hope tugged down the top sheet and stepped back so Matthew could lower Nanna onto the mattress with tender care. Hope's chest swelled with more than gratefulness and she turned away as a warmth that had nothing to do with appreciation spilled into her veins.

"Bless you, Matthew." Easing back into her pillows, Nanna pressed her lips together to hide a moan of pain. Kirby rushed in with noontime medication and a glass of water to wash down the collection of pills.

Matthew took the older woman's aged hand in his and squeezed gently. "You take it easy now and rest. I can't thank you enough for allowing my boys to stay."

Nanna's eyes glistened. "They made this place feel happy, like it used to when my children were young. I can't tell you what it did for this old heart of mine."

Matthew eased back to give Kirby room to work, and Hope followed him into the narrow hallway, which was warm from the heat of the day. Feelings she couldn't name fought for recognition in her heart as she struggled with the locked window at the end of the hall. It wouldn't budge.

"Let me." Matthew's arm brushed hers as he took

over, efficiently manhandling the stubborn old lock and lifting the equally obstinate wooden window.

The heat from his brief touch lingered on the outside of her arm and didn't go away, even when she stepped farther back, even when she rubbed at the spot on her arm. Was it her loneliness making her feel this way? She didn't like it, not one bit.

"Harold's going to go ahead with the finishing work. He's excellent at it." As if he felt it, too, Matthew backed away, creating distance between them, and his gaze locked on hers, warm and intimate.

Way too intimate. Panic leaped to life inside her. "I'm glad you're leaving the boys for the rest of the afternoon."

"It looks like you're managing." He caught hold of the banister and hesitated. "I'd like to stop by and check on my mom."

"Why don't you give her a call from here, and if she's still under the weather, I'll send home some food for her, so she doesn't have to cook tonight. The refrigerator is packed, thanks to your thoughtful words to the pastor."

"That's what friends are for." He tossed her a slow grin, one that lit up the hazel twinkles in his eyes.

"Is that what we are? Friends?"

"Why not, it's better than being enemies, or adversaries or afraid of the matchmaking women in our lives."

The confusion coiled in her chest eased. Yes, they were friends. And there was nothing she would like more. Friends were safe. Friends didn't demand a vulnerable part of your heart.

"Speaking of our matchmaking relatives, I'm going to need your help." She swept past him, careful not to brush against him, and skipped down the stairs. "I'm going to make a list of all the eligible men in your mom's age group. I don't know what to do about Harold. I know Nanna is still interested in him, but Helen is her best friend. That's the way Nanna is, and I love her for it. So we'll have to find her someone as nice."

"That's going to be hard." Matthew's step echoed in the kitchen behind her. "Look."

Hope eased the screen door open to get a better view of Harold running in the calf-high grass, arms spread, making airplane noises with his three great grandsons.

"I think we should leave it up to the Lord." Matthew's grin broadened, and he was handsome enough to make Hope's senses spin.

Somehow she managed to speak. "What about Helen?"

"'And we know that God causes everything to work together for the good of those who love Him.'" Matthew splayed both hands on the porch rail and squinted through the sun to watch Harold dive-bomb Ian, then pretend to have engine trouble and drop to the ground. The boys giggled. "We'll let Him work it out. Whatever's meant to happen will. I have a suggestion, though."

"I'm almost afraid to ask."

"I think Nora might be happy if Harold refinished every last one of her cabinets. Think how shiny and new they'd look."

"I like the way you think." Let Harold and Nanna spend time alone in this house, and if they were meant to be together, then the Lord would work it out in His own way. "Consider refinished cabinets my treat to Nanna. How about new linoleum and countertops?"

"I'm miraculously booked up, but I bet Harold might do it."

"Then we have a deal." She sidled up next to him at the porch rail, leaving enough space so their elbows wouldn't brush, and it felt good having a friend in Matthew.

She felt different, better than she could ever remember feeling.

Chapter Seven

The sun slanted low in the sky and thunderheads were gathering on the horizon in tall pillars of angry clouds by the time Matthew headed his pickup down Nora Greenley's drive. The tires crunched in the gravel, and the warm breeze from the open window blew against his face. It wasn't hot enough for air-conditioning yet, and with the approaching storm, the dusty air felt muggy.

He rounded the last corner and Nora's old white farmhouse rolled into view, a sprinkler casting arcs of water across the front lawn. The shade trees shivered in the gentle breezes as he pulled to a stop in the graveled area in front of the detached garage. He cut the engine, and the familiar sound of his sons' laughter came distant but welcome.

So, Hope had survived the threesome after all. Warmth gathered in his chest, an emotion he couldn't name as he hopped from the truck and strode down the garden path. The rich scents of pollen, blooming plants and new roses felt as mellow as the late afternoon light.

He rounded the corner of the house and stopped in his tracks at the sight of his boys racing around on the back lawn, squealing whenever Hope hit one of them with a blast from the garden hose. Drenched, Ian darted one way, Kale the other, and Josh got hit full-force in the stomach.

"It's cold!" he shrieked, face pink with delight.

"Catch me, Hope!" Ian waved both hands, then took off running the instant she turned the nozzle toward him. With a shout, Ian hopped away from the cold water jet, laughing as Hope took off after him, hose snaking in the grass behind her. Water sprayed over him, drenching him from head to toe.

"Gotcha!" Hope called victoriously, then quick as a whip shot water at Kale, who wasn't expecting it.

"Run, Kale, run!" Ian urged, and the three took off toward the garden gate, trying to outdistance the arcing geyser that was quickly catching up to them.

Then Josh spotted him. "Daddy! Daddy!"

"Daddy!" They headed toward him talking at once, their bare chests glistening in the warm sun and their brown locks sluicing water as they ran.

"Hope sprinkled us with the hose and not the grass," Ian shouted over his brothers. "It's real cold. We want pizza."

"Pizza, pizza!" the other two demanded.

"You boys have food on the brain." Matthew knelt down as they launched toward him and didn't mind their wet hugs one bit. "Ready to head home?"

"Is Hope comin', too?" Kale wanted to know.

"Hope has to stay here with her grandmother." Matthew stood, and the tiny hairs on his arms and the back of his neck prickled when Hope padded close.

"I sure had a lot of fun with you three today." She'd rescued their shirts from the porch railing, and she held them out now. "Let me run inside and grab some towels. I'm afraid I got your boys a little wet."

"They're sweet, but they won't melt. Already tried it." He winked, and he liked the smile that shaped her face. His fingers brushed hers as he took the shirts, and for the life of him he couldn't stop looking at her.

She simply glowed, out of breath from chasing his boys, dripping wet, her hair tumbling in thick shanks, and he wanted to pull her close to him. To take her in his arms and hold her, simply hold her, as if her brightness could chase away the shadows inside him and make right every wrong in his world.

But he hesitated, knowing he had no right. There was too much to stop him.

The moment was lost, and she stepped away, heading toward the porch. "I'll be right back."

"Don't bother with the towels. They'll dry off in the truck. It's hot enough. Okay, boys, time to head out and give Hope some peace and quiet."

"Why?" Ian demanded. "Wanna get sprinkled by the hose."

Matthew recognized the signs. A long, exciting day and no nap. "Looks like I'd better get them home and fast. Thanks again for watching them."

"I hope it helped you out. Heaven knows you've done more than enough for me."

He couldn't look at her any longer, torn between the past and something that felt frightening to think about. "I was able to finish another job this afternoon. It made a huge difference."

"Good." A world of goodness shone in her eyes as their gazes met and held.

It felt like a deep chasm breaking his heart into pieces and he stepped back, searching but not finding words to begin to explain.

"Bye, boys," Hope called, lifting a hand, looking as attractive and beautiful as morning, and he wished....

A part of him wished.

The boys called out in answer, grumbling first, then telling him about every aspect of their afternoon with Hope. How she'd let them dig holes for the baby corn plants, how they'd watered the garden and got into a water fight, and the chocolate cookies she'd given them.

She'd taken their pictures, and they climbed trees and ran through the sprinkler until they were cold. Their happiness filled the cab of the truck but it didn't touch him as he first belted each boy in tight, then climbed in behind the steering wheel.

He could see Hope through the shivering leaves of the willows as she set the sprinkler in the backyard. Then the boughs moved, blown by a harsher wind, signaling the first edge of a storm and hiding her from his sight. But not from his mind.

Wishing, aware of a great emptiness in the deepest

part of him, he headed down the road, straight toward the dark shadow of gathering angry clouds, already dreading the night ahead.

"I happened to see you and Matthew talking alone together," Nanna commented, patting the sheets smooth over her legs to make a place for the supper tray. "You two sure look like you're getting along well."

"Why wouldn't we? We're on the Founder's Days planning committee together, thanks to you and Patsy, so we have to find a way to cooperate. And what were you doing out of bed?" Hope set the tray into place and checked the wooden legs to make sure they were locked and sturdy. "Don't tell me you got up without anyone noticing."

"I could hear you two talking because my window is wide open." Nanna's bright eyes spoke of something more as she unfolded the paper napkin and spread it over her lap. "Sounds like those boys of his have really taken to you."

"They're nice boys, and I know where you're headed, so don't go there and say grace instead."

Nanna chuckled. "'Fools think they need no advice, but the wise ones listen to others.' I've told you before and I'll tell you again, you need roots, Hope. You're like me, and I watched you with Matthew's boys today. You had joy in your eyes for the first time since you've come back, and it makes my heart glad."

"I like children. I never said I didn't. You have to stop this pressure, Nanna. I know what you expect from me and what you want from me." Her stomach burned, and she could feel the day's lightness slipping away.

A great emptiness opened up inside her, an emptiness that hurt. How did a person know that love would last?

Love didn't come with guarantees.

Tucking away her fears, Hope decided to take charge of the conversation. "Now say grace because I'm starving."

Over the pleasant supper, Hope steered far away from Matthew and made a point to ask about the people in town she'd known as a teenager and how they were doing now. Nanna's exhaustion caught up with her. Her nighttime medication put her to sleep before she had time for her prayers and chamomile tea, so Hope took the pot with her to the living room.

Wind whipped through the open windows, lashing the lace curtains without mercy. With the scent of imminent thunder and rain strong in the air, Hope wrestled with the stubborn, warped wood window frames and wondered how on earth Nanna had managed to strong-arm these windows for so long.

A spill of light through the archway from the kitchen filled the room with shadows, and Hope flicked on lamps, listening to the sound of her footsteps loud in the emptiness. Even though Brittany, the new nurse she'd hired from the agency in Bozeman, was busy with her paperwork at the kitchen table, Hope felt the solitude as keenly as a punch to her chest.

Maybe it was because she'd had so much fun with

the boys today, watching over them and marveling at how three identical children could be so different. Somehow she felt lonely without their constant noise, energy and happiness.

The old house echoed around her as she dug through the rolltop desk in the far corner. How could Nanna stand this night after night, year after year? Distant thunder boomed and the wind gusted, knocking a lilac bough hard against one of the windows.

Finally, Hope found what she was looking for and carried the small stack of spiral-bound paper to the wing chair in the corner. She eyed the phone sitting there and grabbed the cordless receiver from the kitchen since there was an electrical storm on the way.

She dialed the number, listened to the four rings and felt her smile the minute Matthew answered. "It's Hope. Do you have the boys in bed yet?"

"I've got them last-minute water and found a missing teddy bear. The light is out, the door is closed and so far I haven't heard anyone hollering for me." The rich warmth in his words spoke of his deep love for his boys, something that couldn't be mistaken, and chased away the shadows in the room.

"Any luck with a housekeeper yet?"

"I've put an ad in the Bozeman paper. Mom's been against it, but she can't keep up with those three forever and it's too much to ask her to do full-time." He sighed, a sound of pent-up frustration.

"I'd be glad to help out again, if you get in a bind."

"I can't impose on you like that. How's Nora feeling after a day with the boys?"

"Her spirits are high and that's got to make a difference. She looks better, but it's going to be a long road for her. She initially refused the option of surgery. You know how stubborn she is. Tomorrow I'm taking her to the doctor in Bozeman and we'll see what he says. They're going to run some tests and if there's no sign of bone growth, I'm going to talk her into surgery. She'll have no choice."

"I'll be praying for both of you."

"Thanks, Matthew." Outside the house, the wind gusted so hard, shrubbery slammed against the windows, and the sound of wood scraping and clawing at the glass gave Hope the shivers. She curled up in the wing chair. "I have the church directory in hand. Do you have time to go through it looking for eligible bachelors?"

"For Mom and Nora." His voice smiled. "Sure, I've got time for a good cause."

Clutching the receiver between her ear and her shoulder, Hope opened the well-worn booklet to the first page and scanned the names until she spotted a man listed singly, without family members. "How about Brad Birch?"

"He's twenty-something."

"Okay, I'll cross him off the list. How about..." She ran the ballpoint pen down the page. "Austin Chandler?"

"He was a few years ahead of us in school." Matthew laughed. "Try again."

"Dr. Andrew Corey?"

"Hey, he's Mom's age." Across the wire came the

sound of rustling, as if Matthew was looking for paper and pen. "I think they went to high school together."

"This is going to work, it has to. Patsy and Nanna are still young, considering. They shouldn't have to spend the years they have left alone. How about Zachary Drake? Wait, he's too young. Joseph Drummond?"

"Put him on your list."

Ten minutes later, Hope was staring at names of five lonely widowers, men who might be suitable for either Nanna or Patsy. "I have no clue what to do next. I've never done this before."

"Leave it to me. Got anything going on Saturday?"

"No real plans. Why?"

"It's a surprise." The deep rich timbre of his voice rumbled with expectation. "I'll pick you up at around eleven. Oh, and Hope? Wear sneakers."

"Sneakers? What are you up to? I won't necessarily need sneakers to hunt down the men on this list."

"You'll have to live dangerously and find out."

Laughing, she leaned back in the chair cushions and stretched her legs out, propping them on the corner of the coffee table. "Do I need to bring anything else?"

"Just your lovely self. Good night, Hope."

"Good night."

And then he was gone, the line went dead and the shadows returned.

"Are we there, Daddy?" Ian's question filled the cab of the pickup like a thunderclap. "Are we, are we?"

Matthew snatched a brief glance at his son in the

rearview and couldn't hold back a grin. Hope had sure won over his boys. "We're almost there."

"But I wanna see Hope!" Kale complained, and Josh nodded in grave agreement.

"I'm turning into her driveway this very minute." Dust kicked up from the gravel road. The storm earlier in the week had dropped a bucket load of rain, but there was no sign of it now. The countryside shone green and gold from the distant hills to the fields on either side of the road, where tall grass waved in the temperate winds.

The minute his truck shot around the last curve, he spotted Hope sitting on the front porch next to her grandmother on the old wide-benched swing. The way Hope lifted her hand in greeting made him glad he'd invited her along.

"Hope! Hope! Hope, we saw a hay truck," Ian shouted, then was drowned out by his brothers. Three boys strained against the confines of their car seats to get Hope's attention.

"Hi, boys, Matthew." She rose from the swing and her gaze snared his, but there was only a flash of friendliness there. A warm, sweet friendliness. She turned to kiss her grandmother on the cheek, an equally sweet gesture, and the love and concern on her face left no doubt how grateful she was for Nora's slow improvement. "Nanna, I can still stay, if you need me."

"Goodness, I've got twice as many nurses as I need and an afternoon with nothing to do but feel the breeze on my face." Nora still looked pale, but the sparkle was in her eyes. "Go have some fun. It's past due."

"I'll make sure she does have some fun." Matthew called out his window and earned another one of Hope's smiles. "Nora, you're looking better."

"Nonsense, but I *am* feeling better," answered the spry woman, frail but determined, with her casted leg propped up on a stool. "The doctor said my bone is healing just fine and in another week I'm going back to my crutches, no matter what a certain pushy granddaughter of mine says. So you do me a favor and make sure my Hope relaxes, will you? She's worked herself to the bone the last few weeks, and it's time we put an end to it."

"Like I can't take care of myself, Nanna. Really." Hope skipped down the steps, the hem of her untucked cotton shirt fluttering around her waist and hips as she moved.

Matthew tore his gaze away and hopped from the truck. "Nora looks like she's happy about this outing of ours."

"Sure she does. She thinks we're going out on a date." With a wink, Hope accompanied him around the tailgate to the passenger side. "I heard her say that to your mom on the phone last night."

"You were eavesdropping?"

"No, but I heard her anyway. Don't worry, I didn't let her get away with it. I changed the subject to the list of eligible men at church, and I got a few clues."

He opened the truck door for her and held out his hand. "It's a step up. Here, let me help."

"I've climbed into your truck before," she argued but surprised him by placing her hand on his. Her touch was warm, her presence captivating and when he breathed in, he smelled the sunshine fragrance of her hair.

With the sun hot on his shoulders and a strange tingling down the back of his neck, he helped Hope into the truck and shut the door. Through the open window he could hear the boys yelling over each other, trying to win her attention.

As he circled around the hood, he watched Hope twist around in the seat and heard the velvet gentleness of her voice as she spoke to them. By the time he'd slipped behind the wheel, the boys had quieted down and were talking in turns about the trucks they'd spotted so far today.

Hope made a bet she could see more trucks than they could. Through the entire drive to Harold's ranch, shouts of "logging truck" or "gas truck" or "milk truck" peppered the air until Matthew joined in, spotting a coveted fire truck ambling along the country roads.

"Like picnics?" Matthew asked after he'd pulled off the paved road and onto a narrow dirt lane.

"Love them."

"Good, because I hoped you might take it in stride. Believe it or not, I thought you might like to see something of Montana, considering the pictures you take for a living and all." He braked and killed the engine. "Now I know this isn't an Italian countryside, but it's not bad."

"I guess not." She gazed ahead to the tall rim of white-capped mountains in the distance, jagged proud peaks spearing the forever-blue sky. "I hear a river."

"The Gallatin. Runs all the way from Yellowstone Park to the Missouri headwaters." This had always been his weekly retreat with the boys, and it felt right including her, this woman who had everything but seemed lonely in many ways. He knew a thing or two about loneliness.

"Want out, Daddy!" Kale demanded.

"Is Grampy Harold comin', too?" Josh asked.

"I'm hungry!" Ian announced, and Matthew knew there'd be no peace unless he unleashed his sons and let them run around in the sun and grass.

"Stay where I can see you," he warned Ian as he swept him from the car seat and let him go. "Kale, you, too."

"'Kay, Daddy." As soon as Kale's sneakers hit the ground, he was off to join his brother, who was running through the tall grass.

"Hurry, Daddy!" Josh squirmed in his seat and made it harder to unbuckle him. The minute he was free, he tore off toward his brothers.

Matthew grabbed the picnic basket, and Hope was beside him, dark eyes laughing as she watched the boys burning off energy. His chest felt too tight to breathe. "Come on. I'll show you the river."

She smiled, and he felt its warmth all the way to his toes. His step seemed lighter as he herded the boys toward the copse of cottonwoods hiding the bank from sight. As she walked beside him, he heard her step in the grass, felt the whisper of the wind between them and heard the gentle rhythm of her breathing.

Her presence, her scent, her being felt so female, so

womanly. She filled his senses, making his heart twist and ache. The emptiness inside felt too much to bear. He would miss Kathy, he would always miss her. But right now, he realized he was missing something even more.

"Oh, Matthew." Hope froze in her tracks, face lifted to the beautiful peaks in the background, taking in the simple rugged beauty of the river that winked with quiet confidence in the midday sun.

Across the wide river, a fragile antelope lifted her white muzzle from the water and studied them. The fawn at her flank stared hard at the boys, then in a flash both mother and baby leaped into the grass and disappeared.

The wind, the sweet-smelling fields, the powerful river and the mountain's beauty couldn't hold his attention the way Hope did. The awe on her face showed as she spun around slowly, gazing upstream at the beavers working in the waters of a nearby creek that emptied into the river. At the distinct white face and hooked yellow beak of the American eagle soaring overhead on a hunt, black wings spread in a breathtaking glide. And then at the river cutting its path through the rich Montana earth and clay, a deep silent force.

Hope breathed the words. "It's a different kind of beauty, wild and simple, better felt than seen."

Matthew merely nodded, his throat tight, captivated by this woman who made her living photographing sunsets in French vineyards or the play of light in the remains of a medieval cathedral. He knew without asking that she understood what he saw here—endless peace, the ever-turning circle of time and God's hand in the world.

"How would I capture this wind, I wonder?" Her hand lighted on the top of her camera case, but she didn't open it. "Or the feel of this river?"

"I'd planned on taking you downstream. Harold keeps a boat not far from here. He's a serious fisherman, but I don't like to mix three-year-olds and fish-hooks."

"I can't imagine why."

Before he could answer, the boys charged toward them, their calls carrying on the wind, waving the sticks they'd just found high in the air.

"I got one for you." Josh handed the dry length of what had been once a tree branch to Hope. "The bestest one."

"Thanks, Josh." Hope knelt to take the gift offered with three-year-old pride. "You are a thoughtful boy."

He gave her a beaming grin before he took off with his brothers to try to get inside the picnic basket Matthew carried. But Matthew was slow to lift it out of their reach because he was too busy watching Hope hold that length of wood as if it were a treasured gift.

"It's not every day a girl gets a stick as good as this one," she told him with a smile that dazzled, that reached down to the chasm in his heart and warmed him like spring sunshine. "Your boys are acting like they're about to keel over from starvation."

"Thirsty, Daddy!" "I'm hungry, Daddy!" "Kale's pushin' me!" The words rang with deafening force, but Matthew moved by rote, sending the boys to pick out a picnic spot in the dappled shade.

All he could think of, see, hear and feel was Hope as she helped the boys settle the dispute over where to sit, with the wind in her hair and the sunlight caressing the soft curve of her face.

The way he longed to do.

Chapter Eight

Hope bit into the cold chicken thigh and moaned. Crispy, moist, seasoned just right. "Did Patsy make this? It's delicious. I'm going to have Nanna ask for the recipe."

"Well, she's going to have to ask me because I made it." Across the blanket, above the boys' chatter, with the food spread out between them, Matthew spooned a generous helping of potato salad onto his paper plate. "Everything you see here, I did, and I'll be glad to share the recipe with a woman as beautiful as you."

"Compliments will get you everywhere." She laughed, feeling more at ease with her friend, and her opinion of him rose another notch. From what she could see, he was everything that a father should be.

When the boys got into an argument, he quieted the situation with kind words and a fair solution. When they were on the brink of a potato salad flinging fest, he stopped them with a word that was firm and not threatening. Love shone in his eyes whenever he looked at his boys.

It was so easy to see the depths of this man's heart, and she knew that's why she liked him. Why, when she'd spent her adult life avoiding any kind of relationship with a man other than in her work, she felt safe at Matthew's side—as his friend.

"Piggyback ride, Daddy!" Ian demanded, after finishing two helpings. His two brothers eagerly abandoned their plates to beg for rides, too.

"Okay, but don't wear your old dad out." Amid cheers, Matthew scooped Ian from the blanket and swung the boy onto his broad shoulders.

"Go, Daddy, go!" Ian chanted before he broke into laughter as Matthew raced through the knee-high grasses. "Faster! Faster!"

Hope snatched her pocket-size Nikon from her camera bag, uncovered the lens and focused. Frame by frame she caught Matthew's easy lope through the fields, the blue bunch wheat grass snapping against his tanned knees, scattering butterflies and startling larks.

Through the eye of the camera she caught the easy intimacy between father and son as Ian lifted both hands in the air, fingers extended as if trying to touch the sky. And then how he hugged Matthew hard, his arms banding around Matthew's forehead. Behind them stretched the vastness of crystal blue sky and puffy white clouds and the snow-capped Bridger Mountains, purple-blue and breathtaking.

With a final click, Hope captured father and son, profiles matching, dark shanks of hair tumbling over identical brows as they laughed, facing the wind.

"We wanna ride now!" Kale complained.

"I'm always last," Josh sighed to her.

Okay, she was a pushover. Every stray cat she'd ever come across had her pegged. And so did Josh as he toddled over the wrinkles in the blanket and reached out for her camera with sticky hands.

Too quick for him, Hope tucked it back into her bag. "I can give piggyback rides, too."

"You can?" Twinkles just like Matthew's sparkled in Josh's hazel eyes. "And run fast, too?"

"Just as fast as your daddy." She knelt, giving him her back. "Climb on."

Hot sticky fingers caught hold of her neck, tugging on a few strands of her hair. Then a knee dug into the middle of her right kidney. Hope reached around and gave Josh a boost, and his legs swung one at a time into place over her shoulders.

"Hold on tight, and we're good to go." As soon as she felt Josh's hands on her neck, she stumbled to her feet.

"Faster!" Josh squealed in her ear.

Hope caught hold of his shoes, holding him steady as she broke into a jog through the fragrant grasses. Josh was a sweet weight on her shoulders, bouncing and giggling with glee.

"I'm not last, Daddy!" he shouted with jubilation as Hope sprinted past him.

"Hey, wait a minute!" Matthew's back had been turned, and the surprise on his face transformed into an approving wink. "I'd race you, but I'd win."

"Don't count on it." She took off into the wind, pushing hard.

"We winnin', Daddy!" Josh twisted backward to shout, nearly throwing Hope off balance.

She managed to keep him right side up on her shoulders, but Matthew took advantage and sprinted alongside her.

"You're pretty fast, Hope." He wasn't winded yet, and there was a challenge in his eye as he paced her. "I'm faster."

"You sound a little too confident to me." She leaped over the remains of a dead limb, and Josh shouted his approval.

Matthew sailed over the thick cottonwood bough, his gait smooth and steady. Kale's shouts spun Matthew around, and he stopped. Hope waited, too, as the third boy raced after them. "I want up now, Daddy! Please, please!"

Matthew knelt to let Kale crawl up behind Ian and somehow settled one on each shoulder. The boys seemed used to it, holding on tight, their heads leaning together to touch at the brow, their grins identical, and Hope's fingers itched for her camera.

"I'll race you back to the river. How about it?" Matthew's challenge was answered by the boys' shouts.

"I'm ready if you are."

His half grin turned saucy, as if he already figured he was the winner. "Ready? Go!"

He waited half a beat before taking off, and Hope leaped ahead of him. Let him try to be a gentleman, he was still going to lose. But the added weight of two boys didn't seem to slow him down any, and she fought to stay ahead of him as they swung along the fence line and headed straight for the river.

A hawk lighted on a post, took one look at them and soared skyward, wings spread, so majestic Hope longed to turn and watch the beautiful creature, but she didn't dare take her gaze from the ground. A prairie dog poked up from its home in the earth, chattered as if scolding them and ducked.

Matthew sailed over the hole, gaining on her. He was at her side, breathing hard, working to pass her. She wouldn't let him.

Shoulder to shoulder, neck and neck, they raced side by side, the boys urging them on. Matthew started pulling past her, running all out, breathing hard. Gasping for air, reaching down for the last bit of strength, she pushed past him and soared beyond the blanket's edge. She'd won!

"I can't believe it!" Matthew dropped to his knees, letting the boys tumble off his shoulders and into the grass, giggling.

Breathing hard, Matthew stretched out on the sun-baked grasses. "You're pretty good for a city girl."

"You're not bad for a country boy." On wobbly legs, she lowered herself to the ground. Josh dove off her shoulders into the soft grass, rolling around with his brothers. Out of breath, she sank back into the sweet fragrant grasses and stared at the sky, the exact color of a robin's egg.

Sunlight shot in streamers through the trailing wisps of cotton white clouds. High overhead were the twin tracks from an airplane, and if she squinted she could barely see its silver body flitting across the face of the sky.

"Daddy! Look." Kale stood up, pointing toward the far end of the blanket.

Hope watched Matthew roll on his side. "Why, you little thief. Get away from our basket." He climbed onto his feet, unfolding easily to his six-foot height. "Hey, those are our brownies."

Hope twisted around to see two little prairie dogs trying to help themselves to something inside the basket. They looked up defiantly as Matthew loped toward them, then settled for stealing a biscuit before scurrying back to their home in the grass.

"Can you believe that? A guy's brownies aren't safe anywhere, I guess."

"Maybe we'de better eat them now so they aren't temptation for more wild creatures." Hope sat up and dusted grass from her hair.

"Good idea."

Already the three boys were helping themselves to the plate Matthew held out for them, taking a brownie in each hand. Anyone could see what a good man he was—no, what a great man he was. His humor and patience with the boys made her heart hurt in a way she couldn't explain and didn't much want to think about. They were friends. Just friends.

She inched over to her camera bag and tugged out the Nikon. She uncovered the lens and framed Matthew as he knelt with his boys, their adorable identical faces smeared with brownie frosting. The shutter clicked.

Matthew looked up, seeing her camera for the first time.

"I've been missing working, and I couldn't resist," she confessed. "You don't mind?"

"Nope. Not at all." He set the plate down between them and crouched with his back to the sun. "Now that you're sure Nora's leg is on the mend, will you be heading back to wherever it is you call home?"

"I have a condo in Malibu. And don't give me that look," she admonished as she stole a decadent-looking brownie from the plate. "It's a modest place, believe me. Just a one bedroom, something to call home, even if I'm hardly ever there."

"Sure, well, I have a vacation home in Maui, but I'm hardly there, either." A slow jaunty grin tugged at the left corner of his mouth. "Will you be around to go to the Founder's Days dance with me?"

"Well, since we're two of the committee members, we might as well go together. Especially since your mom and my grandmother are expecting us to announce our engagement."

"Mom was ecstatic when I let it slip I was seeing you this afternoon."

"You saw the joy on Nanna's face when you drove up." Hope nibbled the edge of her brownie, and the rich chocolate sweetness melted on her tongue. "Whatever you do, don't let her know you can bake like this. I'll never hear the end of what a fine husband you'd make."

"Hate to break your illusions about me, but this is from a box." He held up what remained of his brownie.

"I'm really good at following directions, especially if they come with step-by-step pictures."

He didn't know where it came from or how it happened, but one minute Hope was laughing and the next he had to fight to keep from claiming her mouth with a kiss. The need to hold her tenderly and cover her lips with his burned like a steady flame inside him.

Hope, unaware of his struggle, leaned on one elbow and lifted the camera. After a moment, the shutter clicked. "I think I found the angels in them, chocolate fingers and all."

Her gentle humor wrapped around his heart and it only made him want her more. Shocked at himself and at his feelings, he hopped to his feet and rescued the empty plate from the ground.

"It's getting late." He couldn't look at Hope as he turned away. He just couldn't bear to look at her. "If we want to float down the river, then we'd better get going."

"Sounds like fun." By the sound of her voice, she had no idea what he was feeling and what he wanted from her. "Boys, let's get you cleaned up before we head out. Such a strong chocolate scent might bring out more than just the prairie dogs."

As she knelt down to do her best to wipe chocolate off the boys' faces, his heart broke open a little wider. She was like sunlight on summer afternoons, and how she warmed him.

Peace drifted on the winds and whispered in the swift deep waters of the Gallatin River. Hope drank in the beauty of the land sparse with trees but rich in wild beauty. The boys played with their bright green plastic fishing poles that sported no dangerous hooks, Matthew guided the boat by oar, and they drifted in the swift current. She slipped the camera out of her bag.

For the fun of it, she snapped shots of the boys and of Matthew, who merely shook his head at her, a dimple revealed in his left cheek.

"Don't you city girls know how to play?"

"I'm here, right?" How did she admit work was the only thing she had in her life, besides God? No one was waiting for her at home, no one missed her when she left town, and there was no one to hold close through the long nights. "This is my idea of fun. I know, amazing but true."

"Nora ordered me to make sure you relaxed."

"I *am* relaxed." She tilted her face to the sunlight and drank in the feeling of sun and wind and freedom against her skin.

"I've been hearing tales about you."

That drew her attention. Hope twisted around and settled into the curve of the bow. "Out with it. I want to know what you've heard."

"Afraid, huh?" He dipped the tip of one oar into the water and eased them along with the current. "I've heard a few things, actually. It seems quite a few people noticed the two of us together at the Sunshine Café for brunch after church that day. I've been asked by about four or five people just exactly what's going on between the two of us."

"Oh, as if we were there alone together instead of with our families."

"Exactly. From the sound of it, you'd think the two of us were having a romantic tryst." There was no sadness in his eyes as he met her gaze. "Don't worry, that particular rumor will die down. But there's another rumor I do believe that's being spread around this town and it's about you."

"I'm in trouble now."

"Yep, everyone's saying how hard you work taking care of Nora. Even Harold mentioned it to me. He said you'd taken over all the housework and cooking, besides helping the nurses day and night."

"Nanna's doing better, that's all that matters."

"You'll rest later, is that it?"

She felt her stomach tighten and begin to burn. "Nanna is all the family I have. Or at least it seems that way."

"What about your brother?"

"Oh, he's so busy making money in New York that he doesn't have two seconds of spare time. And either of my parents—" Her stomach felt on fire. "They wouldn't come here. When they heard about Nanna's fall, Mom offered to pay for a nursing home. A nursing home!"

Anger licked through her, and she knew it showed. "Nanna has always been there for me. She took me in when I was lost and alone that horrible year my parents were divorcing, and hers was the first real love I'd known. I can't leave her to fend for herself now."

"No, you wouldn't." The way he said it sounded like he believed in her.

And it comforted her like nothing else. That's what

friends did, comforted one another. So why did she keep noticing the play of muscles beneath his T-shirt? Why was she feeling an electrical charge from being so close to him?

She *wasn't* attracted to him. She just *couldn't* be. She was off balance, that was all. Yes, that had to be it. She was out of her usual environment, like a fish out of water. That had to be why she was feeling this way.

The reason she'd let herself close enough to see Matthew's heart and feel her own respond.

"I catched a fish!" Kale's shout of delight shattered the definite tug of attraction between them. The boy hopped up and down, clutching the taut line of his play fishing pole. "Looky, Daddy! I got the big one!"

"Harold is always trying to catch the big one." Matthew winked as he tucked the oars into place and stood from the bench seat. Kneeling beside his son, with the other boys burrowing close to him, he reached over the gunwales and tugged on the heavy plastic line. An old leather boot popped out of the water, caught on the green plastic bobber.

"Sorry, son, but the big one fooled us again." Matthew kissed Kale's brow in comfort.

"Kale catched a shoe!" Ian giggled, and soon all three of them were laughing, the merry sound traveling across the gurgling river like birdsong, attracting smiles from a group of onshore fishermen.

"I bet Grampy Harold never caught a shoe before." Matthew winked at Hope as he wrestled the boot that was mysteriously tangled in the sturdy plastic line.

"Hope, we're drifting toward that snag up there. See the way the water currents move around that spot in the river?"

"You mean the spot where we're heading?" She uncurled from the bottom of the boat.

"That's the one. Can you untangle this for me so I can steer the boat? I'd hate to capsize us on our first official date—you know that's what my mom's gonna call this. I'd never live down the embarrassment."

"Give me that pole." She towered over him with the wind in her hair and the sun haloing her with golden light. "I may be a city girl, but I know a thing or two about fishing. Move over, Kale, and I'll show you how it's done."

"You know how to catch fishes?" Josh asked, eyes shining. "Really, really?"

"Really. I went on a fishing expedition off Cabo San Lucas and saw big blue fishes the size of this boat."

"Did ya eat it?" Kale wanted to know. "Grampy Harold cooked the trouts we catched."

"No, I didn't want to kill anything so beautiful, but I got some great pictures of the sea." Hope twisted the boot, tugged on the waterlogged laces and the plastic bobber popped free. "Now, let's go fishing."

"Maybe you can catch the other boot," Matthew quipped as he guided the boat safely past the dangerous spot.

The way Hope laughed, easy and sweet, made him laugh, too. In fact, he'd drifted this river hundreds of times and he couldn't remember it ever being this beautiful or the day so bright.

* * *

Matthew hated pulling his truck into Nora's driveway and knowing the day was at an end. The sunset gathered in bold splashes of crimson, gold and purple along the jagged peaks of the Rockies, casting a lavender sheen over the peaceful land and regret through his heart.

"I'm going to call Patsy tonight," Hope said as she gathered her camera bag from the floor. "You've got three tired boys to deal with, so no arguments. Let me do it. I'll catch you at church tomorrow and let you know how it went."

"Matchmaking is harder work than I thought." They'd talked of nothing else on the drive back and had come up with an idea that just might work, or at least provide them some direction. "Fine, you talk to Mom. But I'm warning you, she's going to bombard you with questions about today. Nosy, probing questions. Be prepared."

"I'm brave, I can take it." Hope's hand moved toward the door handle.

"Wait right there, city girl. Sometimes you're too fast for me. Just slow down." He hopped out, circled the truck and opened the door for her. "Old habits."

"Nice habits." She smiled and covered his palm with hers, although the independent flash in her eyes didn't fade.

Longing filled him, and he fought it. He stepped back an appropriate distance when he wanted to sweep her into his arms and nestle her against his chest.

Instead of being able to hold her and feel her sweetness, he had to be content with the springlike scent of her as she climbed down from the truck and released his hand.

It wasn't enough.

"I guess I'll see you in church tomorrow," she breathed, spinning around to face him, bathed in the soft lavender glow from the setting sun. "Nanna insists she can make it, so I'm going to let her try."

"I'll volunteer to carry her into the church and back out again, if she needs it. If she's not strong enough for the crutches."

"That's a wonderful offer, thank you." She looked so independent, so beautiful. "But strength isn't the issue. Nanna is plenty strong enough, and thank the heavens her pain is back under control. I just don't want her doing too much."

"Let me know if you need anything, okay?" He took a step back. He had to go. The boys were starting to yammer in the background, and the rising urge to reach out and kiss her was overwhelming him. He ached for her brightness, her sweetness, her sanctuary, and he had no right to feel this way.

No right at all.

"I told Nanna we're making a short day of it. Just church and nothing else. So, at least we're safe from another surprise brunch."

"Don't count on it. There's still the Founder's Days committee meeting coming up."

"Yes, but Nanna will be staying home and your mom won't be there, so how bad can it be?"

Famous last words, Matthew thought. It would be

tough sitting beside her through the hour-long meeting, smelling the shampoo in her hair and fighting an impossible attraction to her.

"The day was the best I'd had in ages." Hope retreated to the porch, sincerity dark in her gaze as she looked at him one final time. "I'll never forget it."

"Neither will I."

Then she hopped up the stairs and, with the bang of the screen door, disappeared from his sight.

But not from his heart.

"Have a good time with Matthew and his boys, did you?" Nanna asked from the kitchen table. A playful glint sparkled in her eyes. "Looks like you've got a little sun. Or is that the first bloom of romance I see?"

"Definitely the sun, Nanna. Keep on dreaming, because marriage and I aren't happening." Hope plopped her camera bag on the counter and snapped open the refrigerator. "Did you get some supper?"

"No, Roberta decided to starve me. Figured it was the best treatment."

"I can tell you're feeling better, you're starting to get sassy." More happiness wedged into Hope's heart. Yes, it had been a good day indeed. "In the mood for some iced tea?"

"Now there's a good suggestion. We'll sit down right here and you can tell me all about your date with Matthew."

Hope rolled her eyes. "It wasn't a date and you know it."

"I know what I see."

"Let's just agree to disagree on this, okay?" She set the pitcher on the counter with a thunk. "It wasn't a date, I'm not looking for love, and poor Matthew is still grieving his wife."

"Grief doesn't last forever. The loss does, but grief is like a wound." Her voice grew serious. "In time a heart does heal."

"Oh, Nanna." Hope heard the truth in her grandmother's words. "I didn't mean to bring up something painful to you."

"I'm strong, and I learned how to be a long time ago. The day I buried Jonathon was the saddest in my life, and the lowest point. The very lowest." Nanna stared hard at the table to hide the tears in her eyes, tears that never fell.

"I never told anyone this, not one soul, but I was furious with God. And I mean furious. He took more than my husband from me, He took my life, my reason for being."

Hope took the chair closest to her grandmother and realized for the first time just how deep love between a man and woman could run, deeper than any river, higher than any mountain and stronger than death. "I can't imagine you being angry at God, Nanna."

"I was hurting, honey, and let me tell you, the word 'rage' wouldn't have described it. I'd always seen Jonathon as the gift from God that he was, and the greatest light was our love together. And then one day Jon was so sick and soon gone. I'd shared most of my life with him, and after twelve long years I'd still give anything I have for one more day.

"Of course, I know I'll see him again. But it took me a long time to accept His wisdom, to understand that for everything there is a time. 'I trust in your unfailing love. I will rejoice because you have rescued me. I will sing to the Lord because He has been so good to me.'"

Hope didn't know what to say and didn't know if she could speak for the tears knotted in her throat. So she simply reached out and held her grandmother tight and safe. But in her arms, Nanna no longer felt fragile, but strong. She felt strong.

"We are so alike, Hope," Nanna said when she'd pulled back to dash at the tears shimmering on her lashes. "We both came from families where there was no love, only war. Like you, I vowed I would never marry. I'd never trust any man like that. I'd never live with hard words and dark anger."

"I didn't know. I thought…." Hope looked around at the old house where Nanna had raised her children, where Hope's own mother had grown up in the bright sunshine of Nanna's love, and not even that love had protected Mom from a bad marriage. "I don't know what I thought. That you came from a happy family."

"I fought falling in love, I can tell you that. But God found me a patient man, one with fortitude and a loving heart as infinite as eternity. I trusted in God's love, and so I trusted in His gift of Jonathon's love."

"You found your happily ever after."

"Yes, I did. But Jonathon was on loan to me. Every day is precious, and a day filled with love ever more so. Please, don't waste your time stubbornly protecting your heart, Hope. Life is far too short to forsake God's gifts because we are afraid to accept them."

Later that night, after tea, prayers and reading Nanna to sleep from her Bible, Hope felt the truth of her grandmother's words. Or maybe it was the contrast between the laughter-filled day and the unsettled aloneness of night.

She was glad Nanna had found love in her youth, one that had given her great joy, but Hope also knew the reason behind her grandmother's story. Nanna would not give up her stubborn desire to marry Hope off. Couldn't Nanna understand that Hope didn't need a husband? She had faith, she loved God, she tried to live her life the right way, but the memories of her and her fiancé's last fight echoed in the darkness surrounding her until her stomach burned and she flicked on as many lights as she could find.

Restless, Hope dug out her laptop computer and popped the small disk from inside her camera. As always, her work calmed her and centered her. She scanned some of the hundreds of images she'd taken on her interrupted trip to Italy, making notes of which ones she'd use for her next book.

Then she came across the pictures of the triplets she'd taken both in the garden and at the river. As she studied the images on her computer screen of three identically charming smiles and sparkling eyes, happiness slipped into her heart.

Nanna said that time was precious. Hope was glad she'd spent this day the Lord had given her with Matthew and his boys.

Chapter Nine

Matthew bolted awake, sitting straight up in bed in a room bathed in darkness, breathing hard. The wisps of dream remained before his eyes, the vision of Kathy at his side as they hiked through the mountains, her features blurring and her voice fading away into nothing, nothing at all.

The darkness felt choking and he kicked off the sheet, desperate to force the memory of the dream from his mind. But it wouldn't leave. The image of nothingness at his side remained.

Maybe he'd been unfaithful to her, to her memory. The vows he'd taken were until death do us part, but it was more than that. Love didn't stop with death, and he was at a loss what to do.

He tiptoed past the boys' room and found his way by memory and feel to the kitchen, where stardust and moonbeams silvered the bay window of the eating nook. A cold glass of water didn't dislodge the knot of emotion wedged in his throat or wash away the twisted-tight feeling in his stomach.

It's time. He heard those words like a voice surrounding him, more mysterious than the moonbeams slanting through the window. As he stepped into the silvery cast of the light, he felt the chasm in his heart tear open a little more.

He knew it was time to let go, to stop mourning. He couldn't bear to. For as long as he grieved Kathy, he still had a part of her. He was terrified that if he let go of his grieving then he would lose her completely.

His grief was all he had left of his beloved. And he felt guilty that he was ready to move on, ready to welcome sunshine on his face and feel again. And he was lonely. So very lonely.

Father, how can I do this to Kathy? Please, show me what is right.

His Bible was in the center of the table where he'd left it earlier in the evening, and he reached for it now, the smooth cover welcome against his fingertips, the weight in his hand an old comfort, the papery crisp flutter of the weightless pages soothing. The moonlight slanted over the type, and it was just enough to read by if he squinted.

"There is a time for everything, a season for every activity under heaven. A time to be born and a time to die." Matthew rubbed his thumb over the words, read so many times since Kathy's death. "A time to cry and a time to laugh."

He remembered talking on the phone with Hope the night of the last storm, and they'd laughed together. That wasn't the only time. On the picnic, Hope had made him laugh so many times that she'd chased away the sorrow in his heart.

The image of her, sun-kissed and gentle, flashed into his mind as she'd knelt with the boys in the boat.

Hope made him laugh. Made him feel. They'd run together through the field with the boys on their backs, racing each other through the sweet wild grasses, and he'd felt joy breeze over him like the wind.

"A time to grieve and a time to dance."

The moonlight slanted lower across the page, across words already committed to memory. Matthew closed his eyes, hating to admit it and knowing he could no longer deny it. For whatever reason God had brought Hope Ashton to town, the effects were felt in his heart. Her friendship had shown him exactly how alone he was.

As she'd fished with the boys, she'd illustrated unknowingly how much the triplets needed a woman in their lives, not a housekeeper but a mother. She'd shown him that the empty place at his side could be filled. Yesterday had been a gift, and Hope was a true reminder of what could be for him again.

In time.

Pain filled him, and it felt as if his heart were breaking all over again. But this time, unlike when he'd buried Kathy, there was no anguish. Now there was only peace.

After a long time, he opened his eyes and watched the moonbeams fade as the moon set. Soon the blackest point on the eastern horizon grew shadowed, then gray. Birdsong began like the most reverent of hymns—quietly, gently, building to a song of joy, of melody and harmony and hope.

Dawn broke softly over the Bridger Mountains, burnishing the snow-capped peaks with a rose-pink glow, and the stillness was shattered as three sets of bare feet pounded down the hallway. Three little boys wearing cartoon print pajamas bolted into sight, shouting good morning and racing to be the first to hug their daddy.

"Want waffles, Daddy," Josh asked as he fought his brothers to climb onto Matthew's lap. "Please, please?"

"Blueberry waffles," Ian specified.

"And lots of sausages," Kale added. "Please, please?"

Looking at the faces of his three boys, the truth struck Matthew like lightning out of a blue sky. He could never truly lose Kathy. She was here in their sons, in the shape of their smiles. And always would be.

Judging by the din of laughter and conversation spilling out of the open door of Manhattan's only specialty coffee shop, Hope figured she was late, at least by country time standards. It was still ten minutes to ten, but when she stepped through the threshold, she saw that hardly any chairs were available.

"Hope, you came." Helen pressed her hand in welcome. "How is Nora today? Did you let her up on her crutches yet?"

"She's doing better and no, not yet. She might be

hopping around on them right now when I'm not there to watch her, but she'd better be off them when I come home."

"Atta girl." Approval beamed in Helen's smile. "You make Nora toe the line. She's far too strong-willed to listen to her doctors or her best friend. Come, we saved a spot for you. This Founder's Days dance will be the best one yet."

"I thought you were on the decorating committee," Hope began as she and Helen wove around the crowded tables.

"Yes, but you, Matthew and Harold might require a hand from time to time. A few of the committees overlap, like decorations. Believe me, you'll appreciate my help when it comes to making all those tissue paper flowers we'll need."

A waitress swept past with an empty tray, and suddenly Matthew was there, rising out of his chair, his smile easy and his gaze focused only on her. Even though he wore a work shirt and jeans, he looked exceptionally handsome and Hope felt as light as air as he offered her the chair beside his.

"I was saving this," he confessed. "With Harold in our group, our table has suddenly become very popular. I didn't want you to have to sit on the floor."

"You wouldn't have offered me your chair?"

"Not a chance." He waited until she was seated, then helped her scoot her chair in.

She couldn't remember the last time she'd experienced this courtesy. Not that she couldn't situate her own chair, but a cozy feeling wrapped around her as

Matthew settled at her side, and with every breath she took she was aware of his presence.

"Look what I have for you." He pushed an index card across the table to her.

"Your fried chicken recipe."

"Remember, this is my secret formula. I'm trusting you with it."

"I'll guard it with my life. Wait, I have something for you, too." She reached into her handbag and presented him with a bound four-by-six book. "I couldn't resist. When you see them, you'll know why."

"What did you do?" He looked at her, his gaze speculative, his brow furrowed as he reached for the small photo album.

Hope watched as he focused on the first picture of the boys in Nanna's garden, contentedly playing with their trucks in the dirt. Their differences were evident in Ian's puckered brow, Kale's frown and Josh's sucked-in bottom lip. The boys were cute playing side by side, identical and yet distinct.

Matthew must have thought so, too, because when he looked up at her, his eyes shone with an emotion she didn't dare name. "I can't believe you did this."

"It was fun. Look at this one." She flicked the thick, plastic sheeted page to two more pictures, one on each side. "Look at the boys here. Running through the sprinkler. And here, when they noticed I was taking pictures."

"They started preening. Look at them." Matthew's gaze raked over the glossy photographs of his sons, first caught in action as they leaped into the sprinkler's spray and again as they posed for the camera, each showing his best smile.

"Keep turning. I took a lot at the picnic." Hope waited, buzzing with anticipation as Matthew flipped the pages, admiring the pictures of the boys running in the fields. She held her breath at the picture she loved of Matthew, with the wind ruffling his hair and Ian perched on his broad shoulders.

"I like this." Matthew tapped the image where three boys were caught in the act of devouring brownies, chocolate smudges and all.

"Look at them in the boat. This is my favorite." She leaned closer to turn the page. They were close. Maybe too close, but Hope couldn't force herself to move away. She turned the album toward Matthew so he could see the pictures of the boys, kneeling at the wooden gunwale and clutching bright green fishing poles.

"I don't know how you did it, but their personalities shine. You can see the differences in them at the same time you see they are exactly alike."

"I had to wait until they were unguarded." Hope didn't tell him that was the challenge of her work, finding the extraordinary in the ordinary, in color and light, in faces and landscapes. "Plus, the boys are good subjects. Kids don't come much cuter than this."

"I'm biased, so I gotta agree." Dark hazel sparkles lit his eyes, and she realized more intensely this time that they were too close, shoulder to shoulder, nearly chin to chin.

"You two are looking cozy," Harold commented as he pulled up a chair.

"Look what Hope did." Matthew turned the little book so that the older man could see the individual shots that Hope had taken of each boy.

Of Ian with fire in his eyes as he perched on his father's shoulder. Of Kale determined to catch the big one with his play fishing pole. Of Josh reaching with gentle wonder for a dragonfly as it hovered for one brief moment over the rippling waters of the Gallatin River.

"I hear those pictures you take go for thousands of dollars at fancy galleries." Harold shifted to get a better look at the photographs. "What would something like this cost a fellow like me?"

"How about a mocha with whipped cream?"

"It's a deal." Harold stood, heading for the front counter to order, and he was followed by three older women, all asking if he needed help on the dance committee.

Hope realized her arm was touching Matthew's, so she leaned back in her chair, breaking the contact. But the buzzing attraction she felt remained.

"Poor Harold. It's been like this ever since he moved back to town." Matthew flicked the book closed and ran his fingers across the blue flowered pattern. "Thank you for this. Kathy and I took a ton of pictures of the boys, but after the plane crash, I just stopped. Didn't have the heart for it, I guess. Or the time."

She could see there was more, but it was probably private and he paused, the appreciation lining his face unmistakable. "Thank you."

Hope nodded. She hadn't meant to make him

remember his loss. "When I make prints for Harold, I'll copy off a set for Patsy, too. I should have thought to do it in the first place. My only excuse was that it was late at night and I was brain-dead."

"You're working at night?"

"Nanna's sleeping through the nights now. In fact, she's doing a lot better, but I'm going to be overprotective of her whether she likes it or not."

"I guess tomorrow night we'll test your overprotective skills." The sorrow in his eyes eased, and his smile returned.

Why did his smile scatter every thought in her brain? It took a moment, but she finally remembered what she was going to tell him. "When I talked to Patsy on the phone about inviting the Bible study group out to the house, she asked how our date went."

"What did you tell her?"

"I said we had a fabulous time, which was the truth. I'm getting fearless, here. Probably because I know the joke's on them."

"So, I take it you were able to invite more than Mom's Bible study group out to the house?"

"I thought we should celebrate Nanna's feeling better with an old-fashioned barbecue and potluck." Hope lowered her voice so it wouldn't carry across the table where Harold returned with coffee cups in hand. Helen took one side, and Mabel Clemmins took the other. "I even asked Harold to man the grill for me."

"How's Harold and Nora getting along?"

"Terrible." She leaned close to whisper and caught Matthew's man and soap fragrance. Awareness buzzed

through her, and she fought to control the breathless-
ness of her voice. "Nanna won't look at the cabinet
work until he's gone for the day, and she won't speak
with him."

"How's he going to know if she's happy with his
finishing work?"

"Good question. Twice he's come out to talk to her
and both times she hardly looked at him. I hate to
admit it, but so far we're dismal failures at matchmaking."

Matthew frowned, his gaze traveling across the
small table to where Harold sat, seeming uncomfortable but unfailingly polite to Helen and Mabel. "She
won't compete with her best friend for Harold, is that
it?"

"Exactly." Hope looked sad. She thanked Harold for
the coffee cup he pushed across the table. Lowering her
voice, she leaned close enough to make Matthew's senses
spin. "Nanna would never hurt her oldest friend. Maybe
we'll have better success with your mom tomorrow."

"We'll just have to watch and see. I've interviewed
a new housekeeper and she's going to take a trial run
with the boys tomorrow night, so I can come help with
the barbecue. If you want."

"I want. And that's great news. I hope she works
out." Hope took a deep breath, but it didn't disperse the
tangle of emotions tightening in her chest. She reached
for her mocha and took a drink, letting the melting
whipped cream and chocolate-flavored espresso roll
over her tongue. But instead of soothing her, it only
made her warm. Much too warm.

She leaned back, feeling flustered and embarrassed. What was wrong with her? Goodness, she *wasn't* attracted to Matthew. She wouldn't *let* herself be. Okay, he was handsome. About as handsome as a man could get. And he was nice, funny, kind and strong, dependable and more responsible than any man she'd ever known.

Not that it mattered. She wasn't going to forget the pain of her childhood and the fact that she'd almost repeated those patterns. The wall around her heart was in place. She was still safe, and Matthew's friendship wasn't going to threaten it.

It *had* to be Nanna's influence. Yep, that's what it was. Nanna's story of her husband and the love that still lived there had touched Hope's heart, that's all. Made it seem like maybe, just maybe, true love could be possible for everyone. For her.

Okay, maybe that kind of love did exist, but it was rare. And the odds of finding it had to be astronomical.

No, a person couldn't go around hoping a fairy tale would happen to her. Hope turned her chair as Helen stood and called the room to order and the last of the waitresses hurried to serve the coffee and tea.

She'd been alone all her life and wanted to keep it that way. At least if she stayed single, there would be no husband's angry words and no insults hurled like sharpened arrows.

Relying on love had been the worst mistake of her life.

She'd never make that mistake again.

* * *

Matthew couldn't take his gaze off Hope. She wore a white dress that draped her gently and brought out her rose and cream complexion. Wisps of her hair danced in the cross breezes from the open windows and doors.

"I'll handle contacting the band," Helen offered. "Last year's country players had such a great time, they wanted to come back. I don't think we'll have a problem getting them."

"Thanks, Helen." Hope jotted something down in a small notebook she had open on the table before her, and thick locks of her hair tumbled over her shoulder to flutter against his forearm, soft as silk.

She riveted her gaze on Harold. "You'll make sure the community hall is still reserved?"

"I'll make sure of it." The older man nodded.

"Great." Hope turned. The smile touching her lips looked rose-petal soft. The impact of her gaze was like a touch to his soul. "Matthew, do you have anything to add?"

"N-no," he stammered, a little embarrassed that he was staring at her beautiful mouth. "I guess this means we're done. Until next week."

Their small meeting broke up, although the coffee shop was loud with the laughter and good-natured arguments of other committees trying to nail down the details for the big event.

Hope looped her purse over her shoulder. "Are you off to another job?"

"Not until this afternoon." He waited, gesturing for

her to pass, then followed her around the edge of a table toward the door. "How about you? Do you have to get back home to Nora?"

"Eventually. I'm hosting the barbecue and potluck tonight, remember?"

"I remember." He reached over her head and gave the screen door a shove before she could catch hold of the handle. "How about you and I grabbing lunch together?"

"I'd like that since I'm absolutely starving."

"Starving, huh? Can you make it across the street to the diner?"

"If I can find the energy."

"Here, you'd better take my arm."

She looped her arm lightly through his, and they fell in stride as they hopped down the stairs and across the street. There were only a few cars to dodge. Too soon he was holding open the door for her and she breezed past him, her dress whispering around her, and led him to a booth in the back where geraniums were blooming in a pot on the windowsill.

Matthew snagged the menus from behind the salt and pepper shakers and handed one to Hope. "People are staring at us. Maybe this wasn't such a good idea."

"I'd forgotten this about small towns. Everybody probably knows what Patsy and Nanna are up to."

"And they think it's working."

"That's right." Her gaze met his full force. "We've become friends, and I'm glad."

"Me, too." Friends. Matthew skimmed the menu, feeling her gaze on him, feeling…just feeling. The loneliness in his life remained, but being with Hope made him happy. Friendship was more than he expected from this woman different from him in fundamental ways. "If you're back to work, does that mean you'll be leaving soon?"

"I have a book I'm supposed to be starting, but I'll have to put it off until Nanna's able to take care of herself." She looked wistful, as if she missed her work, but the love for her grandmother shone unmistakably. "I just wish my mom showed some interest in her welfare."

"Besides suggesting a nursing home?"

"Exactly." Hope nodded, her throat working, her gaze troubled. "My brother offered to take care of Nanna, but Noah's in New York, and she didn't want to leave her home. At least he calls every week. Mom, well, it's hard to believe she came from here."

The waitress arrived, an old friend from high school, and so the ordering took longer with the exchange of hellos and news. Jodi Drake lifted one brow at him, the question clear in her eyes. *What is a woman like her doing with you?*

Matthew shrugged. It was a good question, but this was no date. It was two friends having lunch. Jodi returned with two sodas in tall glasses and finally left them in peace.

Of course the entire café had quieted, as if the people he'd grown up with and gone to school with, and whose houses he repaired, were straining to listen in on their conversation.

Hope's eyes laughed as she tore the paper from the

end of the straw. "I'm resisting the terrible temptation to say something really scintillating, not that I could actually do it."

"You mean, like starting a rumor? That could be dangerous. We're probably already engaged according to the gossip that's out there."

"I said it was tempting, not that I'd do it." Hope took a sip of cola, eyes sparkling with laughter.

Their food arrived, and he told himself to put a stop to his budding feelings for her. Hope Ashton might be out of his league, but she was his friend. And for that he gave thanks as he bowed his head in prayer.

Across the table he heard Hope's gentle amen, and he wondered if she felt this, too—this feeling of harmony, as if the angels smiled down on their friendship.

"I never answered your question," she began as she spread the paper napkin across her lap. "Since I'm stuck here in Montana—"

"Stuck?"

"Okay, happily visiting Montana, I won't be able to fly back to Italy to work, but I figured I might be able to work here. I got some great pictures the day you and your boys let me tag along."

"You really did enjoy the trip downriver, didn't you?" He liked the way she lit up at his words.

"I loved it. Montana's beauty is spectacular, and I think I can get some work done while I'm here."

"You happen to be in luck." Matthew grabbed the ketchup bottle from the end of the table. "I happen to know my way around this countryside."

"Oh, boy." She stole the ketchup bottle from him. "I suppose this means you're volunteering to be my tour guide?"

"Yeah, I guess it does." Friends. That's what they were.

But that wasn't a satisfying thought. Not at all.

Chapter Ten

"I take it your lunch date with Matthew went well?" Nanna asked, eyes sparkling. "Because he's speeding that truck of his down my driveway. Probably in a rush to see your lovely face."

"Ha! He's bringing over his barbecue like a good *friend*." Hope slipped an aqua barrette into place in Nanna's gray hair. "I'm not even going to ask how you know Matthew and I had lunch together. A *friendly* lunch, nothing more."

"How did I know?" Nanna's chuckle was as merry as lark song. "It wasn't noon yet, and my phone started ringing. Notice how it's been ringing all afternoon?"

"It often rings all afternoon. You have a lot of friends, Nanna." And maybe one male friend would change her life. Hope took solace in that thought as she clipped the matching barrette into place.

Nanna had found true love once. She certainly could find it again. "You look beautiful."

"I would look better if you'd let me back up on my crutches."

"There's no chance of that. You'll overdo it, I know you. It's only a few more days until we head back to the orthopedist. If he says the bone is still mending to his satisfaction, I'll take your crutches out of hiding."

"You're awfully bossy for a young woman. Does Matthew know about this? Maybe he won't discover it until after the wedding."

"Sure, go ahead and tease. I can't imagine where I get my bossiness from."

"From your father's side of the family, surely."

"Certainly not from you." Hope laughed as she held the small silver hand mirror for her grandmother. "What do you think?"

"You work magic on me, that's for sure." Nanna peered around the mirror to see out the bedroom window as Matthew parked his truck alongside Harold's and called in greeting to someone at the back of the house. "Who all is coming to supper tonight?"

"You'll just have to wait and see. Now, if you'd agree to let me put your bed downstairs, we wouldn't have to negotiate those stairs."

"This is only temporary, young lady. By this time next week I should be in a walking cast, so hide my crutches all you want." Merriment sparkled in Nanna's eyes as she scooted off the edge of the bed and straightened, standing on one leg.

"You fall down now and you can say goodbye to that walking cast." Hope shook her head and retrieved the light aluminum crutches from the corner of the room. "How about I find a handsome man to help you down the stairs?"

"That Matthew is terribly handsome, isn't he? Makes a woman turn her head twice and wonder if he's a good kisser."

"Nanna." Hope nearly stumbled over her own feet, and the crutches slipped from her fingers. The crutches clanged as they clattered to the floor, and she bent to retrieve the awkward things. "You are incorrigible, you know that?"

"I know."

"You look far too pleased with yourself. Well, fantasize all you want. You'll eventually see how wrong you are." Hope held the crutches upright in front of her grandmother. "Now, careful. I don't want you falling."

"'You can make many plans, but the Lord's purpose will prevail.'"

"What is that supposed to mean? You're the one matchmaking, not God." Hope fit one crutch under Nanna's arm. "And no, don't try to tell me it's part of His plan for me. I'm independent, I'm happy and I don't mind staying single. It's better than the alternative, believe me."

"But Hope—"

"No, not another word." Hope helped Nanna with the second crutch. "And don't tell me about Grandfather again, okay? I know you found happiness, and I'm glad. I believe there can be happiness in some marriages, I do. Just not for me."

She nearly tried the alternative, and what did it get her? Heading toward the same kind of misery that her parents lived through. She'd made the right decision and broken off the engagement, but she wasn't going to spend her life wishing for the kind of rare, impossible love.

She wasn't about to believe that true love would happen to her.

A floorboard creaked behind her, and she spun around to see Matthew outside the open door, a sheepish look on his face. "I came up to ask where you wanted the grill, Hope. Nora, you look breathtaking."

"And you are a shameless charmer." Nanna took a wobbly step. "Now, help me down the stairs, young man, and tell me, do you plan on flirting with my granddaughter over supper?"

"I was thinking of flirting with her *after* supper." Matthew winked at Hope over Nanna's head.

"You aren't helping, Matthew," Hope warned.

"I do think there could be some flirting." He tossed the words back as he took Nanna's elbow and held her steady as she hobbled into the hallway.

"And you, Matthew Sheridan." Nanna's step was wobbly but her voice rang as strong as ever. "Those boys of yours need a good woman to mother them. And a woman doesn't come any better than my granddaughter. Maybe you've noticed that by now, if you're as smart as I think you are."

"I noticed that right away, Nora." Matthew's gaze found Hope's and held it. She could see so much on his face, in his eyes, in his heart. Strength. Kindness. Humor. A goodness that ran soul deep.

Hope's step was shaky as she led the way down the

stairs, keeping a few steps ahead of Nanna in case she needed assistance. But she didn't, and after the older woman was settled on the garden bench in sight of the grill Harold was setting up, Hope pulled Matthew aside in the kitchen.

"'The wicked are trapped by their own words,'" she reminded him. "You deliberately misled her and now she's going to have our wedding planned before she's off those crutches."

"She'll be too busy with her own to worry about us, you wait and see. I'll be right about all the flirting that will be going on, it just won't be between us." A saucy grin tugged at the corners of his mouth. "Anything is possible."

"I'm not going to argue about that."

"Are you two lovebirds done flirting in there?" Nanna called from the garden, her voice drifting through the open window. "Do you need a chaperone?"

Hope felt embarrassment creep up her neck and heat her face.

Matthew splayed one hand on the counter and gazed through the ruffled curtains. "Nora, behave."

Laughter rose on the wind, and Hope realized Nanna wasn't alone. Good grief. Who was out there listening to them? She squeezed next to Matthew and peered across the budding roses, clematis and hollyhock to the bench where Nanna sat, surrounded by half the senior citizens from church. Patsy was seated beside her, and the two of them were beaming.

"We're in trouble now." Matthew laughed as he looped his arm around her shoulders, and Hope didn't step away. Cozy warmth seeped into her, and for the first time since she could remember, she felt safe. Completely safe.

Boy, it was a good thing they were just friends. Because if they weren't, she might really fall for Matthew. And what good could come of that?

While Matthew and Harold cooked beef patties and hot dogs on the grill, Hope made sure gray-haired but dapper Joseph Drummond was on Nanna's left and polite Claude Winkler on her right. Helen was one of the women helping with the food, and Hope noticed her at the grill, holding a platter steady for Harold to fill with hamburger patties.

But Harold wasn't responding to Helen's gentle flirting. He was merely being polite. After Helen left with a look of longing on her face, carrying the platter to the table crammed with potluck dishes, Hope caught Harold's quick glance across the lawn to where Nanna sat, making conversation with two men.

So, Harold *did* like Nanna—a lot. Hope plopped a scoop of Patsy's baked beans onto the sturdy paper plate she carried and watched Harold turn away. He looked troubled and filled with regret. Mabel scurried up to him with adoration in her eyes, and the distinguished man merely smiled politely as he checked the thick German sausages that Matthew was turning to see if any were done.

And because Nanna didn't want to hurt Helen, she wouldn't acknowledge Harold, much less act on their mutual interest. Hope's heart sank as she squirted a thick ring of mustard on the top half of a fresh hamburger bun. It didn't take a genius to realize that both Jake Drummond and Claude Winkler liked Nanna, especially Claude. A retired rancher and a new widower, Claude had a genuine smile and the tough wiry look of a man who'd earned his way in the world. Jake Drummond was all gentleman as he took Nanna's paper cup to refill it from the pitcher of iced tea in the middle of the table.

Hope finished the garnishes on Nanna's hamburger and carried the full paper plate across the lawn. She wanted her grandmother to be happy. She wanted her to find a love to brighten the rest of her days. With Harold?

Nanna looked happier than Hope had ever seen her, with color high in her cheeks and her eyes twinkling like stars. "You, my dear, are a fine granddaughter. Surprising me by bringing all my dear friends here."

"Now you know why Matthew and I were conspiring. To figure out a way for you to attend Bible study without going very far on that leg."

"You can't fool me, young lady, but I won't press you tonight. No, tonight we will have fun, fellowship and take time to remember our Lord." Nanna pressed a kiss to Hope's cheek. "Now, go on, have some fun. See if you can get Matthew to take a break from the grill."

Hope shook her head at her incorrigible grandmother and left her in good company. The din of happy conversation and the rise and fall of laughter lifted on the sweet evening breezes. The mouthwatering aroma of sizzling hamburgers scented the backyard as Hope grabbed a paper plate for herself.

Matthew stepped behind her, and the memory of his cozy warmth lashed through her. "Leaving Harold to handle the grill?"

"Yeah, he told me to eat, then we'll switch. He doesn't look in a hurry to sit down and let the single ladies fawn over him. Notice how he keeps glancing in Nora's direction and not in Helen's?"

"I noticed." Hope added a handful of carrot and celery sticks to her plate. "And Helen keeps watching Harold. Let's face it, we're doomed as matchmakers."

"Nora seems to be getting a lot of attention from Jake and Claude."

"Yeah, but she doesn't have that look in her eye. The one that Harold puts there. Or used to before Nanna realized Helen was serious about Harold." Hope grabbed the salad tongs. "We're not faring any better with your mom."

"I've been watching her all night. She hasn't shown any interest in any of three single men her age." Matthew heaped a helping of pasta salad onto his plate. "Want some?"

"Sure." Hope stepped close to his side and it was a nice place to be. "Have you noticed your mom avoiding anyone?"

"What?" As if considering the question, his brow furrowed and his eyes narrowed, and he scanned the crowd scattered around the half dozen picnic tables. "Well, yeah. Dr. Corey. She's got her back to him. I noticed him behind her in the food line earlier, but she didn't talk to him."

"And your mom talks with everyone. Is she always like this with him?"

"Beats me. I know she goes to his son for medical treatment, but not Andrew."

"Right, for her allergies." Hope wrestled a hot dog bun from a plastic bag and dropped it on her plate. "Isn't that weird, that she'd see someone our age instead of a man she'd gone to school with? A man with more medical experience?"

Matthew nodded slowly, his gaze pinning Hope's as bold as a touch. "I'm going to look into it. You're not half bad to have around in a pinch."

"I've been known to be useful now and then." But she heard the deeper meaning behind his words, and her heart twisted hard enough to make her catch her breath. Matthew liked her. And that knowledge made her feel good. Very good.

Too good. The caring bright light in his eyes was one of the most beautiful things she'd ever seen, and for no reason at all, she felt that after a lifetime of battling uncertain seas, lost and alone, she'd found her safe harbor. She longed for him to wrap her in his arms and pull her against his iron-strong chest.

For this one moment the loneliness vanished, replaced by the sweetest tenderness she'd ever known or felt from another human being.

And he was someone she could never call her own.

"So what's the holdup?" Mira McKaslin asked from behind them.

Embarrassed at herself and laughing, too, Hope tucked away those wishful thoughts, no, *foolish* thoughts, and reached for the potato salad spoon.

As twilight deepened in thick shadows, Hope retreated to the kitchen to fetch the box of citronella candles and tried not to watch Matthew as he worked with several men to push the picnic tables together to form one big square. But it was impossible to look at the bunch and stretch of his muscles beneath the cotton shirt he wore and not ache to be held by him.

A warm wind gusted through the window, bathing her with the sweet scents of wild grasses, roses and moonflowers, and she remembered what she'd come to the kitchen for in the first place. She grabbed a book of matches from the top drawer by the steaming coffeemaker and was turning around when the air in the room changed. It became electrified, and then Matthew was striding through the threshold, his dark hair tousled by the ever-present wind and his big hands loosely fisted at his sides.

Aching, just aching, Hope took one step back, knowing with the lights on in the kitchen that anybody in the yard who was looking could see them clearly. Not that she was in danger of reaching out to Matthew. Wanting and reaching were two separate things.

"I pulled Harold to the side of the house to wash off the grills and asked him what was going on with Helen. She seemed awfully interested in him." Matthew joined her at the counter and took the matchbook from her. "He assured me he's done nothing to lead her on.

The day they went to church together, they'd accidentally met in the parking lot and since she had no family with her that day, he didn't want to leave her alone."

"He's a gentleman." Hope tore at the shrink-wrapped box, trying to act unaffected. "Let me guess. He felt obligated to invite Helen to brunch that day."

"Exactly. He told me that he'd explained to her that he wanted to be friends."

"Did you ask how he felt about Nanna?" Hope wrestled open the box and began setting candles on the counter.

"We didn't get that far. Mabel came up and interrupted us so she could flirt with Harold." Dimples flashed in his cheeks as Matthew lit a match. "Ever since he's moved back to town, he's been a real popular fellow. But have no fear, I promise I'll try to get the truth out of him. Nora's cabinets are nearly finished, so we're running out of opportunity."

"Did you find out anything about your mom and Dr. Corey?" Hope set the last candle on the counter and stepped back so Matthew could light it.

"The night's still young." Matthew blew out the match and tossed it into the sink. "It's strange thinking of finding love for my mom. She's been without Dad for a long time."

"Having second thoughts?"

"No way. I want her to be happy. And I'm trying to look at it this way, a guy's never too old to get a new stepdad." His gaze dropped to her mouth.

Hope shivered. Heat spilled through her veins, and she didn't know what to say.

Together they carried the lit candles out to the tables where the party was calming down and Bibles were appearing out of handbags. Men and women settled on the benches as Hope carried out pitchers of iced tea and a thermos of decaffeinated coffee.

"What a wonderful surprise." Nanna caught her hand when Hope handed her a paper cup filled with brisk iced tea. "I've so missed Bible study."

As Hope kissed her grandmother's cheek, love warmed her heart. Love for this rare woman of substance and joy, of gentleness and affection. Hope didn't know where she'd be without Nanna's love, and she was grateful for it. Nanna was her family—God had truly blessed her with a beautiful grandmother.

"Hope, I saved you a place," Patsy called out as the group quieted. "Right here between me and Matthew."

Hope tried not to blush as she circled around to the far table. Matthew stood, shrugging one wide shoulder, the apology already in his eyes.

"I tried to stop her," he whispered, his breath hot against the shell of her ear. "But she just wouldn't listen to reason. This matchmaking thing has gone to her head and affected her judgment. I'm considering looking into medication."

"Some nice antipsychotic drugs, you mean?"

"Exactly." His hand cupped her elbow as she swung her legs over the bench. His touch was like midsummer, and all too soon he'd pulled away.

But the memory of the touch remained.

His mom led the way across the darkness of Nora's driveway, the rhythm of their steps sounding loud in the peaceful night. "Wasn't that just the best time?"

"A real thrill," Matthew said.

"Now, don't go being sarcastic with me. I know you had a good time. I *saw* longing in your eyes for Hope Ashton."

"What you saw is none of your business." He opened the car door for his mother.

"Admit it. You're finally over Kathy and ready to move on with your life."

He winced and nearly dropped the casserole dish his mom handed to him. Kathy wasn't someone he would ever be able to erase from his life and forget. "I'm not looking for a replacement for Kathy. I'm not going to forget her and what she was to me."

"But she's in your past, dear." Mom sighed. "I didn't mean to hurt you, but Matthew, look at what's in front of you and not behind. Can you try to do that for your mother, who loves you more than anything?"

"Sure, use guilt and manipulation to get what you want." He kissed her cheek, the familiar scent of White Diamonds perfume and baby shampoo reminding him of a lifetime of her good-humored affection. "I'll follow you home to make sure you get there safe."

"A son who dotes on his mother. I'm glad to know I raised you right." She brushed her hand along his jaw. "Now indulge me in finding me a daughter-in-law. Not a replacement, but an addition. Someone for me to shop for. Someone to force to go to lunch with me and who'll raise my grandsons right."

"I see where this is heading." Matthew slipped the

dish on the floor behind the driver's seat and stepped back so his mom could climb behind the wheel.

He would follow her home, make sure she got in all right so that she wouldn't face a dark, empty house alone.

As if he could feel Hope's gaze, he turned around and gazed up at the white, green-gabled farmhouse, but the lit windows were curtained. Maybe it was wishful thinking, or maybe it was because he wanted to hold her in his arms.

"Matthew's a wonderful man, isn't he?" Nanna asked as she eased onto the edge of the couch. "I doubt there's a kinder man running around loose in this town."

"I don't know about that. Harold seems like an awfully nice man. Don't you think?"

"Sure, but he's not for me, little one." Nanna's smile faded. "I could sure use a cup of chamomile tea."

"I can take a hint." Hope grabbed the crutches and leaned them against the wall, walking past the spot where Matthew had almost kissed her. Uncertainty balled hard in her chest. "I'm not going to badger you the way you badger me, but consider this. You've got a lot of years ahead of you still, and wouldn't it be nice to have someone to share your future with?"

"I can ask you to consider the same."

Laughing, shaking her head, Hope crossed the room and headed toward the bright lights of the kitchen. She saw a flash of movement and heard a rustling sound in the corner, but before she could become alarmed,

Harold strolled into sight wrestling with a garbage bag.

"A raccoon found its way in while the last of the crowd was leaving," he explained with a simple shrug and the steady, kind gaze of an honest, good man. "He was probably attracted by the smell of food. I scooted him on out of here and thought I'd make sure all the garbage was tight in the can before I left. Don't want you girls having any troubles tonight."

Hope bit her lip to keep from chuckling. She wasn't afraid of a raccoon, but Harold's thoughtfulness was a kind gesture, and she didn't want him to think that she didn't appreciate it. "You and Matthew did a fantastic job cooking tonight. I'd never had corn cooked on a barbecue before."

"Imagine that. You had to travel the world over to find good corn on the cob."

"They do a lot of things right here in Montana."

"That they do." Harold finished knotting the big white plastic bag. "I'll just take this out. Got to do one more thing and then I'm out of your way."

Hope watched him leave, a man still tall and strong, unbowed by the years. Anyone could see he had a good and genuine heart. If only there was a way to bring Harold and Nanna together. Two lonely people deserved love, and there was no mistaking the longing in Harold's gaze whenever he looked at Nanna.

After she put tea water on to boil, she punched the playback button on the answering machine. The tape screeched and clicked, then began to play. Her brother's voice, as deep and nearly as overbearing as her father's, apologized for missing them. Hope glanced at the clock. It would be after midnight in New York, but Noah would be up. She punched his number and waited. Sure enough, he answered the phone on the second ring.

"You should be in bed sleeping," Hope told him.

He laughed. "Now don't start on me. You know I'm a night owl. How's Nanna?"

As they talked, the tight uncertainty in her chest began to ease. Her big brother always had been able to make everything right—well, as right as anything could be in their family. And he hadn't shed the scars of their childhood, either.

Hope feared those wounds would never heal. For the time it took the water to boil and the tea to steep, they talked of his work and hers, of Nanna's progress and of her and Matthew's matchmaking scheme. She had him laughing by the time she asked if he wanted to talk with Nanna.

Carrying the phone into the living room, she wasn't paying attention until it was too late. Harold was with Nanna. He must have come in the front door. He was offering a bouquet of flowers to the stunned-looking woman on the couch.

Hope took one silent step back before they noticed her. She hid in the shadows, afraid to retreat farther because of the squeaky floorboards. Could this be it? Was Harold going to start courting Nanna?

"I'm sorry, Harold." Nanna lifted her hand to refuse the beautiful bouquet. "I don't like cut flowers. Maybe there's another woman who'd appreciate them."

Harold mumbled an apology, obviously hurt, and tried to make pleasant small talk as he retreated toward the front door. Hope's jaw dropped, and she couldn't believe her ears. Sympathy for him welled within as he tossed one last look of longing toward Nanna, then quietly left the house.

"I'm not interested in him, so don't look at me like that."

Hope didn't argue. She didn't know what to say. This matchmaking scheme of hers and Matthew's wasn't turning out like she'd planned. Pain darkened Nanna's eyes and made them bright as if with tears.

"Noah's on the phone. He says he's looking for a gorgeous woman to talk to."

"That flatterer." Nanna took the receiver, the pain lingering even as the pleasure of speaking to her only grandson lit her smile. "Noah, you ought to start flirting with women your own age and then maybe you'll find one who'll marry you."

Hope retreated from the room to check on the tea. It had steeped long enough, and the earthy freshness of chamomile steamed when she lifted the ceramic lid. She loaded the sugar bowl and creamer on a tray and found one of Nanna's favorite china cups in the dining room hutch. She carried the tray upstairs, the faint sound of Nanna's voice keeping her company as she wandered down the lonely hall to the room at the end.

She set the tray on the corner of the nightstand and walked to the window. Since she hadn't bothered to turn on the lights, the room was as dark. With the lacy curtains fluttering around her, she gazed out on the night. Bright stars twinkled in a velvet sky so black it glowed.

Unlike in the cities, here it was dark enough to see the smaller, dimmer stars that winked from so far away, stars nearer to the edge of heaven. The pink haze of the Milky Way swirled across a piece of the night with no moon to dim its amazing radiance.

And lower, she could see the faint cut of headlights illuminating the landscape where the end of Nanna's long driveway met the county road. A car followed by a pickup slipped out of sight as the road lifted and dipped. It was Matthew's truck. She knew it. It had to be. Aside from Harold, he and Patsy had been the last to leave.

What was she doing? Aching for the chance to be held safe and warm in Matthew's arms?

Please, Father, show me what to do.

But there was no answer as the night seemed to darken and the chirping of one raccoon calling another sounded from the fields. The echoes of the happy evening and of Matthew's warmth remained, and not even the night breezes could disperse them. There was nothing she could do to erase the longing to be in his arms—his strong, safe arms.

Or the way her blood felt strange, tingly warm in her veins. Why was she feeling this way? It was more than friendship she felt for Matthew. Much more.

Love could hurt. It could tear a person apart. It could take a whole heart and reduce it to dust. She trusted God to keep her safe from it, and He had. He'd kept her from marrying Christopher. He'd reminded her that to some He gave the gift of singleness.

And that meant Matthew was no threat to her heart. Her feelings for him were just a reflection of her wishful thinking, of the little girl inside her still looking for love.

That was all. Hope was sure of it.

The night was silent, and she felt small and alone. So very alone.

Chapter Eleven

"Harold told me what happened." The sound of Matthew's step echoed against the bare walls and high rafters of the community hall. "He crashed and burned."

"Nanna actually lied and said she didn't like cut flowers, like the entire house isn't filled with them." Gladness radiated through her at the sight of Matthew, dressed in denims and a royal blue T-shirt. "Harold came this morning to finish polishing the cabinets and attach new handles. I brought Nanna out to see, and she wouldn't look at him."

"Wasn't she happy with his work?"

"The cabinets are beautiful and they match the new linoleum so nicely. She told him so, but in this distant voice that's so unlike her. I know she likes him very much, but when he went to say goodbye, he'd brought her another gift. A beautiful rosebush. She turned it down."

"How did Harold take it?"

"He just nodded, grabbed his toolbox and left. She's doing this because of Helen."

"Then that woman's a bigger fool than I gave her credit for." Helen tapped across the polished wood floor on her low-heeled pink sandals, her spring dress fluttering with her rapid movements. "I know what you two are up to. I overheard Patsy and Nora chattering on about their success with you two, and it doesn't take a fool to figure out why half of the unmarried population over fifty was in Nora's backyard."

Hope couldn't tell if Helen was angry with her, too. "I wasn't trying to force Harold and Nanna together. I know you like him, and so I made sure Nanna had plenty of handsome men to talk with at the table."

"I saw." Helen's eyes sparkled even though her mouth was pinched. "And I saw how Harold kept looking at Nora. Over and over again. Now, don't get me wrong. I'd grab hold of that man in a second, but only if he wants *me* to grab him. And what about you, Matthew? Trying to marry your mother off, too?"

"If I can."

"Well, that explains the time you're spending together, doesn't it? You're letting everyone think you two are an item to keep those two matchmakers from matchmaking again. I see what you're up to. Marry them off instead, and they won't mind so much that you were only fooling them."

"It sounds awful when you say it like that." Hope looked to Matthew for help, but he only shrugged. "We're not being deceitful. Matthew and I are only friends, and I've told Nanna that over and over again."

"Just be careful, dears." Helen clucked, shaking her head and changing the subject. "Now, since I'm in charge of the Founder's Days decorations, I get to meddle in every subcommittee. Let me tell you, the balloons and tissue paper flowers we had in here last year were stunning."

Hope fell in stride beside Helen who tapped merrily around the hall, making suggestions that would tie the theme of the celebration together. Over the top of Helen's carefully hair-sprayed curls, Hope caught Matthew's puzzled gaze. He seemed to be asking, what have we gotten ourselves into? Hope shook her head, completely at a loss.

After they'd surveyed the hall, Helen hurried off, digging in her big purse for the car keys to her beloved Ford Falcon. "One word of advice for you, Matthew. Consider this. Your mother planned to go to the senior prom with Dr. Corey. I know because my Jenny is the same age and they were friends. There was a terrible falling out. Have you noticed how Patsy drove all the way to Bozeman to see a doctor until Andrew's son joined the practice?"

Matthew shook his head. "I don't see how she's going to marry a guy she won't even talk to."

"I didn't say she wouldn't marry him." Helen winked as she turned over the engine. "You two *friends* be careful."

"You're an angel, Helen." Hope waved as the Ford Falcon crept out of the parking lot and inched toward the empty street. Helen honked, stuck her hand out the open window to wave and inched down the street with great care.

Hope turned to the man towering beside her, casting her in his shadow. "How did your boys like the new baby-sitter?"

"Good enough so that I hired her. Millie's easygoing and gentle and nothing seems to faze her, so I think she'll work out. Least, I hope so." A slow smile tugged at the corner of his mouth—his very handsome mouth. "I hear from my mom that Nora is up on her feet with a walking cast, which has got to mean she's healing."

"It does. She's not getting around a whole lot because there's still quite a bit of pain, but that shouldn't last for much longer."

"So, is she feeling well enough for you to spend the afternoon with me? I promised you some sight-seeing, and I mean to deliver on that promise."

"You want to show me that you're a man of your word, is that it?"

"Sure, or my reputation will suffer. Is that a yes?" He strolled into the shade made by her Jeep and his truck, parked side by side. A tow truck slowed to a near stop on the street behind them. The driver gaped at them through the open window.

He waved and Matthew waved, then the truck sped off with a roar. Matthew shook his head, chuckling. "My reputation is going to suffer when you leave town. Everyone is going to shake their heads and say, that Matthew Sheridan, don't know what he was thinking of, but he didn't have a chance with that beautiful Ashton woman."

"No, they'll be saying, what's wrong with the

woman because she won't grab hold of a man like that." Referring to Helen, who'd said the same about Harold, she made Matthew laugh. "She gave us a good clue about your mom. What are we going to do next?"

"Try to put them together, I guess." Matthew shrugged. "Not that it worked so well with Harold and Nora."

"Putting them together isn't going to work unless they'll talk to each other. Maybe what you should do next is ask your mom why she won't speak to Dr. Corey."

"I wanted to avoid that, because she'll tell me to mind my own business." Matthew winked. "But I'm not afraid of my own mother. She's a secretive sort, but I'll uncover the truth. Don't you worry. My sanity depends on it."

A car passed on the street, slowing down for a good look. Then it zipped off, and Hope thought she recognized one of the waitresses from the café.

"See what I mean?" Matthew crooked one brow, his humor as warm as the sun above.

Hope liked this man far too much. "I need to stop by Nanna's to change and grab my camera before you can steal me away."

"Now, if my mother heard you say that, think what ideas that would give her."

Laughing, Hope tugged open the Jeep's door. Although she fought, it was strange how places in her heart felt alive whenever she was around Matthew.

Matthew squinted against the harsh sun and shouldered open the door to Harold's stable. "How long has it been since you've been on a horse?"

"When I'm home, there's a stable I ride at."

"Then you own your own horse?" He followed her inside the dim warmth where light sheened against wood and off the straw-strewn floors. Where the scents of sweet hay and horse lingered in the air.

A wistful look tugged at Hope's features as she nodded. "I miss her when I travel. She's a good friend and a great mount. I learned to ride during the year I stayed with Nanna. She kept cattle on the land, and I rode her mare out to check on them."

"I remember." The neighbors rented the vast pastures that comprised most of Nora's land, Matthew knew. "I thought you might like seeing Montana on horseback."

"You thought right." Hope breezed past the empty stalls. "Where's the tack room?"

"At the end of the row on your left." Matthew grabbed the saddlebags Harold kept just inside the front door, ready to go and packed with essentials like antivenin for snakebites, binoculars and a first aid kit. Slinging the bags over his shoulder, he caught up with Hope, who was in the tack room hefting a saddle onto her shoulder.

"Grab the other one, will you?" She tossed him a sassy grin with a hint of challenge in it. That city girl sure liked to do things for herself.

Well, he wasn't going to argue with her. This time. He tossed two blankets over his forearm and grabbed Firebrand's saddle. The small room felt smaller as she breezed past him so close that they almost touched.

Then she was gone, tapping away in those fancy

leather boots, looking like a million dollars in worn Levi's and a turquoise shirt. Her luxurious hair was tied back in a ponytail, which swung in a gentle rhythm with her gait.

His skin burned, and he felt the need to hold her, to take her in his arms and tuck her against his chest. He hurt with wanting to hold her, and it took all his will-power to let her walk away.

He heard her steps hesitate. The jingling sounds told him she'd snagged the bridles from their hooks just inside the corral door.

The two horses had already come to investigate. Friendly, they stood side by side and nosed Hope's hand. Then, when they weren't satisfied, they started bumping against her.

"Hey, you two," she scolded lightly, adjusting her balance due to the heavy saddle she carried.

Matthew scooped a handful of sugar cubes from the box on the shelf, then loped down the aisle into the corral. "This is what they're looking for. Harold always hides treats in his pockets, which is fine until a guy comes along unknowingly and gets accosted by these greedy brutes."

Firebrand whinnied a welcome and shook his head, his platinum mane sweeping along his golden neck. Spying the treats, he neatly scooped four cubes off Matthew's palm. "Watch out, they're spoiled gluttons."

"Yeah, and vicious, too." Hope laughed as the more polite of the two Arabians lipped her hand in a persistent, gentle request. "Matthew, give me some of those sugar cubes if you know what's good for you."

"Or what, you'll feed me to Firebrand?" He dropped a half dozen cubes onto her palm. Those hands—why did they keep attracting his attention? Everything about her did, the way her smile lit her eyes, the dark silken wisps that framed her face, how she laughed. All he could think of was the way she touched the world—with gentle, loving hands.

And a gentle, loving heart.

He noticed she'd looped the bridles over the end post of the corral, and that gave her one free hand to deal with Morning Glory. The horse managed to get a couple of cubes before Hope slipped the rest into her jeans pocket.

"Now, stand still and be good." She tipped the saddle onto its side and stole a blanket from him. "Harold must do a fair amount of riding."

"He's an true outdoorsman. Now that he's moved back to his family homestead, he heads out on horseback into the wilderness to fish and camp. Sometimes, if Mom's feeling brave enough to take care of the boys for a few days on end, Harold and I head out together."

Hope smoothed every last wrinkle from the blanket she'd tossed over Morning Glory's withers. Matthew did the same on Firebrand, and the horses stood patiently, eager for a run. Matthew's heart squeezed when he watched Hope lift the saddle as if she'd done it every day of her life, and then tighten the cinch. Morning Glory settled down once Hope tugged the chestnut forward a few steps and pulled the cinch in a notch.

Matthew finished saddling Firebrand and tied the

saddlebags into place. "Let me know if you need help with Morning Glory. You're going to need gloves and a hat. You might as well use Harold's. I'll fetch 'em for you."

"Thanks." She exchanged the mare's halter for the bridle with quick efficiency, then dug a sugar cube out of her pocket.

Matthew's fingers faltered on the buckle, and he could only stare at the woman who seemed to be able to do anything—even make his heart feel again.

Here in the sunshine, the loneliness ebbed away until he felt only the heat of the sun on his back and the longing for Hope in his arms.

"I'll be right back." He left the reins trailing to the ground and Firebrand nickering with a demand for more sugar and retreated to the stable's dim interior.

Matthew knew he was feeling this way for a reason—it was time to move on, time to start living again. That was all. It couldn't be more, even if he wanted it to be.

He found Harold's hat and gloves and stepped into the sunshine where she stood watching and waiting for him.

"It's going to be a little big," he warned as he dropped the black Stetson on her head. "But it will keep your nose from burning."

"Hey, I'm not picky. I'm just glad to be here." Hope took the gloves and slipped them over her slender hands one at a time. Delight shimmered in her eyes, and she made him feel far too much.

"Need a boost up?" he asked, even though she was already reaching for the saddle horn.

"Not a chance, cowboy." With easy grace, she eased into the saddle and tightened the reins as Morning Glory sidestepped.

"That's a girl," Hope praised when the mare calmed, and she patted her hand, lost in Harold's glove, against the horse's velvet neck.

She straightened in the saddle like the seasoned rider he'd figured she was, and he mounted Firebrand. The gelding pranced, scenting the wind, eager for the chance to stretch his strong legs.

Hope's appreciative gaze scanned the Arabian he rode and then higher. Matthew felt a spark of realization zing through him—he wasn't the only one affected by their closeness. But before he could think that through, Morning Glory broke into a trot toward the heavy wooden gate at the end of the corral. Dust rose in the horse's wake, and Matthew didn't have to urge Firebrand into a trot.

"Sure, show off your riding skills." His voice might be teasing, but he couldn't deny the flicker of warm pride in his chest as Hope opened the gate, backing the Arabian with skill. Morning Glory tried to balk, but Hope soothed her with firm assurance. The Arabian gave up the fight and obediently stood.

"After you." He sidled Firebrand alongside her. "I thought you might like to ride into the foothills. We can keep to the river if you want, but something tells me—"

"I want to get closer to those mountains." The Bridger Mountains shone like polished amethysts, the rugged range of snowcapped peaks so close they filled the entire eastern horizon. Hope shone, too, and he couldn't look away.

Sweet native grasses and wildflowers in vivid purples, yellows and oranges rustled in the warm winds. The sun burned warm on his back as Firebrand tugged at the bit. Matthew knuckled back his Stetson so he could get a good look at the woman at his side.

He saw the challenge in her eye and the toss of her head as she pushed the too-large hat out of her eyes. And in a flash, he knew what she was thinking, saw her grip loosen as she gave the mare more rein. Hope leaned forward in the saddle.

At the same moment he gave Firebrand his head, and the gelding stretched out with his long legs. Shoulder to shoulder the horses ran, and only wind and air separated Matthew from Hope. He couldn't tear his gaze away from her, so different as her ponytail came loose and her ebony locks danced and rippled in the wind. His heart felt alive, like a dark place touched by a new sun.

Happiness like spring bloomed inside him, and he laughed as he gave Firebrand his head and the gelding broke into a full-out gallop, shooting in front of Hope and Morning Glory. He laughed at the surprise on Hope's face and then he was in the lead, leaning into Firebrand's windswept mane and feeling the horse's amazing power as he flew across the earth.

The wind in his ears and the drum of Firebrand's hooves kept him from hearing Hope's approach, but when he glanced over his shoulder, there she was, leaning low over Glory's neck and whispering quietly to her. The mare's ears were flattened, her nostrils flaring as she chewed up the ground, drawing closer. Anyone could see the challenging tilt to Hope's chin.

Matthew could feel his pulse pound in his ears as Firebrand reached the fence marking the pasture's northeastern boundary. Breathing hard, he spun the Arabian around to watch her ride in. She was grace and fire and it made the happiness inside his heart burn hot as the sun above.

She reined in, at ease in the saddle. Her hair was wind-tossed and Harold's hat had fallen down her back, dangling by the string that had caught around her neck. "You had a head start, or we would have beaten you. And I'll prove it to you on the way back."

"Is that a dare?"

"Count on it." She sparkled, and she made him sparkle, too.

"Is that an eagle or a hawk?" Hope leaned back in her saddle to squint at the perfect blue sky. A great bird the color of brown sugar lowered her wings as if she were stroking the wind, then soared over the rise of a hill.

"Looks like a golden eagle to me." Matthew pulled a pair of binoculars from the saddlebags and handed them to her. "Here she comes again."

The brush of his fingers on hers made her feel safe somehow, as if no harm could come to her. She lifted the binoculars with one hand and searched the sky for the majestic raptor, aware of the world around her. The wind sang through the needles of the lodgepole pines and the Douglas firs lining the trail. Pine grass crunched beneath the horses' steeled hooves, and saddle leather creaked as she shifted her weight.

"Right there." Matthew's words tickled against her ear as he nudged her wrist toward the east.

The snowcapped peaks stood in high relief, and she searched the sheen of glaciers until she spotted a blur of golden-brown. The eagle soared closer until she seemed near enough to touch. Hope watched breathless as the great bird nosed into a swift dive, swooping toward the grassy earth, talons hooked and outstretched. In one smooth motion the eagle brushed the ground and in an arc soared straight into the sun.

Inspiration struck, and Hope shoved the binoculars in Matthew's direction and snatched the small camera buttoned in her shirt pocket. In the space of a breath she caught the eagle on film, flying on the shafts of the sun, light gleaming on copper wings.

"See where she's heading?" Matthew asked from behind his binoculars. "Look at the cliffs above the river. She's got a nest there. She must have new babies because she's keeping close to home."

Morning Glory was stretching her neck to lip at some of the sweet grasses in the shade of a boulder. Hope switched the lightweight Nikon to her left hand and leaned over the saddle horn to snare the fallen reins.

They rode with the sun at their backs and the wind in their faces in companionable silence. It was enough that she was with him.

"Look down there." Matthew halted Firebrand at the

rise of the hill, where the rugged earth plunged downward into a steep river canyon. The waters of a silent river winked in the sunlight below where five or six dark objects were wading into the current.

It was too far away to take a good picture without a different camera, but she could make out the thick, wide bodies covered with brown-black wool and the humped back and shoulders of the creatures as they crept ever deeper into the cool mountain-fed waters.

"It's like something out of the old west." She lowered her camera and slipped it into her shirt pocket, then buttoned it in tight. "They must be wild."

"Yep. There's a buffalo range for them that backs up to the national park. Now admit it, this isn't something you'd see on those worldwide travels of yours."

"I freely admit it." Wonder shone in her eyes as she dismounted with one graceful movement. "I can't believe in all this time I've never been back. Nanna loves to travel, and so it's easier to fly her to where I am. But to come here…I guess I've avoided it."

"Too small-town for you, is that it?"

"No." She led Morning Glory to the very edge of the rise and she stood alone facing the majesty of mountains and sky. "Nanna's house was the first real home I'd known when I was a girl. I came here with a world of hurt inside me, and to tell you the truth, it's almost like coming back to that place in my life. Not exactly. I'm different, life is different, but it makes me remember."

"And it's coming home."

"Yes." She said the word on a sigh, quietly, and it touched him like nothing else.

Matthew had always known the security of a home, the nurturing love of his parents and then of his wife. Even with the grief and loneliness of missing Kathy, he'd never been truly alone. He'd had God's assurance, his mother's love and friends he could count on.

He dismounted, the saddle creaking in the vast peace of the hillside, and joined Hope on the edge of the precipice where only wind filled the enormous canyon. "With Nora up and walking, I suppose you'll be leaving soon."

"Afraid I'll be leaving you to coordinate the Founder's Days dance single-handed?"

"Sure. I guess I have the right to know if you're going to dash off to Europe and leave me holding the bag, or if you'll stick by me just in case things get tricky."

"Do I look irresponsible?"

No, but she didn't belong here. She might look at home with the wind teasing her ebony locks, dressed in a casual shirt and jeans, but she had no reason to stay, not when the entire world stretched out before her like a big red carpet.

"Now that you mention it, you *do* look irresponsible," he teased, because there was no way to say what was in his heart. "Everyone here knows you can't trust someone from a big city."

That made her smile, a brightness of her being that lured him closer. Like a rainbow at the end of a storm, like the first brush of dawn's light after a dark night, and he longed to hold her, just hold her.

"I've got Nanna to marry off, remember? And your

mom. Which reminds me." She flicked a lock of dark hair behind her ear, a simple gesture, but one that left him riveted. "Since we're at such a dead end with Nanna, we've got to concentrate on your mom. It's too bad there isn't a way we can get her and Andrew together."

"Already tried that. She ignored him."

"Okay, we have proof. We're total and complete failures as matchmakers." Hope sat on the ground and crossed her legs. "Maybe this means I'm doomed to endure Nanna's advice for the rest of my life."

"So, I take it this means you never plan on marrying?"

"What's wrong with that?"

"Nothing." Matthew eased down beside her. "Even a big-city girl has to have an admirer here and there."

"Being from the city is a big flaw, is that it?"

"Sure. At least around here." He liked watching her laugh, light and sweet, liked the way her beauty shone from within. "You must have wanted to find someone."

"I did once." She stared down the canyon wall at the Gallatin River threading through the lush green valley below, and she looked lost. Her easy confidence faded and her voice saddened. "I thought that just because I'd come from a painful family, it didn't mean I was stuck with those patterns. That I could break them and find the home and family I'd always longed for."

"You fell in love?"

She nodded once, and he watched the muscles in her jaw tighten. "His name was Christopher and I thought he was so wonderful. I really thought—" She paused, looking hard at the buffalo so very far below. "I thought he was everything my father wasn't. Gentle, encouraging, loving and kind. We dated for three years, because I had to be sure. Absolutely sure before I agreed to marry him."

"But you didn't marry him."

"No." Her shoulders slumped perceptively. "After we were engaged, he started changing. I don't know, maybe it was me. Maybe I made the ultimate mistake of thinking I could make a marriage work, that love could last. But when I let my guard down and trusted him, he changed. He tried to limit what work I did and started checking up on me when I traveled. I was working as a photographer for an ad agency and living with my brother in New York at the time. I was working very hard at my job, and Christopher became possessive. He didn't want me to work."

"I know a lot of men feel that way because they want to be good providers," Matthew said evenly. "But this was about control, wasn't it?"

Hope nodded. "I tried to talk to him about it, and he became so angry. It was like he'd been hiding this other side of his personality, and I recognized my father in him. I knew if I married Christopher, then I would be sentenced to a life like my mother's. She married Dad for his money, and I wasn't going to make a similar mistake of marrying someone because I needed to be loved. It would have ended the same."

"I'm sorry that happened to you." Matthew could see her sorrow and something larger and deeper, and it saddened him. "Believe it or not, there are men in this world who aren't like that. A few outstanding, handsome individuals a woman can trust."

"Like you, is that it?"

He laughed. "Are you saying I'm not?"

"It's certainly debatable." But her heart ached with what could never be. "I took Christopher as a sign that I was better off forsaking my dreams of happily ever after."

"Or maybe it was a sign not to marry that particular man."

"With my past, maybe marriage isn't an option. I know that's what God was telling me." She tried not to let the words hurt. "I must have gotten the bad marriage gene that runs in my family."

"There's a gene for that?"

"Sure. Apparently there's a recessive gene on Nanna's side and a great big dominant one on Dad's. He comes from a big wealthy family and everyone's been divorced at least twice, I think."

"Now see, we have more sense than that in Montana." He winked so she knew he was kidding, and his gentle humor was like the sun's touch to her heart.

"The light is changing. Wait, I want to get a picture." She had to move away from the comfort of being by his side. He felt suddenly too close, and she'd revealed far too much of herself.

Dark-bottomed thunderheads gathered in the sky behind them, threatening to cover the sun. Shafts of light textured the background of turbulent clouds, bright against dark. If she climbed on that boulder, she'd get the right angle.

"Do you always work when you're supposed to be having fun?" Matthew asked, saucy.

"This *is* fun." She crawled onto the huge rock, powdery dirt clinging to her knees and hands as she scaled to the top. *Perfect.* She framed the shot. "I'm having a rip-roaring time."

When she turned the camera on him, he lifted one hand. "No, you don't. I'm getting camera shy."

"Too bad." She captured his slow easy smile and the wind ruffling his hair before slipping the camera into her pocket. "It's getting late. I bet you have to get home to relieve your baby-sitter."

"Right you are." Matthew gave his horse a sugar cube from the palm of his hand. "I'm looking forward to our race. Firebrand and I intend to win, just so you know. And the winner gets…"

"A meal cooked by the loser?" Hope offered as she climbed from the rock.

"It's a deal."

The instant her boots touched the ground, she heard the chilling clatter of a snake's distinctive rattle. Right next to her ankle.

Chapter Twelve

Fear struck her like lightning, leaving her weak and terrified.

"Don't move. Not an inch." The quiet strength in Matthew's calm voice penetrated her panic. "That rattle is his warning. He won't strike first, not as long as you back away nice and slow."

"Are you s-sure about that?"

"Positive. He's probably more scared of you than you are of him."

"I don't know. I'm pretty scared. And his mouth is open. I can see his fangs." The snake, curled up in the sun, hadn't awakened from his nap in the best of moods, and his V-shaped head swiveled toward her as if taking accurate aim.

"Just back up like I told you," Matthew's voice soothed. "Slowly."

She heard a snap as he tore a dying limb from a spindly fir and stalked toward the boulder, out of the rattler's sight. "I don't think I can move."

"Standing there is making him nervous. Come on, just lift your right foot. Trust me, Hope."

"Okay." Every instinct she had screamed at her to run, but she took a deep breath. *Please, help me, Lord.* She shifted the weight off her front foot and eased back a single step.

The snake didn't strike. Coiled tight, tail rattling, he watched her with cold eyes, front fangs glistening.

"That's it, another step, Hope." Matthew's voice rang with calm assurance.

She managed another step away and still the snake didn't strike. Shaking, she spun and flew at Matthew. Before she knew what she was doing, her arms were around his neck and she was safe against his strong, wide chest. The fast beat of his heart beneath her ear told her he'd been just as afraid. Her feet lost touch with the ground as he lifted her to a safe distance from the rattling snake.

"You're okay, Hope." His hand curled around the back of her neck, his fingers winding through her long hair. "He didn't get you."

"He startled me. I should have been watching where I was going." Her words were muffled because her face was pressed into his shirt. *Thank you, Lord.*

"Next time we'll do a rattlesnake check before we let you start climbing around with your camera."

"Good idea."

She felt like heaven in his arms, like forever and a day, and he wanted to tip her chin up and kiss her gently until her fear vanished. But kissing her wasn't a good idea. Not a good idea at all.

She broke away, thanking him for rescuing her, and he caught Morning Glory's reins for her because she was shaking badly.

He wanted her in his arms again, but the moment for that had passed. Visibly shaken, she mounted and took the reins from him. The brush of her hand on his lit a warmth inside his heart. A warmth that didn't fade as they headed to Harold's land, racing toward the barn with Morning Glory nosing Firebrand out of a win.

The warmth in his heart lingered far into the evening, when the lonely hours stretched before him like an endless sea. All he could think about was her smile, her brightness, her grace. All he wanted was to hold her in his arms again.

The ringing phone snapped Hope's concentration from her computer screen to the clock above the stove. It was nearly midnight, and she grabbed the receiver before it could ring again.

"Hope?" Matthew's cello-rich voice rumbled across the line. "Is it too late to call? I figured you'd be up working."

"You're starting to figure me out. That can't be good." Hope rubbed her tired eyes, exhausted from staring at the computer screen for hours on end. She'd been working because it was better than remembering the exciting, protective shelter of Matthew's arms. "I'm taking a look at the images I took today. I'm really happy with a couple of them."

"The eagle and the thunderheads?"

"Among others."

Hope tapped her mouse, and the image on the screen changed from the golden eagle soaring to heaven on a sunbeam to the image of Matthew's half smile and twinkling eyes. The light burnished his strong shoulders and highlighted his wind-tossed hair. In a single frame she could see the laughter in his eyes and the character in the man.

She grabbed the glass of soda on the table next to her computer and leaned back in her chair. "Are you calling with plans for the meal you owe me?"

"I have to show you that I'm not a sore looser. The only question I have is do you want to eat with or without the boys. I mean, it's hard to enjoy a quiet meal when they need refereeing."

"I've been brushing up on my refereeing skills."

"Then you'll have a chance to put them to use." His voice so far away felt like a touch, comforting and welcome. "How does Saturday sound? After the planning committee meeting?"

"It's a date. How are the boys doing with the new sitter?"

"So far so good. Josh takes a while to get used to change, but he's doing better. All three have been asking to see you. They want to go fishing with you again. They even told it to my mom, and boy, did that make her smile."

"I bet it did. Is she hearing wedding bells?"

"Imaginary ones. Her hold on reality is slipping. It's a shame. I wonder if this happens to all grandmothers?"

"It looks that way to me. When you dropped me off, Nanna had to hear all about our date, as she called it. I told her you had romantically raced me on horseback through a field and I nearly stepped on a rattler. Just your typical dinner and romance kind of date."

He chuckled, a mellow, attractive sound that touched her deep inside. She couldn't remember ever laughing with a man like this, maybe not even in her entire life. He made all her worries fade until she felt as light as air.

"Oh, I have news on the matchmaking front, but not good news." Hope stood up and paced to the window, the cordless phone propped between her ear and her shoulder. "Apparently Helen and Nanna had a heart-to-heart today about Harold. Helen told Nanna to go for it."

"What did Nora say?"

"That it wouldn't be right to set her cap for Harold now. She won't compete with her best friend, even after all this."

"That woman is stubborn, but principled. I can't imagine who she reminds me of."

Hope laughed. "Go ahead and charm me. It's not going to ease the sting of failure."

"At least we haven't messed up the Founder's Days dance so far."

"Not yet. There's plenty of opportunity left."

"What does that mean? That you're counting on failing?"

He laughed and although miles separated them, she felt as if he were with her. "I've got Millie to promise she'll baby-sit for me that night. That means there won't be three little boys at our knees tripping us when we dance."

"You're actually going to dance with me? In public?"

"It's a rough job, but someone's got to do it. Besides, five of my buddies have called wanting to know if I've snared the most eligible woman in Gallatin County."

"The most elusive, you mean. I had a great time today. I mean, a *really* great time. Thank you, Matthew."

"Any time."

She heard in his voice that he'd enjoyed their afternoon, too, and so she hung up the phone with a smile. No man had ever made her feel like this. No man had ever made her feel as if there was really such a thing as romance, really such a thing as a man's honest love.

"When's Hope comin', Daddy?"

Matthew felt a tug on his jeans and looked down to see Joshua gripping a dump truck in his free hand. "She should be here soon. We'll have to wait until she gets here."

"Why?" Innocent hazel eyes gazed up at him.

At about a thousand whys a day, times three, Matthew merely rolled his eyes and tried to ignore it. "Go out and play with your brothers."

"They wanna know when Hope's comin', too."

"Tell them to be patient." Matthew passed a plate beneath the faucet and plunked it into the bottom rack of the dishwasher.

"Then can we have more cookies?"

"You boys just had some. Outside and get some fresh air." Matthew wiped his hand on a nearby towel and reached down to ruffle his youngest son's hair.

"Why?"

Finally Josh was convinced enough to head outside, leaving a trail of sand in his wake on the clean floor. Watching them through the window, Matthew finished up the past-due breakfast plates. By the time he turned off the faucet there were more tracks of sand across the kitchen.

"Is Hope coming *now?*" Ian asked, rubbing a clump of sand out of his hair.

"Right now?" Kale seconded.

"Now, Daddy? Now?"

"You boys are impossible." But Matthew wanted to see Hope, too. All it took was one trip down the river for the triplets to like her. And Matthew figured it had taken him even less time. He'd liked her the moment he'd spotted her broken-down Jeep alongside the road that stormy night. Every time he saw her, he liked her more.

"So, is she comin'?" Ian rubbed more sand out of his tousled hair. "She squirted us with the hose, and we gots a sprinkler."

"Yeah, Daddy, we gots a sprinkler." Kale and Josh spoke nearly in unison, their identical faces upturned with the widest, sweetest pleading looks on the entire planet.

Okay, so maybe he wanted to see Hope, too. "Go outside and play and she'll be here before you know it."

Three little boys opened their mouths to protest and were cut short by the chime of the doorbell. Cries of "Yippee!" and "Hope! Hope!" preceded him to the front of the house. His heart was beating fast with anticipation as he reached for the brass knob. But it was Mom standing on the front step, arms full of plastic containers.

Matthew swallowed his disappointment. "You didn't have to bring vats of food."

"Well, Nora and Hope make two extra to feed, and if Harold shows up to grill his specialty burgers, I swear he can eat a big bowl of potato salad all by himself."

Matthew lifted the heaviest containers from the collection in his mom's arms and held the door for her as the triplets shouted, "Gramma! Gramma came, too!" and threw their arms around her knees, holding tight.

Matthew managed to speak above them. "Harold isn't coming. He found out that Nora would be here and bowed out."

"That's a shame. Doesn't that woman know he's carrying a torch for her?" Patsy blew kisses at her grandsons and agreed to their pleas to see the big hole they dug in the sandbox. "Helen told me what you two kids were up to, trying to play matchmaker for Harold and Nora. I think it's sweet, but you need a professional's touch, dear."

"A professional like you?" He shut the door with his foot and followed his mother and the trail of sand left by his sons down the hallway to the kitchen. "You were so successful with Hope and me. We're planning a June wedding."

"You are?" His mom turned, a brief second of joy on her face, then she shook her head, scowling. "I can't believe a son of mine would tease me like that. Your brothers have better manners, but you, Matthew Joseph, are the scoundrel of the bunch. I actually believed you."

"How does a dose of your own medicine taste?" He set the containers on the counter next to the refrigerator. "Come on, Mom. There's no way Hope Ashton is going to marry me, so stop dreaming."

"Who's dreaming? Anyone can take one look at that girl and see she needs a family." She thunked several containers onto the counter and told the boys, yes, she would be right there. "Hope Ashton looks lost and alone, and besides Nora, what true family does she have? She's got a good heart. Anyone who would take the time to care for her grandmother is certainly good enough to marry my son and raise my grandsons."

"Sure, but next time you matchmake, try to find me someone a little more realistic, okay?" He opened the refrigerator and started stacking the containers inside.

"What's this, you aren't scolding me for trying to marry you off? Can it be that God has answered my prayers?"

"Don't go dancing a jig or anything, but if I fall in love again, I'll remarry. Sometime in the far future." He smiled as his mom wrapped her arms around his middle and hugged him fiercely.

"Now don't make me wait too long for more grandchildren. I love my triplets, but Matthew, they are growing up and pretty soon I won't be able to bribe hugs and kisses out of them." She stepped back as the doorbell rang again. "Well, not unless I use my car as a bribe. I bet that's Hope."

"Hope!" "It's Hope!" The cries rang through the air as the boys pounded from the kitchen and raced down the hall.

"Son, let me sweep up after them while you greet your *girlfriend*." His mom waggled her brows.

Matthew swung the refrigerator door shut and shook his head. "I'm going to talk to the pastor about you. I think you need some serious counseling."

She laughed, shooing him away with the broom she'd snatched from the corner.

The boys had already flung open the door to reveal Nora with Hope standing in the bright threshold. Hope had a wicker basket slung over her forearm, and her hand was on Nora's elbow.

Matthew's heart stopped beating when Hope turned her attention from the doting, noisy triplets and greeted him with a smile. A genuine smile from her gentle heart, and everything inside him—all his hopes, his dreams, his needs—remembered holding her in his arms. He craved the feel of her sweet and warm against his chest and the peace that came with it. A deep, abiding peace.

"I brought Nanna's special secret baked barbecue beans." Hope lifted the basket just enough to emphasize it. "And baked cinnamon rolls."

"Yippee!" The shout filled the air. "Cinnamon rolls!"

"I know how to be popular with the three-year-old set." She laughed when Ian took hold of her basket.

"I carry it, Hope!"

"That's my job." Matthew lifted the heavy basket from Hope's arm and breathed in her scent. Memories of their day on the mountainside assailed him, and the peaceful feeling in his heart doubled. He knew he shouldn't feel this way, but he couldn't help it. "Boys, out of Nora's way. Nora, it's been a long time since two such beautiful ladies have graced this house."

"You big charmer, you." Nora wasn't fooled as she took the arm he offered. "No wonder my granddaughter has fallen for you."

"Nanna, you're impossible. You see, Matthew, Nanna has this lovebug theory. That eventually everyone is going to get bitten."

"And here I forgot to put on my flea collar this morning," he quipped. "Knew I'd forgotten something."

"I remembered mine, so never fear." Hope winked at him. "Can the lovebug bite a person at any age?"

"That's what I've heard," Matthew answered.

"You two!" Nora huffed, amusement glittering in her eyes as she took a careful step on her walking cast. "I'm going to go out into the yard with Patsy and sit a spell. We have a world of visiting to catch up on."

"As long as you two beautiful women aren't plotting our wedding, I'll allow it." He said it just to make Hope laugh again.

After sending the boys outside to play and escorting Nora to the comfortable shaded chairs beneath the old maple trees in the backyard, he realized he'd lost Hope. He found her kneeling in the grass next to the sandbox, intently listening while the boys talked in triplicate, demonstrating with their trucks.

He had a perfect view of them through the kitchen window above the sink—a perfect view of her. Dressed in tan pleated shorts and a melon tank top, she looked like the girl next door and not a woman of means. When the boys started throwing sand and a spray hit her in the arm, she merely laughed and gently admonished them. Then she helped Kale brush sand from his face.

Something inside Matthew changed as he watched Hope with his sons. Her touch was as caring as any mother's, her words as gentle, her manner as nurturing. He could hear the melody of her voice through the open window, carried by the warm breezes. Kale thanked her and, with a child's open heart, threw his arms around her and hugged her tight. Hope hugged him back, sand and all, and a smile touched her face as Ian and Josh hugged her, too.

His heart ached with an emotion he dared not name, because he *couldn't* be falling for Hope. He wouldn't let himself. *Lord, please don't let me feel this way,* he prayed, but his feelings remained, growing stronger with every breath as Hope kicked off her sneakers and climbed into the sandbox, claiming a bulldozer as her own.

Hope felt the touch of Matthew's gaze as she played trucks with the boys and through the entire time she spent running around his backyard with the hose, squirting the giggling triplets with cold water. On the sidelines, Nanna laughed and worked at her knitting, her needles clicking along as she chatted with Patsy.

After the boys were thoroughly drenched and shivering, she turned off the hose. "Time to dry off, boys."

"But we're firemen!" Ian argued, grabbing the nozzle for himself.

Hope stopped him before he could turn it on and blast his brothers with it. "Firemen also have to dry off and get ready for lunch. They all eat together at the firehouse."

"Hamburgers?" Kale asked skeptically.

"Lots of hamburgers." Laughing, Hope looked up and nearly dropped the hose she was coiling as Matthew stalked across the lawn toward her.

The muscles in his legs rippled beneath sun-bronzed skin and other muscles worked beneath his navy-blue T-shirt as he tossed a towel to each boy. "The coals are on hold. I put cinnamon rolls on the picnic table, one for each of you. Sit down and use your manners."

"Cinnamon rolls!" The triplets raced, towels fluttering behind them like capes, their voices lifting on the warm breezes. "No, Josh. Don't sit there." "That one's mine." "Don't push." Then they turned quiet as they started eating.

"Food works every time." Matthew leaned close, so close she could see the smooth shaven texture of his jaw and the green-brown flecks in his hazel eyes. "The boys had a blast. Thanks for taking time with them."

"My pleasure. Can I have that last towel you're holding?"

"On one condition. Go horseback riding with me again."

"What about the boys?"

Matthew's grin dimpled as he pressed the beige terry towel into her hands. "Mom can watch them. We'll tell her we want to spend time alone."

"Are you sure that's wise?"

"Mom deserves what she gets. Look at her, gloating over there with Nora. Guess what I did?"

Hope bent to swipe the towel down her lower legs. "I'm afraid to ask."

"Invited Dr. Corey over for lunch. He just called— he had an emergency he had to deal with but he's on his way here. He lives next door." Mischief flashed in his hazel eyes. "He was outside watering his rhododendrons when I stepped outside to fetch the morning paper, and I couldn't resist."

"Leave it in the Lord's hands, you said." Laughing, Hope stood on one foot to dry off her toes. "Your mother doesn't know, does she?"

"Do you think she'd be looking so happy and relaxed if she did?" Matthew caught hold of her wrist, and his touch brought back the memory of being held by him, of sunshine and laughter and the safe protection of his arms.

She yearned for that security again, to feel the thump of his heart against her cheek and his muscled strength. Even though she knew it was a dream she could never believe in.

"Sit right here," he whispered, and she gasped in surprise to find a bench directly behind her. When she sat, Matthew knelt in front of her.

He cupped her right foot at the heel and rubbed the

towel across her arch with slow care, then over the ball of her foot and down the length of her toes, leaving a tingling trail. Hope felt the tension ease from every muscle she owned, and she leaned back against the wooden bench with a sigh.

A doorbell rang in the distance. "Hey, Mom, would you get that for me?"

"You're terrible," Hope laughed as Patsy set down her crochet work and hurried into the house. "What if she scares him away?"

"I don't think so. Funny thing, when I told Dr. Corey that my mother would be here, he agreed to come." Matthew dragged the towel over the top of Hope's foot, finishing with slow caresses.

Her breath caught sideways when Matthew's warm, callused fingers caught her other foot and began a wonderful, luxurious massage that left her unable to think. She felt as if she were floating on clouds and sighed again.

"There. Let me grab your shoes." He reached for her canvas slip-ons and eased them onto her feet. This man who'd spent the last few years of his life caring for his sons now took care of her.

No one had ever pampered her so much. Hope felt lost when Matthew stood and offered her his hand to help her from the bench. She placed her palm to his, and his fingers curled around the side of her hand. At his touch, fire shot through her veins and tenderness welled in her soul. Her feet touched the ground and she suddenly stood breathless in front of him.

They were so close, their breaths mingled. So close

she could see his pupils dilate and his bottom lip quiver. His hand skated in a slow caress up her wrist and forearm to band around her elbow. For one second the world, the boys' shouts, the wind in the trees, Nanna's cheerful welcome to Dr. Corey, faded away until all Hope could feel was the tight, tingly plummet of her stomach to her knees. Her mouth quivered with anticipation as Matthew's lips hovered closer, a fraction above her own, waiting, just waiting.

"Matthew!" Patsy's shrill voice rang through the air from very far away. "Matthew Joseph Sheridan, I want a word with you. Oh...my. Not right now."

Matthew groaned, winced and moved away. Over his shoulder she could see Patsy just inside the back door, hands to her face, horror-struck that she'd interrupted.

"I'd better go calm Mom down," he said, apology rough in his voice. His gaze slid one more time to her mouth and then he moved away, leaving her wanting, leaving her wishing for a fairy tale she wouldn't believe in. A fairy tale that could never come true.

"One more time, Hope. One more time." Ian, secure in his jammies, leaned back against her and tipped his head up to stare at her with big innocent pleading eyes, exhaustion bruising the delicate skin. "Please, please."

"Please, Hope." Josh snuggled against her side, warm and sweet, smelling like shampoo and little-boy goodness. Kale on the other side hugged her as he yawned, just as dear.

"You boys know I'm a total softy, but this is the last time."

Yawns were her answer as she flipped the hard-cover book to the beginning and read one more time about the brave fireman, his trusty dog and his bright red fire truck. In just three readings, she had the book memorized and recited the story this time by heart. The boys struggled to stay awake even as sleep claimed them.

First Josh's chin bobbed forward, and then Kale's eyes drifted shut. Ian slumped against her stomach. Sweetness filled her as she set the closed book aside and, still whispering the words, eased the boys back on the mattress. Afraid to move them, she covered them with an afghan she found at the foot of the bed and tiptoed to the door.

The glow of the night-light lit her way and cast enough light for her to take one last look at the triplets, identically tousled dark hair and sloping noses, three miniature versions of Matthew lost in dreams.

She eased the door shut and headed down the unfamiliar hall, snapping on lights as she went. Twilight had turned to darkness while she'd been getting the boys to bed.

A shadow moved across the open doorway that looked out at the night skies. Before she could even panic, she recognized Dr. Corey's voice coming from the porch. "Matthew, is that you?"

"No, he took Nanna and Patsy home. Patsy wanted to talk to him alone, and I volunteered to stay with the boys."

"Getting pretty close to Matthew, aren't you, from what I hear?"

"We're friends, that's all."

"That's how my wife and I started out, just being friends. The next thing you knew I was proposing to her." His shadowed form filled the threshold. "I know what you and Matthew are up to, trying to marry off Patsy and Nora. I've got eyes, I see what's going on. And believe me, you won't get far. Patsy and I go way back."

"To a falling-out in high school. Helen told us." Hope followed Dr. Corey onto the small front porch. "What happened?"

"Nothing major, and that isn't the reason Patsy won't speak to me, leastwise not these days." He eased down onto the top step. "I owned the plane that crashed and killed her daughter-in-law."

Hope's knees gave out and she took the step beside him. The warm night air carried the scent of juniper from the yard, and she breathed it in, trying to find the right words. "I'm sorry. I had no idea. Matthew could have told me."

"Matthew doesn't hold me responsible and he wouldn't see that his mother would. He's a good man that way, he's got a good heart. Not many men could face the loss of a wife and still find the inner strength to raise three infants with care and love. Not many at all."

"I know he's a good man. The best I've ever met."

"Well, in all your travels, you won't find another to compare, believe me." Emotion rang in the doctor's voice, quiet like a deep river. "My wife died in that plane, too. I was stuck in surgery and they didn't tell me until later. Until it was too late."

"I didn't know. I'm sorry for your loss."

"Me, too." Andrew Corey took a shaky breath. "Grieving is a long journey, slow and painful. But one day, it's over. Not the loss, but the desolation, and you start feeling again. I want Patsy to forgive me, but I don't think she will. Tell me, is that ulcer you had still bothering you?"

Hope didn't comment on the change of subject, surprised that he would remember the few times Nanna had hauled her in to his office over a decade ago. "I wound up in surgery my sophomore year of college. It bothers me now and then, usually whenever I have to deal with my parents."

"Not everyone deserves the parents they get or the children they bear. Families can be tricky things, but luckily they don't need to be permanent. You've grown up and now you can pick your family. And it looks like you're doing a fine job."

Andrew gestured toward the pickup pulling into the paved driveway at the side of the house. She wanted to correct his misimpression, but he was already walking away. Matthew hopped out of the truck, and the two men spoke briefly in low murmurs. Then Dr. Corey waved good-night to her and crossed the driveway to his house.

"How were the boys?" Matthew asked as he paced toward her in the darkness, a shadowed form with shoulders immovably strong. "Did they give you any trouble?"

"Nothing I couldn't handle. You have nice sons. Energetic, but nice." She'd spent many years convincing herself she didn't want children, didn't need them. And yet the tenderness of caring for Matthew's boys lingered in her heart and made her wish. He made her wish. "How did it go with Patsy?"

He hunkered down beside her. "I haven't been in that much trouble with my mother since the night when I was sixteen, took the car without permission and didn't come home until three in the morning."

"You were a bad boy."

"Mom thought I was even worse tonight." He shook his head, tousling his hair. "She told me never to try to marry her off to anyone. Imagine that. I told her I was just following her example."

Remembering Andrew Corey's words, Hope's heart ached. "Maybe she blames him."

"No, she doesn't blame him. She condemns him. I had no idea she was holding this in her heart. It wasn't Andrew's fault. His wife made a pilot error. It might not have happened if he'd been at the stick, but it did. I reminded her that our faith teaches forgiveness, that it isn't her right to hold Andrew accountable. It didn't comfort her."

Matthew looked down at the shadowed ground and didn't tell Hope how helpless he'd felt.

"I'm sorry." Hope's hand, satin-soft, covered his, a connection of affection that made his eyes tear and his heart ache in ways he'd never felt before.

The night brushed her with faint stardust, a silver, shimmering radiance that caressed the high cut of her cheekbones, the delicate shape of her chin and the lush curves of her mouth.

He moved closer to her across the cement steps until only inches of air separated them. "It seems to me we were interrupted earlier, and I want to correct that."

Her eyes darkened. "You mean when I was helping Josh with the ketchup bottle?"

"Before that." It seemed he couldn't look anywhere but into the depths of her eyes, so dark and luminous. "After I dried your feet with the towel."

"I remember now." She'd remembered all along, her eyes told him that, but she was nervous. And yearning for closeness. And afraid of it.

Just like he was.

"I want you to know that I'm a man who finishes what he starts."

"So, you're going to kiss me?" Her words were tremulous, her lips so close he could sense their movement as she spoke.

"As often as I can." Then not even air separated them, and his mouth slanted over hers. The kiss was like coming home, like comfort and love and contentment all wrapped up in a single, growing emotion filling his heart and spilling over into his soul.

When she withdrew, she was smiling. "Good night, Matthew. I'll see you in church tomorrow."

He watched her breeze down the driveway, a slim shadow against the darkness of the night, her hair blowing in the wind. Holding his heart, she hopped into her Jeep, found her keys and started the engine. He couldn't look away, still unable to breathe, until her vehicle's taillights disappeared in the darkness.

He sat on the step for a long while, lost in thought,

forgetting to breathe, watching the stars move across the face of the night. The truth remained as invincible as the stars above.

He loved Hope. With all his heart.

Chapter Thirteen

"It's good to have the house all to myself without a nurse underfoot every time I look." Nanna turned from the counter where her china teapot sat next to an opened package of butter cookies. "Although I will miss you when you go."

"I'll miss you, too." Hope closed the back door and hung her key ring on a row of hooks near the light switch. "It's nearly June. I can't believe time has passed so quickly, and look at you. Another week and you won't need me at all."

"I'll always need my Hope." Nanna held out her arms, and Hope moved into them for a sweet hug. "Tell me all about you and Matthew. Don't look so shocked. I can recognize love when I see it."

"I don't want to be badgered about this tonight. Please." Hope pulled a chair out from the round oak table. "Sit down and stop meddling."

Nanna settled onto the chair's cushion, still frail. Far

too frail. "I just thought you might be in need of my advice. Since I've been in your shoes once before."

"Seems to me you're still in those shoes." Hope crossed to the counter where she grabbed the teapot. "Sounds echo in this big old house like loneliness."

"I don't mind so much. I've spent some good years in this house." Nanna smiled. "I have a good many more years to go."

"Yes, you do." Hope set the teapot on the table and the cookies next to it, then spun toward the corner hutch to grab the china cups. "And remember, those years don't need to be spent alone."

The smile faded from Nanna's face. "I know what you're up to and I never should have confided in you. I was like a teenage girl, young again, daydreaming about a man I thought was handsome. But that was all."

"I don't believe you." Hope placed saucers and cups on the muslin cloth, then tapped on the worn leather cover of the closed Bible in the center of the table. "You've been deliberately trying to marry me off to Matthew, proclaiming all the while about the blessings of marriage and the existence of true love. When all this time you're too chicken to take the same advice."

"I give good advice." Nanna's chin shot up. "And I'm not afraid."

"Yes, you are. Helen knows Harold will only see her as a friend. He's made that clear to her, to everyone. Even Helen has told you she thinks you should go for it. She understands. She wants you to be happy."

"She is the oldest friend I have, and if there's any chance that she and Harold will find happiness together, then I will never stand in the way. I could never do that to my friend."

"Your friend wants that happiness for you."

"'The greatest love is shown when people lay down their lives for their friends.'" Nanna's lower lip trembled, and she pressed her fingertips to the Bible's cover. "'Love is patient and kind. Love is not jealous or boastful or proud. Love does not demand its own way.'"

"'Seek His will in all you do, and He will direct your paths.'" Hope knelt down beside her grandmother and pressed a kiss to her cheek. "You are not in control of Harold's heart. And what did you tell me? Life is far too short to forsake God's gifts because we are afraid to accept them."

"This is what I get, sharing all my wisdom with you." Nanna smiled through unshed tears. "It comes right back at me when I don't need it. Now sit down and tell me. Matthew kissed you, didn't he?"

"I told you, don't go there." She felt too confused by what had happened. The claiming brand of his kiss still lingered on her lips, and she needed to be alone to think. "I'm going to be leaving soon. You know it. I know it. Matthew knows it. Now, read your Bible and let me make my paper roses in peace. The dance is coming up, and Helen needs these so she can decorate the community hall early."

Hope pulled the box Helen had brought over from the corner, lifted a thin crackling sheet of carnation pink tissue paper from a pile and began scrunching it in one hand.

Nanna shook her head. "Stubborn people always learn the hard way. You wait and see."

Later, after putting Nanna to bed and checking the doors, Hope retreated to her room beneath the eaves. Restless, that's what she was. The loneliness of the night called to her, reminding her of the sweetness of putting the triplets to bed and the precious comfort of their little bodies tucked against hers. Of the day on the river. Of racing Matthew on horseback with the wind on her face and feeling happier than she'd ever been in her life.

Closing her eyes, shaking her head, she sat down on the bed. The ancient springs creaked and the old iron bedstead groaned, and then all was silent. Completely silent.

The memory of Matthew's kiss still touched her lips, and an ache gathered in her chest, so sweet that it brought tears to her eyes.

Hadn't she made this mistake before? Memories of her parents fighting whispered like ghosts in the dark. Memories of the devastation when Christopher had shattered her trust. Broken hearts, isn't that where love led? Even Nanna, with one happy marriage behind her, was afraid. Didn't that show how rare true love really was? What if she was making a mistake?

Troubled, Hope lifted her Bible from the nightstand and cradled it. She'd liked Matthew's kiss and she wanted the excitement and the sweetness of being in his arms again.

But was it right? The thought terrified her. Love terrified her. The walls defending her heart were stout ones, built over time by necessity. How could she take them down now? Did she trust in Matthew?

The night wind ruffled the curtains at the open window, sending the scent of roses and honeysuckle into her room. Hope opened her Bible and flipped through the pages until a verse from Psalms caught her eye. *Let the morning bring me word of Your unfailing love, for I have put my trust in You. Show me the way I should go, for to You I lift up my soul.*

God was holding her heart in His hand. He wouldn't fail her. Feeling that truth all the way to her soul, Hope flicked off the light and let the breezes caress her face. Calm settled over her as she watched the stars wink and dazzle in a night that felt full of dreams.

He couldn't get Hope out of his mind. Even though it was after midnight, Matthew couldn't get to sleep. He threw back the sheet and paced through the house in his bare feet, the sound echoing in the infinite darkness.

He ran the water in the tap a long time until it was cold and he filled a glass. The liquid slid down his throat cool and refreshing, but it didn't satisfy him.

Nothing would, unless it was another of Hope's kisses.

Frustrated at himself, he paced to the back door and turned the knob. The warm breeze didn't help any, and the shadows only made him feel more alone, left him remembering the sound of Hope's laughter in this yard. How the boys had clung to her, laughed with her, played with her.

She was wrong for them. He knew it. He didn't have the right to love Hope. They were friends, nothing more. And if his heart felt differently, then that didn't change the facts. She would be leaving as soon as Founder's Days were over. Sure, she might not have said the words, but he knew them to be true.

Nora was nearly well, and after Hope's obligations were met, she had no reason to stay. Not with the world at her feet and a job that kept her traveling.

"Where's Hope?" Josh's quiet whine cut through the night. "I waked up and she ain't here."

"She had to go home, tiger." Matthew knelt as the boy toddled up to him, sleepy and sweet, and nearly tumbled into his arms.

"I want her to read. I wanna hear my fireman story." Josh rubbed his ear, his whine bordering on a cry.

"Does your ear hurt?"

"Yeah. I want Hope to read." Josh buried his face in Matthew's T-shirt and wept. "I want Hope."

It wasn't until that moment that Matthew realized what he'd done. If he risked his own heart, then he was risking his sons', too.

It wouldn't be an easy visit to make. Matthew drove slower than usual up Nora's driveway and over the whir of the air-conditioning wondered if he had the courage to actually tell Hope what he'd been practicing all morning.

He didn't want to hurt her feelings. He'd never want to do that. Love in his heart burned for her; that was the one thing that hadn't changed. But after three days with a sick boy who didn't understand why Hope couldn't come, Matthew knew he had his answer. There was no other way. He had to ask Hope if she felt what he did, if she loved him and the boys enough to stay before this went any further.

Even if he already knew what her answer would be.

The old farmhouse looked alive with the trees in full leaf and the gardens prospering. Parking in the shade of one of the mature maples, he cut the engine and hopped out into the heat of the day.

"Matthew, is that you?" Hope peered from behind a big flowering bush, a smudge of dirt on her cheek. She was kneeling in the dirt. "I left a message last night and you didn't return it. Is everything okay?"

"Josh has been sick, that's all. Nothing too serious, just a minor earache, and thanks to Dr. Corey he's better now." Matthew stared at the big wicker basket he held. "You and Nora left this at my place."

"Thanks." She stood, brushing dirt from her bare knees as she approached with equally dirty gardening gloves.

It was hard not to remember the feel of her kiss and the sweetness of her in his arms. Hard not to wish for what might never be. He handed her the basket. "Heard from Helen that Nora's getting around well on her cast now."

"This last trip to the doctor showed the bone is nearly mended. Another week, and the cast comes off." Hope set the basket on the nearby bench and wondered why Matthew wouldn't look her in the eye. Was he remembering their kiss? "Helen said we've got the go-ahead to start decorating for the dance. I know it's a busy time of year for you, but maybe you could drop by. We're working tonight."

"I'll see what I can do." A muscle in his jaw jumped, and he stared hard at the ground. "Got a few minutes? I want to talk."

Not about the dance, but the kiss. She knew it. Feeling her face heat, Hope gestured where the garden path led to the back porch. "We can sit in the shade, if you'd like. I'll fetch some iced tea from the kitchen. It's hot today. Summer's definitely here."

"Sounds good."

He didn't sound right—he didn't sound like Matthew. She started to tremble as she led the way across the flagstones and toward the shade at the end of the house. Don't be silly, she scolded herself. Matthew was her friend. Okay, secretly she might, just might, want him to be more.

He clumped up the steps behind her, his work boots heavy on the wood, and cleared his throat. "Hope, I—"

The screen door swung open and Nora held the cordless phone in her free hand. "Matthew, it's about time you showed up to pay attention to my granddaughter. Hope, this is for you. It's your agent. Maybe I'd better tell him to call back...."

"No." Hope grabbed the phone. "Matthew, I'm sorry, but I need to take this. It will only be a minute."

Matthew watched her retreat into the kitchen, already talking. "Her agent, huh?"

"Why, yes," Nora said, with the sparkle back in her

voice. "She's got a deadline coming up and whatnot. Her next book is coming out and they want some signing tour or some such. Still, it's important work she does. Have you seen any of her pictures?"

"The ones she took of my boys. They were good."

Pride shimmered in Nora's eyes. "Good? Why, she's better than good. Sit down in that chair, young man, and I'll fetch you an iced tea."

He obeyed, noticing how spry Nora was even in her cast. It was true. She was healing and anyone could see she would be as good as new. And soon.

If he leaned to the left, he could see Hope through the open window. She'd settled into a chair at the far end of the kitchen table and was scribbling something down on a piece of paper.

"Here you go." Nora plunked a glass on the rail beside him and shoved a book into his hands. "Take a look at what my Hope does, photographing light, reminding us of God's brightness."

Matthew had never seen Hope's hardback book of pictures. The cover showed a solar eclipse above an endless sea, both sky and water reflecting all shades of light and darkness. The title and Hope's name flowed in gold print, and beneath, in the corner, was a verse from Job. "Your life will be brighter than the noonday. Any darkness will be as bright as morning."

Inside were powerful images—shafts of light impaling an ancient cathedral's spire, dew droplets on grape vines reflecting the rising sun on a new day, page after page of stunning photographs that made him feel and verses from the Bible that inspired, that gave hope.

"Guess what?" She stood in the doorway, excitement snapping in her eyes. "I just got asked to do a Christmas book."

"This is a good thing." Nora tapped across the porch, arms wide, and wrapped her granddaughter in a hug. "Don't tell me you have to leave now."

"Well, not this minute." Hope turned to him and shook her head. "Matthew, I'm sorry. I've told Nanna not to force my pictures on innocent, unsuspecting people but she does it anyway."

He closed the book and handed it to Hope, but the beautiful images remained, tucked in his heart. "Congratulations on your good news."

"Thanks. Taking pictures on our outings rejuvenated me, I think. I feel ready to start some serious work again."

"So you're leaving." He could see the excitement shimmering in her eyes, bright and unmistakable.

"Actually, I'm not sure what to do." Hope handed the book to her grandmother and looked vulnerable, far too vulnerable.

He wanted to take her in his arms and protect her, but it wouldn't be right. He had his answer. He'd asked the Lord to guide him, to show him the way.

And this was the answer. Hope would be flying who knew where to take pictures for her books. And he had three little boys to raise.

"Like I said, this is my busy season, and I've got a lot of work piling up." Matthew headed down the steps, heart aching. "I'm going to talk Mom into taking my place on the dance committee."

"I see." She looked crestfallen. "The one she forced you into in the first place?"

"That's right."

"Well, I'll certainly miss you."

Her eyes looked so sad. Was she disappointed in him? "Harold's decided to help me out, but there's still more work than I can do. Plus, I have the boys."

"Sure, I understand." Her chin lifted. "Is there anything I can do for Josh? I could bake more cinnamon rolls."

"No, don't do that." He didn't want to sound harsh, but he was breaking into pieces and he couldn't let her know. "The boys are just fine. Take care, and I really am glad for you."

"Thanks." She looked lost as he stormed away from her, her eyes pinched, her hands loosely clenched at her sides. From her ponytail all the way down to her dirt-streaked sneakers, she looked every inch a country girl, every inch the woman who'd stolen his heart.

But she wasn't. And down deep, he'd known it all along.

Hope thought about Matthew's behavior all through the decorating meeting where about a dozen women sat around tables stacked high with brightly colored tissue roses, making more. Patsy looked awkward when she tried to explain how Matthew truly was busy. The jobs kept coming in and there wasn't enough time in the day.

Hope tried not to read anything into it, but she knew in her heart something had changed between them. It was that kiss, that soul-touching, wondrous kiss that had done it.

He's no fool, she told herself. He has three small boys and more responsibility than she could understand. The last thing he wanted was a romance with a woman who didn't know the first thing about a family, about what made love last.

But that didn't stop her heart from hurting. It was as if the light had gone from her world.

As the evening passed, she felt at home here among old acquaintances renewed. Her best friend from high school showed up and invited her afterward to the café for ice cream sundaes like they used to do when they were schoolgirls.

By the time Hope pulled into the spare stall in Nanna's garage, twilight was advancing, draining the last of the daylight. An owl swept past her when she shut the garage door, and she almost didn't see the green pickup parked in the shadows near the house.

Through the windows open to the fresh breeze, she could see the living room. Nanna looked as if she'd just opened the door for Harold, who was holding something in his hand. Then he moved and she could see he held a potted rosebush.

Accept it, Nanna. Please. Hope watched breathlessly as Nanna hesitated, studying both Harold and his offering, then nodded. Maybe accepting more than just the plant.

Joy filled Hope's heart. Matthew. She had to tell Matthew. She could imagine the twinkle of happiness in his eyes when he heard the news. She could picture how his smile would stretch slowly across his mouth and he would nod, glad for his grandfather-in-law, glad for Nanna.

Then she remembered how Matthew had behaved today and how he'd looked at her. He'd put that distance back in place between them, as he'd done at the beginning. And because of the kiss. The beautiful memory of that tender kiss faded away, tarnished by a growing feeling of failure.

She'd kissed a man who didn't want her, a man who didn't want to be more than friends. Hadn't she known better? Both of them had emphasized over and over again that all they wanted was friendship. She was foolish even to be tempted by a kiss and a dream.

Pain tore at her heart and she stumbled through the darkness, aching for the solitude of the garden, silent and cool this time of night from a late watering. The bench was dry so she sat on it and listened to the night sounds, the harmony of nature, of insects, frogs and owls and the chatter of a nearby raccoon probably playing in the birdbath out back.

She ached to spend one more sun-filled afternoon with Matthew. She wanted his kisses and to find refuge in his strong arms. She missed the sound of his easy laughter, the jaunty tilt of his half grin and the way he made her feel.

But she should have known. She should have realized that nothing that good could ever happen to her.

Her life alone stretched out before her. If she cried, it was only because she'd touched and lost a dream that had never been hers.

* * *

Hope realized why Harold had sounded so eager on the phone when she'd called not twenty minutes ago, and her grip on the steering wheel tightened. Had he turned into a matchmaker, too? Even from a quarter of a mile away on Harold's gravel driveway, she could see Matthew perched on the roof in the hot morning sun.

Okay, I can do this. She guided the Jeep into the shade of the house and tugged a small photo album from beneath the seat, then an envelope and two cardboard portfolios. By the time she'd stepped down from the driver's seat with her arms full, Harold was already halfway down the nearby ladder.

"Howdy, missy. Good to see you this morning. Are those my pictures you got there?" He nimbly hit the ground and started toward her.

"As promised. I can't believe how many pictures I ended up taking of the triplets." She handed him the photo album first.

He flipped through the pages right there, delight on his face, love for his grandsons bright in his eyes. "This is mighty fine work. Mighty fine, indeed. Sure I can't pay you for this?"

"Now how can I charge the man who will be taking my grandmother out on her first date in forty years?" She held out the portfolio and watched as he unfolded the cardboard to reveal three framed blown-up prints, one of each triplet.

"Hope, I don't know what to say."

"Then don't say it. Those are mighty special great grandsons you have."

"Don't I know it. Now, if my plans to court your grandmother work, then that will make you my granddaughter. What do you think about that?"

"I'd be proud to call you my grandfather." Hope's heart ached, and the sound of Matthew's step on the gravel startled her. She hadn't noticed him climb down and now she couldn't look anywhere else. Even if the sight of him reminded her of the terrible mistake she'd almost made by falling in love with him.

His hair was dark with sweat and tousled by the wind. Both the white T-shirt stretched over his broad shoulders and his denim jeans were streaked with dust. "Harold bent my arm and forced me to help him reroof his house. It's good to see you, Hope."

But he didn't look very happy. She noticed the strain tight around his eyes and mouth. "I have some things for you, too. More pictures of the boys for the album I gave you and a set of prints like Harold's."

It was hard, holding back her heart, acting as if she wasn't hurting on the inside. Pride sustained her as she held out the prints and the thick envelope. She hated that her hand trembled.

Matthew stepped close enough to take them, then retreated. "Thanks, Hope. It's mighty good of you."

"It's what I do every day of my life." She didn't know what to say, how to keep from telling him that those prints were a labor of love. If things were different, maybe he might understand, but he was standing a good two yards away, a statement she couldn't miss.

Feeling awkward, hiding her hurt, she took a step toward the Jeep. "I tried to reach Patsy several times before I came out here. I have a set of pictures for her, too."

"Mom took Josh to Dr. Corey this morning for me—saved the baby-sitter a trip."

"Is he still doing better?"

"Sure, just a minor ear infection. He gets them all the time. Andrew was good enough to take a look at him late at night for me, so I made Mom take him back to Andrew, not his son. Should be interesting to hear how it goes."

"Well, let me take these in the house and leave you kids to talk," Harold said. "Hope, if you want to give me Patsy's pictures, I'll make sure she gets them today. Should be going to town anyway later this afternoon, and it'd save you a trip."

"Thanks." Hope leaned across the driver's seat and grabbed the duplicate album and prints. Harold took them from her with a wink, then headed for the house, leaving her alone with Matthew.

"I'm hoping to finish this roof before the heat of the day." He backed toward the ladder, but something flickered in his eyes that she couldn't read. Regret? Sadness?

"I just have one thing to say first." Hope took a deep breath. "I'm sorry about the kiss. It had to have bothered you, but I don't want you upset at me because of it."

"*You're* sorry." He repeated the words, weighing them. "I am, too. Should we leave it at that?"

"Sure. And I realize that you might not want to take me to the dance, especially since we're no longer on the committee together, so consider yourself free of the obligation."

Matthew nodded, seeing the hurt shadow her eyes and feeling a similar pain in his heart. They'd let it go too far. It was nobody's fault. Knowing Hope, feeling her warmth and sharing her laughter had changed his life for the best. How could he be sorry about that? "Everyone figures you'll be leaving town as soon as Founder's Days are over. Is that true?"

She nodded. "Nanna's getting around so well, she doesn't need me anymore. Her cast comes off Monday morning and so I booked a flight out that afternoon. Since I don't have any other reason to stay." She paused, looking frail and lost somehow. "Do I?"

Did she? This was the chance to ask her how she felt, how she truly felt. To find out if his love was enough to keep her here. He fought the urge to wrap her in his arms, fought every urge to hold her. "You've got pictures to take for your new book. I suppose you need to fly somewhere far away for that."

"Not really. The sun shines even here in Montana." She spoke quietly, leaving much unsaid, and he knew what she was asking.

No, his heart answered. She might stay, but she had the world at her feet. The images from her books lingered in his mind, brilliant, subtle, sublime. She had a calling, and it wasn't here in rural Montana.

On a prayer, he took a deep breath and said the hardest words he'd ever had to say. "Looks like I'll see you at the dance Friday night."

The silent appeal faded from her luminous eyes. "Yes, I'll see you there."

He watched her turn and hop into her Jeep. Her

head was bowed, and she didn't look at him as the warning chime dinged and she shut the door. The photographs he held in his hands felt as heavy as his heart as she fastened her seat belt and started the engine. He couldn't watch her head down the circular lane, driving straight toward the horizon.

His vision was blurry when he went to look at the matted prints—one of each boy, the pictures she took the day they'd drifted down the river with the boys, images captured with a gifted eye and an affectionate heart. Ian's sparkling mischief, Kale's concentrated intelligence, Josh's humble wonder.

If Matthew needed more proof, this was it. He wouldn't be floating the river with Hope through the summers of his life.

Sure, he loved her. He loved her more with each breath he took and with each kindness she showed him and his sons. Even knowing she wasn't right for him didn't stop the love in his heart, or change it, or lessen it, and Matthew felt shattered.

Simply shattered. When Hope left, he would lose his heart again.

Chapter Fourteen

The week had been a tough one for Matthew, dreading the dance to come. He'd tried to get out of it, but Mom hadn't wanted to go alone like some poor middle-aged lady who couldn't find a date, and he'd agreed to be her escort for the night. Oh, he knew what his mom was up to, especially since she wouldn't stop talking about the beautiful pictures Hope had taken of the boys.

The night was warm, the skies clear and the bright lights flooding the street and community hall's parking lot could be seen for blocks. A band was playing bluegrass on a makeshift platform in the far corner of the paved lot, and their snappy harmony lifted spirits and the dancers' feet. Observers ringed the sidelines, drinking from flowered paper cups. The scraps of conversation Matthew heard as he passed included remarks about the current low cattle prices and concern over a possible summer's drought.

Then he saw Hope through the double doors opened

to the night breezes. She worked beside one of the McKaslin girls restocking the dessert platters on the cloth-draped tables. Pain filled his heart looking at her. She wore a simple blue dress, understated and elegant like she was, and pearls at her throat. She was busy talking and hadn't noticed him yet.

It hurt to look at her, at this woman who was all of his heart, this woman he couldn't have. Think of the boys, think of her future, and just walk away. He gently guided his mom in the opposite direction. "Let's go look for Nora and Harold. I bet they're dancing."

"Look, there's Hope." Mom tugged him through the door. "Now explain to me again why you've got me on your arm and not that wonderful woman?"

"Can't admit defeat, can you?"

"Not when it comes to my son's welfare." Her hand on his arm squeezed gently, a show of a lifetime's love.

"I'm just as concerned about your welfare." He caught sight of Dr. Corey, only because he'd walked up to the table Hope was restocking. "You wouldn't tell me how it went with Andrew when you took Josh to his office."

"There wasn't much to tell. I was polite."

"I guess that means I can count on you to be polite a second time?" Now it was Matthew's turn to tug his mother gently toward the white-draped tables.

"Matthew, now don't you dare—" Mom started, but Andrew turned around from surveying the refreshments and she stopped protesting, for politeness's sake, apparently. "Hello, Andrew," she said stiffly.

"Patsy." Andrew nodded a welcome. "Matthew. How's young Josh feeling?"

"As good as new. The triplets are with the sitter tonight." Matthew watched Hope behind the table, her lithe shoulders now stiff, her jaw tight as she worked. She'd seen him. "Andrew, would you do me a favor and dance with my mom? I promised her a dance, but there's something else I need to do first."

"Matthew," Mom sputtered. "Andrew, surely you don't need to—"

"Do this for me," Matthew whispered in her ear. "And forgive the man while you're at it." He laid her hand on Andrew's palm and watched the doctor's face change, saw the reaction on his mother's.

"My son is far too bossy," Patsy commented to Andrew as he led her through the crowd. "That's what happens when they grow taller than you. I should never have spared the rod with that boy—"

The noise of conversations, the crowd, the music and the beating of his own heart cut out the rest of Mom's words. The crowd swallowed them.

"Looks like your mom's had a change of heart." Hope didn't look at him across the table as she lifted a small slice of frosted angel food cake on a doily from her tray and placed it on one of the serving platters. "I hope it works out for the best."

"I heard about Harold and Nora. Double-dating with Helen and Claude tonight. That's amazing."

"If only we could take credit." She kept working, filling the platter with angel food. "I guess God is the ultimate matchmaker. We're just mere mortals."

"We're failures, face it, but at least now maybe Harold and Nora might find happiness. What my mom chooses remains to be seen." He didn't want to make small talk with Hope. He didn't want to keep watching the graceful line of her arm as she worked refilling the platters, her wrist slim and her movements elegant. Had she come alone? He didn't know, but he bet that when she was done helping out, there would be plenty of men willing and able to dance with her.

If only he could be the one with her tonight. To dance with her. To fold her in his arms and kiss her over and over again beneath God's handiwork of stars and sky. He wanted to hold her, just hold her.

But how he could reach out? What good would come of that?

How could he resist wanting to be with her one last time?

"Would you care to dance?" He heard the words and couldn't believe he'd said them, but he knew in his heart it was what he wanted more than anything else.

"I don't want you to feel obligated." She didn't look at him as she turned and set the empty tray on the pastry cart tucked between the back wall and the tables. The vulnerable sound to her voice made him think that she was hurting, too.

"You know if we aren't seen on that dance floor at least once tonight," he said by way of an excuse, "your grandmother and my mom will be plotting ways to trick us into it."

Her chin sank a notch as she faced him, and the hurt he saw there startled him. "You're right. I know you are. Those women think they're succeeding."

"They're delusional. It's a shame in otherwise

sensible women like that." He teased because he couldn't bear to say the words. To admit Nora and his mom had been successful in their matchmaking. He loved Hope with his entire heart.

It didn't hurt so much to admit now. He let some of the self-doubts slide away, and peace filled his heart.

He led her through the crowd, knowing the entire town was watching as the snappy tune ended abruptly and the sweet chords of a Garth Brooks love song filled the air. Harold climbed down from the platform, slipping his wallet into his back pocket, and winked at him.

"Nanna and Patsy have corrupted Harold." Hope shook her head, but the smallest grin shaped her mouth. "I can't believe what old people are like these days."

"It's a shame. I don't know what this world is coming to." Matthew held out his arms.

He watched her hesitate. Something he couldn't name flickered in her eyes, showed in her heart, and then she stepped forward and he pulled her to his chest.

Holding her was like coming home, like finding respite in a weary world. She was his spring after a hard winter, his dawn after the darkest night. Holding her in his arms made him feel rested and safe, renewed and strong.

Gossamer strands of her silken hair tickled his chin, and he breathed in the spring scent of her and remembered the fields they rode through, dotted with wildflowers. He could hear the faint rhythm of her breathing, feel the beat of her heart, remember the sweet taste of her kiss beneath the midnight sky. How he ached to kiss her again.

If only the song could go on forever, verse and chorus, melody and harmony, lyrics and music, so that he would never have to let her go.

There was a time for everything, and the song ended. Hope slipped from his arms and he wanted to snatch the moment back, anything to keep her close to him.

But he had the boys, and she had the world. Taking her pictures made her happy, he'd seen it with his own eyes.

"Look." Her touch to his sleeve had him turning.

He hadn't realized another ballad had started, and there was his mother in Andrew Corey's arms with one hand on his shoulder. Saying something low in the doctor's ear, she chuckled as if she didn't have a care in the world.

Matthew had to clear his throat to speak. "I've never seen her look so happy."

"That's something everyone deserves." Hope glanced toward the ring of people and the quiet street beyond. "I need some fresh air. Excuse me."

She took off through the crowd, heels clicking. Too full of longing, too confused, too everything. Her senses spun from being held in his arms, and her heart broke with wanting him. Wanting everything about him. His smile, his humor, his gentleness, his strength.

He was everything she'd ever dreamed of and couldn't have. A family. A real home. His love that threatened to claim every vulnerable place in her heart.

"Hope! Don't run off." His voice echoed eerily on the empty street, nearly drowned out by the loud background noise of the dance. "I just want to make sure you're okay."

"I'm okay."

"You're not *really* okay." He loped easily at her side, and his fingers curled around her forearm, stopping her.

Steady and strong, his hand. Steady and strong, the man. Her heart made a strange series of bumps as she realized she couldn't escape. Breathless, feeling more vulnerable than she wanted to be, she withdrew from his touch. From the touch she craved. From the closeness she wanted more than anything else in the world.

And what was she going to say to him? Tell him the truth? Tell him that being held by him was a dream she didn't deserve?

"Go back to the dance, Matthew. I can take care of myself." She retreated, walking fast, breaking a little with each step away from him.

He's not going to love you anyway, she told herself, marching down the shadowed street, thankful that he wasn't following her yet. When she looked over her shoulder, he looked ready to, hands fisted, legs braced, the wind tousling his hair.

Their gazes met and locked, and the night stilled. She could only hear the sound of her breathing and the drum of her heart.

He didn't want her. Pain clawed at her heart. Tears blurred her vision and she blinked hard, refusing to let them fall. She kept right on walking down the lonely street, feeling the knot of emotion expand in her chest until she couldn't breathe.

What a fool she'd been. She couldn't deny it any more. She loved him. Loved a man who couldn't love her back. She started walking, stopping only to throw off her heels before heading out of town and into the endless night.

She loved Matthew, with the breadth of her heart and the height of her soul. She wanted to be with him with an intensity she'd never before felt. He was her night and her day, her winter and her spring, and without him, she had nothing.

Choking on a sob, she sank into the tall wild grasses at the side of the road. She let the pain wash over her. Let the storm break inside her heart.

Only God's love lasted. She had that assurance. But what about this love she harbored for Matthew?

She'd forget it, that's what. She'd bury herself in her work and go on. Loneliness didn't hurt as much as love could, as the darkness that came with it.

A darkness she never wanted to know again.

Chapter Fifteen

"**N**ow you're sure about leaving." Nanna crossed the gravel drive at a strong clip, thanks to her new wooden cane. "You can stay here as long as you like. This will always be your home."

"I know, but work's waiting." Hope shut the Jeep's back door, struggling not to give in to the grief heavy in her heart. Leaving was the right thing to do. It was the only thing to do. "Everything's loaded, and I have a plane to catch."

"Give me a call when you head back this way." Nanna lifted her free hand and brushed stray wisps from Hope's face. A gentle touch. A gentle love. "I'm glad they liked those pictures you took while you were here and want more. At least you won't be so far away."

"I'll be close enough to fly in for the weekend now and then." A horrible pain tore through her, blade-sharp, and she blinked back burning tears. She didn't want to leave, to let go of this woman and this magical place. "I'm still going to miss you."

"Now, don't get me started or I'll just cry all afternoon." Nanna held her arms wide, and Hope stepped into them.

"Just keep this in mind, dear one," Nanna whispered in her ear. "'Anything is possible if a person believes.' Let the Lord guide you to the happiness He has in store for you, all right? You're so headstrong and independent, making up your own mind on everything. And always remember that your nanna loves you."

"Not as much as I love you." Hot, painful tears spilled down her cheek, and Hope wished she could hold on forever.

But Nanna moved away, and somehow, Hope managed to climb into the Jeep, find her keys and turn on the engine. Somehow she managed to say goodbye to her grandmother who no longer looked frail or old, but infinitely beautiful standing in the shadow of the giant maples, waving with her free hand.

Hope drove away with more regrets than she could name and more sorrows. She watched the farmhouse become a dot in her rearview mirror and then nothing at all.

This was for the best, she told herself. She had a flight booked for California and home, where she would plan more of her travels. She had deadlines and responsibilities to face, and that's where the Lord was leading her. That's where she was meant to be. She believed that. She had to believe that.

Matthew hadn't asked her to stay, hadn't said he loved her, and even if he did, she'd made up her mind. She was better off alone just like she'd known all along.

Across the golden fields of grasses and up on a small knoll, she could see Matthew and Harold perched on the McKaslins' sloping roof. She saw them turn in unison to look at her as she sped toward them on the paved road. Loss beat at her heart as she watched Matthew straighten from his work. Even across the span of the field and through the barrier of the windshield, the impact of his gaze felt like a punch to her soul.

She *wouldn't* love him. She refused to let her heart love him. What she felt was a mistake on her part. Chanting that over and over, Hope turned down the McKaslins' driveway and circled around to the rambling ranch house.

At the first sight of Hope's Jeep barreling down the dirt road, Matthew knew she was coming to say goodbye. He kicked himself one more time for not running after her the night of the dance. He'd wanted to comfort her, to find out what was wrong, but fear held him back. Fear that he wasn't enough for her.

"Go on down and say goodbye." Harold didn't look up as he adjusted the new flashing around the chimney. "Maybe this time you can get it right."

Matthew tugged off his work gloves and climbed down the ladder. She was already out of the Jeep and lifting something out of the back by the time he got to her, looking like heaven and the purest of dreams, like the woman who could be the love of his life.

What she didn't look like was a woman who belonged in California. Dressed in jeans and a cotton top, wearing a leather belt and riding boots, her hair long and unbound and dancing in the breeze, she looked like she belonged here in the shadows of the Rocky Mountains where every now and then buffalo still roamed.

He hurt with wanting to hold her close, to kiss her like he had that night when she'd felt a part of him— the best part of him.

Two whole days he'd been praying, searching for a way out of this anguish. Surely God hadn't brought him this far to break his heart all over again. Yet that's sure what it looked like He was doing.

"I got this for the boys. I couldn't resist." Chin up and firm, she held out a colorful box showing a picture of a green lawn and kids in swimsuits running through some kind of child's sprinkler. "I thought they might like it."

"Like it? I'll never get them to stop playing with it." Matthew tried to smile, tried to insert humor into the uneasiness between them and failed. So he took the box. "That was mighty thoughtful of you."

"I really care about your boys." She turned away and shut the back with a snap, but not before he saw her suitcases.

Nothing could be clearer. She was leaving for good. He wanted to stop her. More than he'd ever wanted anything.

The Lord had led him to Hope, led him to Hope's presence and warmth, and for the life of him Matthew couldn't understand why God was letting him hurt like this. Especially after losing Kathy, especially after finding the courage to let go of his grief for her.

*Wherever you are leading me, Lord, I go willingly.
But show me the way. Show me the way through this.
Give me the right words to say.*

"I guess this is goodbye." Her words sounded heavy
with sorrow. "I've got a flight to catch."

"I know." He choked on the words, wanting to take
away her pain and her anguish. *Say what's in your
heart*, a voice within urged him. *Just tell her how you
feel.*

But how was he going to do that? How could he find
the strength to reach down and speak the truth?

He cleared his throat, wanting to keep her close
when he knew he had to set her free. The thing was,
she didn't look happy. Her soft oval face looked tight
with strain and lined from lack of sleep, and her eyes
held shadows dark and deep.

A passage from Isaiah came to him with quiet assurance. *Don't be afraid, for I am with you. I am your
God. I will strengthen you. I will help you.*

What did he truly want? Hope. He wanted Hope. To
cherish her and treasure her. The world separated them,
but could it be possible? What if there was a way to
work this out? Did she love him enough to stay and
marry him?

The thought terrified him. How could he find the
courage to say the words?

He wasn't alone. God was with him. God had led
him here.

Strengthened, Matthew took a step closer to the
woman he loved with all his heart. "I know you've got
a lot of opportunities ahead of you and everyone here

figures you'll go far. But if there's ever a way you think you could stay in Montana—"

He stopped short of touching her and gazed into her eyes, into her very soul. "If there's a way you could stay, I want you to know that I love you, deeply and truly. It's as if you complete me, and I've never felt this way before. I want you to marry me. If you think you could settle for a man like me and still be happy."

"Marry you?" Hope couldn't believe what she was hearing. Had Matthew just proposed? Had he just said he'd loved her? He stood with his hand out, waiting for her touch and she couldn't believe it.

This couldn't be happening. Panic banded around her chest. He'd said the words she longed to hear— words she'd never expected. And there were no more excuses. Not one.

Only the fears in her heart.

A terrible blackness gathered down deep and seemed to fill her. She wanted to run. She needed to escape. Her heart wanted to say yes to the man of her dreams.

What if she failed him and his boys? What if she wasn't enough for him? He was gallant and strong, tender and kind, everything she could never be. Everything she could never deserve.

She could see that now.

"Marry me, Hope." His hands covered hers, and his touch made it clear. He thought she was the most precious love he'd ever known.

The wall protecting her heart crumbled just enough to let in a ray of light. Of hope. She loved him so much. She hadn't realized the power of three simple words. Tears filled her eyes and she tried to find the words. All she had to do was say yes, and he would be hers to love and hold forever. For better or worse.

It was the worse that worried her. The worse, she believed in that. But the better... How did she know if their love would last through the times ahead? It was strong now, but that was no guarantee.

She could fail him. Again, the horrible doubt ripped through her joy, blotting out her one ray of hope. A verse flashed into her mind, one Nanna had recited to her. *Love is patient and kind. Love is not jealous or boastful or proud. Love does not demand its own way.*

She couldn't marry Matthew. Grief clawed like sharp talons across her soul, and she tore her hand away, tears blinding her even though she didn't know she was crying.

"This is because of your job? We could compromise. We could work that out. The boys might like riding in airplanes." So sincere, so steadfast, this tender man who deserved more than she could give him.

True love broke in her heart, deeper, bigger, a new rose budding for the first time, fighting the hard covering that protected it.

"I wouldn't make a good wife," she confessed, battling the tears pressing into her eyes. "I do love you. More than I've loved anyone in my life."

"Whew. I was worried." He smiled, his tender goodness shining through. He was an incredibly good man.

She broke into a million pieces. She spun away,

running blindly, finding the Jeep by a miracle, turning her back on a wonderful, perfect dream come true because she couldn't believe in it.

She couldn't risk destroying it.

Anything is possible, a voice inside her urged. But she couldn't trust those words. She couldn't.

To some God gave the gift of singleness, at least that's what she told herself as she drove away.

If anything were possible, then this traffic jam in the middle of the freeway would disappear, Hope thought. But for thirty precious minutes she'd been stuck in a backup a mile from the airport. According to the radio, a wild moose had strolled up an exit ramp onto the freeway, and the game department had to stop traffic to shoo her back into the woods.

While Hope waited, she tried not to think. She didn't want to think about how she'd left Matthew. No, not left him. Ran away from him like a frightened child. Shame filled her. She'd hurt his feelings, hurt him. But what was she going to do? Follow a path that wasn't meant for her? That would end badly for them both? She loved him too much to hurt him and his sons.

Finally they were moving again. Hope raced down the off-ramp and along the service road, palms sweating. She *had* to make this plane. The line was long at the express check-in, and she barely had time to sprint across the terminal, praying the flight was running late.

But there was a line at the security check, and she couldn't find her driver's license, which had fallen out of her wallet and had to be fished out of the depths of her purse. Frustration rose, and she bordered on tears.

Lord, please help me make this plane. Home awaited her—a quiet, one-bedroom condo in a pleasant palm-tree-lined street. A place where she didn't know her neighbors and no one waited for her. There was nothing there but a safe life. The life she wanted God to give her.

Well, that didn't sound right, but it was the truth. The simple unguarded truth.

"Looks like you can catch your flight if you run for it." The security guard smiled at her as he finished inspecting her laptop. "Good luck."

She slid her computer into her carry-on and started running, but the concourse was crowded and she had to slow down to circle around an impenetrable wall of people.

Father, I could use a little help here. She was doing the right thing, and she could see the coming year unfold before her. Maybe a trip to Italy to finish the photography work she started there, then a long tour of the West. Starting with the Zion National Park in Utah. Yes, that's what she'd do. She'd always been captivated by the vivid beauty of that rugged landscape.

Yes, that's just what would happen. Hope felt the panic like a hard prickly ball in her chest fade into peace. She darted around the last slow-moving person, and the carpeted concourse was clear. And empty.

Please, God, don't let that flight leave. She started running again, her bag banging against her hip, her new boots rubbing at her heels. She passed an empty gate where a flight had already departed. Not hers, but seeing it made her run faster.

She had to get out of here before her heart broke completely.

There it was—the gate agent was taking the boarding pass from the last passenger. The seats were empty, the entire corridor was empty as she sprinted breathlessly toward them.

"Wait! I'm on that flight!"

The agent whipped the ticket and boarding pass from the ticket sleeve with swift efficiency. "They'll hold the door for you. Hurry!"

Hope hitched her strap higher on her shoulder and started running. Her steps pounded like thunder in the narrow passageway, and she could hear the whir of jet engines and the distant sound of a plane taking to the skies.

Nanna's words lingered in her mind. "Anything is possible if a person believes."

She did believe. In God's goodness, in God's grace. But the love with a man was something entirely different. Even one as once-in-a-lifetime as Matthew's love.

We live by faith, not by sight. Remembering the verse made her slow from a run to a walk. *He will not let you stumble and fall; the One who watches over you will not sleep... The Lord stands beside you as your protective shade. The sun will not hurt you by day, nor the moon at night.*

She turned the corner to see a flight attendant

holding the door open for her. "Hurry!" she called. "First class is to your left."

Did she keep walking? Or did she trust the Lord with something this frightening? She didn't know. She didn't know what to do.

Then peace filled her heart. She'd spent her entire childhood protecting herself from her family's painful neglect. She'd spent her adult life making sure it didn't happen again. God had been beside her all the way, but she had not trusted Him with this. In everything else— her life, her health, her friends, her travels, her career— but not with the innermost place of her heart.

"Anything is possible if a person believes."

And no matter how it frightened her, she would trust in the Lord. And if He brought Matthew to her, she would find a way to believe. Because the Lord meant good things for her life, and not hurt, not pain.

"I'm sorry," she told the flight attendant.

On shaking knees, Hope took one step back, then another, not knowing what the future held for her— Matthew's rejection or Matthew's love.

Matthew skidded to a halt, his heart breaking at the sight of the passenger jet rolling away from the gate. The sign over the ticket desk confirmed it. Hope's flight to California. A fierce sense of loss, greater than he'd ever known, battered him, and he sank to a nearby bench and put his head in his hands.

She was gone. And it was his own fault. He had no one to blame—not God, not Hope, only himself. He'd lacked the courage to say all the words she needed to hear. The kind of words that didn't come easily to a man who'd lost a wife once before, and in protecting his heart, in keeping back that deepest vulnerability, and he'd lost Hope.

Footsteps tapped toward him, and when he looked up he had to blink to make sure. But it truly was Hope running toward him, tears streaking her face and the carry-on slipping from her hands.

He was on his feet in a flash and his arms were folding her to his chest before he could breathe. In the space of a heartbeat his lips found hers and claimed her with a kiss that reached from the depths of his soul and every last recess of his heart. His entire being sang with the sweet contentment of holding her in his arms, and when she broke the kiss to bury her face in the hollow of his throat, he realized that she was shaking with sobs.

"I couldn't leave." Her tears thickened her voice, already resonant with heartbreak. "But you're here. I can't believe you're here. That you would come for me."

"I will always come for you." He curled his hand around her nape, caressing gently, and yet she shook all the harder.

"You hate me now, don't you? I don't know what to do."

He pressed kisses to her brow, tender with all the love in his heart. "I was afraid all this time. Afraid I could never be enough to hold you here. But God has led me to you, and you are an incredible, impossible gift. I love you, Hope, with all that I am, all that I have, all that I will ever be. And I promise you, my love will never fail you. Never."

Beautiful words. She knew he believed them. She wanted to believe in them, too. But a hard place inside her, the place that had protected her heart all her life, stood fast, like a great unbreachable wall. She couldn't trust. She couldn't believe.

She wanted to. More than anything she'd ever wanted before.

He drew her to his chest again, to the warm shelter of his body, where she could feel his breath in her hair and his heart against her cheek. Where she could feel the anguish fade and the dream begin.

"If you will honor me by being my wife—" he cupped her chin and gently tilted her head back so they were eye to eye, vulnerable one to the other "—then I will promise you this. 'Your life will be brighter than the noonday. Any darkness will be as bright as morning.'"

A terrible rending tore through her, shattering her heart. Aching tears rolled down her cheeks, released from her past, setting her free.

"Now, I'm going to ask you one more time." Love shone in his eyes, the truest of loves, the greatest of dreams. "Will you complete my life and marry me?"

She was crying too hard to speak. God had led her here, the greatest of matchmakers, the One who knew for certain that their love would last. He'd given her her heart's desire and this man so rare. All she had to do was believe. "Matthew, I'd love to be your wife."

Epilogue

Two months later

"I wonder how Harold and Nora's trip to the travel agent is going?" Matthew asked as he shifted the oar in the water, sending the drifting boat safely around the wide river's bend.

Holding Josh's play fishing pole for him, Hope couldn't get enough of looking at her husband. They'd arranged a quick but meaningful ceremony at their church and had spent an impromptu honeymoon in Italy so she could finish up her work there and spend the rest of the summer close to home and the boys.

She caught Ian by the belt before he tipped over the boat. "There's nothing like a Hawaiian honeymoon to start off a marriage."

"Second only to an Italian honeymoon, right?" Mischief twinkled in Matthew's eyes and he grinned, slow and tantalizing. "If my Mom and Andrew keep going the way they're going, then we'll be out of the matchmaking business completely."

"Sure, as if it wasn't in God's hands all along." Contentment filled her. She had her work, she had her family, and she had Matthew, her love for him growing more with each passing day.

"Careful, Kale," she cautioned. "Don't lean too far over the side. The fish might get a look at you and swim off."

"But I wanna see 'em!" Kale answered, although he eased back down on his heels.

"Mama, gotta hold me." Josh crawled onto her lap and snuggled against her. "Gonna say the fireman story?"

"Lucky thing for you, I know the whole thing by heart." She set down the pole and ran her free hand lovingly through Josh's tousled hair. Her dulcet voice rose and fell like the breeze with the story's rhythm.

Shade dappled them, mother and sons. Matthew watched, captivated, unable to tear his gaze from the sight of her beauty, of her loving heart. Peace filled him, cool like the river, tranquil like the drowsy afternoon. Hope finished her story and pressed kisses to the boys' heads.

"I love you," she whispered across the length of the boat as the boys snuggled against her.

"I love you more." His heart ached with it, sweetly, so very sweetly. "Forever."

"Forever." Her hand covered his, and his heart

soared at her touch. With a quiet prayer, he gave thanks for this beautiful woman he would love for the rest of his days.

* * * * *

Dear Reader,

I was on vacation with my husband, driving through Montana, when I saw an exit sign at the side of the highway. Manhattan, it said, was the next exit. I immediately thought of New York skyscrapers, which seemed completely at odds with the peaceful farmland and majestic mountains surrounding us on all sides. Horses grazed in pastures, and combines could be seen harvesting distant hillsides.

I reached for my notebook. I could feel a story starting, one with the small-town values that I know so well, having grown up in a very small town. I could imagine Matthew, widowed and sad, and a mother who ached at seeing him alone. I could hear the voice of Nanna, a woman wanting true happiness for her granddaughter who doesn't believe in love.

This, I knew, would be a story about the ways in which the Lord sends us blessings—rain or shine and without end.

Thank you for choosing *Heaven Sent*.

Best wishes to you,

Jillian Hart

HIS HOMETOWN GIRL

You should be known for the beauty that comes from within, the unfading beauty of a gentle and quiet spirit, which is so precious to God.

—*1 Peter* 3:4

Chapter One

Karen McKaslin scrambled out of her car in the small back lot behind her coffee shop. The gravel crunched beneath her sneakers as she strolled toward the back steps, squinting against the first fingers of sunlight. Dawn painted the eastern skies with bold strokes of crimson and gold, and larksong merrily drifted on the temperate breeze.

Another beautiful Montana day.

"Hey, Karen!" Jodi Benson called out from the alley as she hurried, the hem of her short skirt snapping with her fast gait. "I heard about you and Jay. How are you feeling this morning?"

"Fine, except that everyone keeps mentioning that man's name." Karen lifted one hand to her brow to shield her eyes from the low glaring sun. "You're late for work, too."

"Don't mention it to my boss, will you? He won't be in until seven. Hey, don't let this get you down. Every bride-to-be has cold feet. You and Jay will patch things up."

Not in this lifetime. Karen hiked her purse strap higher on her shoulder. "Thanks, Jodi. Have a good day."

Jodi was already at the end of the alley and lifted a hand in answer.

It's not as if they were close friends, Karen thought, so there was no reason to try to set the woman straight. Rumors were rumors and they didn't matter.

She knew the truth, but her troubles felt heavier as she hurried up the back steps. Sweet peas tumbled from the planters on the wooden rail and waltzed with carefree happiness in time with the breeze.

Karen's key clicked in the lock, and she pushed open the glass door with one elbow. She wasn't going to worry about small-town rumors and setting everyone straight, because Jay wasn't her true problem. No, the real problem was before her as she stepped into the little dining room she and her older sister Allison had decorated together.

Today was the third anniversary of Allison's death. Karen had vowed to try to live this day like any other, but at 6:10 in the morning, she'd already failed. She only had to close her eyes to see how this shop looked four years ago when she'd unlocked the door for the first time.

Allison's footsteps had tapped across the subflooring as she'd held her arms wide. "Imagine all these windows with ruffled gingham curtains. And a counter over there. Our coffee shop is going to be a success, I can *feel* it."

Karen opened her eyes, the remembrance slipping away, her heart aching. The echo of her sister's voice bounced off the walls, an eerie echo of a memory that felt too real.

Gone were the days when she'd made plans with her sister to run the coffee shop together. Plans cut short by a small-plane crash on this day three years ago. Allison's loss would be forever felt.

Sell the shop, Jay had told her. *When we get married, I won't have my wife working for anyone but me.*

Red-hot rage sliced through her like a sharp blade, and she hated it. Hated both the force of her anger and Jay's unsympathetic demand to sell this place she loved so much.

"Karen?" A man's chocolate-smooth voice broke through her thoughts.

Startled, she spun around. Zachary Drake stood in the doorway, wearing his usual gray Stetson, a white T-shirt and jeans.

Wide and strong and a little rough around the edges, Zach nodded once in greeting. "Standing around daydreaming?"

"Wishing I could pay someone else to get up this early every morning and open for me." She pasted on a smile, since her problems were her own. "You're early today."

"Got a busy morning. Saw you pull in the alley and figured you might make me some coffee even if you aren't open yet." He ambled inside, bringing with him the scent of fresh morning breezes and Old Spice. "So, how about it?"

"For the man who keeps my trusty car running, anything." She slipped behind the counter without another word and stowed her purse.

"Looks like you'll have a busy day, too." Zach couldn't stop his gaze from following her every movement as she broke open a fresh bag of coffee beans. "What with all the tourists dropping by for a cold glass of whatever you've got."

"The tourists are too busy staying on the highway heading for Yellowstone." She flashed him an easy smile, one that didn't reach her beautiful eyes. "Besides, it'll be too hot for anyone to want coffee."

"I might stop by later and get one of those iced things you make."

"That's why you're my favorite customer." Karen grabbed a pitcher of water. "Let me set up and I'll get your cappuccino. It'll take just a minute."

"Appreciate it." Zach turned toward the window, pretending to watch the activity out on the street. Except at eighteen minutes past six on a weekday morning in this small town, there was no activity to watch.

Larks roosted on the edge of the green planter boxes on the wooden rails out front. The streets were empty, and the stores still closed up tight. In the window of the diner just down the road, Jodi Benson appeared and turned the Closed sign to Open.

Truth was, he'd rather stare out at nothing because if he turned around and watched Karen work, she just might notice the way he was looking at her. Mooning after her like a man with a secret crush.

Sure, she'd broken off her engagement. Normally a man might take hope in that. But Zach knew, figured like everyone in this town, that Karen and Jay belonged together. Whatever had torn them apart a month before their wedding would be easily fixed, he was sure, and the two would marry at the end of the summer.

He could deal with that. His heart took a blow every time he talked with her, every time he saw her.

"Here you go. One cappuccino, double shot." She set the paper cup on the counter and held up her hand when he reached into his back pocket. "No, I don't have my till set up yet, so don't worry about it."

"I'll catch up with you tomorrow."

"I'm real worried." She flashed him a smile, a friendly one that had entranced him since his first day of kindergarten. She leaned both elbows on the counter and studied him for a moment. "Can I ask you for a favor? I know you said you're busy, but could you possibly find a spare minute to take a look at my car?"

"You mean that rusted-out rattletrap you drive?"

"That rusted-out rattletrap is paid for, cowboy. That's how I can afford the luxuries of being self-employed."

"Sure, you can't afford a vehicle that runs."

"Hey, my car runs. Sometimes." She lifted one shoulder and made an attempt at a smile.

"Since I'm the only mechanic in town, I guess the real question is, can you afford to have me look at it?"

"Now you're getting greedy."

"Lots of folks accuse me of that." He winked. "But for you, being my favorite customer, I'll make an exception."

"Oh, boy," she teased back, but the sadness in her eyes remained, dark and steady.

And he knew why. He didn't know if he should say anything. Didn't know if bringing up the subject of her sister would give her more pain. Comforting her... well, it wasn't his right. That right belonged to the man whose ring used to sparkle on her left hand, a small diamond on a gold band.

"I'll come over and take a look when things get slow. On a hot day like this, I never know if I'll be bored to death or if radiators will be boiling over all around town."

"I'm running late. I've got to get in the back and start the muffins baking. Thanks again, Zach."

"No problem." He watched her move away, heading toward the kitchen with ease and grace, leaving his heart hammering.

Longing filled him, and he controlled it. He didn't want her to suspect how he truly felt. Not today of all days, with the memory of her sister's death and the pain of her breakup written on her face.

Zach grabbed his cup of coffee and headed out into the morning. The sun didn't seem quite as bright.

Thank heavens for a busy day, Karen thought as she laid two slices of bread on the cutting board. A few hours ago, a tour bus had limped into town, blowing blue smoke out the back. The stranded senior citizens had divided themselves between the coffee shop and the town's diner. Add that to the regulars and she could hardly make sandwiches fast enough.

"How are you, dear?" a kindly woman asked from the other side of the counter. "I heard about the breakup. You look like you didn't get a wink of sleep last night."

Karen reached for the mustard jar and slathered a knifeful on both slices of bread. "I'm doing fine, Mrs. Greenley, and don't believe those rumors you're hearing."

"I never do. Just don't you worry about what people are saying. What matters is doing what's best for you." The older woman turned around in line. "Helen, come up here and take a look at your granddaughter. She appears exhausted to me."

"I'm not exhausted." Karen layered ham and cheese slices on top of the mustard-coated bread.

There was a shuffle in the line, and Karen saw Gramma elbowing her way up to the counter.

Great, just what she needed—the woman who could see past her every defense.

Karen concentrated very hard on laying thick slabs of fresh tomato and crisp lettuce leaves just so, before she sliced the sandwich in half. "Gramma, I'm fine. Go back to your place in line. You're cutting."

"I'm doing no such thing," Gramma protested, causing a louder ruckus as she pushed her way to the edge of the counter and circled behind it.

Karen laid the sandwich neatly on a stoneware plate and set it on top of the glass barrier. "And, no, I don't need any help."

"Hogwash. Nora's right. You're as pale as a sheet, and the only place I've seen dark circles like that is on a raccoon. You need to hire help so you can take a day off now and then, missy," Gramma admonished as she grabbed Nora's five-dollar bill and marched to the cash register. "Now, go. Scoot. Nora and I will cover the rest of the lunch crowd."

"You bet," Mrs. Greenley said eagerly. "I've made a sandwich or two in my time."

"There's no way." Karen shouldered against her grandmother and counted out change from the till. "I'm perfectly fine. Make yourself a sandwich, go sit with Mrs. Greenley and have a good visit."

"You can't fool me, sweetie." Gramma's arm settled firmly around Karen's shoulders. "Use that line on someone who hasn't been around as long as I have. You haven't been sleeping."

"I have a long line of customers—"

"*Karen.*" Gramma's voice was firm but caring. "I don't know all that's going on between you and Jay, but I'm on your side. Never forget that. And I know what day it is. Allison would want you to visit her, you know."

"I can do that later—" Karen turned away, hating that Mrs. Greenley had stepped behind the counter and was taking the next order. "I can't afford to pay you—"

"That's good, because we're volunteering." Gramma gave her a grandmotherly shove toward the door. "I know, it goes against your grain to accept help, but you're always doing for others, Karen. Don't deprive me of the pleasure or I'll drag you to my Ladies' Aid meetings for the rest of the year."

Suddenly the shop was too loud. The clatter of plates, the scraping of silverware and the cackling din of voices all scraped over Karen's raw nerve endings.

A hand closed over hers, one whose touch was dear and loving. "Sweetheart, let me finish up for you."

"No, I'll be fine." She *would* be fine.

"Go outside and get some air. Give yourself all the time you need. Nora Greenley, I can't read your chicken scratch on this ticket. Does that say turkey and Swiss?"

"Of course it does," Nora answered back, digging through the commercial refrigerator. "See? I told you that you need new bifocals."

"That's the *last* thing I want to hear." Gramma grabbed a pair of plastic gloves from the box on the counter.

Just like that, Karen was superfluous in her own business.

"Hey, are you all right?" someone asked. A hand lit on Karen's arm, the touch warm and caring.

"No, Julie, I just need some air." Stumbling away from her friend, Karen headed straight to the back, threading around customers and cloth-covered tables to where sunlight glinted on the glass door.

Her hand hit the brass knob and she sprinted into the hot sunshine.

Hot aching tears that wouldn't fall turned the world into a blurred mass of green, blue and brown as she tripped down the walkway, running her hand along the banister so she wouldn't lose her way. A nail head gouged into her skin and pain jolted through her palm.

She felt the wet sting of blood and dropped to the stairs, burying her face in her uninjured hand.

Mom was tumbling into another bout of depression and it seemed like nothing could stop it. The coffee shop was on the brink of disaster—the shop her sister had loved. And she'd just broken her engagement to a man her parents practically worshiped. She couldn't stop the weight of failure pressing like a thousand-pound rock on her chest.

Worst of all, she still missed Allison with a fierceness that nothing could erase. Not time. Not grief. She'd lost her best and lifelong friend and even now she felt as if she had no one to turn to.

"Hey, it looks like you need a handkerchief." A rugged male voice broke through her thoughts.

Zachary Drake settled onto the step beside her. Grease smudged his cheek and was smeared across the front of his otherwise white T-shirt.

He certainly was a handsome man. Her heart kicked at the sight of him. He looked tough as nails, as if growing up the way he had could never quite be taken out of him. But she knew Zachary Drake was as strong and dependable as the day was long.

He pressed a folded handkerchief into her hand. Only then did she notice that her car's hood was up. He'd been taking a look at the troublesome engine and she hadn't noticed him.

Ashamed and embarrassed to be caught crying, she rubbed the cloth across her eyes and down her face, wiping away the wetness of her tears. "Don't tell me you have bad news about my car."

"Okay, I won't." He caught hold of her right wrist. His touch was hot and unsettling. "You're bleeding."

"It's nothing serious."

"I'm not too sure about that. Looks like a lot of blood to me." He stood and strode down the steps, his big body moving with an athlete's power and ease. He disappeared in the shadow of his tow truck, parked behind her car in the alley.

She heard the click as he opened his truck's door and the crunch of his gait on the gravel as he returned.

Even without his motorcycle, which he frequently rode through town, Zach still looked a little untamed as he'd always been in school. Maybe it was the way the wind caught his dark hair and whipped it across his brow, or the slight swagger to his walk.

"Let me clean this up and we'll see who's right— if it's nothing or not." He knelt before her, opened the first-aid kit on the step between them and reached for her injured hand.

At the first touch of the gauze to her cut, she winced.

"Sorry about that. It's got to hurt."

"It does," she lied, because that was the easiest explanation. She felt jumpy, as if every nerve had been laid open from his touch.

It's only Zach, she told herself. I've known him forever. But her heartbeat picked up as he leaned closer, his fingers a warm touch on her skin.

He swabbed the blood away from her cut with careful brushes of the sterile gauze. Each swipe was gentle. Soon he'd exposed the two-inch gash along the side of her palm.

"See? I was right." His words were a smile of victory, but his gaze felt like something else, something deeper. "This is going to require some expert care."

"You're a *mechanic*, Zach, not a doctor."

"No, but I get a lot of scrapes, so I know how to take care of them."

"That makes you an expert?"

"It ought to make me something."

"Clumsy?"

"Watch what you call me. I'm the only mechanic around, and let's face it, Karen, if your car's any indication, you need me. Badly." He dug through the small plastic kit and produced a sealed packet of antiseptic.

The air caught in her chest when he leaned even closer and rubbed the salve across the tear in her skin. Like a bee's sting, sharp pain traveled the length of her cut. "I hate to break it to you, but you'll never be a doctor. That hurts."

"Is that so?" He lifted one brow as he laid a butterfly bandage across her wound, his voice warm with teasing. "What are you? A wimp who can't take a little pain?"

"Thanks. I suppose you're one of those tough guys who never admit to a weakness like pain."

"You've got that right." He tore open another package and removed a bandage, a wide pad that covered her entire wound. His fingers were a warm pressure in the center of her palm as he made sure the adhesive stuck. "There. An expert repair job."

How could it be that she was smiling? The weight

on her chest remained, but it was easier to breathe, easier to find a way to face what she had to do. All because of Zach. "Now I owe you two favors."

"Good. I like it when pretty women are in my debt." He snapped the kit closed.

When he straightened, unfolding his six-foot frame, he towered over her, casting her in shadow. The sun gilded his hair and the width of one shoulder. The wind caught in his brown locks and tousled them.

He held out his hand. "You look like a woman who needs a friend. Lucky for you, I just happen to be available."

"Is that so?"

"Absolutely."

Karen fit her good hand to his. Her pulse jumped, leaving her shaken.

Normally when she was with Zach, she didn't react like this. But today, everything was off balance. She didn't know what was wrong with her.

"Thanks, Zach." The words caught in her throat, and the lump of tears was back, thicker and hotter than ever. "I appreciate the patch job. Now tell me what's wrong with my car."

"I'm still working, but I can tell you it looks like a cracked head. We're talking about a whole new engine."

The strength went out of her knees and Karen leaned against the banister post. She stared at her poor car.

A new engine. There was no way she could afford that. No way at all. "It's still working, right? How much longer can I drive it?"

"Hard to say." Zach raked one hand through his thick hair, stepping closer, casting her in his shadow again. "I'd say you have anywhere from an hour to a week. It just depends. I can find you a rebuilt engine if money's a problem."

"Money's a problem." This was the *last* thing she needed. "Are you sure it doesn't need a new belt or hose or anything cheaper?"

"I'm sure. I can order a rebuilt engine and have it here in a couple of days. Since you're my favorite customer, you wouldn't have to pay for it all at once. I trust you."

"A dangerous move. I could be a bad credit risk. I've got a balloon payment on the building coming up at the end of next month." Karen sighed, feeling the weight of stress clamp more tightly around her chest. "Even if I scrape everything together to pay for it, it'll be tight for a long time."

"I know what that's like." He lifted a big round car part from the ground and dusted it off. "Take some time to think about it and let me know if you want an estimate."

She looked at the raised hood of her poor car and the grease-coated engine beneath. "How long will it take you to get all these parts back where they belong so my car's running again?"

"Ten minutes tops."

"I have a few errands to do. I'll be back. Thanks again, Zach."

"That's what I'm here for. Hey, Karen, are you going to be okay? Do you want me to call someone for you? Your grandmother or your sister Kirby?"

"No, I'm fine." She had to be. She had no other choice.

But she suspected Zach didn't believe her as she hurried down the alley.

She didn't believe it herself.

Chapter Two

An emergency call came when he was finished with Karen's car. The early '70s model with a rusting olive-green paint job managed to start after several attempts. There was no doubt about it—the car needed serious help.

He shut off the ignition, tucked the spare key back into place behind the visor and climbed out into the scorching sunshine.

Karen's scent from her car seat—a combination of baby shampoo and vanilla—clung to his shirt. A sharp ache of longing speared through him, old and familiar, and he ignored it. Over the years he'd gotten good at ignoring it. The scent tickled his nose as he ambled across the gravel lot. He ignored that, too.

The coffee shop looked like it was quieting down. The group of tourists must have headed out, now that their bus was as good as new. He didn't have time to step inside and wait for Karen to get back from her errands, not with an elderly woman's radiator boiling over in this heat.

There was nothing else to do but to hop into his truck and let the air-conditioning distribute the faint scent of vanilla and baby shampoo.

Great. That was going to remind him of Karen for the rest of the afternoon.

When he'd been patching up her cut, he'd been close enough to see the shadows in her dream-blue eyes. He hated that there wasn't a thing he could do to comfort her.

Anyone could see a woman as fine as Karen belonged with a man like Jay, a man with a big future ahead of him. And even on the off chance that Karen didn't marry Jay, it wasn't as if Zach had a chance with her. Not a man who'd grown up on the outskirts of town in a rusty old trailer.

He took a ragged breath, vowing to put her out of his mind. He checked for traffic on the quiet street and pulled out of the alley.

As he drove down the main street, he saw Karen coming out of the town's combination florist and gift shop. His pulse screeched to a stop at the sight of her. She didn't see him, walking away from him the way she was, so he could take his time watching her. Karen was fine, all right, and as beautiful as a spring morning. Head down, long light brown hair tumbling forward over her face, she carried a live plant that was thick with yellow blossoms.

No, he wasn't going to wish, he wasn't going to want.

Some things weren't meant to be.

Zach headed the truck east away from town and did

the only thing he was allowed to do for Karen McKaslin. He said a prayer for her.

Karen watched as her gramma's spotless classic Ford eased slowly into the cemetery parking lot. The rumble of the engine broke the peace of the late afternoon.

She stood, squinting against the brilliant sun, and left Allison's flower-decorated grave. She waited while her grandmother parked her car and then emerged, clutching a bouquet of white roses.

"I recognized your rattletrap of a car in the lot." Gramma held her arms wide. "How's my girl?"

"Fine. I'm just fine." Karen dodged the bouquet and stepped into her grandmother's hug. More warmth filled her, and all the worries bottled up inside her eased. "I shouldn't have left you with the shop like that. I shouldn't have let you bully me."

"You were powerless to stop me." Gramma stepped away, squinting carefully, measuring her with a wise, sharp-eyed glare. "Don't try to fool me, young lady. You don't look fine. You look like you're missing your sister."

"She was my best friend."

"I know." Gramma's voice dipped, full of understanding. "Let me go set these on her grave. She loved white roses so much."

Tears burned in Karen's throat, and it hurt to remember. She remained in the shade of the oaks, so that her grandmother would have time alone at Allison's grave.

Karen watched as the older woman ambled across the well-manicured grounds, through lush green grass and past solemn headstones.

Sorrow surrounded this place, where bright cheerful flowers and a few colorful balloons decorated graves. At the other end of the cemetery, she could see another family laying flowers on a headstone in memory.

Time had passed, taking grief with it, but Karen didn't think anything could fix the emptiness of Allison's absence in her life or in her family. Not time, not love or hope.

She waited while her grandmother laid the flowers among the dozens of others. She waited longer while the older woman sank to her knees, head bowed in prayer.

In the distance, a lawn mower droned, and overhead, larks chirped merrily. It was like any other summer afternoon, but this day *was* different.

"Now that I've given thanks for the granddaughters I still have, I'm ready to go." Gramma took Karen's hand. "I closed the shop for you, so there's no sense hurrying back this late in the day just to open it for an hour. Why don't you come home with me and give me a hand?"

"You know I can't say no to you."

"Good, because I promised your mother that I would make sure supper's on the table tonight, not that anyone will feel much like eating. But since she's my daughter, I'll do whatever she'll let me do. And if that's to make my famous taco cheese and macaroni casserole, then so be it."

"What about Mom? Dad's busy with the harvest. Maybe I should run home first and see how she is. Make sure she isn't alone."

"One of your sisters is with her—Kirby, I think. I called from the shop before I came here."

Karen felt the sun on her face, the wind tangling her hair and the disquiet in her heart. So many responsibilities pulled at her, but she could feel her grandmother's love. Because they were standing in a cemetery with both life and death all around, she nodded, unable to say the words.

There was never enough time on this earth to spend with loved ones. It was a truth she couldn't ignore, not after losing Allison. Time was passing even as she let Gramma lead her toward the parking lot where their cars waited in the shade.

"Do you need me to stop by the store and pick up anything?" Karen asked as she opened her car door.

"I already did. No grass grows under these feet," Gramma answered, her blue eyes alight with many emotions.

Karen's throat tightened, and she climbed into the driver's seat. Even with the windows rolled down to let in the temperate breezes, she could still smell the scents of mechanic's grease and Old Spice, evidence of the man who'd sat behind this wheel only hours ago.

A rumble of a powerful engine drew her attention. In her rearview mirror she caught sight of Zach's blue-and-white tow truck rolling up the driveway.

She turned the key in the ignition and gave the gas pedal a few good pumps, and the engine started and died. Started and died. Started and coughed to life. Gramma was parked at the edge of the lot, patiently waiting.

Karen put her car in gear and pulled around, having only enough time to wave to Zach as he rumbled into one of many empty parking spots. He lifted a hand in return. The tips of yellow blossoms waved above the dash, and she sped away, somehow touched beyond words.

She knew without asking that he'd brought flowers for her sister's grave.

"Is this why you asked me over?" Karen turned to her grandmother the minute she stepped foot inside the kitchen door. "Don't tell me you've taken up Mom and Dad's cause?"

"What cause, dear?" Gramma set her purse and keys on the nearby counter.

"Trying to show me how wrong I am to call off my wedding." Trying to control her anger, Karen pointed at the sunny picture window. Over the top of the short cedar fence, she could see Jay mowing his mother's lawn next door. "I'm not going to be pressured about this."

"I'm not trying to pressure you." Gramma circled around the polished oak table and headed for the refrigerator.

"No, but silence speaks volumes." Karen turned her back on the window. She wouldn't let the guilt in. "You think I'm going to forgive him and marry him anyway, just like Mom does. Like everyone does."

"I respect your choice, either way." Gramma set two cans of diet cola on the counter. "Of course, Jay *is* awfully handsome. He's dependable and easy on the eyes."

"He doesn't love me, Gramma."

"Then why on earth did he propose to you?"

Karen didn't answer. She couldn't admit the truth. If Allison were alive, she would have been able to confide in her, but who else would understand?

Karen watched as her grandmother calmly scooped ice into two glasses. She worked methodically, easily, content with the silence. Tall and slim, she looked comfortable in her usual flowered dress and low, sensible shoes.

"Sit down." With a clink Gramma set the glasses on the round oak table and looked through her glasses perched on her nose. "Tell me all about it."

"About what?"

"What's taken away my favorite granddaughter's smile."

"I don't want to talk about Jay." Karen pulled out a chair and settled onto the cushioned seat. "Or how I'm looking thirty in the face and don't have any better prospects."

"Fine. Then we won't talk about Jay." Gramma took a sip of soda, understanding alight in her eyes. "Most of my friends have great-grandchildren by now. Nora was one of the last holdouts. Then her granddaughter married Matthew and got those triplet boys. I don't suppose I'm going to be that lucky."

"Don't count on it. I see where you're going with this. You're trying to get me to talk about my breakup with Jay."

"Not at all. I'm just sharing some of my troubles with you for a change. At my last Ladies' Aid meeting, Lois had new pictures of her adorable great-grand-daughter."

"You're feeling left out. Is that it?"

"Yes, but you don't look very sorry for me."

"Sure I am. I'm hiding it deep inside."

Gramma's eyes twinkled, full of trouble. "If you went ahead and married Jay, then in a year or so I'd have my own great-grandbaby to show off. I've got to keep up with my friends."

"I see. It's a status thing. Like having a new car or the right house?"

"Exactly."

Karen ran a finger through the condensation on the outside of her glass. "Jay has one semester left at seminary, and then he wants me to sell the coffee shop."

"Why is that?"

"He needs me to help him with his career. A pastor's wife belongs at her husband's side, he told me. Then he asked how much equity I had in the building."

"I see." Gramma nodded sagely. "You and Allison opened that shop together. It would be hard to sell just for the money."

"I got angry and so did he. He said some harsh things—" She took a deep breath. "He told me the real reason he wanted to marry me. Because I was someone he could count on. I work hard, I know how to run a business and I'm comfortable, like an old friend. He needs someone dependable to help him with his career."

"I see." Gramma lowered her glass to the polished

table. Ice cubes clinked in the silence between them. "Those words must have been hard to hear from the man you loved."

"I was in love with him."

"Not anymore?"

"How can it be love, if he doesn't love me back?" Anguish filled her. "Everyone tells me I'm wrong. I should be lucky to have a man like Jay who wants to marry me. He's going to go far, and he'll be a good husband."

"They don't know the real story, do they? You haven't told this to anyone but me."

"Not even Mom." Karen let out a shaky sigh. She'd never felt so confused in her life. "I don't know what to do. Am I wrong? I love Jay—at least a part of me did—and is that enough? Do I settle for friendship? Or am I throwing away something good? It feels as if I've done the right thing and the wrong thing all at the same time. You were married to Granddad for thirty years, so tell me what you think."

"I know one thing." Gramma reached across the table and her warm, caring hand covered Karen's. "Love without passion is like lukewarm water. It's not good for much."

"Then you think I did the right thing?"

"I think you should do whatever makes you happy. Forever is a long time with a man who doesn't love you the way you want to be loved."

Some of the weight lifted from her chest, and Karen managed to take a sip of soda. "I thought you wanted great-grandchildren."

"I want my granddaughter to be happy. That's more important to me than anything in this world, even keeping up with Lois." Gramma's fingers squeezed gently, a reminder of the love Karen had known her entire life. "It's tough when the man you're interested in thinks you're a cup of lukewarm tea. I have the same problem with Clyde."

"Clyde Winkler, the man you've been seeing?"

"You look surprised." Gramma took a long sip of her cola. "What? You don't think a woman my age can have a love life, is that it?"

"I'm speechless."

"And do you know what I've figured out? Men are all the same. They haven't changed a bit since 1940. Still as thickheaded as ever."

"Surely not every man in existence."

"The one I'm interested in, at least." Gramma stared out the window, where the drone of Jay's mower grew louder, then began fading away. "I'll tell you something I've never told a living soul. Once, I was in the same situation you're in."

"You called off a wedding?" Karen leaned closer. "With Granddad?"

"I almost did. I was younger than you are now, but back then, girls married much younger. All my friends from school had husbands, and I desperately wanted to get married. More than anything. Oh, what plans I had! I wanted a house of my own, children to raise and a man to take care of."

"Which you did. Granddad was wonderful."

"But he wasn't the love of my life." The confession

was a quiet one, hardly loud enough to be heard above the hum of the air-conditioning.

Karen dropped her glass. Ice cubes and soda sloshed over the rim and onto the table.

Gramma calmly reached for the napkin holder and began mopping up the mess. "Surprised you, didn't I?"

"But you loved Granddad. I know you did. I saw you together."

"I did love him in a hundred different ways. As my husband, as the father of my children, as my best friend. But not in the most wondrous way. He never said, but I know that he felt it, too. He tried and I tried. While we made a life together, we lacked something important." Gramma rose and dropped the wet napkins in the garbage container. "We didn't have a deep emotional connection. That was something we couldn't make together, no matter how hard we tried."

I don't believe it, Karen thought. Denial speared through her. Her grandparents had always been happy together.

No, *seemed* happy together, she corrected herself. And as she watched her gramma's shoulders slump and felt the truth in the air, Karen realized the pain her grandmother must have silently lived with every day of her marriage.

When Gramma straightened, what looked like sadness and regret marked her face. "Your granddad told me once that he was glad to be with such a reliable woman. That out of all the women he could have married, he'd been lucky to wind up with me.

"Reliable." Her voice shook a little. "I loved

Norman deeply, but not deeply enough. Just as he could never love me. Even now I wonder what it would have been like for us if we'd managed to figure out what we were missing. We were never really happy. We were never truly unhappy. Lukewarm."

Karen stood and paced to the window. She could see Jay in his mother's backyard, pushing the mower. Tall and dependable, he was a handsome man with golden hair and sun-bronzed skin. The faint growl of the engine rumbled through the glass, and looking at the man whose ring she'd worn made sadness weigh on her heart. "Granddad wasn't your true love."

"I made a life with him and it worked out fine. I was blessed. I won't say otherwise." Gramma paused, letting the silence fall between them. "But a woman yearns to be something more than 'reliable' or 'comfortable' to the man she loves."

Karen turned from the window, relief filling her. "That's the real reason why I broke the engagement. It wasn't only about the coffee shop. He doesn't really love me, so how will he feel about me in ten years?"

"Love *can* grow and deepen with time." Gramma slipped an arm around Karen's shoulder. "But there are never any guarantees. Are you having regrets?"

"I know I hurt him. He's a fine man, but he's not the right one. I've prayed and prayed over it. Mom thinks I'm being foolish. But you don't."

"No, I don't. Did the Lord answer your prayers?"

"No. No confirmation either way."

"You're a good girl. God will answer you. Be patient."

"See, that's my problem. I'm not good. I'm just average."

"Average? My granddaughter? Nonsense." Gramma marched Karen to the table and gestured for her to sit. "You are a bright, beautiful young woman and as good as can be. I ought to know, since I'm your grandmother. A woman my age is wise about these things."

"You're biased."

"I guess love will do that." Gramma ran her fingers through Karen's brown hair. "Do you know what I think?"

"I'm afraid to guess."

"You might look good as a blonde. Ever think of that?"

"What do you mean? Color my hair? What does that have to do with this conversation?"

"You'd be surprised." Gramma looked up into the mirror on the wall behind the kitchen table. "I've been thinking about getting rid of this gray hair. Maybe that's my problem. If I dyed my hair red and bought a sports car, I wouldn't be the same old reliable Helen."

"You wouldn't be the grandmother I know and love."

"I'm not getting any younger, so why wait? And at my age, what am I waiting for? I want something different than spending most of my days in this lonely house. I want to know passion in my life. That's what I want."

Karen twisted around in her chair, surprised at the unhappiness etched on her grandmother's face.

"You and I have the same problem, Karen. We've

been good girls all our lives and in my case, it's been a few decades too long."

"What do you mean?"

"I've been living a lukewarm life for sixty years now, and that's not how I want to be remembered. I don't want people to say, 'Helen was nice,' at my funeral. I want them to say, 'Remember the fun we had the day Helen drove us through town in her new convertible.'"

Karen's hand trembled, and she didn't know what to say. Today at the cemetery, she'd felt the same—that time on this earth was too short to spend with regrets.

Sympathy for her grandmother filled her. "If you want, I'll go with you to the beauty shop. We'll get your hair done so you'll look beautiful."

"Thank you, dear. I knew you'd understand." Gramma held her close, and Karen hugged her long and hard, grateful for this grandmother she loved so much.

Chapter Three

Karen was placing fresh flowers on the tables in the quiet hours before the lunch rush started when an engine's rumble on the street outside her shop caught her attention. A gleaming black motorcycle pulled into an empty parking spot out front, ridden by a man wearing a white T-shirt and jeans.

"There's trouble," matronly Cecilia Thornton, Jay's mom, commented over her iced latte.

"With a capital *T*," Marj Whitly agreed.

With the way Zach's muscled shoulders and wide chest stretched out that T-shirt, there was no word other than 'trouble' to describe him. Karen watched him swing one leg easily over the bike's seat and unbuckle his helmet. Shocks of thick brown hair tumbled across his brow.

Zach might look larger than life, but she knew at heart that he was a good man.

He strolled down the walk in front of the row of windows and winked when he caught sight of her.

Eager for the sight of a friendly face, Karen quickly set the last little vase in the center of the last table.

The bell above the front door chimed. Zach strode through the door. Her pulse skipped and she didn't know why.

"Working hard on a Saturday, as usual. Don't you know you're missing a fantastic morning out there?" Zach raked one hand through his tousled locks, rumpling them even more. He lowered his voice. "I'd offer you an escape on my bike, but I don't think Jay's mom will approve."

"You noticed her glaring at you?" Karen circled around the counter.

"Always." His eyes sparkled, holding no ill will toward the woman who frowned at him from the far corner of the dining room.

"Is it too early for lunch?"

"Not in my shop."

"Then I'll have a bologna and cheese with mayo and mustard, on white." Zach nodded in Cecilia's direction. "Good morning, ladies."

The two women's eyes widened in surprise. Cecilia managed a polite response, even though it was clear she didn't approve of the likes of Zachary Drake.

See? With that kind of attitude in Jay's family, it was a good thing she'd broken her engagement.

Zach leaned over the counter, a mischievous grin curving across his mouth. "I don't think they approve of my mode of transportation."

"It's not the bike, Zach."

"Are you saying those woman don't approve of *me?*"

"You're crushed, I see."

"Devastated. Is Cecilia's death-ray glare of disapproval getting to you?"

Biting her bottom lip to keep from laughing, Karen donned clear plastic gloves. "Cecilia's death-ray stares aren't hurting me any. I missed you this morning. You didn't come in for coffee. Are you two-timing me over at the diner?"

"I wouldn't dream of it. I'm a devoted man. Not even the diner's full breakfast menu can tempt me away from your charming shop."

"A loyal customer. Just what I like to hear."

"I have to confess I made my own java and took a thermos of it fishing with me this morning."

"I didn't know bachelors could make coffee."

"You see, there's this little scoop that comes in the can. It's easy to measure."

"A can? You didn't even grind your own beans?" Karen unwrapped a loaf of fresh bread. "I'm disappointed in you."

"I know, but I've learned my lesson. Next time I'll bring my thermos over and let you fill it for me."

How did he do it, she wondered. With that dazzling smile and his melting-chocolate voice, Zach could chase away her troubles and leave her smiling.

"How's that car of yours?"

"Still running, and don't look so surprised."

"Only prayers are keeping that heap going, believe me. When it finally breaks down for good, give me a call and I'll help you out."

"Unlike you, I have complete faith."

"Unlike you, I've looked under the hood, and that car's doomed, Karen. I'm telling you this as a friend. I've already ordered a used engine."

"I can't afford it."

"We'll work something out or we can barter. Car parts for sandwiches?"

"That's a lot of sandwiches."

Zach sent Cecilia a brief, imposing glare. "Mrs. Thornton still hasn't forgiven you for dumping her son?"

"Does it look like it?"

"If she's upset, what's she doing in your shop?"

"This is the only place in town to buy a latte." Karen sighed.

"You're doing the right thing, giving it time." He meant to be comforting. "Everyone knows you and Jay will get back together."

"Everybody doesn't know me, not if they believe that. I'm never going to marry Jay." Karen concentrated extra hard on her sandwich making. "I suppose that's what you think, too, isn't it? That good, dependable Karen will do what's sensible. And why not? It's what I've always done."

"That's the problem with a small town. People make up their minds about what kind of person you are, and it doesn't matter how honest you try to be when it comes to their repair bills, they still see what they're used to seeing."

"I know what you mean." Karen's pulse skipped again. Had Zach's eyes always been so blue? "Have a good afternoon."

"Good luck surviving Cecilia's death-ray stare." He tossed a five-dollar bill on the counter and took the paper sack from her.

His hand brushed hers and burned her like a hot flame.

Why was she feeling like this? Confused, she watched Zach push open the door, causing the bell to jangle overhead. For a brief moment he glanced at her, his eyes dark with unmistakable sympathy.

Then he turned and was gone. The bell chimed again as the door snapped shut, and Karen felt as if all the warmth had gone from the room. What was wrong with her? What was going on?

She didn't mean to be watching him, but there he was. Striding down the walk with the wind tousling his dark hair. He looked as rakish as a pirate, and yet as dependable as the earth. He hesitated at the top of the stairs and then he disappeared from her sight.

Caffeine, that's what she needed. Karen reached for the pitcher of iced tea and poured a tall glass. The sweet cool liquid slid down the back of her throat, but it didn't ease the confusion within her.

The bell chimed again. Zach—had he come back? Karen held her breath as the door swung open to reveal not her handsome mechanic but someone just as welcome. Her grandmother swept into the room wearing a red T-shirt, a pair of denim shorts and tennis shoes.

Karen nearly dropped her glass. "What happened to you?"

"I raided Michelle and Kirby's closets. I've been wearing dresses all my life. It's time for a change."

Gramma set her purse on the counter. It was a neat slim red pocketbook instead of the sensible black handbag she always carried.

What was going on?

Gramma faced the dining room and clapped her hands. "Ladies, Karen sure appreciates your business, but she's going to have to close up shop for a few hours. I know you understand. Here, Cecilia, let me get a paper cup so you can take your latte with you."

Cecilia's disapproving glare gained new intensity. "Helen, whatever have you done to yourself?"

"What? A woman can't wear shorts in the heat of summer?" Her grandmother looked nonplussed as she transferred Cecilia's latte from the mug to the paper cup. "Now, head on out so I can lock the door."

"Gramma!" Karen stepped forward before her grandmother took over completely. "You can't do this. It's nearly time for the lunch crowd."

"But you have to leave right now." Gramma flipped the sign in the window so it read Closed. "It's the only time Dawn over at the Snip & Style could fit us into her schedule."

"What do you mean by 'us'? *You're* the one getting your hair colored. I'm going for moral support. That's what we agreed to."

"That's not how I remember it. Come on, get your keys. I'm not about to be late, not when Dawn has promised me a whole new look."

"Gramma, I'm glad you're doing this. I'm thrilled, really. But lunch brings in the biggest sales of the day. I can't miss it. Maybe Michelle can—"

"Your sister has a client scheduled—you. I mean it, ladies, out of those chairs. Hustle." Gramma gave a good-humored clap, looking as if she were herding reluctant deer from her rose garden. "Thanks, ladies. Karen sure appreciates it."

"Anything for our Karen," Marj Whitly said warmly. "That's just the thing she needs, Helen. Time for herself at the beauty parlor, a complete shampoo and facial. Restores the spirit, it does. Then she'll be over her wedding jitters and can get down to the business of marrying your son, Cecilia."

Karen opened her mouth to protest, but Gramma winked at her, so she offered Marj a lid for her cup instead.

Gramma locked the door after the women departed. "Leave your purse. This is my treat."

"What treat? I'm going to say this one more time so you understand. I'm going along for moral support *only.*"

"Of course you are," Gramma said indulgently. "Now get a move on, because I don't want to be late for my new life."

See? This is what always got her into trouble. In the end, she hadn't been able to disappoint her grandmother. Look what that had gotten her.

"It wasn't supposed to do this," Michelle, her youngest sister, apologized. "Working with hair is always tricky. You have a lot of naturally gold highlights in your hair, which was a surprise considering it's such a dull brown—"

"I never should have agreed to this." Karen wished she had Cecilia Thornton's knack for a death-ray glare. "I should've never trusted you."

"I guess I left the color in too long."

"You *guess?*" She could only stare in the mirror at her wet, scraggly hair. It hung in limp, ragged strands and shone perfectly gold. Except in about ten or twelve places. "Look what you did to me. My own baby sister."

"Sorry. This is the first time I've ever turned someone's hair green. Honest."

"Fix it. Whatever you have to do, do it now."

Michelle grabbed a fresh towel. "I know what to do. I think."

"You *think?* What did they teach you at that school anyway?"

"They warned us never to work on our own relatives. Now I know why." Michelle dashed away and disappeared from sight.

"It's certainly different, I'll grant you that," Gramma said from the neighboring chair. "With those green streaks, you could be in the latest fashion. Anywhere but in Montana."

"Thanks, I feel so much better." Karen peered at her reflection, her heart sinking. What if Michelle couldn't fix it? "I didn't mind being mouse brown. At least my real color wouldn't glow in the dark."

"That's the spirit. Don't worry. We'll turn you into a dazzling blonde yet. Michelle might be new at this, but Dawn here has decades of experience. She can work wonders. Why, look at me."

"I'm looking." Karen couldn't believe her eyes as the other beautician switched on a blow dryer and began styling Gramma's hair.

No more gray curls. Rich auburn locks fell in a short, feathery cut. She looked beautiful. Infinitely beautiful.

"I've always wanted to be a redhead," Gramma confessed above the hum of the dryer. "It's a whole new me."

"You don't need any improvement." By contrast, Karen's hair looked like a cosmetology school disaster. "Look at me. I could sure use something. Michelle, I want you to put this back the way it was."

"Don't be silly," Gramma admonished. "You promised moral support, so don't think I'm going through this alone. You're staying at my side every step of the way, missy. It'll be good for you."

"I don't want a makeover."

"You need one more than anyone else I know, my darling sister." Michelle returned, armed with a cup that smelled like varnish. "I don't know how it happened, but you got all the recessive genes in the family. A shame it is. Gramma, you wouldn't know a good plastic surgeon, would you?"

"Mess up my hair again, and you'll pay," Karen threatened.

Michelle didn't look a bit afraid. "I know you too well. You're all bark and no bite. How about platinum blond streaks? What do you think, Gramma?"

"No! No streaks. No blond anything." Karen couldn't help panicking a little. "I've come to adore mouse brown. Really. It's the way God meant me to be. Just give me a rinse or something to get this color out of my hair."

"Trust us, Karen." Gramma winked. "They say that blondes have more fun. Let's find out if it's true."

Seeing the happiness on her grandmother's face, how could she refuse—even if disaster loomed?

Zach felt the hot midday sun burn the back of his neck as he twisted the bolt with his pliers. "Your car should start fine, Mrs. Greenley."

"You, my dear boy, are nothing short of an angel." The older lady blew him a kiss. "Tell me why a handsome man like you doesn't have a ring on his finger."

"No girl can catch me, I guess." Zach shut the car's hood.

"Doesn't a smart fellow like you know not to run too fast?"

He wiped the grease smudges from his fingers off her gleaming hood. "No one said I was a smart man."

"You can't fool me, Zachary Drake." Nora Greenley shook her head at him, watching every movement he made as he reached around the steering wheel and turned the key. "You're not as bad as you seem, even with the motorcycle. How much do I owe you?"

The engine rolled over, purring contentedly. He released the key. A movement caught his gaze on the sidewalk across the street. Karen with hair as gold as summer sunshine breezed out of the Snip & Style. She looked more beautiful than he'd ever seen her.

Then he remembered Mrs. Greenley was watching him. Anyone with good eyesight would be able to see how he felt for Karen, so he closed his mouth and turned to his client. "I'll bill you for the battery. Have a good afternoon."

"I'll sure try." The older woman glanced across the street before she climbed behind the wheel. "You behave yourself, you hear, young man?"

Zach closed Nora's car door and waited until she pulled away. Alone, he dared to look across the street again. There she was, with her grandmother at her side, talking with a group of women who'd spotted them on the sidewalk. Their conversation rose and fell with merry energy, but all Zach could see was Karen.

She looked great as a blonde. The lighter color made her eyes bluer. Somehow it made her seem more wholesome, if that could be possible, as if she'd spent all summer outdoors in the sun.

Karen's words from earlier in the day echoed in his mind, replaying over and over again. *Everybody doesn't know me, not if they believe that. I'm never going to marry Jay.*

Words like that could give a man hope.

Home. Finally. Zach snapped on the light switch just inside the door of his apartment over the garage. A bulb popped with a bright flash, leaving him in darkness.

Great. Just great. Too exhausted to even summon up a little anger, Zach rummaged around in the dark. His closet was too messy and so he couldn't find his flashlight. His stomach grumbled in loud protest, not wanting to wait a second longer for supper. He'd change the bulb later and make do with the light in the kitchen.

Sweat trickled down the back of his neck, and he tugged off his T-shirt. Man, it was hot. He headed straight for the air-conditioning window unit and flicked it on high. Tepid air sputtered reluctantly, and the fan inside coughed. A lukewarm current breezed across his heated face.

What? No cold air? He flicked off the machine, marched across the small apartment to the kitchen and yanked open the window above the sink. Humid air blew in. As he circled his apartment, opening the windows wide, his stomach clamped with hunger.

Food. He needed it bad and he needed it now.

Not overly hopeful, Zach scoped out his kitchen cupboards. At the sight of the practically empty shelves, his stomach twisted harder. A can of olives, a stale box of cheese crackers and there was mold growing on the remaining slices of three-week-old bread.

Okay, maybe the refrigerator held more promise. He jerked open the door and stood in the welcome icy breeze, surveying the empty metal racks. There was only a half-empty jar of mayonnaise, the butter dish and an empty container of salsa. His stomach growled so loud, it hurt.

Maybe there was something in the freezer.

Bingo. He'd found supper. Even if it was two beef franks, heavily iced in their original package stuck to the empty ice tray, which was iced to the bottom of the freezer. This was not a problem—he was ingenious and he had a knife.

Using it like a chisel, he inserted the blade's tip between the thick bed of ice and the frozen franks. Cold air wheezed across his face as he leveled a careful blow.

The phone rang—the shop phone. It was work and he couldn't ignore it. Reluctantly he set down the knife and knocked the freezer shut with the flat of his hand. A meal, air-conditioning and time to relax—was it too much to ask?

He grabbed the old black phone in the corner by the door.

"Zach's Garage." He tucked the receiver between his ear and his shoulder.

"I know it's late." Karen's voice came across the line, tight with strain. "But remember that offer of help you made? I could really use it."

"You called the right man. Don't tell me your engine went and died, just like I said."

"Okay, I won't, but that's why I'm calling." Static crackled across the line. "No one at home is answering the phone. They're probably outside on the deck, so I'm stranded. I'm at the grocery store."

"I'll be right there."

"Thanks, Zach."

"No problem. That's what friends are for." He eased the receiver into the cradle and grabbed his keys.

Dinner could wait. Relaxing could wait. Karen needed him. Even if it was only as a mechanic, only as a friend.

He grabbed a clean shirt before heading out the door.

He spotted her sitting on the curb the minute he turned onto Railroad Street. The night breezes ruffled her silken hair around her delicate face. Her slender shoulders slumped with either exhaustion or defeat. He couldn't tell which.

She turned at the sound of his truck and waved. Behind her, the lights of the closed grocery store were dim and cast a faint glow over her, emphasizing her willowy shape. She stood, holding a plastic grocery bag in one hand.

He stopped the tow truck in the middle of the road and leaned out the window. "Hey, good lookin'. Need a lift?"

Her new blond locks danced against the side of her face, driven by the wind. "Do you like the new me?"

"There was nothing wrong with the old you." He reached for his door to climb down and assist her, but it was too late to help her in. She was already breezing through the beams of the truck's headlights, so he leaned across the seat and opened the door. He gave it a shove for her because it was heavy. "What's with Helen? I saw her new hairdo."

"Gramma is having a midlife crisis three decades too late."

"Good. Everyone needs to try something new now and then."

Flashing him a grin, Karen climbed inside the cab as if she were used to climbing into big trucks. And then Zach remembered she was a ranch girl and had probably helped her father in the fields through the years by driving hay trucks and tractors.

What would it have been like to grow up as she did, with a solid and close-knit family and hundreds of acres of land to roam on? It was a far cry from living at the edge of town where he'd called a single-wide trailer home. And where he'd struggled to take care of his younger brother and sister.

The bench seat dipped slightly with her weight. The air-conditioning circulated her vanilla and baby shampoo scent. Yes, a man had to have hope. That's all it was—hope—and not the right to be more than a friend.

Not knowing what to say, Zach released the clutch. The truck eased down the street in a smooth rumble.

He headed north, away from the lights of the small town where rolling fields stretched into the deepening twilight. The roar of the engine and the whir of the cool air through the cab covered up the silence that fell between them. But it didn't change the fact that she was sitting next to him with only two feet between them.

Yes, it was good for a man to have hope.

"What are you looking at?" she asked, her hand flying to the sassy ends of her hair. "You hate this, don't you? I can't get used to looking at myself."

"Neither can I." He fought the urge to tell her just how great she looked. He thought her beautiful before, but she looked better now. Not because her hair was different, but because there was a sparkle in her eyes he hadn't seen in a long while.

"Gramma forced me into this."

"She strong-armed you, did she?"

"She guilted me into it. Works every time." Karen shook her head and her jaunty locks swept her slim shoulders. "I'm a soft touch when it comes to her."

"When it comes to everyone."

"Sometimes." She looked unhappy, and he never much thought about the pressures she might face always looked to as one of the well-behaved McKaslin girls, even now when she'd been an adult for many years.

"I have the same problem," he confessed with a grin. "I'm always a real softhearted guy. That's why I drive my motorcycle through town at least once a week. So no one suspects the real me."

"It's a good disguise. It fools a lot of people, but not me."

"Really? Maybe I shouldn't have left the leather jacket at home." He tossed her a grin as he slowed down to turn into her family's long gravel driveway.

How she liked Zach's smile. Kind and warm with a hint of charm, and when his smile touched his eyes, she could see the goodness in him. In fact, there was a lot to like about the man.

Aside from being a dependable friend, he was probably the most handsome man in town. He'd certainly been considered the best-looking boy in her high school class. All the years since had only improved him.

Even in the dark interior of the truck and silhouetted by the encroaching night, he looked amazing. His profile was strong with a dark shock of hair tumbling over his forehead, a straight nose and a well-carved jaw. Just looking at him made her pulse drum.

Zach slowed the truck down to take the final corner of her parents' long gravel driveway. She looked through the windshield and saw her family's home up on the knoll. The lit windows shone like beacons in the descending darkness.

The truck eased to a stop in front of her house, and the silence between them lengthened. Light from the house spilled through the open windows to cast a glow on the trimmed juniper bushes lining the driveway.

She didn't want to walk through that door. The pressure of her parents' disappointment in her pressed like an anvil against her chest.

"I can take that in if you want." His voice startled her, and his big warm hand curled over hers.

His heat seared her like a jolt of electricity and she jumped at the contact. Then she realized he wasn't trying to hold her hand. He was taking the plastic bag from her grip.

To her amazement, he opened the door and hopped from the cab. His boots crunched in the gravel and then tapped on the brick walk. The light from the windows burnished him with a golden glow. His silhouette was impressive—broad shoulders, wide back, tapered hips and long legs.

He was all male, that was for sure. Hard and strong and powerful. Something she'd never quite noticed to this degree before.

Her heart kicked for some unexplained reason, and

she fled into the fields where the darkness swallowed her. She knew every bump in the dirt path that led from the house to the stable.

She splayed both palms on the worn smooth curve of the top rail and let the calm of the night surround her. Dark clouds blocked out the stars. She didn't know how long she waited before she heard Zach's gait on the path behind her and felt his presence, substantial like the night.

"Karen? I'll head back to town and rescue your car. I can have an estimate ready for you sometime tomorrow."

"There's no hurry. It's not like I can afford that engine."

"Stop being so difficult. In my book, you're a good credit risk. Besides, you've got a business to run. You need your car."

"I do." Trying not to give in to her troubles, she took a breath and let the wooden rail take the weight of her head. Too late—her neck muscles had coiled into one hard aching mass.

Gathering her hair in her free hand, she held it up in a loose ponytail so the winds could caress a warm current across her knotted muscles.

His work boots tapped behind her. "A little tense?"

"That's an understatement."

"Let me see what I can do about that."

She felt a swish of air over her exposed skin and then his warm fingers settled on her neck. She stiffened at his touch, but the heat of his palm felt like heaven.

A sigh escaped her as his big, callused hands

caressed and soothed the pain from her muscles. Her tension melted with every glide of his fingers over the back of her neck.

Too soon he stepped away, leaving her breathless. His touch was like nothing she'd known before— electrical and enlivening and comforting all at once.

She was grateful for the dark. She didn't know what to say, and even if she did, how would she say it?

As if he were flustered, too, Zach walked away without saying a word.

The thick blanket of clouds broke apart overhead, and thin, silvery moonlight brushed the ground where Zach walked. A verse from Matthew came to her as soft as the breeze. *"...and He will give you all you need from day to day."*

There was no doubt about it. She was blessed with Zach for a friend.

She stepped into the swatch of moonlight and began jogging to catch up with him. "Hey, where do you think you're running off to? Did you get supper?"

"No. I was in the middle of chiseling frozen hot dogs out of my freezer when you called."

"*Chiseling?* Unbelievable. I've heard bachelor stories before, but I didn't think they were true. Even my father can cook well enough to make an omelet in a pinch."

"I've been busy. I didn't have time to get to the grocery store."

"Sure, a likely story." She met him halfway across the yard. "Zachary Drake, you're pathetic, but I can't in good conscience let you starve."

"Pathetic? C'mon, give me a break, I'm not that bad. Usually."

"Sure, like I believe you." She led the way up the brick steps and onto the porch. "A man who thinks crusted-over hot dogs is a worthy meal is a danger to himself."

"Does this mean I'm in luck and you're going to feed me?"

"Somebody's got to."

He laughed, a rich, wonderful sound that warmed her all the way to her soul.

Chapter Four

The microwave beeped and Zach watched Karen pop open the little door. The light inside snapped on to reveal the sight of a steaming cheesy casserole. It made his mouth water.

"That's the best thing I've seen all day."

Karen smiled breezily. "If you're really nice to me, I'll give you the recipe. If you can fix a car, you can learn to make this."

"That's a bet I'm not willing to take. If I could cook as good as I can build a transmission, my stomach wouldn't be growling. I haven't had a decent meal since my little sister left for college."

Karen set the plate on the kitchen table. "What have you been eating for the last year?"

"They have these boxes in the freezer part of the grocery store. I buy 'em, take 'em home, and when I'm hungry, put one in the oven. They're called frozen dinners."

"Shocking." Teasing glints lit her eyes and chased

away the worry lines across her brow. She tugged flatware from a nearby drawer and set a knife and fork on the table. "Sit. Eat. It's a wonder you haven't spontaneously combusted with all the chemicals you've been ingesting."

"It's not that bad. They've got these healthy frozen meals that taste pretty good. But nothing like your grandmother's cooking."

"I won't argue with you about that." Karen set two soda cans on the table. "Go ahead and get started. I'll dish up a nice bowl of salad."

"You're going to torment me with vegetables?"

"Even a man as handsome as you needs his antioxidants."

"Antiwhats? That sounds suspicious. Let me guess. It has something to do with broccoli."

She peered around the edge of the refrigerator door. "What's wrong with broccoli?"

"It tastes like cellophane, for one thing. As a general rule, I never eat anything green."

"It's a wonder you've made it this far, Zachary Drake. A tough guy like you needs his vitamins." She shook her head, golden locks shimmering as she shut the door. "I've got a bowl of carrot sticks. Do me a favor and eat a few. Hey, don't look at me like that. They're orange, not green."

"Orange is a good color. Lots of junk food is orange."

She rewarded him with another smile, one that chased away all the shadows from her eyes and the strain from her face. A smile that made her look like the Karen he remembered. Happy and wholesome, with the kind of beauty that settled in a man's heart and never faded.

Those are dangerous thoughts, Zach. He tried not to notice the way his skin felt prickly when she sat down beside him.

He bowed his head in a quick prayer and reached for his fork.

Delicious spices and creamy cheese melted across his tongue. "This is great. I'm so grateful, I'm liable to give you the engine you need for free."

"Don't you dare, although Gramma will appreciate the compliment." Karen popped the top of the cola can and sipped.

No ring sparkled on her finger. He couldn't forget what she'd told him. That she wasn't going to marry Jay. *Ever.*

Hope was a bright blessing as the night darkened and he could see his reflection in the white-paned glass of the kitchen's bay window. And of the woman sitting next to him, her bouncy hair sparkling like pure gold, her presence as sweet as the cut roses scenting the air.

This was definitely something he could get used to. Forget coming home to an empty apartment and eating alone in front of the TV.

A door opened behind him and the hot, evening wind whipped across the back of his neck as Karen's mother and grandmother entered the kitchen.

"Mom." Karen bolted out of her chair and circled around the table, her arms extended.

Zach watched as she wrapped her mother in a comforting hug. Mrs. McKaslin looked frail and ashen, but when she glared at him over Karen's shoulder, she looked as tough as nails.

Mrs. McKaslin didn't need to say the words. Zach had lived with the same looks from half the town since he was a boy—looks of disdain and judgment. Looks that said he wasn't quite good enough, even twenty years later. He'd worked hard to become a man of integrity, but he was still Sylvia Drake's son from the wrong side of town.

"I'm in the way here, Karen." He grabbed his empty plate and carried it to the sink. "Let me rinse this off and I'll be on my way."

"What? No seconds?" Karen released her mother and moved to stop him, her beauty just as bright and her friendship as genuine. "Let me grab the casserole from the fridge and I'll dish you up another—"

"I'm good, Karen. Thanks anyway."

"You haven't had dessert yet."

Mrs. McKaslin's gaze grew sharper, and Zach could feel the man he was fade a little. "It's getting late."

"Are you sure? Mom, would you mind wrapping up a few of your brownies? If Zach has to go, at least he can take heaven with him." Karen's smile shot straight to his heart.

She was heaven.

Good thing she couldn't read his thoughts. Embarrassed, he set his plate in the sink.

"Oh, no, you don't." Karen sidled up to him and curled her hand around the hot water tap. "I'd still be sitting on that lonely sidewalk if you hadn't shown up tonight. Thanks, Zach. I owe you big-time."

"Pretty lady, you don't owe me a thing."

Her soft mouth stretched into a quiet smile. She smelled like heaven. He wanted to breathe her in, wrap his arms around her and pull her against his chest.

He'd give about anything to have the right to hold her.

"Karen." Mrs. McKaslin cleared her throat from the other side of the room. "It's been a very hard day for me. I want my bath now."

Strain tightened in the corners of Karen's eyes and mouth, stealing away her beautiful smile. "I'll be right there, Mom."

"Nonsense. I can do it," Helen called out and set a paper sack on the counter. "Zach, don't forget to take this with you. A man can't live without a dose of my double-chocolate fudge brownies. I sprinkle them with powdered sugar just to make them sweeter."

"Thanks, Helen." He took the carefully folded sack and avoided Karen's gaze. "Karen, I know you're busy. I can find the door on my own."

"Don't you dare." Her hand brushed his arm as she escorted him from the room.

He could feel Mrs. McKaslin's prickly gaze on his back, and he tried to ignore it. Karen walked quickly beside him, and without a word pulled him through the foyer toward the front door. Her shoulders looked tight and a muscle jumped beneath the smooth skin on her jaw.

"I'm sorry about my mother. She's battling depression again and it turns her into a harder person."

"Hey, I'm fine. I'm sorry that she's not feeling well." He felt sorrier for Karen.

The phone rang in the kitchen behind them as he

pulled open the elaborate front door. "Now that your car is dead, just like I predicted, will you need a ride to town tomorrow? I could be bribed into swinging by to pick you up."

"I'll take Mom's car." Karen's hand settled on his forearm, light and steady. "I can't begin to tell you what your friendship means to me. If I didn't know better, I'd think you're an angel in disguise."

"Me? The last time I looked, angels don't ride Harleys."

"There's a first time for everything." She pressed a kiss to his cheek, warm and sweet, just like her.

Friends. He didn't miss the message in the words. She wanted friendship with him, not romance. His hopes fell like a star from the sky.

Tucking away his disappointment, he stepped into the shadows.

She stood bathed in the gentle glow of the overhead light, and there was no mistaking the grateful gleam in her eyes. She watched him not with attraction or interest or affection. But with gratitude.

"See you tomorrow," he said, a dutiful friend and nothing more. "Thanks for supper."

Before she could answer, Mrs. McKaslin's voice called from inside the house. "Karen, honey, it's Jay on the phone. He's waiting to talk to you."

Zach was glad the shadows hid him from Karen's sight. "Sounds like you'd better take that."

He walked away and didn't look back. He was halfway to the truck when he heard the door close with a quiet *click,* leaving him alone.

On the outside.

Just like always.

Footsteps tapped in the dark aisle behind her and tightened her grip on the currycomb. The stall was shadowed, lit only by the moonlight that cut through the top half of the open stall door. She couldn't see who was heading toward her. Star shifted, her hooves clomping on the concrete floor, and cut off Karen's view of the door.

"It's me," Michelle said quietly, pain in her voice. "I got Mom to take a sleeping pill and stayed with her until she fell asleep."

"I'm glad she's resting." The mare she was brushing nickered low, as if in comfort, and Karen leaned her head against the old horse's warm shoulder. "I shouldn't have made her so angry."

"You didn't want to talk to Jay. You had every right to refuse to take his call." Michelle paused, as if she had something on her mind and decided not to say it. "Tomorrow will always be better. At least, that's what Pastor Bill says."

"Tomorrow is almost here, and I have to get to bed." She felt weary all the way down to her soul, but she feared another sleepless night was ahead. "You go on back to the house. I'll be up in a few minutes."

"Okay. I just wanted to make sure you weren't still mad at me. About the green hair, I mean." How unsure Michelle seemed, her voice thin, clinging to the shadows.

"I could never be truly mad at you. You're my baby sister."

"If you want, I can give you back your dull, mouse-brown lifeless color. That is, if you don't like the golden beauty you've become from my expert touch."

"Expert touch? Ha!" Karen meant to tease, but her heart weighed down her words.

She wrapped her arms around her sister, frail-boned like a colt still growing, and hugged her long enough so there could be no doubt the hair disaster was forgiven.

What blessings she had in her sisters and in every aspect in her life.

"Hey, Karen." Michelle halted at the moonlit doorway. "Wake me up when your alarm goes off in the morning. I'll drive you to town and help you at the coffee shop before church."

"*You?* Help? You don't know the first thing about a kitchen. I'm afraid you'll burn the place down."

"Just keep me away from all electrical appliances and I'll be fine."

"Then it's a deal. See ya in the morning."

"How much are you going to pay me per hour?" Michelle asked, her teasing as bright as the moon. "What? You think I'd do that for free? No way. I need the cash. I've got a lifestyle to maintain."

As her sister disappeared into the night, Karen was laughing for the first time since she'd refused Jay's call and disappointed her parents even more.

Maybe now they believed her that there wasn't going to be a wedding.

Tonight, her future seemed empty. She didn't know what was in store for her.

Help me please, Father. I'm trying, but I just can't hear Your will for me.

No answer came to her. Star nudged her hand in a show of comfort, a reminder that she wasn't alone. Even when it felt that way.

"Hunky Zach's at the front door." Michelle wandered into the coffee shop's small kitchen, a mop in hand. "Should I do you a favor and let him in?"

"Absolutely. He may have news about my car." Karen slipped the last pan of muffins onto the oven racks.

"I figured you might say that. He's too handsome to leave out on the street, isn't he?" Michelle winked, laughing. "Are you actually blushing?"

"It's the heat from the oven," Karen explained as she closed the door gently.

"Sure." Michelle stole a fresh muffin from the cooling racks. "I'll help myself to breakfast and you answer the door. He wants to see you anyway."

"Hey, leave my muffins alone." Karen set the timer. "Did you finish mopping the floor like I asked?"

"Are you kidding? What do I look like? A manual laborer?" Michelle leaned against the counter and peeled back the paper baking cup.

"No, but you do look like a freeloader who's eating my profits for the day."

"Well, I *did* get up early to drive you this morning. You ought to at least feed me."

"What am I going to do with you? When the buzzer for the next batch rings, will you take them out?"

"I can do that." Michelle picked out the raisins and flicked them into the garbage bin across the room. "Oops, I missed that one. Don't worry, I'll pick it up."

"Don't burn my muffins," Karen warned as she found the courage to leave her little sister to watch the oven. Which was probably a big mistake.

Her sandals tapped an echoing rhythm through the dining room, but the noise was nothing compared to the thump of her heartbeat when she saw Zachary Drake standing on the other side of the glass door.

It ought to be illegal to make men that exquisite. The morning breeze tangled his dark, unruly hair. Today he was dressed for church. A dark jacket shaped his magnificent build and tan pants encased his long, lean thighs.

Why was she noticing?

She opened the door to the scent of Old Spice. "Don't you clean up nice."

"I try. You aren't looking so bad yourself." His gaze slid lazily from her French-braided hair to the tips of her sandals. He quirked one brow. "Blue toenails?"

"Thanks to Michelle." She gestured to the kitchen door where her little sister was spying on them. "Gramma and I had the complete works over at the Snip & Style. Even a pedicure."

"At least your toes match your dress. Not everyone in church will be able to say that."

"Lucky me. Can I get you something to eat? I have blueberry muffins ready to come out of the oven—" An alarm in the kitchen buzzed and Michelle reluctantly tore herself away from her spying duties. "They're ready right now. Come and join us."

"How can I say no to that?" Zach reached into his pocket and handed her a slip of paper. "I've got your estimate. Like I said, the engine's ordered. I can get started in a few days. Be done by the end of the week."

Karen stared at the precise numbers in the bottom right-hand column. She didn't need to ask Zach to know he'd given her a discount. And probably had charged very little for his labor.

It was still more than she can afford. "I can't pay for this. Maybe you could hold off for a couple of months. Let me make my balloon payment and see if there's anything left over."

"We've already discussed this. You pay me when you can." He ambled across the dining room. "In exchange, you'll let me help myself to those delicious-smelling muffins."

"I'm not putting a strain on our friendship because I owe you money."

"Like I would want you trying to get by without a working car? C'mon. I'm a better friend than that." He flashed her a dazzling wink before he stepped into the kitchen and out of her sight.

Why was she noticing that his wink was dazzling? Or how strong he looked when he crossed a room, all man and might and charm?

She was *not* attracted to him. Not a chance. It was caffeine deprivation, that was all. Because after the royal mistake she'd just made with Jay Thornton, she'd wasn't about to turn around and make another one.

Besides, romance was the best way to mess up a good friendship.

"Michelle, is that pot of coffee ready?" Karen snapped the front door shut, making sure the lock caught, and resolved to solve her caffeine-deprivation problem immediately. "How are the muffins?"

"Yeah, yeah" came Michelle's response through the open door. She sounded very distracted.

Karen knew why. Michelle was leaning against the counter again, picking at her muffin, gazing at handsome Zach as if he were Mel Gibson.

Apparently Michelle was coffee deprived, too. Maybe all men looked better right before a jolt of caffeine.

Well, that was easy enough to fix. Karen grabbed three paper cups and reached for the steaming carafe. She poured with unsteady hands and sloshed coffee over the rim of one cup.

"These are good. Thanks." Zach held up one of two muffins he'd pilfered from the cooling racks. "They'll keep my stomach from growling during the service."

"Unlike last time?" Karen teased.

"I'm on my best behavior today because I'm hoping that you two lovely ladies will accompany me to church. I always show up alone and that's why I can't get any dates. I don't look desirable."

"You? Desirable?" Karen took a big sip of coffee.

"See? I get that all the time. Girls always see me as good old dependable Zach. The guy who helps them when their cars break down. That's all. They can't see that beneath the engine grease and the tough-guy mechanic's image, I'm a heck of an eligible bachelor. A real catch."

"You're a real something, that's for sure." She laughed, reaching for a muffin. "I don't think Michelle and I can do anything to help *your* sorry image."

"Sure you can. Other women will see you two clinging to me, and they'll get curious. I'll have them flocking around me in no time. It's the least you can do for me." He nodded toward the written estimate she'd laid on the counter. "Since I'm giving you a line of credit."

"You drive a tough bargain and I'm in no position to argue. But sitting next to you in church with adoring looks on our faces? Do you think we can stand it, Michelle?"

"Oh, I don't know." Michelle shook her head, feigning disdain. "It might ruin my reputation as the best beautician in town. People might begin to question my sense of taste and style and flock to Bozeman for their cuts. Dawn would fire me."

"Exactly." Karen turned off the oven and removed the last batch of muffins. "My customers will migrate to the diner across the street. I'd be destitute."

"You girls sure know how to deflate a guy's ego." He fought to keep from chuckling. "Okay, new deal. Sit with me, but no adoring looks. I'll survive. I'll never meet a woman, fall in love and marry. One day I'll be known to all as the old man who fixes cars and who can't cook for himself."

"Everyone has their crosses to bear." Karen tried not to laugh, shaking so hard with the effort that a muffin tumbled from her fingers.

Zach scooped it from the floor. "Tell me you won't put this on the discount display?"

"No, that's only the day-old stuff." Karen unplugged the coffeemaker. "Everything that falls on the floor I save for you."

Zach's laughter filled the room, echoing warmly as Michelle flicked off the overhead light. In the darkness, his hand lighted on her shoulder, just for a moment, and his breath was warm and pleasant against her ear.

A friend, that's what he was. That's all he was, even if she couldn't help noticing him.

I need more caffeine, she thought, glad she'd brought her coffee with her.

"There you are. Knew you'd be behind this counter. You sneaked out of church before I could grab you."

Karen took one look at her sharp-eyed grandmother as she marched past customers in the crowded coffee shop. "Hey, what do you think you're doing back here?"

"Helping out my granddaughter." With a twinkle in her eye, Gramma stashed her purse next to the sink and turned on the faucet. "Thought I could make myself useful."

"You should be over at the café with your friends for Sunday brunch."

"The truth is, I need you to do a favor for me. So I figured I would do one for you first."

Words of doom. Karen sliced the sandwich she was making down the center and placed it on a plate. "What kind of favor?"

"A big one. One a loving granddaughter does for her grandmother, no questions asked."

"I was afraid you were going to say that." She rang

up the sale at the cash register and counted back change. "No, Gramma. Whatever it is. I've lost enough business this week, taking a whole afternoon off to turn my hair green."

"This is the Lord's day. They'll be no talk of profit and losses. Besides, I'm only asking you to close early." Gramma winked, and only then did Karen realize how beautiful she looked with her tasteful auburn curls and a breezy summer dress.

"Is that Mom's?" she asked.

Gramma's eyes sparkled her answer as she stepped up to the counter. "Why, hello, Julie. Don't you look pretty today? What will you have?"

"The special, please." Julie Renton, one of Karen's close friends from high school, lifted a brow in a silent question.

Karen shrugged, whipped up an iced mocha and rang up the sale.

"Watch out. Jay just walked in," Julie warned in a whisper as she slipped a five-dollar bill onto the counter. "I noticed you managed to avoid him at church."

"If only I could be so lucky now." A heavy weight pressed down on her chest, making it hard to breathe, but Karen found solace in her friend's sympathetic smile. She counted back change. "Thanks for the warning."

"I'll try and head him off." Julie dropped a dollar in the tip cup and headed toward Jay.

"Need one of those iced tea things," Gramma called from the counter. "Mr. Trouble here says he wants something cold."

"Mr. Trouble?" Then she spotted Zach at the head

of the line. "Hi, stranger. Wait, I don't see any women flocking around you. I guess Michelle and I didn't help your image like you thought we would."

"You two didn't cling and adore me, remember, so none of the other women got jealous. No one even noticed me."

"Well, you'll have trouble getting anyone in town to do that." Laughing, Karen grabbed a wide-necked bottle of raspberry-flavored tea from the commercial refrigerator and set it on the counter by the till. "Don't even think of paying for this. It's on me."

"Now, I didn't mean—"

"It's *my* treat today," Gramma cut in and handed the generous sandwich to Zach. "He's going to be doing me a favor, too."

"That's news to me." Karen frowned. Just what was her grandmother up to? "Would you mind enlightening me?"

"Not at all, dear. Let's just wait until the rush dies down and I'll tell you all about it. Don't go hounding Zach for any answers, because I've sworn him to secrecy."

"Sorry, Karen." Zach turned away. "I can't break my vow to a lovely lady like Helen."

Gramma looked innocent as she took the next order.

"I know what this is about," Karen whispered to her grandmother as they made sandwiches side by side. "You're going to pay for my car repairs, aren't you? Just like you tried to do last time."

"What? Me? Waste money on that worthless rattletrap?"

"You've tried to do it before, and I know what you're capable of." Karen swabbed mayonnaise across the bread. "I don't want your money. The haircut was enough. Will you promise to keep your wallet in your purse?"

"Fine. I promise."

"That was too easy. Wait, you're scheming and don't deny it." Karen layered the meat with garnishes, then sliced the sandwich in half. "Tell me the truth. What's this favor you want from me and Zach?"

"Oh, it only involves a quick trip to Bozeman."

"Bozeman? I've got my business to run, and after I'm done here I have to head home. Mom couldn't get out of bed to make it to church and I'm worried—"

"Your sister Kirby will be at home with her. Don't forget that you promised to help me."

"I did. I'm just worried what's next."

Karen finished a second sandwich, laid them on plates and grabbed soda cans from the refrigerator. As she rang up the purchases, she spotted Jay next in line. Tension knotted in the back of her neck.

"Hi, Karen." He stood arrow straight and rigid, looking as tense as she felt. And just as hurt. "That's great Helen's here. She can take over for you. Come and talk to me."

"There's nothing to talk about. You know that."

"I want to find out what happened. I know what you said, but you couldn't have meant—"

"I meant it, Jay. I don't want to marry you." Sadness filled her, looking at this man she'd once made dreams with, at the man who couldn't love her.

He'd never love her, not truly. He saw her as a practical choice for his future, that was all. He'd never be able to give her the depth of love she wanted from a husband.

She knew he'd never be able to understand how a practical sensible girl like her would want true love.

"Did you want to order? Today's special is Swiss and turkey—"

"C'mon, Karen, don't be like this. I've got a flight to catch in a few hours. Didn't you listen to Bill's sermon today? It was about letting go of our grief and moving on. Of accepting that God's plan may differ from what we wish for ourselves—"

Karen felt her grandmother's curious gaze and realized their conversation wasn't as quiet as she'd thought. She lowered her voice. "I know you don't love me. Marriage should be about love. Are you going to order or not?"

"No." Jay drummed his fist on the glass counter, rattling utensils and drawing surprised gazes from several diners.

Flushed, he marched toward the door.

He was a golden son of this town, a man destined to be a great minister. Next to him she felt plain as she always did, plain and small.

Because that's how he saw her.

She was doing the right thing. Certainty filled her and all her turmoil faded away like fog to sun.

Gramma wrapped her arm around Karen's waist. "You did good, my girl."

"Not really." Karen leaned into her grandmother's

embrace, grateful for the comfort and for the blessing of this woman in her life. "I'm finally at peace over this."

"I'm glad. I finished filling the last order, so let's treat ourselves to some lunch. I'm in a hurry to get to Bozeman."

Karen reached for two slices of whole wheat bread. "What's in Bozeman? C'mon, tell me."

"I certainly will not. You'll just have to wait and see for yourself."

Karen felt a strange heat, as if someone were staring at her. She looked up, expecting to see Jay's mom and her death-ray glare of disapproval.

Instead, she saw Zach. Seated across the length of the dining room, he winked at her.

The peace in her heart intensified, and she swore that sunlight streamed through the windows, brightening the room.

Chapter Five

The late-afternoon sun beat relentlessly on the paved lot outside the car dealer's office. Karen had to squint against the bright rays to see her grandmother emerging through the glinting glass doors.

"She's all mine!" Gramma had never looked so happy as she approached the shining red convertible, jingling brand-new keys. "I can't believe it. This is a dream come true."

"A beautiful dream. One I hope you share now and then. I'd love to go joy riding with you." Karen wrapped her grandmother in a hug. "You're going to look like a new woman in that car."

"Don't you know it." Gramma beamed. "And yes, I'll treat my granddaughter to a drive, but not right now. You've got to take Zach back to town for me. After all, he did negotiate the price of the car. I can't let him walk home."

"I guess not." Karen considered the man who stood talking with a salesman in the shade of the building.

He'd changed into his usual white T-shirt and jeans. With the wind tangling through his dark locks he looked fine.

Very fine.

"I suppose I can tolerate his presence for a little longer, but I'll need the keys to your old Ford."

"It's not mine any longer."

"Gramma! You traded in that car? You've had it for as long as I can remember."

"I had it brand-new off the showroom floor since long before you were born. It's been my only car for nearly forty years. Forty years! And it never broke down on me once and left me stranded. A blessing, that Ford is, and that's why I'm giving it to you."

"What?"

"I have an extra car, and you don't have one."

"I do, too. It's in Zach's shop waiting for a new engine."

"That old rattletrap? It breaks down once a week. Why would you sink perfectly good money into a wreck like that?"

"Because it's mine and it's paid for. Thank you, but no. I can't take your car. You should hold on to it. It's a classic and—"

"I've made up my mind and I'm not changing it. I'm giving the car to you." Gramma's hand closed over Karen's. "You work too hard, harder than most, and you deserve a little help."

"No, I don't need—"

"You're a good girl for wanting to pay your way, but

indulge me. Take my car and consider it a favor for your doting grandmother."

"It's an entire car. It's worth money."

"Money I don't need. I've spent my whole life scrimping and saving. It's time I loosened my belt just a little. Life is too precious not to enjoy, and I get happiness from helping my grandchildren.

"So here." Gramma pressed the keys against Karen's palm. "Drive home that helpful young man who got me a fantastic price for my new roadster. And treat him to dinner because he's a man and they just don't know how to take care of themselves."

"I don't know what to say. It's an entire car. One that runs. 'Thank you' doesn't seem enough—"

"But it is, sweetie. Don't forget what I said. Take Zach out to a nice meal as a favor to me, because I've got plans." Gramma looked so happy as she brushed her hand across the new car's cherry-red fender. "I'm going for a spin in my new convertible. Wait until my friends see this!"

"You be careful in that thing. It goes from zero to sixty in like five seconds or so. You're not used to that kind of power."

"No, but I'm going to get used to it." With a wink, Gramma slipped into the soft-looking leather driver's seat and placed her hands on the wheel. "I'm going to enjoy every second of this. Bye, dear. Thanks for the help, Zach."

Zach nodded goodbye to his friend and stepped into the sunshine. "Helen, you stay out of trouble."

"I'll try." She started the engine with a twist of the key and put the roadster into gear. "Adios!"

Karen watched the little red car with her grandmother inside zip through the parking lot and pull onto the street. "*Adios?* She's never said that before."

Zach watched as the convertible sped out of sight. "I'm glad for her. It's always a good idea to take some time and enjoy this life we're given."

"I could learn from my grandmother's example—is that what you're telling me?"

"Something like that. Let's take a spin in your new old car, and I'll show you what a great machine you've inherited."

"A great machine?"

"That's right." Zach opened the driver side door. "Climb inside and start her up. You're bound to notice the quick start, the smooth shifting and the powerful purr of an expertly maintained engine."

"That's right. You're Gramma's mechanic, too." Karen leaned against the Ford's polished fender. "Sure this is safe to drive? Not that I'm doubting your mechanical abilities, Zach, but my car was always breaking down. And you are always the one working on it. I see a correlation, and it isn't a pretty one."

"Ah, did you notice how I said *maintained?* Not *resuscitated?* There's a difference. Plus, this is a fine automobile." Zach held the door wide for her and gestured for her to sit. "It's guaranteed not to break down like your old heap."

"Guaranteed?" Karen slipped into the seat and reached to adjust it. "Do I have your word on that?"

"Absolutely. I'm an expert, and I'm telling you that this car has a lot of good, trouble-free miles ahead of her."

Zach shut the door, gentleman through and through. Karen watched him circle around the hood. Being with him made her feel lighter than air, as if all her problems had vanished. The sun felt brighter, the wind fresher as she fit the key into the ignition.

Zach settled on the seat beside her and stretched out his long, denim-encased legs. Nicely muscled, those legs were. Very nice.

And why exactly was she noticing—again? And worse, she was feeling a little woozy. It *had* to be from low blood sugar. She'd had a rushed lunch, and it was nearly dinnertime. "Where do you want to eat?"

"There's a drive-in down the road that serves the best onion rings this side of Missoula."

"A drive-in? I think when Gramma said she wanted me to take you to dinner, she envisioned something with waiters. Where your salad is followed by a grilled entrée and vegetables." She put the car in gear and eased through the lot. "Something healthy."

"Healthy? You think that's healthy? I don't know where you get these ideas. Hamburgers cover all the basic food groups—meat, bread, cheese and lettuce. What more could you ask for?"

"I'm speechless. You are logic challenged. That's the only explanation."

"What do you mean? French fries are just cut-up potatoes. It all makes sense. Growing up on a ranch with all those vegetables everywhere has warped your perspective. It's a good thing you've started hanging out with me. I'll show you the right way to eat."

"I'm not sure the nation's nutritional experts would agree with you."

"What do they know?"

She pulled into the small parking lot where a red-and-white sign boasted the best burgers in town. "Doesn't look like they serve salads here."

"That's the beauty of it. The problem with you is that you're too wholesome, Karen. So come with me and live dangerously."

"Eating deep-fried food *could* be dangerous."

"I'm not talking about the food." Zach winked and climbed out of the car.

Karen could only stare at him, unable to move. He'd had her laughing, and now he was causing her to feel something else entirely. Her skin prickled with awareness as he opened her door and held out his hand. He was so masculine, and he made her very aware of being a woman.

When she placed her palm to his, she felt a zing of energy travel through her. She could no longer deny it.

She was attracted to Zach. Very attracted.

"Hmm." Zach inhaled deeply. "There's nothing quite like the scent of frying burgers. Come, I promise you. A culinary delight awaits."

"How can a girl say no to that?"

She stood, but he didn't release his hold on her hand. His palm to hers felt hot as flame and far from comfortable. Not at all the way she expected. When Jay had held her hand, she'd felt...*lukewarm*.

Zach made her feel unsteady—how could that be? This was *Zach*. Her mechanic. Her friend. A fellow business owner.

"After you." He held the door for her.

When she slipped past him, the fine hair on her arms prickled.

He didn't appear to be affected by her as he ambled toward the red counter. A teenager approached and grabbed an order pad. Zach ordered, but his words sounded far away, and she couldn't make out what he was saying because her ears were ringing.

"Karen?" His hand lighted on her forearm, hot and scintillating, and the buzzing in her ears silenced. "What do you want? I recommend the cheeseburger. Nothing like it on this planet."

"That's an experience I'd better not miss."

"Good. I'm glad I'm with a woman who lives on the edge." He winked and ordered for her with the casual friendliness he'd always shown toward her.

When he withdrew his wallet from his back pocket, she stepped forward. "This is on Gramma."

"Forget it." Zach dropped a ten-dollar bill on the counter. "This is my treat. Your company is payment enough."

"My company?"

"Sure. I'm used to eating alone. Charm me with witty conversation and we'll call it even."

"You know I've never been witty in my entire life. I don't think it's a McKaslin family trait."

"Well, it only goes to show that you can't have everything. Status, beauty and brains will have to be enough."

"See what you're doing? One compliment after another. It's making me dizzy."

"Dizzy? I thought I was charming you."

"Nope. You're expelling too much hot air and contributing to the greenhouse effect."

He laughed, carrying a red plastic tray of food toward the condiment stand. He grabbed packets of ketchup and mustard. "Where do you want to sit?"

"In the corner, right in front of the air conditioner." She led the way, her skirt snapping above her knees and drawing his gaze.

Careful, Zach. It was hard to forget the way Karen's mom had glared at him as if she knew very well what he'd been thinking. And what he wanted when he looked at Karen.

He'd been foolish to hope for more than friendship. With or without another man's ring on her finger, Karen would never be interested in him, the Drake boy who'd gotten into trouble at twelve. Whose mother had spent her days and nights at the local bar, unable to hold a job or take care of her children.

His step faltered. What did he think he was doing? Following Karen McKaslin around and hoping she might suddenly look at him—really look at him—and see the man he'd become. Like that was going to happen.

She slid into the booth as graceful as always. "That's one thing Gramma's car doesn't have—an air conditioner. I'd vowed my very next car would have one. When I *could* afford a new car, that is."

"Just be glad Helen's car has a heater. That's a step up from that rusted-out heap in my lot."

"Speaking of my old car, what do you think I should do with it?"

Zach set the tray on the table and sat across from her. So, he was back to being her mechanic. If he needed any proof of how Karen saw him, this was it.

He tucked away the disappointment. Wanting her was a dream; he'd known it all along.

"Let's say I make you an offer on the car. I'll fix her and sell her to someone really desperate for a set of wheels."

"It's a deal." Karen grabbed an onion ring from the paper holder and bit into it. "Mmm. This is delicious. I'll never doubt you again."

"Glad to hear it. It's about time you acknowledge my wisdom."

"Yes, you have great onion ring knowledge."

"Face it, I'm gifted."

"You're certainly something. I'm not sure *gifted* is the word I'd use."

"Hey. Be kind to me. Beneath all this greatness hides a fragile ego."

Her laughter was a gentle trill that washed over him. Zach couldn't help the zing of satisfaction in his chest or the tug of attraction as she took a second bite of the golden ring. Her mouth was soft pink and bow shaped. A truly beautiful mouth.

He had no right noticing. No right wondering what her kiss would feel like.

"How did you find out about this place?" she asked, taking another onion ring.

"When my brother was an undergraduate, he had an

apartment not far from here. I'd stop by now and then and take him out to eat. I had to save him from his own cooking as much as I could."

"More like you were helping him stretch his food budget. You can't fool me."

"I imagine it's tough being a student. He worked nearly full-time with a full class load. My sister's doing the same."

"That brings back memories. Allison and I shared an apartment when we went to Montana State. Money was tight and we scraped by on what we both made working on campus, but those were good times I'll always remember."

"I took a few years of night classes at MSU," he said, slurping on his strawberry milkshake. "I took courses for the small-business owner from the extended learning center. They helped me figure out how to do my own books. I liked it so well, I made sure my brother and sister could get their four-year degrees."

Karen heard what Zach didn't say. How he'd struggled through high school as the sole support of his younger siblings, and that couldn't have been easy. She realized that he helped them still, giving his brother and sister advantages he hadn't taken for himself.

She saw a new side to Zach and it left her speechless. His wide shoulders really did look like they could carry a family's burdens. Beneath his teasing humor was a strong and responsible man. Respect for him glowed like a warm ember in her chest, steady and strong, and lingered long after the meal ended.

* * *

The sun shot fire across the jagged peaks of the Rockies rimming the horizon, and the clouds burned with crimson and purple. Zach figured it was one of the best afternoons he'd had, spent with Karen.

He'd been stealing looks at her out of the corner of his eye as she drove down the highway. Maybe that's why he didn't notice there was something wrong with the car.

He leaned out the window, hoping to get a better look. It was a bad feeling as much as it was a mechanic's skill that told him the tiny plume of steam rising from beneath the polished hood was a sign of doom.

"Karen? Take a look at your gauges for me."

"Why? Think I'm speeding?" she asked as they left the highway behind, driving through golden fields toward town. "Ha! I never speed."

"I wasn't worried about the speedometer—"

"Heavens!" She gasped. "The temperature needle is on 'H'. Oh, and now there's a little bit of smoke coming from the hood. I'll pull over."

"Good idea." He waited while she stopped the car on the shoulder of the two-lane road. He hopped out onto the sun-baked pavement as soon as they stopped moving.

Not good. Steam hissed with wild venom as he unlatched the hood.

"An expert mechanic, huh?" Karen padded into sight around the front fender. "Guaranteed not to break down. Isn't that what you said?"

"Yep. That's what I said."

"Hmm." She sidled up to him and stared down at the radiator cap. "I'm no expert, but that looks like a problem to me."

"It sure does. We'll have to hike it the rest of the way to town."

"Good thing we don't have far to go, because I'm going to look up the mechanic who works on this car. I intend to give him a piece of my mind."

"That mechanic of yours is obviously not at fault." He joined her on the road. "Even a meticulously maintained car can suddenly crack a radiator. Come to think of it, it was probably the driver's fault."

"My fault? I was driving the posted speed limit."

"See what I mean? You bored the car to death. It decided to spring a leak just for a little excitement."

"You're a bad man, blaming this all on me."

"Then let's blame your grandmother. She's been driving that car for the last forty years. She must have known what condition it was in. She gave you a lemon."

"Stop it. I'm laughing too hard to walk."

"We can take a break. Sit down here next to the thistles and you can catch your breath." He gestured at the nuisance weeds at the side of the road. "Face it, I know how to show a lady a good time."

"Well, I *have* been laughing a lot." How could that be? All her problems felt as if they'd floated away like dandelion fluff on the wind. There was no pressure on her chest, no worries weighing her down.

"Look." He gestured down the block where a

gleaming red car was parked beneath the diner's striped awning. "Helen's already showing off her convertible. I hope she's having a good time."

"Me, too." Karen recalled what her grandmother had said about how she wanted to be remembered. "I hope she's truly happy. Life is too precious to live the way everyone expects."

"Newfound wisdom after sending Jay packing?"

"Something like that." She stopped in the shade of the awning. "I can hitch a ride with Gramma or give one of my sisters a call."

"Then I guess it's goodbye."

He hated to admit it, but he couldn't keep Karen to himself any longer. One of her sisters, Kendra, was pushing through the screen door of the diner, calling out to her in excitement over the new convertible.

He backed away as she waved to him, the wind tangling sassy blond locks around her face, framing her beautiful face that made a man wish.

And keep wishing.

"What's with you and Zach?" Michelle asked as she pulled Karen by the arm into the diner. "You're with him in the morning, you go to church with him. And now it's nearly nighttime and where do I find you? Taking a walk with Mr. Tall, Dark and Handsome."

"Why are you looking at me like that? You know he only went to help Gramma negotiate a good price on her new car." Karen wasn't about to let Michelle know what a good time they'd had. "Zach and I were walking because the car broke down."

"No way. Zach's a great mechanic, and Gramma's car doesn't break down. Not in the history of the world as we know it. I think there's more to this." Michelle quirked one brow.

The last thing Karen wanted to talk about was Zachary Drake and her feelings for him—feelings that had become very confusing.

She spotted her grandmother in a nearby booth and walked over to her, figuring now was a good time to change the subject. "Gramma, how was the ride home?"

"Perfectly exciting. Why, I can't say the last time I had such a thrill. With the wind whistling in my ears and the world whizzing by at seventy miles an hour. I have to confess I had a hard time keeping to the speed limit."

"You lawbreaker." Karen knelt in the aisle next to the booth and said hello to her grandmother's friends. "Your eyes are sparkling. I'm glad you had a good time."

"And I'm taking Nora home in a bit. As soon as we finish our iced tea. And my dear Karen is following in my footsteps. Look how beautiful she is as a blonde. And only happiness can put that color in a girl's cheeks. Did you have a good time with Zach?"

Karen decided not to tell her grandmother about the damaged radiator. "I had a very good evening."

"Perfect. The new car was only one step of many I've been needing to take. Karen, I see a shopping trip in our future."

"Shopping for what?"

"Don't seem so surprised. My makeover isn't nearly

complete and neither is yours, although you're making good progress." Trouble sparkled in Gramma's eyes. "Michelle, I see you and Kirby are enjoying ice cream on a Sunday night."

"Yeah, Gramma. You know us McKaslins, wild girls to the core. C'mon, Karen, my sundae is melting."

"Thanks for the car, Gramma." Karen pressed a kiss to her grandmother's cheek and stood. "You keep out of trouble."

Gramma laughed, and it felt good to see her looking happy.

Michelle leaned close as they made their way down the aisle. "Confess. Is Zach the real reason you broke up with Jay?"

"Yeah, tell us, Karen," her sister Kirby asked from the nearby booth. "Is he the reason you colored your hair? Everyone is talking about it. Going to church with him and not with Jay. Did you really think anyone *wouldn't* notice?"

"There's nothing to notice," she alibied. "Now move over. That sundae looks pretty good."

Michelle grabbed a spoon from the counter and dropped it on the table. "Okay, now we're together, out with it. We want to know what's really going on."

"The truth is that you're just nosy."

"We're your sisters. We have the right."

"Yeah, we have to know which rumors to believe and which to ignore." Kirby nudged the ice cream dish closer so they could share. "Without a doubt, Zach's the most handsome man in this county. Are you going after him?"

"What? It's nothing like that. He's just…" Heat

warmed her face and she couldn't deny the attraction she felt. Thinking of him made her pulse race. "He's a *friend.*"

"And getting closer by the minute." Michelle waggled her brows.

"Don't tease her like that," Kirby admonished, waving her ice cream spoon in the air. "We don't want her to get stubborn and refuse to cooperate. C'mon, Karen. Tell the truth. You two look pretty cozy. He comes by your shop every morning."

"He's a customer, really."

"You're over at his garage quite a bit," Michelle accused. "Oh, and he likes to drive you home."

"When my car dies and leaves me stranded."

"Your car is dying quite a bit lately."

"But it's the truth!" Karen exclaimed.

Her sisters laughed too hard to be able to eat.

So did she. "All right, I give up. I admit it. Zachary Drake is the best-looking man in the entire state of Montana. Are you happy now?"

"I am," Zach answered as he laid the car key on the worn Formica table.

"Zach?" Karen saw his sneakers stop in the aisle next to her table. She didn't dare look up. He'd heard her say—

"I put some stuff in the radiator to seal the crack and parked it out front, but you'll need to bring it in one day so I can fix the problem."

"Great. Thanks." Karen choked on the words as she stared at the fascinating tabletop. Beside her, her sister was shaking with the effort to hold back laughter. "I'll give you a call."

"I'll be looking forward to it. Oh, and Karen, I think you're pretty good-looking, too."

Her sisters burst into howls as Zach walked away. She couldn't get mad at them, because she'd embarrassed herself. "Stop that. Michelle, you had to be able to see him, so you knew he was coming to our table."

"Guilty as charged, but how was I to know what you were going to say? I think he likes you, sis."

Both Kirby and Michelle nodded vigorously.

"I know what you guys are thinking, but I'm *not* looking for a replacement for Jay." Karen grabbed her spoon and dug into the chocolate-sauce-covered ice cream. "My heart has taken enough blows."

"Then Zach can be your rebound romance," Kirby offered sensibly, stealing the cherry from the top of the sundae.

"Yeah, he can help you get over Jay." Michelle seemed pleased with herself as she gestured toward the windows. "Look at him all alone, a man as gorgeous as that."

"He *is* gorgeous," Kirby agreed.

"I know." Karen stared through the dusty window, her heart tugging painfully at the sight of the man ambling across the street. "We're friends, that's all. We have a good time together."

"Still holding on to regrets with Jay?" Kirby asked.

"No regrets." Karen licked the chocolate topping off her spoon, holding back the truth. There were some things she couldn't tell anyone. She was plain and ordinary. She'd never done anything daring or exciting in her entire life, and she was tired of it.

Lukewarm. That's what Gramma had called it.

Karen couldn't give voice to the fear that she would always be seen as sensible, dependable Karen when her heart craved so much more.

"Look, it's Mr. Winkler." Michelle gulped down a mouthful of ice cream. "He's walking over to Gramma. Think he's impressed by her new car?"

Karen scrambled in the cramped booth for a view around the back of the tall seat.

Beside her, Kirby did the same. "Ooh, they're talking. I can almost hear them."

There was no way Mr. Winkler would see Gramma as lukewarm now. She looked so happy, glowing with life and beauty. She was going to charm the socks off of the poor man. Triumph jolted through Karen's chest as she watched Clyde Winkler greet Gramma with a polite nod.

"Nice to see you girls here," Clyde was saying, his low baritone was friendly. "Helen, why'd you go and change your hair like that for?"

"Why, because I felt like it, Clyde. Enjoy your evening." Gramma twisted away from him and she took a long drink from her iced tea, turning her back to the man in the aisle, who gave a shrug and walked away.

"Poor Gramma." Karen knew her grandmother had to be hurting.

"Way harsh." Michelle shook her head in apparent disbelief. "I mean, he didn't even compliment her. Dawn did such a fabulous job with her hair."

"Maybe it isn't about the hair," Kirby argued.

"Gramma's looked practically the same since I can remember. People get comfortable with who you are and expect to always see you that way."

Like reliable. Dependable. Karen peered around the booth to where her grandmother sat, nursing her iced tea and what had to be a wounded heart.

There was no doubt about it. Sometimes a woman wanted more.

Chapter Six

The rattle on the back door echoed through the morning-bright shop. Karen nearly dropped the nearly full frothing pitcher. She eased to the end of the counter and strained to look around the wall.

It's him.

On the other side of the glass door, Zach waved, looking twice as handsome as he'd been the last time she saw him, even in his plain T-shirt and jeans.

Be calm, she coached herself as she snapped the to-go lid on the cup of steaming coffee. Just pretend he didn't hear what you said about him last night. He knows we're just friends, right?

Her face felt a shade hotter as she hurried to the glass door, his gaze as bold as a touch. He leaned against the door frame, with the golden sunlight kissing his dark locks. Had a man ever looked this good?

As if he were perfectly aware of the impression he made, he shaded his eyes with one hand and winked when he spotted her. His eyes sparkled as if he was very glad to see her.

He apparently hadn't forgotten what she'd said—sure, it had been just last night, but was it too much to hope for momentary amnesia?

A strange sense of panic ripped through her, leaving her weak as she tugged open the door. Sweet hot wind breezed between them and, like a hug, pulled her close to him.

"Hey, you were expecting me." He gestured at the cup she held. "Either that, or you're hoping to get rid of me real quick."

"What? Get rid of my favorite customer?" She pushed the cup into his hands and tried to look innocent.

"Your favorite customer, huh? I like the sound of that."

"I meant my *best* customer."

"Sure you did. It's too late, and you can't fool me anymore." Trouble flashed in his eyes. "Mind if I come in? This'll only take a minute."

"I've got my bread delivery to sort—"

"You don't need bread until lunchtime. This can't wait." He pulled an envelope from his back pocket. "Payment for your old car. Got the title?"

"Not with me."

"You look like a trustworthy girl. You can get it to me later." He tossed the envelope onto the nearby table. "There's my best offer. Take it or leave it, although it's a darn good deal."

"I'm afraid to guess. If that old rust heap is worth twenty bucks, I'll be shocked."

"Twenty bucks? I should have negotiated. I bet I could've got the car for a steal. But no, I wanted to be fair." He winked at her.

He was far too sure of himself. And she knew why. "You do know the danger in overhearing other people's conversations, don't you?"

"Climbing cliffs, skydiving—now that's dangerous. But eavesdropping? Last night I was just an innocent guy walking through the café when I happened to hear what you were saying about me. A man's interest perks up when he hears a woman mention his name."

"That's the danger. You didn't listen to the *entire* conversation. My sisters were talking about how homely they thought you were, and I was trying to defend your honor."

"My honor needs defending?"

"Something like that. I was commenting on your looks in the most objective of terms."

"I see." He winked, as if he knew exactly what she was trying to do. As if he could see straight through her teasing to the truth beneath. "It's not like you think I'm handsome."

"Exactly."

"I don't think you're pretty, either." He struggled not to laugh.

This wasn't funny at all. Her attempt to set things right had backfired.

She grabbed the envelope and thumbed through the crisp bills inside. "There's more than a few hundred dollars in here."

"Blue book value."

"No way. This is too much money for an old car that doesn't run."

"A lie for a lie, gorgeous." He pressed a kiss to her cheek, a soft brush of heat across her skin.

Time froze and in the space between one breath and the next, Karen felt the tension knotted in her muscles melt away, leaving her warm and weak.

And aware. Much too aware. He smelled like late-summer sunshine, fresh air and Old Spice, and the day's growth on his jaw scraped against her skin. Every nerve ending felt enlivened.

Through the buzzing in her ears, Karen heard the distant ring of the phone and sound of footsteps as Zach moved away. The sweetness of his kiss remained as she stumbled to the counter and nearly dropped the receiver.

"Field of Beans Coffee Shop, how can I help you?" she said automatically into the mouthpiece, but the familiar words felt awkward on her tongue. Her entire being tingled.

"Karen, is Zach there?" The gravelly baritone of the local fire chief's voice boomed cross the line. "We've got a lost hiker and we need him."

Zach? "How did you know he was here?"

"I've got eyes just like everyone else in town. Tell him to grab his coffee and get his behind over here pronto." The line clicked.

Karen set her handheld phone on the counter.

Zach lifted one dark brow. "That was for me?"

"The fire chief says he needs you." Karen rubbed her forehead because a pain began jackknifing through her skull. "He knew you were here."

"I'm here every morning just about, rain or shine." Zach leaned across the counter and cupped her chin with his hand. His skin was rough and callused but felt more comforting than any touch she'd ever known.

"When Search and Rescue calls, I've got to go." Then he released her, ambling toward the door. "I'll be seeing you, gorgeous. You keep on thinking about how handsome you find me."

"I lied about that."

"You're too nice to do something awful like lie."

"Nice. Is that what you think of me?" It felt like a blow, maybe because that's how Jay had always complimented her. She tucked her disappointment deep inside so it wouldn't show. "Then maybe I'd better tell you the truth I've been hiding all along. You're a homely man, Zachary Drake."

A dimple cut into his cheek when he grinned. "That's not what you told your sisters. I'll see you tomorrow, so be prepared."

"That sounds like a warning. Or maybe a threat."

"Both." He tipped his Stetson and strode through the doors and out of sight.

Leaving behind the scent of Old Spice and the rapid beat of her heart.

I'm not falling for him, she vowed. Absolutely, positively not.

But the memory of Zach's kiss remained.

She let me kiss her. He still couldn't believe it. It was like something from a dream that could never be real. But it *was*.

Her cheek had felt as soft as new silk, and he'd inhaled the scent of her shampoo. Faint vanilla clung to him, proof of what had happened between them.

Nope, he still couldn't believe it. He'd kissed her, and she hadn't pulled away in shock. Hadn't slapped him, called him names or run for the hills.

In fact, she must have liked it. She had this little dazed look on her face, and then a small smile teased at the corner of her soft bow-shaped lips.

Watch it, Zach. He'd only get into trouble if he started thinking about her mouth, because he'd want to try kissing her there next.

He felt a slap on his shoulder, jostling him out of his thoughts.

"Zach, grab your climbing gear. We're here."

"Sure thing, Chief." He grabbed his backpack and hopped over the bed of the four-wheel drive. His feet hit the ground, reminding him of the missing hiker and the team of searchers needing his cooperation.

He had to concentrate and focus, but with the way Karen's vanilla scent clung to his skin, he couldn't forget her. Or how she tried to hide her true feelings this morning.

Karen McKaslin liked him—*really* liked him. Impossible, but true.

He grabbed his water canteen and jogged to catch up with the men.

"Something wrong?"

Karen jumped, and the money she held flew across the table. "Gramma. I didn't hear you."

"Left your back door unlocked." Her grandmother's step echoed in the empty coffee shop. "Saw the car in the lot and thought I'd come in and check on you, and I'm glad I did. You look tired."

"I had a busy day."

"It's more than that." Gramma pulled out a chair, settling down with a sigh. "That looks like a good day's earnings."

"It's from Zach. He bought my old car and paid way too much for it." Karen gathered up the crisp bills and folded them in half. She hadn't decided what she was going to do about his generosity, just as she hadn't figured out what to do about his kiss.

And that kiss was something Gramma wasn't going to know about, no matter how much she pried. "Did you race around in your new convertible today?"

"You're changing the subject, and because I tend to be nosy, I have to wonder why."

"Keep wondering, because I'm not telling you." Karen slipped Zach's money into her shirt pocket. "How's your makeover coming along?"

"There's still room for improvement. I can't keep raiding relative's closets forever. Mine is full of dresses I never really liked, but I bought them because they were sensible and on sale."

"When you wanted something else," Karen guessed. She knew what that was like. Hadn't she purchased her own shapeless purple T-shirt and denim shorts on sale two years ago?

"What I need is a good old-fashioned shopping spree. I heard an advertisement on my fancy new car radio, so I know the mall in Bozeman is having a back-to-school sale. I bet I can find a whole new wardrobe in a place like that."

"The chances are good, but you should take Michelle with you. She's the fashion guru of the family. I don't think the rest of us have ever opened a fashion magazine."

"I have a different assignment for Michelle, so don't you worry about her. And besides, my dear, there is nothing wrong with your fashion sense. I do have the best-looking granddaughters in the county, hands down. Everyone at the Ladies' Aid agrees."

"You aren't going to mention marriage and grand-babies again, are you?"

"Heavens, no! That will come in time, I have no doubt about it."

"Probably not for me." Karen stared through the windows at the quiet, dusty street spread out before her.

She'd grown up in this tiny town, and not one thing she'd ever imagined for her life had come true. She'd always figured she'd be married by now, keeping house, raising children and being a wife. She'd always pictured her husband to be kind. Someone who made her laugh. Someone who returned her love.

Maybe all it had ever been was a dream.

Remembering how Clyde had treated Gramma at the diner and of Gramma's confession about her marriage made Karen sad. Was romantic love a fantasy and nothing more?

Or, maybe, true love didn't happen to women like her.

Karen knew she wasn't particularly pretty or exciting. If she needed proof of that, she had it—she'd won the citizenship award in school every year since the sixth grade. And now, over ten years later, she was still a play-by-the-rules kind of girl who could never inspire a deep, powerful love in a man.

That's what she wanted—a true, abiding love. Not a comfortable sort of marriage without warmth or passion, but the kind of relationship that dreams were made of. And her heart desired.

Gramma's hands covered hers, warm and comforting. "Why does my granddaughter look so troubled?"

"When Zach was over this morning for his cup of coffee, he said I was a 'nice' girl. But I know what he meant—reliable. Dependable. *Lukewarm.*"

"It's hard for stellar women like us to be labeled that way. That's why I'm making over my life. We're stuck in a rut, you and me."

"A big long rut I'll never get out of. It's not like I want to take up bad habits and break laws."

"I know. You just want to find your heart. So do I. That's why I think you and I ought to have a little fun at the mall. We'll shop until we drop, just like the advertisement promised."

"I'd love to, but I can't spare the funds right now. And, no—you're not buying me anything. You've done too much for me as it is. Besides, I can't afford to take any time off. It affects sales and I've got that big nasty balloon payment coming up."

"That's right. I've been thinking about that, too."

"*No.* You're not helping me, so forget it. This is my

business and my problem. Keep your money in your checkbook where it belongs."

Gramma turned thoughtful. "Running a business by yourself isn't easy. In the beginning, you had Allison to take over and give you a break, as you could do for her. Now you're alone without backup. I have the perfect solution. Do you know what you need? Hired help."

"I'm doing fine on my own."

Trouble flickered in Gramma's eyes, as if she'd planned this all along. "Your littlest sister could use a second job. Michelle's position over at the Snip & Style is on appointment only, and isn't full-time yet. Considering how she's been a tad irresponsible with her credit cards, she could use some extra income."

"I'd love to pay her, but I can't dip into my savings to do it."

"Why don't you offer her the job, and maybe things will work out? The Good Lord provides, you know, and He does command us to honor our elders. As I see it, that means you have to come shopping with me."

"You do? That's manipulative and you know it."

"Yes, but you did promise to help me, and there's a coffee shop in the mall. We could stop by and see what the competition is up to."

"I like the way you think, Gramma."

"Then that's one thing settled. You still haven't told me about you and Zachary Drake."

"We're just friends and you know it." Or was he? A *friend* didn't make a woman's pulse race or cause her to think about him when he wasn't in the room.

"Zach's easy on the eyes, I'll grant you that." Gramma winked. "He was such a help with my car purchase. Getting the price so low, I don't know how he did it! Why, he's a gem, and I need to find a way to repay him."

"I'm sure he isn't expecting anything."

"A thank-you gesture is always in good style, expected or not. You know him better than I do. What does he like?"

"I don't know him that well. He fishes. He rides his motorcycle. He likes bologna on white with mustard."

"He's a bachelor. There has to be something I can do for him."

"You could cook for him." The idea came to her like a whisper on the wind. "The night my old car died, he was chiseling frozen hot dogs out of his freezer when I called. So I fed him our supper leftovers, and he confessed he eats frozen dinners."

"Those things from the grocery store? You mean to tell me the poor man can't cook at all?"

"I owe him a big favor, too, so maybe the two of us could spend time in the kitchen and make him a bunch of homemade frozen dinners."

"Perfect." Gramma clapped her hands together. "Oh, he did seem to love my taco cheese and macaroni casserole. Let's do it the first chance we get. That's something he might appreciate."

"You're on. Right now I've got to make the deposit. Want to go with me?"

"We'll take my car." Gramma stole the bank bag from the counter and headed for the door.

That was one problem solved. Karen grabbed her keys. As her fingers closed around the cool metal, she realized this was the exact spot she'd been standing in when he'd kissed her this morning.

It's not like it was a real kiss. Just a brush of his lips to her cheek. A friendly gesture, that was all.

So why had she thought about it through every moment of the day? Or remembered how solid and masculine he'd seemed when he'd stood so close to her?

I'm not falling for him, she ordered herself. She'd never love another man—no matter how good—who wanted nice and dependable.

"You did a fine job today, Zach." Chief Corey halted his truck in the middle of town. "We're lucky to have a climber as skilled as you on our team."

"You were the one who gave the young man medical treatment, not me." Zach grabbed his gear from the pickup's bed. "Bring this piece of junk by sometime tomorrow and I'll fix that misfire. Sounds terrible."

"Yeah, but it makes all the pretty women look at me."

"With disgust."

"We can't all be as lucky as you, dating Karen McKaslin. She looks downright beautiful with her new hairdo."

"John, I don't think you ought to be noticing Karen's beauty. You just leave that to me. I'll do a good job of it."

The chief pulled away, chuckling. Zach slung his pack over his shoulder and headed up the sidewalk. Exhaustion hung on him like a hundred-pound weight, and the sun's heat baking him clear through to the bones didn't help much.

What he needed was a root beer. Frothy and fizzing and so icy it would make a cold trail down his throat.

Too bad he didn't have one in his empty refrigerator.

Zach tossed his pack on the ground and fished through a zippered compartment for his shop keys. Maybe he'd run down to the grocery and pick up a six-pack of root beer and maybe a frozen pizza. He might as well splurge after spending most of the day hiking in ninety-degree temperatures and half the afternoon scaling a tricky canyon wall.

A horn blared. He looked up to see a sporty red convertible with tiny Helen behind the wheel and Karen in the passenger seat.

At the sight of her, he forgot every discomfort. Her golden locks were tangled from the drive with the top down and framed her heart-shaped face. The grape shirt she wore clung to her softly, emphasizing her small frame. The color made her eyes so blue that her beauty astounded him.

How was it that she became more stunning every time he looked at her?

"Howdy, gorgeous." He left his gear on the concrete and ambled over to the street. "I can't believe my eyes. Two lovely women parked in front of my shop. It's good for business."

"You're filthy." Karen shook her head at him in mock disapproval. "Looks like you've been up to no good."

"Like always."

"I heard at the bank that you played hero and rescued a poor stranded tourist who found himself stuck on a cliff."

"He learned scaling a canyon wall is harder than it looks, even if you can afford the equipment. His wife's indebted to me for saving her husband's life and completely adores me. At least *she* has good judgment."

That made Karen laugh. She lit up like a Montana sunset—all quiet beauty that a man never got tired of looking at.

"Get out if you two are going to talk," Helen complained, glancing at the rearview mirror. "I don't want to create a traffic jam because you two are carrying on a love affair right here in the middle of the street."

"We're not carrying on, Gramma."

"Yes, we are." Zach opened the passenger door and held it.

Karen frowned at him as if she were angry, but she couldn't fool him—her eyes were sparkling. Was she remembering that kiss he'd dared to give her? He hadn't been able to think of much else all day.

"See you two kids later." Helen waved as she drove off.

He was alone with Karen. Just the two of them.

Now this was a nice turn of events.

"I've got something for you." Karen reached into her back pocket and withdrew a folded document. "The promised title, signed and everything."

"You were trustworthy after all."

"You say that as if you worried."

"It was a gamble." He could stand here looking at Karen all evening, but he took the title she offered him and led the way up the driveway. "That's the only reason you came over. To give me the title?"

"I really want to argue with you about the money you paid me."

"It's my policy never to renegotiate a price after a deal's been made."

"How did I know you were going to say that?"

"Argue all you want. It won't do a bit of good." He grabbed his keys and slung his pack over his shoulder. "Want to come up? But I have to warn you the air-conditioning only works when it feels like it."

"Can't you fix it?"

"That would be too easy." He led the way up the stairs at the side of the garage. "Have any more trouble with that radiator?"

"No. I noticed you didn't bill me for delivering it to me at the café."

"You didn't charge me for my coffee this morning. We're even, so forget it." He unlocked the door and reached inside to flick on the light. "It's humble, but it's home."

She brushed past him, all sweetness and woman. "I'm speechless. Do you ever dust?"

"Me? Dust? It's a waste of time. It just falls right back on the TV anyway." He tried the air-conditioning and the unit surprised him by coughing to life.

"You don't cook. You don't dust." Karen shook her

head as she paced the length of his small living room. She stopped by the desk in the corner where his computer sat dark and silent. She ran her fingertips over the frames on the wall above it. "Special awards from the governor for your work on Search and Rescue. How come I didn't know about these?"

"You've never been in my apartment before, and I'm too modest to brag."

"You saved people's lives before this, just like you did today."

"The hiker overestimated his abilities, that's all. And besides, I don't work alone. I'm only part of a team."

She frowned as if she didn't believe him, but at least she changed the subject. "This is something I should do. There's attic space above my shop. Maybe I could convert it into an apartment."

"You live with your parents?"

"Not in their house. In the apartment over the garage. It isn't much. Dad always rented it to his foreman, but he hires seasonally now. I talked them into staying there when my mother became ill. It was easier than driving to and from town at night."

"Your family means a lot to you." Zach flicked on the air-conditioning unit in the kitchen window. "How's your mom doing?"

"A little better, although she's pretty unhappy there isn't going to be a wedding. I've disappointed her, she says. I know she was counting on it to lift her spirits."

"So, find another brilliant, handsome and irresistible man and marry him instead." Or me, he added silently. He snared two cups from the shelf and filled them with tap water.

He dropped ice cube chunks iced together into the cups. It was the best he could do under the circumstances. And it was a shame, too, because this was not going to impress her.

"Getting married is the last thing I want to do."

"You don't want to get married? I thought that's what all women wanted." Zach said it casually, crossing the room to hand her a drink.

"Water in a cartoon cup?"

"That's class. You don't get this kind of service just anywhere." Zach shoved grease-smeared truck magazines off the coffee table. "You never told me why you're running around single."

"No, and I don't plan to."

"It's top secret. Is that it?"

"Highly confidential. I could be hauled before a grand jury if I revealed what I know." Karen sipped the water, leaning back on the couch. She was long and lean and looked mighty pretty in his living room. "Do you ever get tired of living alone?"

"Yeah, and every single woman who comes along starts looking mighty attractive. It's tempting to give up my wild ways and settle down, but then how could I move out of this place?"

"You can't fool me. It gets lonely being single."

"It does."

She stared into her cup, unhappiness apparent on her face. "I just don't want to settle."

"Neither do I."

Now he knew what was wrong and what she wanted. He didn't know all that had made her gun-shy about marriage, and maybe it wasn't his business, but he could see how vulnerable she seemed, small on his big bulky secondhand couch.

And so fine. Like rare porcelain, so dainty and fragile. And probably far out of his class—there was no doubt about that. But at least now he had a chance. She liked him, he could tell by the way she smiled.

"What am I going to do with you?" she asked. "We really need to talk about what happened this morning."

"When I ran out without paying for my coffee?"

"That's not what I mean and you know it." A blush stole across her face. "You kissed me."

"No, I thought you kissed *me*."

"Zach!" He was incorrigible, teasing her! "Don't get me wrong. It was very nice, but—"

"You're afraid I'm too handsome for you to resist?"

"I'm not the one who has problems with restraint. You kissed me, remember?"

"Think I might do it again? Or are you afraid you might want me to?"

"You are a bad man. You know that's not what I mean." She set down her cup and stood, marching to the door. "I just want to check and make sure. That was just a *friendly* kiss you gave me, right?"

"Absolutely. That was a one-hundred-percent-friend kiss."

He opened the door for her, so close she could see the rise and fall of his wide chest as he breathed. "We're friends, just like you say."

"Good." At least that was settled.

She stepped into the sunshine and heat, feeling a strange disappointment at leaving him. It was a feeling she couldn't explain.

She didn't want more than friendship. She'd just failed at a romance. The last thing she needed was to fail again because the man she liked thought she was a certain type of person.

"There's just one more thing." She forced her gaze to his. "I'm not nice. Don't ever insult me by saying that again."

He grinned slow and saucy. "I'll try to remember that, you wild, untamed woman."

"That's more like it. I live on the edge and don't you forget it."

"I'll try, *friend*."

She didn't know why the sound of his laughter warmed her clear through to her soul, like comfort and peace and coming home.

Friends. That's what they were, and getting closer with every day.

She took the steps two at a time, wondering if that's what the Lord was trying to tell her. That it was time to make some changes, have a little fun and enjoy this life she'd been given.

Chapter Seven

"I can handle making iced lattes for a few hours, so chill." Michelle looked in command behind the counter that Karen had just finished cleaning. "I've done this before."

"Yeah, but now I'm paying you, so be good, little sister." Karen grabbed her keys, slung her purse strap over her shoulder and headed out the back door.

Freedom. The sun felt sweeter, the breeze gentler as she sauntered along the wooden walk. Her baskets of sweet peas waved as she passed, their scent as welcome as this stolen time.

Gramma was right. Taking some time to herself was a great idea. She felt lighter, freer, as she approached her reliable car, gleaming in the sunshine.

The engine started with a single turn of the key. She loved having a dependable vehicle—except for the small crack in the radiator, which wasn't causing any problems. With the windows rolled down, she cranked up the Christian music station and let the wind blow through her hair as she drove.

She couldn't help noticing that the wide doors to Zach's garage were locked up tight. The memory of his kiss brushed across her cheek, and she felt… No! She wasn't going to feel anything. That was a friendly kiss, and he'd gone to the trouble to assure her of it. He wouldn't mislead her, would he?

Of course not. He'd stood with all the integrity in the world and told her he saw her as a friend. Without blinking or flinching.

So what was the problem? *She* was beginning to feel something more than friendship toward him.

That was definitely the problem.

Troubled, she sang along with the radio as she drove home. The harvested fields stretched out on either side of the road, golden brown and endless. She saw a tall column of dust on the crest of a nearby rolling hill and spotted Dad's tractor, turning soil. She honked and saw him wave his hat in return.

By the time she'd pulled into the shade of the garage, she wasn't feeling calm at all. Muscles knotted along the back of her neck and deep in her shoulders. She might as well have stayed at work!

Just stop thinking about Zach. That was all.

Resolved, she climbed the stairs to her cozy apartment over the garage. When she opened the door, sweltering heat met her and she opened the windows wide. What she needed was an air-conditioning unit, like the ones Zach had.

Okay, she *couldn't* stop thinking about him. What

she needed to do was to distract herself completely. Forget Zachary Drake. But how?

In her bedroom, she changed into a pair of jeans and pulled on her riding boots. After tying her hair back, she found her Stetson. On the way out the door, she grabbed a handful of peppermint candies and stuffed them into her front pockets.

I wonder where Zach is? she thought, then shook her head. Enough, already. This was her afternoon off and she was going to enjoy it.

She strolled down the path from the garage to the stable without thinking of Zach. See, it was possible. Surely she could get through the rest of the day without thinking of him.

Star nickered in greeting, trotting up to the rail fence, her coat gleaming like polished copper. Her platinum mane caught the wind as she sidestepped, eager for company.

"Hey, girl." Karen grabbed the bridle from the rung just inside the stable door, then climbed through the fence. "How about a wild ride, just the two of us?"

Star swung her head, as if in agreement, and tugged at Karen's clothes.

"Found the peppermint, did you?" She unwrapped two candies and laid one on her palm. Star lipped up the mint.

Karen popped the other in her mouth. It took only a minute to secure the bridle and hop onto Star's back. She gathered the reins and urged the horse into an easy lope through the golden fields.

Larks argued in the cottonwoods as Karen and Star

headed for the river. There was nothing like this—just her and her horse, the friendly companionship, the rock of Star's gait and the heat of her coat.

Karen felt the tension melt away from her neck and shoulders. Soon the river came into view and the sight took her breath away. Sunlight sparkled in the lazy waters, and a frog leaped from the shore and out of sight.

Star tugged at the bit, eager to be off, and as she always did, Karen gave the mare her head. The horse leaped into a smooth gallop, stretching full out on the public trail that paralleled the river. There was no one around, so Karen leaned low over Star's neck, urging her faster.

It was like flying without sound, rising and falling, and feeling the strength and life of the animal beneath her. She was right—this was just the thing to forget all her troubles. See how she wasn't thinking of Zach?

There she was, doing it again. Okay, so he was handsome, kind, funny, generous and he made her *feel*. That didn't mean it was a good idea—

She saw a blur of movement careen around a corner in the trail and Star sidestepped, whinnying in fear. The blur became a flashy mountain bike and rider moving fast. She felt the mare tense as if readying to rear, but she was off balance and started to slip.

"Whoa, girl," she soothed, tightening the reins, hoping to draw the mare's head down.

Star's nose dropped to the ground, and Karen kept her seat.

"Hey, sorry about that. I didn't mean to startle your horse." The rider skidded to a stop. Brakes squealed and dust plumed in the air.

Up Star went into a full rear, pawing the air with a panicked neigh. In the back of Karen's mind, she recognized that man's voice, but her legs were sliding out from under her. The ground looked pretty hard. Falling off wouldn't be the best experience.

Clamping her thighs harder around the mare's sides didn't stop Karen from slipping. Her hat tumbled off her head, so she dismounted swiftly, shortening the reins as she went.

Star dropped to the ground, still frightened.

Soothing the mare with her voice, Karen ran her hand up the horse's neck, calming her. "I hope you're happy, you irresponsible—"

"Karen, are you okay?" Zach dropped his bike and raced to her side.

Star sidestepped, whinnying in protest.

"Zach? What were you doing speeding?"

"I wasn't speeding." He grabbed her by the arm. "When I saw your horse rear like that, I had visions of you falling and breaking your neck. Are you really all right?"

"No, I'm not all right." She jerked away from his touch. "You were going too fast and someone could have gotten hurt. What if it had been one of the little girls who ride their ponies on this trail? They might not have known how to handle a frightened pony and—"

"Karen." He cupped the side of her face with his hand. "I wasn't going that fast. I ride fast when I'm on the road, but not on a public trail. Your horse and I startled each other."

"But you just came around the corner so fast!"

"Maybe you weren't paying attention." He drew her into his arms. "Feel that. I was so scared for you, I'm still shaking."

"*You?* Scared?" she quipped. "I don't believe it, a tough guy like you."

"Not so tough. See?" He pulled her all the way against his chest.

Her spine stiffened. The last thing she wanted to be was this close to Zach. Safe and protected in his arms, with the side of her face pressed against his solid chest, she could hear his heartbeat thunder.

His hand curled around the back of her neck, under her hair, holding her tenderly. "I don't see why you want to ride something that can buck you off."

"I love my horse."

"I love my bike." His words vibrated through her, so intimately, it left her breathless.

She desperately searched for a quick comeback to make him laugh, to make them both laugh so she could step out of his arms and everything would be as it was. They would be friends, *just* friends.

She couldn't think of a single quip. Handsome, came to mind. Amazing and wonderful. But her heart broke a little, and she couldn't begin to tell him what she truly felt.

His hand cupping her jaw grew hotter, his touch more tender. This was Zach, she reminded herself. Her mechanic and friend. She'd known him since kindergarten.

Well, she hadn't really known him at all. Maybe she'd

never looked hard enough or noticed the man he'd become.

She noticed now. His chest felt like sun-warmed steel beneath her palm. Her heart began to tumble as he leaned forward slowly, deliberately.

This was going to be a real kiss, lip to lip, the kind that could never be mistaken for a *friendly* kiss. The kind that would mean they were more than friends. The type of kiss a man gave a woman.

Zach's mouth hovered over hers, a brush of heat she wanted to welcome. But how could she? She wasn't ready, so she backed away from the warm haven of his arms.

A crooked smile curved across his lips, but it was the disappointment she saw in his gaze that troubled her. She'd hurt him when she hadn't meant to. She'd only been protecting her heart.

"I know my charm can be overwhelming," he quipped as he rescued his fallen mountain bike. "You'll get used to it."

"You think you're charming, do you?" She grabbed Star's reins from the grass at the side of the trail, where the mare was grazing. "*Charming* isn't the word I'd use."

"Dashing? Captivating?"

"Now you're getting closer." She mounted her horse. "Too bad it's all in your imagination."

"Really? Then why'd you let me almost kiss you? You wanted it. I could tell."

"You have to practice on somebody. Since you seem deficient when it comes to certain social situations, I was only trying to help you out."

"That's downright neighborly of you, Karen."

"That's me. Neighborly to the core." She gazed down at him, the wind tangling the golden strands worked loose from her ponytail.

A pleasant pink flushed her cheeks, and even though she'd stepped away from him, she wasn't mad. The way Zach figured it, she'd wanted that kiss. Judging by the way that her eyes were sparkling, he'd have another chance.

She needed time, and he could give her that. He'd give her anything, truth be told, if only he could have the right one day to make her his.

Marriage was serious business and the thought of it shot a cold chill down his spine, but he wasn't afraid. Well, not *too* afraid.

He'd loved Karen most of his life. God willing, it would be an honor to love her for the rest of his days.

He spied her Stetson in the wild grasses and retrieved it. "Forget something?"

"Thanks."

She swiped it out of his grip so fast, she seemed nervous. Or unnerved. Good. Let her wonder what that kiss would have been like. Because he already knew. Kissing Karen would be like coming home. Like finding the missing piece of his heart.

He mounted his bike. "Where are you headed?"

"To town. Star and I used to always ride to get ice cream, but we haven't done it so much lately." Karen tipped her hat, trying to avoid his gaze.

"Don't tell me your horse eats ice cream."

"She loves butterscotch sundaes as much as I do."

Something changed in the way Karen looked at him, as if she were seeing the man he was and not just the friend he'd been. He liked that. "I have a soft spot for double chocolate fudge cones."

"I don't suppose a tough cyclist like you would want to come along with us."

"My bike scares your horse."

"Not if you ride *slowly*." She laid the reins against her mare's neck, turning the animal on the trail. "Is that a yes?"

"Just promise you won't fall off that animal and break your neck. Horses make me nervous."

"Oh, this from a man who rides a *motorcycle*."

Maybe it was the way she rolled her eyes or the drop of warmth in her voice, but his heart opened wide.

Dust rose on the late-afternoon breezes as they rode side by side through town. Karen noticed several people looking at them. A few cars and pickups passed by, waving a hello.

"You left Michelle alone in the coffee shop?" Zach asked, chuckling warm and deep. "You're joking, right?"

"No joke." Karen felt warm all over from listening to his laugh. He had such a *great* laugh. "I was feeling brave."

"The sister who turned your hair green."

"The very one. It was Gramma's idea, and I hate to admit it, but she's right. A few afternoons off a week is what I need."

"And you trust Michelle not to burn the place down while you're gone?"

"I know where she lives. Just in case."

A few shoppers peered through the glass front window of the combination gift and flower shop to stare at them. Every one of the customers wore a look of surprise *and* speculation.

Like it's their business, Karen told herself. The problem with a small town was that there wasn't enough traffic jams to distract people from noticing every little thing a person did.

Just because she was riding down the street with Zachary Drake *did not mean anything.*

Well, that wasn't true. They were friends. Good friends. Friends close enough to share a friendly kiss now and maybe more. She'd had fun this afternoon listening to him laugh. He had a great laugh. Oh, right, she'd already noticed that.

It wasn't like she was falling for him.

Please, Lord, don't let me fall for him.

"Wow. Busy place." Zach skidded his bike to a stop in the loose gravel. "Don't tell me you're going to ride up to the window. There are little kids waiting in line there. What about your horse?"

"Trust me. Star and I might be out of practice, but we've been coming here together since I was eight."

"I remember." Zach nodded toward a little girl and her pony getting an ice cream cone at the outside window of the little shop. "You and your sister were like that, always together and almost always with your horses."

"Like half the little girls in this town." Karen nosed Star toward the end of the line behind two boys with fancy bikes and money clutched in their fists.

"Hi, Zach," Tommy Clemmins, one of the boys, called out. "Where were ya? We came by to get air in my back tire."

"I was out on the trail. Looks like you guys are going to get some ice cream, too."

"Yeah." Both kids gazed up at him, eyes bright. "You gonna be at the garage later?"

"Only for my friends." He winked at them. "After I'm done with my cone, I'll head over and unlock the doors, okay?"

"That'd be great, Zach. Karen, can we pet your horse? Does she bite?"

"No. She likes her nose rubbed."

The boys turned their attention to the mare, who liked children and noticed right away they had candy in their pockets.

"See what a great guy I am?" Zach whispered in Karen's ear. "Even kids like me."

"Because you have the only air pump in town." She swung her leg over Star's rump, starting to dismount.

His fingers closed around her forearms, stopping her. His touch was both gentle and steadfast, and it rocked her to the core.

"Let me help you. It's a long way down and I wouldn't want you to fall."

"I've been riding since I was four. I think I can dismount all by myself."

"Humor me. I had that scare today, imagining you crashing to the ground, breaking bones. I'd feel safer if I lifted you down."

"Zach, I don't think—"

"Look at this loose gravel. It would really hurt if you fell. Lacerate your knees. Cut up your pretty hands." Trouble flashed in his eyes.

"I'm not going to fall."

"Let's be safe rather than sorry." His grip tightened.

She slid off the mare's back and into his arms as if she belonged there. As if she always would.

Just friends, she vowed. Friendly was all she wanted to feel for him.

But this was more. Much more.

Time froze, the world faded away and she was suspended in the air, held safe by Zach's strength. Awareness tingled through her like a buzz from an electric current. A jolt of realization surged through her so strong, it could have been lightning from the sky.

Zach's eyes darkened and his gaze focused on her mouth. He lowered her to the ground, but she couldn't feel the solid earth beneath her feet, or the sun on her back or the wind in her hair. All she knew was that Zach was holding her, his rock-solid hands banding her arms, his steady gaze holding hers.

Her heart raced, her stomach tumbled and she couldn't breathe.

Zach motioned toward the little window where the two boys were collecting their double cones. "We're next."

"Hi, Karen. Zach." The waitress behind the window smiled and lifted one brow. "Good to see you two together. What can I get you?"

"I'd like a double chocolate cone dip." Zach leaned on the window's ledge. "Karen?"

He appeared as if everything were normal, as if nothing had changed, as if he had no idea what she was feeling.

Karen cleared her throat, managing to speak. She got her order right—at least she thought she did—and reached into her pocket. Zach had already paid. Before she could say anything more, he was handing her a butterscotch sundae with two red plastic spoons.

"There's shade over there." Zach pushed his bike to where a stand of trees shaded a few tables and benches in a patch of mown grass. He gestured toward a lonely table. "How about here?"

She nodded, and he leaned his bike against a tree trunk. Keeping hold of Star's reins, she sat on the wooden table, propping her feet on the dusty bench. Star sidled close. Cradling her bowl of ice cream, Karen watched Zach out of the corner of her eye. Furtively, as if she were afraid to look at him directly.

I *am* falling for him. The realization boomed through the stormy confusion of her mind.

A place deep in her heart warmed when he settled on the table beside her, his elbow nudging hers.

Karen thought about inching away so their arms weren't touching but stayed right where she was. Being this close to him was nice. Comforting. He was steel-strong and she liked it. She didn't want to, but she did.

"Two spoons?" he asked, friendly as always.

"One for me, one for Star."

"You really feed your horse ice cream?" He watched, shaking his head, as the mare neatly lipped the treat from the plastic spoon Karen held out.

"Star and I used to do everything together when I was little. It was a sweet time, riding to town for ice cream and candy, exploring trails in the foothills, playing in the river. You're a boy so you probably don't understand a little girl's love for her horse."

"I had a bike. I loved my bike." How he was teasing her!

"That's not the same." Star nudged Karen's cheek with affection, and she rubbed the mare's nose. "Little girls grow up and don't have all the time in the world to ride through the fields with their best friend or share a sundae."

"Grown-up girls *could* make time for their horses."

"I try, but it isn't easy. It's sad when I see her in the pasture every morning, watching me leave for work. I'd always figured I'd be married and have kids by now—a little girl who would take over feeding Star ice cream and racing her through the fields."

"You dated Jay a long time. Why did you wait so long for him to propose? A lot of girls I know have a time line. After a year of dating, they want to see a diamond ring sparkling on their finger."

"Maybe I wasn't so sure about the man. Or what I deserved." Karen dipped Star's spoon into the ice cream. "That hurt to admit."

"I guess. Maybe the real question is, how could Jay deserve you? Or how could I, for that matter. You're a really nice person, Karen. I'm surprised half the guys in the county aren't trying to knock me over and take my place sitting right here beside you."

"Nice. I thought I told you not to use that word. Maybe I'm not nice."

"What do you mean? You're one of the nicest women in town."

"That's not a compliment. Nice means dependable. Reliable. Boring. It means the kind of woman a man settles for."

"The secret of Jay is revealed." Zach's gaze narrowed as he munched on his cone. "That's why you called off the wedding."

Pain knotted in her chest and she dipped her spoon into the gooey ice cream.

"He's a fool, if you ask me. Anyone with eyes can see that you're no woman to settle for." Zach leaned closer and slipped his arm around her back, strong and comforting and more wonderful than she could ever dream. "A man doesn't settle for a woman like you. He gets lucky. Very lucky."

"You're trying to charm me and it isn't working."

"Fine, then. You're not nice. You're the meanest person I've ever met." He tried to tease and failed.

Memories of how he'd almost kissed her on the lips flashed through her mind. He was so close, she could feel the rise and fall of his chest. See the flicker of want in his gaze.

Her mouth tingled. She wondered—just for a second—what it would feel like to be kissed by him. Would she know the instant their lips met, if he was the one she'd been wishing for? A man who could love her truly?

"Hey, Zach!" Little Tommy Clemmins shouted

across the gravel lot. "Are you goin' to the garage now?"

"I guess I *am* done with my ice cream." Zach flashed her an apologetic grin, as if he were perfectly aware of how attracted she was to him. "Why don't you stay here in the shade, Karen? I'll be right back."

"Think I'll wait around for you, huh?"

"Yeah, I do." Far too sure of himself, he hopped off the table and grabbed his bike, running. In one smooth movement he swung onto the seat, pedaling easily, to catch up with the boys.

Karen watched, mesmerized, unable to look away.

They rode three abreast between the curb and the road, the rise and fall of their voices fading. They pulled into the shop's lot, the boys dragging their bikes up to the door.

Zach dug through his pocket and searched through his key ring. He looked up. Across the half a block where dust eddied along the paved road, their gazes met. There was no mistaking his grin or the pull of attraction that zinged between them.

Okay, maybe I'd like falling for him. And in a big way.

But this was *Zach*. She'd known him since kindergarten, the quiet boy with the secondhand clothes and the saddest eyes she'd ever seen. Zach from high school, a little rugged, a little tough, who kept to himself and held two jobs throughout his high school years. Zach from the garage who'd bought a cup of coffee from her shop nearly every morning for the last four years.

How could a man she'd known forever suddenly seem so different? As if she'd finally met the real Zach?

"C'mon, girl." Karen let Star lick the plastic bowl clean and then she mounted up.

She nosed the mare through the parking lot toward the garage. Her pulse kicked up a faster rhythm as she approached Zach's shop.

There he was, kneeling down beside the air pump between the two little boys. He filled one tire in seconds. The kids clamored to their feet, swinging onto their bikes. Zach listened as the boys told of their latest adventure and what they were up to next.

Karen stopped Star on the sidewalk, seeing in Zach what she never had before. Forget his childhood, his vocation and even his motorcycle parked at the back of the shop.

Zachary Drake was pure kindness. He laughed with the boys and then wished them luck when they raced off.

He liked children, and he was kind to old women. He was a *good* man, heart and soul.

Just like Jay was.

And look how that turned out.

The peaceful glow she felt began to fade. Disappointment filled her, heavy like twilight.

"Hey, Karen." Zach strolled out of the building's shade. "Have any plans for tonight?"

"Gramma's taking me to Bozeman. We're going shopping at the mall."

"Definitely female territory."

"Yep, hazardous for any man." The distance between them felt so wide, and she knew the rift was in her heart.

Moments ago they'd been side by side, touching, nearly kissing. And now the sidewalk might as well be the Grand Canyon.

She kept seeing how he'd treated the boys, easygoing and kind, his eyes gleaming with a quiet hunger.

He wanted to be a father, she realized.

And the truth was, she wanted a family of her own, too. And a man to love her—*truly* love her. To hold her close, to make her laugh, to walk down the road of life at her side. Always at her side.

She had to wonder—could Zachary Drake be that man?

Chapter Eight

"Gramma, look." Karen spotted a tasteful knit shorts set hanging on the circular rack and pulled it from the display. "This would look perfect on you. What do you think?"

Gramma turned from the opposite rack. "That shade of aqua does suit me."

"You'll be beautiful in it. Want me to add it to the stack in our dressing room? I was about to make a trip anyway."

"I'll come with you. I think I'll grab me a pair of denims on the way. My, this is fun. I always hate shopping, but then, I've never bought so much in one place. Goodness, I know I ought to feel guilty, but maybe I'll take a second pair."

"Go for it." Karen took two pairs of denims from the shelf near the dressing room. "A woman deserves to treat herself now and then."

Her grandmother tugged open the wooden slatted door and led the way into the tiny mirrored room.

Voices rose over the top of the dressing room partitions, and the frustrated voices of teenager and mother filled the air in a brief argument.

"For me the tables are reversed," Gramma confessed in a whisper. "Your mother can't believe how I'm dressing. She thinks I ought to act my age."

"You *are* acting your age," Karen assured her, pushing the door shut. "There's no reason why you can't change your image now and then. You're still the gramma I love."

"As I love you, my precious girl. Thank you for coming along with me to help." She glanced around the tiny room where the hooks on the walls bulged with clothes. "This is too much. I don't know where to start."

"That's because you've never shopped with Michelle. Luckily, I have. There's a system." Karen set down her purse next to the already-overflowing shopping bags on the floor and began organizing the hangers. "Jeans first. Those are always the most frustrating. Try this style."

"I've always wanted to own a pair of these. Norman thought they were what forward women wore, not the mother of his children. So I wore dresses." Gramma stepped out of her shorts and reached for the denims. "I saw you in town today, riding that horse of yours. Was I right about taking time off to get some sunshine?"

"You were absolutely wrong. I should have been doing the bookkeeping and serving iced mochas instead of paying Michelle to drive away my customers."

"Don't try fooling me, sweetie." Gramma buttoned the waistband and twirled in front of the mirror. "Oh, my. Is that really me?"

"Yes." Karen felt joy creep into her heart, and she wrapped her arms around her grandmother. "You've always been beautiful, and you always will be. No matter what you wear."

"I sure look modern in these jeans."

Karen bit her lip to keep from laughing. "That means you're taking both pairs?"

"Yes!" Gramma beamed at her reflection.

"Then let's try these shirts." Karen unbuttoned a snazzy silk garment from its plastic hanger. "This color is going to look great on you."

"You are in a good mood, aren't you? I'm so pleased you took some time for yourself."

"Until I take a look at my books and I'll change my mind."

Gramma slipped into the new garment, turning to admire the look of it in the triple mirrors. "Is your little shop really doing that poorly? You know my friends and the women's groups at church always make a point to bring their business to your doorstep."

"I know, and I appreciate their loyalty more than I can say, but profits aren't what I was hoping for." Karen unhooked another shirt from its hanger. "Yet. But my busy season is right around the corner. As soon as there's a nip in the morning air, you watch business pick up."

"You know what you need?" Gramma pulled the second shirt over her head. "A business partner. Someone to share the workload with."

"Then it wouldn't be my shop anymore. It's senti-mental, I know, but I don't want to change it too much."

Gramma tried on a third top, seconds ticking by as she studied the rose-pink knit with the sporty cut. "Does this look too young on me?"

"It looks fun, casual and tasteful. I've seen your friend Nora Greenley in something similar."

"Then put this on the 'buy' pile, too, dear. I have another thought about your little shop."

"I don't want you to worry about my business."

"That's a lot of responsibility to shoulder for a girl your age."

"In a few years I'll be thirty. I think I'm old enough for a little responsibility."

"But when you started the shop, you weren't alone. You had your sister. Comrades-in-arms, I called you. Everywhere she went, you went. I thought of her today, simply couldn't help it, when I saw you riding horse-back through town. Memories rushed back of the two of you, as identical as sisters could be, riding side by side on your mares, giggling and talking in the way little girls do. Hair in ponytails and as sun-browned as can be. You looked happy today."

"It's been a long time since I took Star to town for ice cream. Usually I take her along the river trail so she can get a good run."

"I bet you ordered a butterscotch sundae and shared it with her. Like always."

"I did." Karen handed her grandmother a blue angora cardigan. "This will be just right when the weather turns."

"You're changing the subject on me because you know good and well what I'm about to say next." Gramma's wise gaze narrowed.

"If you saw me in town getting ice cream, then you saw that I wasn't alone."

"Zachary Drake is such a nice man. Good to the core. Sure, he got into a little trouble in his youth, but look where he came from. No father, and no mother that would make sure her kids were cared for, drunk all the time. Sad, it was. But Zach took care of the younger ones, and now he runs a good business. He's a volunteer fireman. Works in the Search and Rescue. Did you hear about that hiker he scaled a cliff to save?"

"You know I did." Karen added the cardigan to the growing pile. "This conversation isn't heading where I think it is, right? You're not going to mention how Lois brought more pictures of her great grandbaby to your last meeting."

"I'm shocked. I wasn't about to mention one word about marriage and babies. Only what a wonderful choice in friends you have."

"I don't believe you." Karen laughed.

"I only have your best interests at heart. He's a handsome one, and that never hurts in a marriage."

"See? You said that awful *M* word."

"I know you want to get married."

"One day. To the right man." Karen unhooked the shorts set from the stubborn hangers, refusing to look at her grandmother in case she guessed the truth. Karen wasn't going to let anyone know she was interested in

Zachary Drake. "According to my sisters, I need a rebound relationship. To help me get over Jay."

"Those girls read too many magazines." Gramma laughed, slipping out of her jeans. "Fold these up for me. Heavens! Look at that pile. This makeover is going to put me in the poorhouse!"

"But think how good you'll look going there. Can we stop talking about Zach?"

"I have only one more thing to say about Zach, so I'll just say it. He's a nice man and as good as gold. He serves his church and his community, he's an honest businessman and kids love him. Bet you noticed that."

"Just how long were you spying on me this afternoon?"

"I could see you from the coffee shop window." Gramma chuckled. "Okay, end of subject. I have another thought on your business troubles."

"My business troubles aren't yours."

Gramma admired the classy shorts set in the mirror, eyes sparkling, full of trouble. "What you should do is find a business partner you get along with. One who works hard, has a positive outlook on life, has money and wants what you want for the shop."

"Oh, and just where would I find this perfect partner? If you mention Zach's name, I won't speak to you for a week, and that's a promise." Karen fought to keep a straight face as she freed a summer dress from its hanger. "I mean it."

"Zach? Why, no, I'm not that sneaky." Laughing, Gramma slipped into the frothy garment. "I was talking about me."

"You?"

"I'm just spending my life sitting in my house and puttering around in my garden. Now, mind you, I love to putter and I love my home, but I've got too much time on my hands. Sure, I have my church commitments and that helps, but I'd like to be a business-woman."

"No."

"I know how to mix up those fancy coffee drinks, plus I make a mean sandwich. I get compliments. Admit it."

"Filling in now and then for me is one thing, but you're retired. You don't need the stress or the respon-sibility of a business, believe me."

"What I want is to feel like I'm making a difference with my life. You're working yourself to the bone trying to keep the shop you love afloat, and I need something to do. Will you help me?"

"You know I will." Karen's heart twisted with grief at the lonely sound twisted up in her grandmother's words. "But the last thing I want is your money. You've given me a car, for heaven's sake, and I'm going to have to pay you for it, you know. Helping me with my business is way too much—"

"You owe me nothing for the car, and as for the business, maybe I have selfish motives. Maybe I won't be helping you as much as I want to help myself." Gramma's chin lifted.

"Why the shop? Maybe there's other things you'd like to do."

"Sure, I can find something else to do with my days,

but what I want most of all is to spend a part of them with you. That would make me the happiest, working in our pleasant little shop. I don't want to, but I will beg if I have to."

Now what did she do? Karen prayed for the right words to obliterate her grandmother's pain—and the guidance to lower her own pride. "How about a test run before we make it official? To make sure you won't have regrets."

"I knew I could win you over." Gramma pressed a kiss to her cheek. "Now, let me change out of this heavenly dress, which I absolutely must have. No, I'm not even going to look at the price tag. And then you and I are going to go check out the coffee shop on the other side of mall. There has to be some more trade secrets we can learn. To think, I'm going to be a businesswoman!"

As good as gold. That's how her grandmother had described the man who was rapping his knuckles on her shop's back door. As he did every morning.

Remembering the kiss that had almost happened, Karen's fingers felt jerky as she waved him in.

He brought the brightness of the morning with him. "Hi, gorgeous. I'm in desperate need of caffeine and figured only you could help me."

"For the right price."

"I knew it was too good to be true. Buy a girl ice cream and she starts taking liberties with you. Like overcharging for her fancy coffee." He set his thermos on the counter. "Fill 'er up for me with regular leaded."

"Sure. Let me get some drip started. It'll take about five minutes."

"I can wait. The fish aren't going anywhere."

She grabbed the bag of freshly ground beans from the freezer. "Heading out to the river?"

"Yep, got to catch me some dinner. My refrigerator's empty."

"The grocery store is right around the corner. Their frozen section is stocked."

"What? And go to all that trouble of fighting the crowds for food? Not me. I'm going to go catch my chow the real man's way."

"How's that—shopping for frozen dinners?"

"I never should have told you about those. I'm leaving now."

"Have you ever actually caught a fish? Or do you just sit there and watch the water stream by?"

"I can't believe this. My favorite person in town is mocking me. Casting doubt on my manly fishing skills." He shook his head, feigning disapproval. "I'm going to start buying my coffee at the diner."

She poured water into the machine and flipped the switch. "Manly fishing skills? Women can be just as good fishers as men. In fact, I always caught the most when Dad took me and Allison."

"Am I hearing this right? Are you challenging me to a fishing contest?" Zach propped his elbows on the counter. "If you think you're better, then prove it. We'll make a fishing date, just you and me. An early-morning contest to see who's the best."

"I haven't fished since I was eight." Karen marched

into the kitchen, far too aware of Zach's gaze on her back. Far too aware of everything about him.

No one had ever made her laugh the way Zach did. Or made her feel happy and full of warmth, like the sun was right in the middle of her chest, lighting her up from the inside.

Gramma straightened from the oven, a heavy muffin tin in both hands. "These are perfect if I do say so myself. I noticed handsome Zach wandered in."

"You were spying on me." Karen grabbed a clean plate from the stack on the counter and stole a plump blueberry muffin from the cooling racks. "Zach and I are friends."

"Clearly."

"I see that look in your eye. The one that says you know better than me. Well, I don't care what my sisters say. I'm not ready for a rebound relationship."

"I'm sure you're right." Gramma transferred the steaming banana muffins from the tin to the cooling racks. "I say Zach's a nice guy, but he's just like Jay. Too lukewarm to lose your heart to. My advice is to keep away from a relationship that will only hurt you in the end."

"Reverse psychology. That's not going to work, either."

"What? I know nothing about psychology." All innocence, Gramma continued to work. "I'm simply saying that we're in this together. We've got to make this place profitable for that big payment due next month. I can't have my partner falling in love and neglecting business."

"I don't believe you. Do you need help?"

"No, you go take those muffins to Zach and make sure you don't flirt with him. It would be unprofessional."

Karen rolled her eyes. "I minored in psychology. I know what you're up to."

"I have no idea what you're talking about."

Shaking her head, Karen pushed through the swinging door. The first thing she saw was Zach, one elbow propped on the counter and looking more handsome than he'd been yesterday—than she'd ever seen him.

How did a man become more and more good-looking? And why?

Okay, she knew. She was falling for him. Hard and fast, and she couldn't seem to help it.

"I heard Helen's voice. Is she helping you out this morning?"

"She talked me into a possible partnership." Karen grabbed a bag from under the counter and snapped it open. "She wants to be half owner."

"No kidding. How did that come about?"

"She played on my sympathies. And if I hadn't caved in, then she would have worked on my guilt." Karen slipped the muffins into the paper bag and folded it neatly. "She claims that she sits alone in her house all day and needs something to do."

"Hey, Helen. You should have gone into business with me. You could be doing oil changes right now."

The door pushed open, showing a slice of the kitchen behind the well-dressed woman holding an empty muffin tin. "Why, Zachary Drake, I didn't know you were in the market for a *partner.*" Gramma winked.

Mortified, Karen shoved the muffin bag at Zach. "Gramma! Zach doesn't need a partner. He's perfectly happy being a sole proprietor."

"That's not entirely true." Zach lifted one brow, trouble shaping his saucy grin. "I've been on my own a long time. The right investor comes along with a pretty smile and I could consider a merger."

"Zach!" Karen threw a napkin at him. "You know my grandmother is talking about marriage."

"Of course he does, honey," Gramma answered. "And what a pleasure it is to cast my gaze on a man who isn't afraid of commitment."

"That's it. You're fired." Karen grabbed Zach's thermos.

"She's only kidding, Zach." Gramma set down her tin and padded closer. "She's grumpy. She works all the time. She took a few hours off yesterday, and apparently it wasn't enough."

"I'm *not* grumpy. Not until you started mentioning mergers." Karen filled the thermos.

"I understand too well," Zach answered, all charm. "I get that way myself when I don't take enough time off. All work and no play."

"It's not how the good Lord intended it," Gramma agreed.

"You two are conspiring." Karen capped the thermos, daring to face them. "Zach, here's your coffee. Happy fishing. Gramma, we've got the last batch of muffins to finish. We open in fifteen minutes."

"Yeah, Helen," Zach drawled. "Look at the stampede approaching the front door. It's going to be a madhouse."

"Yep, looks like they're getting ready to beat down the door," Gramma quipped. "There's not a soul in sight. Should pick up after Labor Day. Come to think of it, I think this is the perfect time for Karen to get out. You used to love to fish."

"Just how much did you eavesdrop while you were making those muffins?"

"I heard everything." Gramma patted Zach's hand. "Be a gentleman and do an old woman a favor. Take my Karen with you this morning. Let her get some fresh air. It's the best thing for her."

"Gramma, you're not a matchmaking service. Zach, you don't want me intruding—"

"Sure I do." Zach grabbed his thermos. "Karen, come with me. We might as well have that contest right now."

"No." She couldn't just leave. "It will be a quiet morning, but it's Gramma's first real day— "

"You know you want to," her grandmother whispered in her ear. "I'll be fine, and you know that, too. You take today off, and I'll take tomorrow off. Is that a deal?"

"Are you sure? I don't want to run out on you."

"This is the reason for having a business partner. Now go and have fun. Isn't that the point of a rebound relationship?"

"A rebound relationship?" Zach quirked one brow, trying not to laugh. "Well, I've been worse. Come on, gorgeous. I've got an extra pole at the shop I'll let you use. I'll even share some of my coffee."

"That's technically my coffee, since you didn't pay for it."

"Yes, but possession is nine-tenths of the law." Zach held the door for her, his hand skimming her elbow.

Karen shivered all the way to her soul.

It was a beautiful morning. He was self-employed and there was no work waiting for him in the shop. It wasn't every day that a man got this lucky. Zach couldn't help but give a quick, silent prayer of thanks as he pulled his pickup into the shade of old cotton-woods.

"Listen to the river." He set the parking brake. The ping-ping of the engine cooling contrasted with the peaceful sounds of nature. "It's saying, 'Karen, leave your troubles behind.'"

"Funny, I only hear a faint gurgle. Maybe the river is saying, 'Karen, you will catch more fish than Zachary.'"

"You're a riot."

He could sit here looking at her all day. She was as refreshing to his spirit as morning, and he wanted nothing more than to pull her into his arms and hold her.

He wanted to have the right to kiss her, gentle and softly, so she would know his true feelings. Deep and tender feelings that no words could describe.

She seemed shy as she reached for the thermos and the small paper bag that proclaimed, Field of Beans, across the front in swirling green script.

"I'll give you my best fishing rod," he told her. "When I win, I don't want you to accuse me of being unfair."

"When *you* win? Ha! I sure hope you're not a poor sport, because you're going to lose." Golden tendrils escaped from her ponytail and fluttered in front of her eyes.

He brushed the gossamer wisps back into place, trying not to think too much about how satiny her skin felt or how silky her hair was.

"Your hands were full," he explained. "I was only being gentlemanly. I wouldn't want you to fall out of my truck because you couldn't see where you were going."

"I appreciate it. Are you ready to go fishing?" She didn't move.

Neither did he.

This is what it would be like if they were a couple. It was a big leap thinking of the two of them as a couple, but why not? Maybe they could be.

Just treat her well. Show her what a nice guy I can be. Twice as nice as Jay. What was it she'd told him? *Nice means dependable. The kind of woman a man settles for.*

One thing was for sure, *he'd* never let Karen doubt how special she was to him.

She walked beside him down the bank. "I'd forgotten how peaceful the river is in the mornings."

"That's why I fish. There's nothing like a quiet morning listening to the river to put things in perspective. Here we are." He leaned the rods against a tree trunk and set the tackle box in the spindly grasses. "I've never shared my fishing spot with a woman before."

"Should I be honored?"

"Sure. If you like this, I should take you to my favorite hideaway. As long as you're willing to climb a mountain to get there."

She uncapped the thermos. "What's that supposed to mean?"

"There's nothing like sitting on the peak you've scaled. With the sweat trickling down your back and your muscles so exhausted they burn. After you've picked your way up a thousand feet of sheer rock, problems don't seem so big and a lot easier to solve. You feel like there's just you, the mountain and the sky, and you're a lot closer to God." He took the thermos from her.

"I've heard rumors that you're a good mountain climber. You climb, you bike, you hike and you fish. Is there anything you can't do?"

"Cook, dust and sew. Other than that, I'm your man."

You could be. Karen caught the words before they spilled across her tongue. She wasn't ready for these feelings, but she couldn't stop them.

Zach poured coffee into the shallow cup, steam lifting in foggy curls. He offered it to her, his silence as powerful as his presence.

The admiration she'd always felt for him had changed. Denying it wouldn't help. She had to acknowledge their relationship had irrevocably changed.

They could be more than friends. So much more.

She took the cup, feeling the warmth though the plastic.

"Enjoy the view." He tucked the thermos into the grass next to fishing poles. "I'll run to the truck and grab the waders."

"Waders? I thought we were fishing from the bank."

"Surprise." He jogged easily through the golden grasses and out of sight. Leaving her alone with her coffee, her awakening heart and a growing question. Did Zach look at her and see a dependable, take-for-granted kind of girl?

She balanced the cup on top of a rock and reached for the tackle box. She opened the lid, amazed at the tidy compartments of neatly tied flies, each a combination of knotted fish line, yarn and plastic buglike bobbles.

"You're laughing." Zach dropped a pair of boots beside her. "What's so funny about my tackle box?"

"You put hours into this. Look, organized by color of yarn. By the type of bobble and hook, Your apartment is a mess and you can't cook, but you have time for this?"

"A man always has time for what's truly important." He knelt beside her and lifted a fly from the tray. "I only have one pair of waders, but I keep my fire boots in the back of the truck. They should work."

"Thanks, but these are huge." Karen moved away to inspect what he'd brought. "The good news is that I don't have to take my shoes off. Look."

He didn't see the too-big boots. He saw *her*. Like

an angel on earth, warm and sparkling. She made him feel both vulnerable and strong, tender and fierce all at once. He wanted to protect her and he wanted to love her for the rest of his life.

She was everything he'd ever wanted. Home and family. Belonging and love. And…just Karen. He'd always had a crush on the quiet gentle girl who was way out of his reach.

Not anymore. Her smile deepened when she looked at him. She was stardust straight from heaven, and he couldn't believe she wanted to be with him.

Unaware, she took the pole from him and clomped toward the river, wearing the heavy boots that went to her midthighs.

He grabbed his fishing pole, pulled his waders to his knees and splashed into the water after her.

"Are you ready?" she challenged with her rod raised, hook dangling above the rippling water. "Stand back. It's been a long time since I've cast."

"That's comforting. If you hook me, I don't count as a fish."

"Why not? We're not going by weight of the catch?" She leaned the pole back to her shoulder, swinging the hook far behind her. With a flick of her slender wrist, the fly snapped through the air, skimming the river's shimmering surface.

"Not bad for a girl. Now watch the master." He cast, satisfaction filling him when he saw the lure slice into the water. "Perfection."

"Not bad for a boy." She reeled in, the fly cutting toward them against the current.

She recast and silence fell between them. A contented peace that felt like forever.

Don't just stand there, Zach. You're alone with the girl. A man doesn't get a chance like this every day.

He edged closer.

She flashed him a smile. "I'm having trouble."

"Good thing I'm here. Since I'm also an expert fisherman, I've got the experience to help you out." That made her chuckle. "You've got a tangle, that's all."

"Did I mess up your reel?"

"Not a chance. There's a knot in the line. Look. It must have happened in the water." He pulled out his pocketknife.

Keeping his pole tucked against his side, he leaned closer to Karen. Close enough to smell the baby shampoo in her hair. That was his favorite scent, he decided. Especially since she was his favorite girl.

"Let me just cut this off here." He inserted the tip of his knife beneath the knotted fishing line, bringing his forehead to hers.

So close. He wanted to kiss her. To show her how he felt and what he wanted to give her—protection, commitment and tenderness. That's what he wanted her to see whenever she looked at him.

"There." The line came free. "Let me tie the hook for you."

"I can do it."

His fingers were fumbling, but he got the job done. "There. No fish is safe now."

Instead of releasing the line, he moved closer.

Karen felt anticipation zip through her. The river's current tugged at her legs, keeping her a little off balance. She wobbled and didn't know if it was because of the river or her feelings for Zach.

He leaned closer and she forgot to breathe. Her eyelids fluttered shut as their lips met in a sweet brush that left her trembling.

How could it be that one chaste kiss could hold so much tenderness?

Zach broke away and she opened her eyes. They were still standing in the river with the sun glinting on the water and the cottonwoods whispering with the breezes—an ordinary morning that was not the same as it had been five seconds before.

Everything had changed.

Zach's hand cupped the side of her face. A gentle, comforting touch that made her heart ache with hope. With a dream of what could be.

She leaned into his touch and welcomed his kiss. The ache within her intensified, making her hurting and happy all at once. Sweet love for him filled her up until she couldn't breathe, until she couldn't tell up from down or feel the rocky riverbed at her feet.

"Your nose is cold," he told her, chuckling, and leaned his forehead to hers to prolong the moment of closeness. "Want me to fetch the thermos?"

She grabbed hold of his arm to steady herself. Heat flamed her cheeks, and how could she tell him how she felt? That he'd affected her so much she was wobbly on her feet?

A tug on the pole jerked her forward. Was it a fish?

Before she could set the hook, she lost her balance and tumbled against Zach's solid chest. His arms banded around her, but it was too late. Her feet lost contact with the riverbed and gravity pulled her down.

She fell with a splash into the river. Water rushed over her and the cold stung her skin. She sputtered, fighting for the surface, and then Zach tumbled into the river beside her bobbing for air.

"Are you all right?" He half swam, half climbed toward her. "Did you hit your head on any rocks?"

Concern furrowed into his brow as he caught her with his strong but gentle hands. "I don't see any bruises. Any lumps? Do you know what day it is?"

"I'm fine, Zach." Her voice came breathy and thin. She stumbled over a rock and pain shot through her bare foot. "I lost my shoes and your boots, but I didn't let go of your pole."

Zach dipped beneath the water and came up with one of her slip-on sneakers. He went down again and surfaced with the other. "What happened? Looks like you lost your hook."

"Guess I got a bite and it took me by surprise." She stared down at the fishing rod, the line a loose tangle. "He got away."

"No, he didn't." Zach swiped water from her face with the side of his thumb. "I've been here all along."

He kissed her again, briefly, sweetly until her toes curled. Then he took her hand.

"I'm holding on to you this time," he whispered in her ear. "I don't want you to fall over, since my kisses have such an impact on you."

"It wasn't you, it was a fish," she alibied as he took her hand, helping her through the current, his strength an anchor that saw her safely to shore.

Chapter Nine

"There you are. I was beginning to worry. Let me help you with those." Holding open her screen door, Gramma wrestled a grocery bag from Karen's arms. "You didn't need to buy all this."

"I didn't want to empty your pantry. Zach helped me, too." Karen stumbled into her grandmother's cozy kitchen, nearly dropping the heavy bags. "Did you make sense of those financial statements I gave you?"

"I've been looking at them all afternoon until my eyes went blurry. I wanted to blame my bifocals, but I know good and well I was nothing but confused. Those classes I signed up for at the university ought to help straighten me out."

"I think Zach told me he did the same thing." Karen set the heavy grocery bags on the counter. "Now he does his own books."

"Zach said so, huh?" Gramma's eyes twinkled.

"I see what you're thinking, so don't even start."

Karen shrugged the purse strap from her shoulder. "It isn't any of your business."

"How could it be, since the two of you are only *friends?*"

"Exactly."

It wasn't a lie, not really. They *were* friends. Then why did the tingle of his kiss remain? So, maybe he could be more than just a friend. "He's going to be really happy that you made your taco cheese and macaroni casserole just for him."

"We have to pay back that man somehow. He's always doing for me, I swear. This afternoon while you were at the bank he stopped by to check on my new car. Says he wanted to keep an eye on the oil, since it's important to a new engine. Imagine that. Didn't charge me a penny."

"Imagine that." Karen reached into the nearest grocery bag, hiding a smile. "So, you're trying to tell me what a nice guy he is."

"Good husband material. Not that you're looking." Gramma set a clean saucepan on the stove. "But believe me, some other girl is going to notice. She'll snatch him up, and then it'll be too late for you."

"That's a risk I'm willing to take." Karen emptied the grocery bag.

"After he was done checking the engine, you know what he did? Told me something shocking. Young lady, you're keeping a secret from your grandmother."

"Secret? What secret?"

"To think I have to hear about this from my mechanic and not my granddaughter. Not one bit." Gramma waved a spatula.

Heat burned Karen's face. "I can't believe it. Zach told you?"

"He surely did. Told me right there in front of my dearest friends. Nora was appalled, and she wasn't the only one."

That didn't sound like Zach. There was no way he would have broadcast news of their kiss to some of the most respected women in their church!

"Just what did he tell you?"

"About the radiator, of course. How it steamed on the way home from the car dealership, and how you had to walk to town."

Relief left her dizzy. "I didn't tell you because I didn't want your feelings hurt. I'm grateful for the car."

"I told Zachary *he* was at fault. A mechanic ought to be responsible for his own shoddy work." Gramma winked. "I told him you would bring the car in for a new radiator."

"I know what you're up to." Karen headed to the pantry. "You're going to try and pay for the repairs and I'm not going to let you—no, don't argue. I don't need a new radiator right away. He fixed it for now."

"You'd better have him give the engine a thorough check. Make sure there isn't any trouble lurking beneath the hood. After all, if he's just a *friend,* you won't mind spending more time with him."

Karen slipped into the large pantry, stocked with shelves of food and jars of homemade jellies. She tucked the folded bags into place. "Are you trying to play matchmaker?"

"Absolutely not! I'm not one of those meddling grandmothers who thinks they know what's best for their beloved granddaughters."

"That's good to hear. Because the last thing Zach and I need right now is a matchmaker."

"I understand completely. I'm glad you and that nice young man are only *friends* because you and I have a business to run."

Karen struggled not to laugh. It wasn't hard to see right through Gramma's strategy.

"Get me the flour canister and a package of noodles while you're over there."

"Sure." Karen peeked over her shoulder. Gramma wasn't looking, so she tugged the money from her jeans pocket. The same hundred-dollar bills Zach had given her for her old car.

She snatched a battered tin from the top shelf and carefully pried off the lid. "Since tomorrow is Labor Day, it should be quiet at the shop, too. Did you want to close early? I did last year."

"That's fine by me. What are you doing in there? I need the flour."

"I'm coming." Karen tucked the money inside and replaced Gramma's secret money tin. It wasn't close to what she owed for the car, but it was a start.

The long day made his apartment seem more homey than usual. Zach tossed his keys on the table. A message light blinked in the darkness. His personal line, not the shop phone.

Did he dare hope it was Karen? He'd thought of her

all day. Images of her accepting his kiss and reaching out for him when she fell. The telltale blush on her cheeks had told him she felt the spark between them, too.

He had a chance with her. A real, honest-to-goodness chance.

He hit the play button and flicked on lights as the tape rewound. "Zach, this is your sister. Just checking in on you. Are you eating right? I worry. Talk to you later."

He liked the happiness in his sister's voice. He'd give her a call as soon as—

"Zach?" Another message started. "This is your mother."

His emotions took a nosedive. Why did his hands shake every time he thought of that woman?

"I need five hundred dollars. I'm in a real fix and I don't know who to call—"

Zach pressed the stop button, cutting off the slurred speech. The thought of her filled him with shame, the old shame that he'd fought all his life. The humiliation of being Sylvia Drake's boy, the woman without a shred of dignity, who spent her life at the Bulldog Tavern, too drunk to care how she behaved or with whom.

Whenever he thought of her, the hungry little boy he'd been didn't seem too far away.

Don't go there. He squeezed his eyes shut against the images of his childhood. He didn't need to remember.

He'd send her the money because it would keep her away.

A knock at the door startled him. He yanked open the door. "Karen."

"Hi, stranger. I've been trying to get a hold of you all evening." She smiled at him over the top of two heavy-looking grocery sacks. "I finally gave up and decided to leave these in the freezer at the shop when I saw your light."

"I'm glad you came by. Let me take these for you." He avoided looking at her as he took both bags. "What do you have in here? These weigh a ton."

"A surprise for you, courtesy of my grandmother and me. Thought you could use some real food."

He saw the foil-wrapped plates, and the faint scent of Helen's taco cheese and macaroni casserole made his mouth water. "Why did you do this? You didn't have to."

"We wanted to. We made them easy to freeze, since you're used to frozen dinners. You can nuke them any time you want, and guess what? They're good for you."

"Did you put any green stuff in there like broccoli or green beans or spouts?"

"No, you're safe. Although Gramma did dice and cook carrots. Before you complain, she smothered them in this buttery sauce and said you'd like it. Carrots *are* orange."

"That grandmother of yours is sly, trying to trick me into eating vegetables." Although he was teasing, his chest tightened until he couldn't breathe.

He turned away and set the bags on the counter. There had to be two dozen dinners inside the grocery bags, each carefully prepared and proportioned.

This was the kindest thing anyone had done for him in a long time.

"Gramma offered to give you cooking lessons, since

she has to keep her favorite mechanic in good health."
Karen leaned against his counter, an angel in a blue
T-shirt and jeans, her hair braided, with little wisps
framing her face.

He loved this woman. With his whole heart. All his
life he'd admired her from afar. Untouchable Karen
McKaslin, a wealthy rancher's daughter.

And now that he knew her better, knew who she was
inside, how easily she laughed, how gently she loved,
he didn't know what to do. Did he reach for her and
hold her? Did he tell her how he felt?

They'd never spoken of their relationship. He was
afraid to break the spell by asking her, as if that would
make her wake up from a dream and see not the man
he'd worked to be, but Sylvia Drake's kid—someone
she would never truly love.

Then she smiled at him, genuinely, from her soul.
"Aren't you going to put them in your freezer?
Gramma was afraid you wouldn't have room, but I told
her about the hot dog story. There's no way you have
anything but ice in your freezer."

"You're wrong about that, gorgeous. I do, too, have
something in here." He jerked open the freezer door.
"Empty ice trays."

"I knew it." Loaded down with plates, she shouldered up to him. "We never did determine who was the
better fisherman."

"I thought I was." He took the plates from her and
began stocking his freezer.

"Why you? You didn't catch a fish. I hooked one, I
think, but it got away. That makes it a draw."

"A draw? No way. I'm not the one who fell into the river, so that means I'm the best."

"I was wearing your enormous boots. They made me trip. I was at a disadvantage."

"Maybe we'll have to have another contest." Uncertainty flickered in his stomach. Did he ask her for a date?

"Another contest? Maybe." She brushed her fingertips along his jaw, a brief contact, and then she moved away. "This time I get to choose what we do."

"Wait, I already know what you're going to say. No way am I going horseback riding with you. I think those creatures are best left alone in their fields."

"What kind of attitude is that for an adventurous guy like you? You can borrow Michelle's horse, and I'll teach you everything you need to know."

"Like how to fall? Trying to put me at a disadvantage, aren't you? Well, you should know that I'm a natural-born athlete." He caught her hand in his. "Prepare to lose and lose big because I've seen you ride, and I have to say you weren't very good at it."

"That's because you scared my horse." Her fingers twined around his, holding tight.

Holding on to him.

Something about her simply made all his doubts fade. Made him feel like a better man than he was.

He followed her to the door. "I'd better walk you to your car. This town is a wild place at night. A girl has to be careful."

"I could use the protection. This *is* a dangerous place."

Not a car passed on the street, and the shops were

silent. Zach felt better, stronger, because there wasn't a safer place than this tiny town in the middle of Montana—Karen just wanted him with her.

He escorted her to the classic Ford gleaming in the starlight. "I guess I'll see you at church tomorrow. Any chance you'd sit with me?"

"It's a good possibility." She waited while he opened her car door. "It's always good for my reputation to be seen with a handsome man."

She didn't let go of him, and his heart started pounding like a jackhammer.

He brushed her cheek with his lips, breathing in the scent of her shampoo. "I'll see you in the morning."

"I'll have your coffee ready."

He shut the door for her. The rolled-down window framed her, and he was jealous of the starlight bold enough to touch her face.

She turned the key. There was a click. The car didn't start.

"Oh, no. This can't be happening. This car worked for Gramma. Never broke down on her once."

"I'll take a look." He circled around the front fender and then disappeared from her view as he popped the hood.

She leaned out the window. "Want me to try again?"

"No. It's the starter. I can fix it tonight if you want to wait, but it'll take a while."

He looked tired. She'd heard about the multicar accident on the highway south to Yellowstone today and figured he'd been called in to help. It must have been a hard day.

She got out of the car and handed him the keys. "I'll call home. Someone can come get me."

"No need. Hop in the truck and I'll take you. For the right fee."

"You're going to charge me?"

"Sure. I'll take you anywhere you want to go for a kiss."

"Wow, that's a pretty high price, but I *am* stranded here. I guess I'll just have to take you up on your offer—except for one thing. Take me on your motorcycle."

He shut the hood. "That'll cost you more."

"Name your price."

"Two kisses. If you want the scenic ride, then it's three."

"Where will the scenic ride take me?"

"Hop on and you'll find out." Zach took her hand, so gallant that he stole her breath away.

"Is this fast enough?"

Karen looked down. Big mistake. The pavement flew by at a dizzying speed. "Definitely fast enough."

"Sure about that?"

"Absolutely. This is my first motorcycle ride."

"Kind of scary and thrilling at the same time, huh?" He revved the engine, the show-off.

"Maybe you could slow down just a little." The surrounding countryside blurred. "Or a lot."

"We're not even going the speed limit. It seems faster when you look at the ground. Try closing your eyes."

"That sounds real smart. Then I won't be able to prepare for a crash."

"I never crash. Trust me."

It was hard not to. Sitting behind him with her arms wrapped around his waist, she could feel the steely strength in his back. He handled the bike with confidence.

She squeezed her eyes shut and it didn't seem as scary. "Okay, you can go faster now."

The motorcycle shot forward, skimming through the night. The roar of the engine, the whir of the wind made Karen's pulse soar. She opened one eye and then the other. It was like flying. Zach was in control, and her fear ebbed away.

They raced through the darkness with only a single headlight to show the way. The road unfolded before them, rising up and falling away like an undulating ribbon. With her arms tight around Zach, she felt safe. Safer than she'd been with anyone. Ever.

Too soon, he slowed the bike and turned off the road. He rolled to a stop and killed the engine.

Her arms were tight around his waist. She didn't want to let go and he didn't move. Finally she released him and scrambled from the bike. She slipped off the helmet, surprised the sense of safety she'd felt holding him remained.

"Do you like the scenic route?" Zach took the helmet and hung it on one handlebar. "I don't want to shortchange you. I'm a man of my word."

"I'm having a wonderful time."

"Good. Come with me." He laid his arm over her shoulder, tugging her close.

Karen cuddled against him as they walked side by

side along the worn path toward the river. Night shadows cloaked the familiar landscape, making it mysterious and new.

What a magnificent night. She couldn't believe how a place she knew so well could transform before her eyes. The cottonwoods overhead whispered a solemn hymn, and the starlight cast a noble glow across the surface of the water. The river, wide and black and seemingly motionless, made no sound as they approached the bank.

"Have you ever watched a moon rise?"

"No," she confessed. "I'm usually inside this time in the evening. If I am outside, then I'm busy exercising Star."

"And you never pay attention to what's in the sky?"

"When do I have the time?" She let him help her to the ground. "Between helping Mom, and the shop—"

"Hollow excuses for a woman who named her horse Star."

"That was when I was eight and I had time to wish on the first stars of the night and watch for meteorites."

"Falling stars." He settled in the grass beside her, his arm drawing her to his side. "That's what you are to me, Karen. A falling star that landed at my side."

"Meteorites are chunks of burned rock."

"Give me a break. I'm new at this." He brushed his lips with hers. "So, I'm no poet and not much of a romantic. I took you fishing for our first date."

"That was a date? I thought it was a contest." She couldn't resist teasing him.

"You're not making this easy for me." He kissed her again, light and sweet.

"That's your second kiss. One more and my debt is paid in full."

"Those weren't real kisses. They were warm-up kisses."

"Kisses are kisses. You only have one left, buster."

"Can I negotiate for more?"

"Why should I? I'm not the kind of girl who kisses just any man for a ride on his motorcycle."

"Then I'll have to change your mind." He kissed her again, light as a breeze. "That's enough of a warm-up to appreciate the moonrise. Look."

Dazzled, she tried to focus on the eastern rim of mountains made black by the night. She caught her breath at the sight of the top point of a sickle moon nudging upward, a lone spear of light changing the landscape. The jagged mountain peaks glowed silver in the night.

She'd seen the moon before but not like this. Nothing like this.

"What do you think?" Zach's breath was warm against her ear. "Was it worth another kiss or two?"

"I only agreed to three."

"I was hoping the moon would inspire you to kiss me one more time."

"A wise plan."

The moonglow cast a silvery light over them and tonight Zach seemed changed, too. He was more than the man she'd known for years—her most loyal customer, her mechanic and a friend who made her laugh.

He was *much* more.

Like a dream, his lips met hers. His slow kiss was tender and true.

Too soon, it was over. Zach drew her into his arms and held her—simply held her—while the moon filled the sky with unquenchable light. The darkest shadows disappeared around them, and the black surface of the silent river turned silvery, reflecting the moon's glow.

All around her, the world felt different. Changed from everything she'd known before. Or maybe it was just a change within her, as if a sleeping part of her heart had awakened.

"Look at the deer." Zach lifted one hand slowly. "Right there in the grasses."

The grasses barely shifted, and Karen caught the glimpse of one white tail and then another. She didn't dare move as the doe led her fawns down to the sparkling water. The babies drank at their mother's side.

Zach's chin came to rest on the crown of Karen's head. Being close to him like this felt right. As if they'd both been led to this place.

Dear Father, tell me I'm not making a mistake, she prayed, but it was too late and she knew it. Tenderness for Zach filled her up so completely she could hardly breathe.

I love him, she thought, turning her face into his neck and letting him hold her. I love him more than I've loved anyone.

But does he love me?

That was a different question, and the answer terrified her. He liked her, he treated her well, but did he feel both enlivened and confused at the same time? Did he look at her and think, she's the one?

He tipped her head back gently. "I'm going to charge you extra for those deer."

"All these hidden charges. I might have to bring up a complaint with the chamber of commerce."

"You'd ruin my professional reputation just like that, huh? Then I'd better try to change your mind." He brushed his lips across hers once and then twice.

The third time left her feeling as if she'd touched the moon. She felt warm and was glowing. Special and so far from ordinary, dependable Karen.

Zach took her hand, as gallant as a knight of old, and helped her rise. With the breeze at her back and the stardust lighting the way, he wound his fingers through hers.

She walked slowly, the grass crackling beneath her sneakers, enjoying the weight and texture of his hand in hers. She wanted to savor this moment, to make it last, to never let it end. But too soon they were at the motorcycle. It was time to go home.

Zach stopped but didn't release her hand. "The Labor Day picnic's tomorrow. Maybe you'd consider going with me?"

"I'd love to, but I'm going with my family. Would you be brave enough to join us?"

"I sure would." He reached around her and retrieved the helmet. "I'll look forward to being seen with a pretty lady like you."

"Then I'll save you a place at my table, handsome."

He kissed her as gently as the starlight and then slipped the helmet over her head.

The ride home was silent-with the moon to guide them. She held him tight and leaned her cheek on his back, her lips tingling from the memory of his sweet kisses.

Had true love finally found her?

He left her on her doorstep with a final kiss. She stood in the dark long after his bike's taillight faded in the moonlight, wishing—just wishing.

Chapter Ten

Where was he? Karen squinted through the crowd gathered in the park, where children played and smoke from the pit barbecue clouded the air. She couldn't see Zach anywhere. His pickup wasn't parked on the street. Neither was his motorcycle.

He said he'd be here, and he'd never broken a promise to her.

"Karen, your hair is getting into your face." Mom opened her purse and began sorting through it. "You need to tie it back."

"I'm fine, Mom." She was glad her mother was feeling well enough to attend the annual picnic.

"Looks like the next batch of hamburgers are done. Would you take a plate and get our meat?"

Karen wasn't fooled. Jay was at the grill, helping Dad and Pastor Bill with the barbecuing.

"Oh, here's a barrette. Clip it back for me so I can see you." Mom pressed the silver barrette into Karen's palm.

"Her hair looks just fine." Kendra came to the rescue, bounding around the edge of the picnic table. "But I can make it better."

Karen handed her sister the barrette. "Mom, I know Jay is here, so don't get your hopes up."

"You couldn't find a nicer boy anywhere. I tell you, he's bound to go places."

"Then he'll just have to go there with some other wife."

"Yeah," Michelle piped up. "Karen's got much better prospects."

Mom frowned. "What could be better than being a minister?"

"A mechanic," Kirby piped up from farther down the table.

Everyone laughed.

Heat splashed across Karen's face and she fought the urge to run for privacy—or cover. Heaven knew growing up with so many sisters wasn't easy. "That is no one's business, let me remind you, no matter how nosy you all are."

"What mechanic?" Mom demanded. "Girls, stop all that laughing. I can't believe what Cecilia told me was true. You're just friends with that Drake boy. Isn't that right, Karen?"

"Right." Whatever else they were or would become, they would always be friends first.

"Yeah, *right,*" Kendra intoned, then stepped away. "There, I'm done. Doesn't she look fabulous?"

"She's blushing," Kirby commented.

"At least that hair is out of her eyes," Mom added.

Karen rubbed her forehead. "I'm trying to remember why going to this picnic with my family was a good idea."

"Because you love us." Michelle hugged her. "I'll get the burgers and save you from dealing with Jay. C'mon, Kirby, I need help." Michelle led the way across the park.

"Sit down, honey." Mom's hand caught Karen's. "I see you looking at him. It's not too late to ask Jay for your forgiveness."

"I'm not looking at Jay." Karen kissed her Mom's cheek. "I'm glad you felt like coming today. Let me get you more lemonade."

"That would be nice."

Karen took refuge at the other end of the table. Kids playing tag raced by, screaming with delight. At the far end of the park, cheers and shouts carried on the breeze from a volleyball game in progress.

Everywhere she looked, she saw families. Hope filled her, strong as the midday sun. Maybe her dreams for a happily-ever-after were not so far away.

"Karen." John Corey, the volunteer fire chief, strolled up to her. "Zach wanted me to find you. I dropped him off at the garage a few minutes ago. We've been out all morning."

"I didn't hear anyone was missing."

"A little kid wandered away from the campsite and got herself in a little trouble. She's safe and sound now, thanks to our Zach. Or is he your Zach?" Trouble danced in the fireman's gaze. "He'll be by shortly, just so you know."

"Thanks." Karen snapped open the pitcher of lemonade.

A good man, that's what Zach is. Not only fair and kind, but concerned about everyone, neighbors and strangers alike. Her heart felt so full of love for him, she hurt with the power of it. Ached all the way to her soul.

When she glanced up, there he was at the edge of the park, waving a hello to the pastor. Dressed in jeans and a T-shirt and with his Stetson shading his eyes, he made her senses spin.

"Hello, Mrs. McKaslin. Karen, don't tell me I got here too late," he quipped, pulling her into his arms for a hug. "Where's all the food?"

"We're running late. Someone forgot the lighter fluid." She breathed in his out-of-doors and warm scent, holding him for a moment longer before she stepped away. "Gramma's not here yet, so you haven't missed the best food."

"Whew. I hurried as fast as I could to get here. I'm starving."

"Then help me take the lids off the Tupperware so we're ready to eat."

"This wouldn't be your potato salad, would it, Mrs. McKaslin? It's good to see you looking well."

"Thank you." Mom squinted at him. "It's my mother's recipe, but Michelle made it."

"Beware, she's not the best of cooks," Karen confided in him. "I tried to keep an eye on her when I was making dessert."

"Dessert? Tell me you made something with chocolate in it."

"Just for you. I was hoping that you might like my cocoa fudge cake enough to take me for another late-night bike ride."

"For the right price."

Aching tenderness filled her as she remembered last night's kisses. She knew, without words, that he was remembering, too.

"Karen, here come the girls." Mom's voice was sharper than usual. "Hurry and pass out the plates. Where's your father?"

"Talking with the other ranchers." She grabbed a bundle of paper plates from inside a grocery bag, but the small smile at the corner of her mouth remained.

Zach snapped a lid off another container—macaroni salad—and tried to ignore the way Karen was making him feel. He wanted to jump right up on the table and shout. It was hard to contain so much happiness.

She gave him another secret smile as she rummaged through the sacks for the plastic knives and forks. He felt like a too-full balloon ready to pop.

He couldn't remember ever being this happy. Not once had he ever imagined that Karen would welcome him into her arms in front of her family. He was here not as a friend, but as her boyfriend.

Boyfriend. Wow, that sounded good.

As one of her sisters brought the barbecued beef and another sister circled around the table, Karen caught his hand and tugged him down beside her on the bench. She didn't let go.

He folded his fingers through hers, her palm small

against his. The breeze ruffled her blond locks against his forearm and he breathed in her vanilla scent.

She was like sunrise to his heart. Sitting beside her as she joked with her sisters, he felt overwhelmed by the depth of his feelings.

Karen called out to her grandmother and made a place for her at the table.

"Zach, it's real good to see you here." Helen winked, as if giving him her approval. "Considering Karen's luck with cars, it's just plain common sense for her to be dating a mechanic."

"Gramma, have some iced tea." Color bloomed on Karen's face as she reached for a plastic pitcher, obviously trying to change the subject. "You look like a million dollars in that outfit. Doesn't she look great?"

Mrs. McKaslin's frown deepened. "I don't know what's gotten into you, Mom. You've always had such good common sense."

"I think you look gorgeous, Gramma." Michelle slipped an arm around Helen's slim shoulders. "Except for one thing. You can't wear sneakers with walking shorts. It's a tragedy."

"It is?" Helen looked bewildered. "But Karen helped me."

"Karen knows the basics, but she's no fashion guru or she would have made sure you had a little gold belt and a pair of strappy sandals."

Karen set a cup of iced tea in front of her grandmother. "When we were shopping, we didn't have much time for the shoe department."

"No time for shoes? I can't believe we're related."

So, this is what a real family feels like, Zach thought, watching as Karen's sisters began arguing so loudly over sneakers and sandals, that they drowned out the pastor's first call for attention.

Beside him, Karen bowed her head. The wind ruffled her golden locks against his arm. Looking at her pretty profile, he couldn't get over how lucky he was to be sitting here beside her.

As Pastor Bill began the prayer, Zach bowed his head. Out of the corner of his eye he caught Mrs. McKaslin's gaze. She shook her head at him once, as if she were warning him. As if she were saying he wasn't good enough for her daughter.

The prayer ended. Karen's sisters dove for the bowls of food, chattering again. But the sun didn't feel as bright, even with Karen at his side.

"Honey, are you down here?"

Karen heard her mother's halting step on the stairs and straightened from the dryer. "Yeah, Mom. What do you need?"

"I couldn't seem to get to sleep. The house is so lonely. It feels empty with most of my girls out on their own."

"You still have Michelle and Kirby. And me." The newly dried towels were hot in her arms as she closed the dryer door with her foot. "Did you take your sleeping pill?"

"I hate taking those—you know that." Mom rounded the corner, easing into sight, wearing an old robe. "You should have left those for tomorrow. It's too late to be doing my laundry."

"When else am I going to do it?" Karen dropped the warm towels on the nearby counter. "Let's get you back upstairs and into bed."

"No, I have too much on my mind."

"A sleeping pill will take care of that."

"I don't want one tonight. What I want to do is talk with my daughter." Mom plucked a towel from the pile. "As long as you have time to talk with your mother."

"I do." Karen kept folding. "What's on your mind? You didn't say much at the picnic. Of course, who could get a word in edgewise with the way Michelle carries on?"

"The picnic is what I want to talk to you about."

Karen took a deep breath. "Okay, I've been waiting for this all day. You might as well get it off your chest."

"It's that Drake boy. I had no idea he would be joining us at the church picnic today."

"Well, he does go to our church."

"Yes, but he didn't have to sit at our table."

"I invited him."

"You should have cleared this with me first."

"What? I haven't done that since high school. I know you don't like Zach, but you don't know him very well."

"Everyone is saying he's your boyfriend."

There was no way she could make this easier for Mom. "Zach *is* my boyfriend."

"That just doesn't sound like you at all, Karen, spending time with a boy like that."

"I'm an adult, Mom. I choose my own friends."

"That Zachary Drake is bound to be a bad influence on you. Normally I would bite my tongue, but I can't do it this time. He doesn't even know who his father is. How can a boy like that grow up to be a decent man?"

"Zach *is* a decent man."

"He's going to take advantage of you."

"What do you mean? He's honest and hardworking." Karen threw down the towel she was folding. "I know you hold grudges, Mom, but to judge other people you hardly know? That's wrong, too."

"You're making a mistake, and it's time you realize it before it's too late. That Drake boy will use you, and then where will you be? For heaven's sake, think about how he's making you behave. Breaking off your engagement, changing your hair, leaving your grandmother to work for you, and that's not all. I know all about your late-night motorcycle ride. Dora Melcher saw you speed by on the way to the river."

"You think I did something wrong last night." Karen grabbed the laundry basket. "I can't believe this. That's what you think of me? That I'd dishonor myself and my faith?"

Mom said nothing at all.

"Thanks for your confidence." Karen bit back her anger and headed for the stairs.

Mom's not going to change, but I have. She stomped all the way to the second story.

"Michelle?" She rapped her knuckles lightly against the closed door. "Are you up?"

"Yeah" came the muffled response.

Karen set the basket on the floor and turned the knob. The warm glow of a single lamp illuminated both Michelle and Kirby on the floor, playing a game of Scrabble.

"We're living dangerously," Kirby quipped. "Sounds like you might want to join us."

"Did you hear me and Mom?"

Michelle gestured toward the furnace vent. "Every single word. We want to know what you and Zach were doing alone at the river. And why are your dear, loving sisters always the last to hear about the really good stuff?"

Karen knelt on the floor and stole the bowl of buttered popcorn. "Zach was giving me a ride home because my car broke down—"

"*Sure* it did." Michelle winked. "If I was going after Zach, I'd have a breakdown, too."

Karen laughed. What a blessing it was to have sisters. "Okay, I confess. I unhooked the battery cable so he had to help me."

"You did not!" Kirby wasn't fooled. "Is Zach romantic? He seems like the type. He's such a gentleman, even though Mom hates him."

"He is a gentleman, and that's all I'm going to say." Karen's heart filled with the same brilliant warmth she felt when she was with him.

She couldn't wait to see him again.

Zach squinted in the bright morning light, wiped his hands on his jeans and turned the key. The engine rolled over and hummed in perfect tune.

There was no way Karen's car was going to break down now. He'd made a thorough inspection, replaced a belt with a little wear on it and put in a new starter. That ought to hold her until the next tune-up.

Satisfaction filled him as he backed the car into the street. He glanced at the coffee shop. It looked like Karen was in already. A light shone in the back windows, and a trail of water dripped from the front steps into the road.

He pulled into the alley, his pulse hammering with anticipation.

There she was, more beautiful than the morning. In faded jeans and a short-sleeve sweater, she was busy watering the flowers on the shop's back railing.

Love filled him, gentle and sweet, and he wasn't aware of parking the car. He couldn't look away from her as he crunched across the gravel lot.

"You resuscitated my car." She smiled at him over the bright flowers. "Is that why you're later than usual?"

"Yep. I wanted to change the radiator. Don't want you breaking down again."

"What excellent service. Now I suppose I owe you a cup of coffee."

"That would be a start. We've got to talk about my charges for services rendered." He cradled her chin in his hand. "You owe me ten kisses for all those repairs. I can put it on your bill or collect right here."

"How about in installments?"

"Sure, but I'm going to need a down payment." He kissed her with all the tenderness in his heart. Slowly, to make it last.

When he broke the kiss, she was smiling. There was no mistaking the affection in her eyes, sparkling for the world to see.

Karen McKaslin *liked* him. Maybe she was falling in love with him. He pulled her against his chest and held her tight. She was surprisingly small and fragile. Holding her felt good. It felt right. Cradling her in his arms brought peace to his heart.

The door whispered open.

"Break it up you two. I've got a business to run." Helen clapped her hands. "I'll finish up the watering. Karen, make this man his coffee and get him on his way. Remember, I don't want any romance to interfere with the running of this shop."

Karen rolled her eyes. "Reverse psychology. Gramma's become an expert."

"I heard that, young lady." Helen stole the hose from Karen. "Go on. And, Zach, I don't want to see any kissing on this premises."

He held the door for Karen. "Then I'll wait until your back's turned."

"You're smarter than you look." Helen winked at him. "So, are there any wedding bells in the future for you two? I think I ought to know, since I am in business with Karen. I don't want her to leave me in a lurch during the honeymoon."

"Gramma! Zach, let's run before she starts in on the great-grandchildren." Karen grabbed him by the wrist and led him inside.

He let the door close, then kissed her again. "Don't worry. Helen isn't looking."

"She's gotten incorrigible. I'd better have Pastor Bill talk to her." Karen leaned back in his arms. "I'll get you a cappuccino. There are oven-hot muffins in the kitchen if you want to help yourself."

"Hey, I like dating the owner. Good perks." He hated letting go of her, but he had to. He couldn't hold her forever. "I see it's another busy morning at the coffee shop."

Karen measured espresso. "Wait until tomorrow. Everyone will be back to school and back to work."

"Then it looks like you'll still be able to get off early?"

"Count on it. Does this mean our competition is still on? You're not backing out?"

"Me? I'm no coward."

"Well, I just thought I should give you a graceful way out."

"You don't have enough faith in my natural athletic abilities. How hard can it be to ride a horse? As far as I can tell, you just sit there."

"This is going to be such an easy victory."

"Victory? No way. Get ready to lose, Karen, because I'm already the winner." He kissed her on the cheek. "I get to spend the afternoon with you."

"Like you said, this can't be hard at all." Karen led Michelle's gelding forward, then stopped to adjust the cinch. "You just climb up and sit there."

"You're mocking me. I can feel it."

"Nope, you said you were a natural athlete. So prove it." She checked the buckle, then gathered the reins. "Mount up."

"Does he bite?"

"Yes." Karen patted Keno's silky neck. "He bucks. He rears. He's a real challenge. I didn't want to give you an easy horse."

"You're kidding. I know you are." His lips grazed her cheek. "I'm already plotting revenge. Maybe I'll take you mountain climbing for our next date."

"Well, sure, if you're out of the hospital by then."

"Is it too late to ask for mercy?"

"I'm fresh out of mercy, but I do have mints." She handed him a roll of candy. "It'll put Keno in a good mood. Stick your foot in the stirrup. No, the other foot."

"I'm losing my balance."

"Put your hand on the saddle horn. That's it."

Watching him was a sight to behold. He was all muscled control and male grace as he rose up in the saddle and swung his leg over Keno's rump.

"See?" He looked proud of himself. "What did I tell you? I'm a natural."

"We'll see about that." She adjusted the stirrups for him and slipped Keno another mint. The gelding nudged her hand in thanks.

"He's pretty fierce," she teased. "Ready to go?"

"Go? We could stay here. Sitting still is fine by me. I've got a view of the mountains." He gestured toward the rugged Rockies rimming the horizon. "When we get hungry, we're close to home."

"I packed snacks, so there's no reason to hang around here." She hefted the lightweight saddlebag from the fence railing and secured it into place behind her saddle. "Besides, we might want to be alone."

"Without your mother watching from the windows?"

"Watching and scowling." Karen gave Star a peppermint and a gentle pat. "I hope Mom's not making you uncomfortable."

"Well, I do read that 'stay away from my daughter' look loud and clear."

"It's Mom's problem, not yours. She hasn't forgiven me for canceling the wedding. She really wanted Jay for her son-in-law."

"He was good enough for you, being of the respectable Thornton family."

"And about to become a minister." Karen mounted up. "You're twenty times the man Jay is and don't you forget it."

She blushed because she'd spoken without thinking. She couldn't believe she'd exposed her heart like that. And so easily.

But Zach only smiled. "I'm glad you think so. I happen to think you're pretty great, too."

His kiss was a promise, unspoken but deeply felt. A promise that seemed as brilliant as the sun and as real as the earth.

What had Gramma said this morning? *Are there any wedding bells in the future?* As Karen headed Star down the path toward the river, she braced for the same familiar panic she'd associated with the idea of marriage ever since Jay had proposed.

But panic didn't come. Instead, peace filled her, as slow and steady as the wind through the grasses. When she looked into her future, one with Zach at her side, she saw only happiness and laughter.

And love. True love.

She felt it when he reached out to take her hand. They rode side by side, fingers entwined, in silence. They rode toward the river. Keno was used to sharing the trail with Star, and so all Zach had to do was keep in his saddle.

And hold her hand.

Slowly the pasture gave way to low bushes and the path turned onto the public trail that ran the length of the river. Cottonwoods tossed dappled shade over them, and the happy sounds of kids playing rose above the gurgling water.

Karen released Zach's hand and pulled Star to the side of the trail.

Two boys pedaled by on their bikes. "Hi, Zach!" they called.

"Hey, there." He lifted a hand in greeting and suddenly the horse he rode started running.

"Karen. Help!" The saddle rose up to meet him with a slap, tossing him in the air just enough so his seat lost contact with the leather. He grabbed the saddle horn with both hands, tugging back on the one rein he was still holding.

"Whoa, Keno," Karen called out between giggles. "Zach, just pull straight back on the rein. Not hard—"

"It's not working." The ground was a blur. He was slipping to one side and slapping hard against the saddle. The up-and-down motion was hard enough to rattle his teeth. "This is giving me a headache."

"Keno!" Karen was closer now, but not close enough.

Keno skidded down the bank and splashed into the

water. Zach tumbled forward, lost contact with the saddle and began to slide. He grabbed the saddle horn with both hands and managed to stay on the horse's back.

"I meant to do that," he called over his shoulder.

The kids watching from the bank howled with laughter, but all he saw were the sparkles dancing in Karen's eyes.

She halted her mare at the water's edge. "Of course, you did. You're a natural. I never doubted it for a minute."

"Thanks for leaving my pride intact." He straightened his Stetson before it tumbled into the river. "Now, how do I turn this beast around?"

"I'll come rescue you." She sent her mare into the water and sidled up to him. "I'm going to have to charge you for this. I hope you're willing to pay my price."

"Depends on what you're charging. Maybe I want to get a couple of other estimates, so I can go with the better deal."

"This *is* the better deal." She brushed a feather-soft kiss on his cheek. "Five kisses. Payable today."

"Wow. That's pretty steep. No payment plan?"

"No. Take it or leave it."

"Then I'd better take it. Five kisses, huh? This must mean that you really like me?"

"You could say that." Tenderness warmed her voice, rare and true.

Karen grabbed Keno's bit and headed for shore. She said nothing more, but she smiled—a little mysterious grin—that told him more than words could ever say.

No one had ever cared for him like this.

His heart soared and gave thanks right where he sat. A whole new future stretched out before him.

As soon as they were alone on the trail, he pulled the horse to a stop and Karen into his arms. "Just so you can't say I'm not a man of my word. Five kisses, like I promised."

He kissed her gently, with all the love in his heart. Tenderly, so she would know. He meant to live every day of his life for her.

Chapter Eleven

The tow truck's headlights slashed through the dark night, casting enough light on the narrow two-lane country road to see the grassy banks.

Zach recognized the crooked signpost that stood forgotten in a spray of dead weeds. A battered mailbox used to perch on that post. It was long gone now, but he could picture it in memory.

Right there in the dirt drive, taken over by grass and wildflowers, he'd waited for the school bus every morning.

He thought about the lost little boy he'd been, in tattered jeans and falling-apart sneakers. How he'd never been able to hold his head up, even when he was that small.

That Drake boy, he'd been called. Sylvia Drake's son. The woman who had three children by three different fathers. Who'd spent days and nights at the local bar, too drunk to make her way home.

Zach pulled the truck to a stop and let the engine idle.

He hit the high beams and brightness slashed through the fields. Cows grazed on what was once an unkempt lawn.

All signs of the trailer were gone. Lord knows it had been nearly rusted through when he'd lived there. He tried to shut out the memories of the long nights when hunger gnawed at his stomach. And of the many mornings when his mother made it home, foul smelling and abusive, with one of her endless boyfriends. Zach had felt the sting of their belts more times than he cared to remember.

He'd worked hard to put the chaos of those years behind him. A lot of townspeople still saw that Drake boy in the man he was today, the kid who'd gotten caught stealing to feed his hungry little sister.

In a small town like this, family reputation seemed written in stone. He'd felt that his past would always be a part of him. That no matter how good a man and how honest a businessman, he could never completely wash away the stain of his childhood.

When he was with Karen, she made him a better man. When she looked up at him with affection in her eyes, he felt as if his past didn't matter.

He loved her in a million different ways. He couldn't believe how lucky he was.

God was truly good, to give him Karen's love.

Zach put the truck in gear and drove toward the lights of town. The night was cloudy; a storm was coming in. Wind whipped the trees and put a chill in the air. Christian country music hummed low on the radio, and the song's lyrics got him to thinking.

Maybe I should propose to Karen. Buy her a ring. Ask her to be my wife.

The thought filled him with joy *and* scared him to death. It was a big step, but he was ready. He had a good job, so he could provide for her, whether or not she wanted to keep her coffee shop. He'd worked hard and saved, so his nest egg was plentiful enough to pay for a new house in town.

Maybe he'd stop by a jewelry store on his next trip to Bozeman. He'd get a ring of gold and diamonds that would look perfect on Karen's hand.

Yes, that's what he'd do.

Zach felt better, at peace, as he drove through the silent town and parked in the dark lot behind his garage.

The wind had a bite to it. Walking through the gravel lot, he shivered. Looked like autumn wasn't far away. He'd better make sure he took Karen hiking in the mountains before colder weather hit.

Halfway up the stairs, he realized he'd forgotten to leave his porch light on. He had the eeric feeling he wasn't alone. The stairs were shadowed, and something at the top moved. A chill snaked down his spine and he didn't know why.

The shadows moved again, and he saw a woman huddled on the top step, a tattered paper shopping bag beside her. She stood, swaying from side to side.

The strong scent of alcohol fouled the air. Zach stared at the pathetic woman. The shape of her face looked familiar—

Recognition hit him like a pallet of bricks.

This woman was his mother.

"Is that you, boy?" Her voice slurred as if she were heavily drunk. "Don't jus' stand there while your mother's freezin'."

Zach wanted to run. He wanted to pretend this woman didn't exist.

"I haven't seen you in over ten years," he growled. "What do you want?"

"Found myself in Butte the other day and ran into a buddy of mine from here. Maybe you remember him—Chuck Derango. Used to own the Bulldog."

"The only time I went into that place was to drag you home." He stared down at his keys. He didn't know what to do.

A thousand conflicting feelings coursed through him, burning like acid in his gut.

"Chuck said I'd be proud of you. That you've made a real success of yourself. And here I thought you were still working for old Ray Emry." His mother—Sylvia— laughed. "A place like this must make a lot of money."

It all came clear. "That's why you're here. You think you can get even more money out of me."

"I raised you. I ought to get my due."

"We'll see about that." All he wanted to do was hop on his Harley and ride until the cold pain in his chest vanished. He wanted to outrun the sight of this woman and the memories that came with her.

He was a man now, not a boy. He would deal with this problem.

Pushing past her, he unlocked the door and hit the lights. "Come in for now while I make a few calls."

"Nice place you got here." Sylvia ventured in, clutching her shopping bag. She swayed a little, and inside the bag, bottles clanged together.

She sunk into the couch and leaned back. Tufts of short gray hair stuck straight up, and her face was shriveled and yellow tinged. Her aqua slacks and smock were wrinkled and dirty.

"Here." He pushed a soda can into her hand. "Are you hungry?"

"Don't got any Jack Daniel's in that kitchen of yours?"

"You know I don't." It was wrong to hate her—he knew that—but his heart filled with dark, ugly hatred. "I don't want you staying here. I'll find you a room for the night."

Sylvia's eyes gleamed as she studied the apartment. "This place is big enough for you to take in your mama. You could sleep right here on this couch and I'd have a room all to myself."

"You're not welcome here. Ever."

"I could stay here a while." Sylvia acted as if she hadn't heard him. "Maybe get on the wagon for good, once and for all. You must make a lot of money in that shop of yours. Who would have thought a son of mine would be a respectable businessman?"

Zach walked away. He'd let hate into his heart, and he'd never felt so low. He leafed through the Yellow Pages and punched in the local motel's number. No vacancies, the desk clerk explained.

He dialed again, anger roaring through him like a twister, chewing up all his happiness. He tried

Bozeman. No rooms there—even at the Y. Full up with holiday travelers.

Now what? There was no way he was spending time under the same roof as this woman. Looking at her brought it all back, the shame and scorn he'd felt as a small, helpless boy. He needed help.

But who could he turn to? Not Karen. There was no way he wanted her to see Sylvia. The last thing he wanted to do was remind Karen of his roots, of what he was deep inside.

And maybe would always be.

There was Pastor Bill, who'd been like a father to him, but he didn't want to trouble the man.

Defeated, Zach hung up the phone. "You can stay, but only for tonight."

Sylvia smiled a cat's smile, as if she thought she'd won.

She couldn't be more wrong.

"Come morning, I'll give you a thousand dollars and a ticket on the first bus out of Bozeman. But that's it. If you bother my brother in Bozeman or if you show up here, then I'm cutting you off. Next time you want money, I won't give you a cent."

She nodded, but her manipulative smile remained.

Pounding on the door startled Zach awake. He bolted upright and the blanket tumbled to the floor. It took him a second to realize he wasn't sleeping in his bed. He was in his living room.

"Zach? You in there?" It sounded like Dan Drummond, the local sheriff.

Dread shivered through him. He stumbled to the door and yanked it open.

"Got a little problem," Dan explained. "Your mother's passed out on the library steps. Seems she had a private party last night."

Zach opened his mouth to argue, to say that couldn't be. He'd tried not to sleep too deeply so she couldn't sneak past him. But she'd obviously waited until he'd been in a deep sleep.

"I know this is a sensitive thing, having a mother like that, but I've got her in lockup."

There was no way news this scandalous would stay a secret. "How long are you keeping her for?"

"Twenty-four hours. I'll give you a call when it's time to come get her."

"Thanks, Dan. I appreciate it." Zach closed the door and buried his face in his hands.

Alone in the early morning shop, Karen's thoughts kept drifting to Zach as she worked.

I'm too much in love with the man for my own good. I can't even get through the day without wanting to be with him.

The horse ride had been a success. It would take him a long while before he'd be accomplished enough to make Keno behave, but that was all right. They'd had fun riding into the foothills and back to town for ice cream.

Tomorrow, she hoped to take the afternoon off. She and Zach were going hiking.

The rest of my life could be like this, she realized. Happiness filled her, sparkling and true.

She'd never been so at peace. She felt as if everything in her life was in the perfect place, and it had to be. The Lord had led her here. He'd answered her prayers in a way she'd never imagined. She was so thankful.

The door swept open behind her. Was it Zach? She spun around, aching to see him.

Gramma waltzed into the shop. The smile on her face had never been so bright. "Isn't this a fine morning? I can smell autumn in the air."

"You're certainly in a good mood." Karen set the morning's freshly ground espresso next to the machine. "Did you have a good time at your class last night?"

"Did I! It was so informative, but the really good stuff happened before class even started." Gramma tucked her purse under the counter. "Guess what? I have a date for Friday night."

"A date? What about Clyde?"

"What about him? He didn't appreciate the new me, and that's just fine because I found someone who does."

"Who?"

"A very handsome professor of literature. I stopped for an iced tea after the ordeal of the campus bookstore. I was stirring sugar into my tea and he asked to share my table. His name is Willard and he's the nicest man. His birthday is three days before mine. Imagine that!"

"I bet he was blown away by your beauty and wit."

"How did you know?" Gramma chuckled. "I still can't believe it. He's taking me to dinner and the symphony. To think I love classical music, but I've never been able to get anyone to go with me. And now, after all these years, I meet someone who loves Mozart as much as I do."

"Way to go, Gramma. I'm happy for you."

"So am I. Whatever happens, the least I've done is make a friend. What a blessing."

"That explains why you're late," Karen teased as she finished her prep work. "I hope this doesn't get serious. I don't want any romance to interfere with the running of this shop."

"Reverse psychology isn't going to work on me, missy." Gramma collapsed into the nearest chair. "You wouldn't happen to have another pair of shoes with you?"

"What's wrong with the ones you have on?"

"I haven't worn them for twenty minutes and my feet are killing me. I don't care what Michelle says. I'm wearing sneakers every day for the rest of my life."

"That's what you get for listening to anyone who believes beauty comes before comfort." Karen frothed a cup of milk, speaking to be heard over the noisy machine. "I have a pair of sneakers in my car. You're welcome to them."

"I'm not even going to ask what they're doing there."

"I'm used to breaking down and having to walk. What can I say?" Karen poured vanilla flavoring into the bottom of a cup. "You've really changed my life. I have a car I can depend on and a fabulous business partner. Thank you."

"I haven't helped you half as much as you've helped me." Gramma gave Karen a hug. "Is that for me?"

"Yep. We've got customers waiting outside. Go change your shoes while you can. I can handle the shop until you get back."

"You're a dear." Gramma grabbed her latte and Karen's keys from the counter.

Yes, how her life had changed and all for the good, Karen mused as she flipped the sign in the window to Open and unlocked the front door. Several women were already waiting—commuters on their way to work in Bozeman.

It was eight-thirty when Karen looked up again. Gramma carried out a fresh batch of banana muffins, so rich and fragrant that some customers in line groaned at the aroma.

Karen made latte after mocha after cappuccino, chatting with her regulars while Gramma rang up the orders.

Still, there was no sign of Zach. Maybe, when things slowed down, she'd take him a cup of coffee.

The bell on the door jangled, and Gramma's friends crowded in.

"Helen, are those your banana muffins I smell?" Lois led the way up to the counter. "I have to have one of those and your coffee special."

Karen sent Gramma to sit with her friends and whipped up four chocolate-peanut-butter lattes and served them at the table.

"Have you talked with poor Zach this morning?" Lois asked.

"He hasn't been by yet." Karen withdrew a handful of honey packets from her apron pocket.

"I noticed his shop door was closed when I drove by. It's no surprise that poor young man can't show his face." Lois turned grave, shaking her head. "With his mother coming back to town. Drunk. Heard Dan Drummond arrested her and that fellow who's a janitor at the tavern."

"No doubt Zachary's too ashamed to be out and about among us decent folk," Cecilia Thornton commented as she walked into the shop. "I always say that blood shows. I've seen it time and time again."

"That's a terrible thing to say." Karen faced her ex-fiancé's mother. "Zach is a fine man."

"And what about you? You have your mother so upset. What is she going to say when she hears about this?"

"Karen, take a break." Gramma stood. "I'll get Cecilia some coffee and one of my banana muffins."

Karen squeezed her grandmother's hand in thanks. See, it was a doubly good thing she wasn't marrying into the Thornton family.

She headed to the back door and skidded to a stop. Zach was sitting on the bottom step, his face in his hands.

"Zach? Are you okay?" She slipped onto the step beside him.

He shook his head, straightening up.

She'd never seen such sadness on anyone's face. She put her arm around his shoulder. "I heard about your mother coming to town."

"Sounds to me like you heard a lot more than that." He couldn't bear her touch, so good and kind, and bolted from the step. "I've got to get back to the garage."

"Zach, wait." She breezed after him. "Did you want some company? I'd be glad to come over. We could talk."

"I've got work to do."

"You didn't happen to overhear what Cecilia said, did you? She's not the most compassionate person in town. You can't let her words affect you."

"This has nothing to do with that," he hedged, knowing he wasn't telling the truth. It was wrong, but how could he admit it? How could he say, yes, I heard everything Cecilia said, I opened the door at the right second and it was like hearing my own thoughts.

Karen's touch lit on his forearm. "I care so much about you. This has to be a painful time with your mother back in town."

"I'll be all right." He moved away from her touch again. She was goodness and grace—everything he thought was beautiful and worthy.

"You don't look all right to me." She wouldn't stop caring. "I seem to remember a while ago when I was upset, you sat with me on the step right there. Do you remember what you said?"

He shook his head.

"'You look like someone who needs a friend. Lucky for you, I just happen to be available.'"

"I've got enough friends. See ya." He pushed away from her, the sun in his eyes blinding him. The rush of blood through his ears left him unable to hear anything except the crunch of gravel beneath his boots.

The main street was busy today—just his luck. Maybe if he walked fast, no one would have time to notice him. But he wasn't that lucky. Karen's mom and sister were on their way into the grocery store and Mrs. McKaslin stopped to glare at him.

He knew what she was thinking—not the right kind of man for my daughter.

Heat stained his face, and he stared at the sidewalk and the tips of his boots as he half jogged, half ran to the garage. Sharp whispers rose on the wind.

Shame filled him. With every step he took, he felt the man he'd worked hard to be fall away like a mask.

Maybe that's all it had ever been—just a facade to cover up who he really was inside. An unwanted child born out of wedlock and raised in the shadow of his mother's shame.

The shop phone was ringing, and he let it ring. He couldn't face anything today, not even work. He closed the front bay doors and locked them. The phone fell silent and after a few minutes started ringing again.

Karen. He knew it. It was like her, to take care of people, to check up on him, to make sure he was all right.

Images he'd dared to dream seemed embarrassing now—foolish to think he could propose to Karen and buy her a house. To make a life with her.

The plain and simple truth was that he'd never really had a chance with Karen. He remembered something Helen said. What had she called him? A rebound relationship.

Zachary Drake, you are such a fool.

He hopped on his Harley and headed east, where the sun rose in an endless sky.

Karen turned off the water faucet, the sprinkler silencing in the thick twilight. Should she try calling Zach again? She'd dropped by his shop twice, only to find it locked and empty. There was no answer at his apartment. She'd left message after message.

He hadn't called.

She was worried about him. He'd been so upset this morning. He'd pushed her away, but she'd refused to take his words seriously.

He's hurting. Maybe he doesn't know how much I really care. It isn't as if I've told him.

She headed inside and picked up the phone. His voice mail answered. There was no sense in leaving another message, so she hung up.

Where was he? Was he with friends? Maybe Pastor Bill? Or was he alone and hurting?

If he doesn't answer the next time I call, I'll drive into town.

That made her feel better, but she couldn't stop shivering. It was as if the night's coolness had settled into her bones.

Chapter Twelve

Seeing Zach lying on a creeper beneath an old pickup inside his shop made Karen's worries fade a little. At least he was okay. He was back to work.

She'd stopped by last night and again early this morning, and he hadn't appeared to be home. He hadn't answered her knock, at least.

Maybe he'd needed space to deal with the sad situation of his mother. It was common knowledge the woman ran off with a man when Zach was only fifteen. Except for yesterday, she'd never been back.

"Hello, handsome," she called out, rattling the paper bag she carried. "You didn't come over, so I brought lunch to you."

He glanced at her from beneath the chrome bumper. "I already ate."

"Then you've got a substantial afternoon snack. I saved you some of Gramma's potato salad. It was gone before the lunch rush was over."

"Karen, stop being so nice to me. If I wanted to eat

at your shop, I would have gone there." A tool clanged on the cement floor.

"You don't sound all right and you didn't return my calls."

"Busy" came his terse response.

"Are you angry with me? Did I do something to upset you?" She knelt down to peer at him beneath the bumper. "You have to forget what Cecilia Thornton said. She's wrong. I know it. My gramma knows it. And you do, too, right?"

He sighed, dropped his tool with a *clunk* and rolled out from under the vehicle. Grease stained his hands and his shirt. Exhaustion bruised the skin beneath his eyes. He looked terrible, as if he'd been up all night.

Sympathy flooded her. She wanted to hold him until all the pain he had to be hiding faded. She went to him, but he didn't step into her arms. He turned away and hunted for a clean rag to wipe his hands.

"Is your mother still here? I could help you if you needed anything—"

"She's on a bus bound for Phoenix. I'm praying she stays on it." He kept his back to her as he wiped the grease from his hands.

His shoulders looked slightly hunched, and she didn't doubt he was hurting.

She should tell him he's not alone and say the words she longed to—*I love you.* She should take the risk and tell him how cherished he was. To her. As the one man she wanted to love for the rest of her life.

Just do it. She took a step toward him. "Zach, I—"

"Look, I don't have time right now. I've got to get

this finished." Zach tossed down the rag, his shoulders dipping more. "Thanks for the lunch. Next time, wait until I come to the shop, okay?"

Karen stared, unbelieving, as he held out a five-dollar bill. "What's going on? You don't have to pay. I—"

"Take the money." He shoved it into her hand. "See you."

She stared at the money, creased and worn. What was happening? "Zach, would you listen? I want to tell you how I feel—"

"Summer's over, and I've got to get back to work." He rummaged through his toolbox. "Maybe you can find someone else to help you get over Jay. I'm no longer the man to do it."

"But—" Tears burned in her throat. "What about all those kisses?"

"They were nice. No strings attached, right?" He found the tool and gripped it, white-knuckled, in his hand. "I don't want to hurt your feelings, Karen, but did you really think anything could work out between us? I live above a garage. I've got a family reputation that would put yours to shame. Cecilia Thornton is right. Your mother doesn't want me around you."

"But they're wrong. You're gentle and intelligent and kind, and I—"

"I don't want to see you again." The words tore him apart, and he said them as quietly as he could. It was for her own good, even if she couldn't see that.

All those sweet kisses had come to this. It tore him up watching the tears fill her eyes, but then she blinked them away.

Her chin shot up. "I'm not a fair-weather friend, and I thought there was more to you than this. We had a good time together. I thought—"

"That's all we had. A good time." He cut her off, turned his back, afraid she'd say the words that would make him start to believe again. Believe in what could never be. "I know you're thinking this is about my mother coming to town and what Cecilia said, but you're wrong. You're too nice for me."

"I see." Her words sounded stilted, without emotion. She looked shell-shocked.

"I don't want to hurt you, Karen, so maybe it would be better if we didn't see each other again."

She fell silent.

He doubted she knew just how much she meant to him. There was nothing more to say, so he stretched out on the creeper and scooted back under the pickup.

Safely hidden, he released a deep breath. Sylvia Drake's son had no business loving a woman like Karen McKaslin.

He watched her walk away. Her slim ankles and dainty white sneakers whispered across the cement floor and then out of sight.

His heart broke in a million sharp pieces.

Zach knew as sure as the sun was in the sky that Karen was out of his reach.

And always would be.

You're too nice for me. Zach's words rang like a bell, over and over in Karen's mind. Somehow she made it down the street, the sidewalk a blur at her feet, the storefronts hazing together. She choked out a hello to Nora Greenley who was waiting at the curb while a box boy loaded groceries into the trunk of her car.

Karen stumbled up the steps of the coffee shop, passing by the flower boxes that smelled sweet like summer.

Summer's over, and I've got to get back to work, Zach had said.

Is that all it was? A good time?

The bell clamored in the nearly empty shop. A group of women sat in the sunny corner, devotionals and Bibles stacked in front of them. Thankfully, they were busy and didn't notice her. Karen turned her head anyway. She didn't want anyone to see the tears in her eyes.

At least he was honest with me, she thought. At least Zach wanted nothing but a good time, a few motorcycle rides and a fishing trip.

But that didn't seem like the truth or keep her heart from rending.

Be calm, she told herself, blinking back tears. She wasn't about to let anyone see her so sad and wonder why.

She grabbed her purse and keys from under the counter as Gramma shouldered through the kitchen doors.

"Good, I'm glad to see you're ready to go. Did Zach like my potato salad?"

"You know he does." Karen kissed her grandmother's cheek. "I'm off. The rest of the afternoon should be quiet."

"I can handle it. I *am* a businesswoman."

"And an excellent one. Look how successful the shop has become. I'll open up early tomorrow, so don't bother to come in until late."

"Maybe that's not a good idea." Gramma followed her to the back door. "You look pale and your eyes are glassy. Are you ill?"

"Just tired." Which was the truth. "I've got to go."

"You have a fun time with your handsome young man."

Karen couldn't answer. Zach wasn't hers. He never had been. She closed the door and dashed down the stairs, the pain inside her hurting more with each step she took.

How could she have been so foolish? No man was ever going to love her deeply. She was too ordinary, too dependable. True love didn't happen to girls like her.

She settled behind the steering wheel and turned the ignition. The old Ford coughed to a start—hadn't Zach promised her that this car was in good shape?—and she headed into the alley. The street through town was quiet, but it took her past Zach's garage.

What had he said about her kisses? They were nice. Lukewarm.

Dear Lord, I thought he was the one. She swiped wetness from her cheeks. *I loved him, and I thought he loved me.*

How could she have been wrong?

Dust lifted behind her on the driveway and clouded the air when she parked the car in front of the garage at home. The sun was hot, but the wind was definitely cooler.

Zach was right. Summer *was* over. No more fishing trips or rides along the river. No more kisses beneath a star-filled sky.

"Karen!" Mom called from the front steps. "Are you going to be home for dinner? I feel up to cooking. You aren't going out with that Drake boy again, are you?"

"No, Mom."

"That's my sensible girl. Supper's at six sharp. See you then."

Sensible girl. The words pierced Karen's soul and stayed there like a barbed wire hooked firm, words that made her feel less than valuable. She'd colored her hair, changed her life, but had it made any difference?

Sensible, plain and responsible. Was that all Zach saw in her? He'd had fun, he said, but he'd only been helping her get over Jay. That's what he'd said. Part of her didn't believe him —or couldn't.

I want someone to love me, Lord. Is that too much to ask? I don't want to be alone the rest of my life.

But she didn't want to settle, either. She didn't want a lukewarm marriage.

What was God's plan for her? She didn't know.

Star nickered from the far end of the corral and trotted over. Karen grabbed the lead rope looped around a fence post and snapped it onto the mare's halter.

"We're going for a run, girl." Karen crawled through the fence rails and mounted. Her horse was something a girl could always count on.

They loped through the fields toward the river trail.
Karen squeezed all thoughts of Zach from her mind.

Maybe there was no such thing as true love. It was
only a fairy tale, and nothing more.

She wanted the Lord to guide her, to show her the
answers for sure. She felt so very lost.

So alone.

Zach looked up, recognizing the sound of the
engine—Karen's car. The morning was calm and
almost cool, and she drove past with her windows up.
He could hardly see her through the sheen on the glass.

Stop thinking about her. There's no point in
dwelling on what was past. Aching tenderness cut like
a blade through his chest, and he turned his attention
back to the engine he was in the middle of rebuilding.

His relationship with Karen was over. He didn't
like it. He'd give anything to have the right to marry
her.

But last night, prayer had put everything in perspective. He had to trust God's will for his life. He had
to believe that everything happened for a greater
reason—and there were some things a man couldn't
have. That's all there was to it.

This morning, he planned to buy his coffee from the
diner and stay away from Karen McKaslin.

"What is with this car?" In the parking lot behind
her shop, Karen gave the tire a kick. Steam was wafting
from beneath the hood and the temperature gauge had
been climbing all the way into town.

"I'm going to find another mechanic." She wasn't about to ask Zachary Drake to repair her car again. Especially since he'd been doing a lousy job.

"Morning, Karen!" Jodi called out as she cut across the alley. "Your car is smoking."

"I know. I have bad car luck." Karen slung her purse over her shoulder and hurried up the stairs. She was late, and she was opening the shop alone. This morning Gramma had a meeting at the church.

Karen was unlocking the door when she heard a car pull into the lot. For a second she thought it was Zach come for his early-morning coffee. Then she remembered he said that he didn't want to see her again.

Gramma parked her snazzy car, climbed out and shut the door. "Surprised to see me, aren't you? I woke up before the alarm and the house seemed lonely. I figured if I showed up here, I could sweet-talk my granddaughter into making me a cup of coffee."

"You've got that look in your eye." Karen wasn't fooled as she held the door. "Why are you really here?"

"Nothing." Gramma appeared perfectly innocent as she dropped her purse and keys on the counter. "I happened to notice yesterday that Zach was in his garage working all afternoon. When he was supposed to be on a date with you."

"No, I'm not going to talk about that." Karen headed straight for the kitchen.

"Did you two have a disagreement?"

"Not a disagreement. I wouldn't call it that." Karen yanked open the freezer and grabbed the heavy bag of coffee beans. "That's all I'm going to say."

"Fine. All right. I respect your privacy." Gramma took the bag from Karen's arms. "Let me do the grinding. You don't look like you slept a wink last night."

"It's your morning off." Karen regained possession of the bag. "Sit down, put up your feet and relax. I'll have your latte ready in a few minutes."

"If that's what you want." Gramma went around the dining room, opening the curtains and tying them back.

Sunlight washed into the room. It felt like any other day. The sun rose and soon people would be hurrying to work and taking their children to school.

When Karen felt as if her life would never be the same. How could it be? She'd lost her dreams of Zach. She'd lost his friendship, too.

By the time she finished Gramma's latte, she found her grandmother in the kitchen, whipping up muffins.

"Just set it there on the counter, dear," Gramma said as she filled the tins. "Are you ready to tell me what happened?"

"No." Karen reached for the mixing bowl and rinsed it in the sink. "Oh, all right. I'll tell you. All this time I thought Zach...well, it turns out that he's not interested in me."

"That's nonsense. I've got eyes. I can see that boy's in love."

"No. He said he was just having fun."

"That sounds ridiculous." Gramma slipped the tins into the oven. "I was married for a long time, and you learn to break the code. Seems to me that this happened after his mother's arrest. Maybe he thinks he has something to be ashamed about."

"Nice try, but you don't want to admit your granddaughter is plain and unexciting. I spend my days making coffee and helping my sisters look after my mom."

"Maybe he figures he'd reject you before you reject him."

"Maybe, but he thinks I'm too nice. That's the problem." Karen dried off the bowl and fit it into place in the mixer. "It isn't because of his mother. He told me that."

"That man's protecting his heart, if you want my opinion." Gramma set down the oven mitt and wrapped Karen in a hug. "Zach has never had a real family. He's never known what it's like to have unconditional love. The kind that can never be broken. Maybe God sent you into his life for a reason. To teach him that."

"Nice try, Gramma, but I don't think so."

"Talk to him. Find a reason to go to his shop and try to make him listen. I've seen how happy you two are together. A love like that is worth fighting for."

"Even if it's one-sided?" She was afraid to believe otherwise. "He said—"

"People say lots of things to protect their hearts. Now trust your grandmother, make him some coffee and go talk to the boy."

"I can't." Karen turned to the flour canister and started measuring.

"Hey, Zach." Tommy Clemmins rode his bike into the garage, his book bag dangling over one handlebar. "My tire's flat again. I guess I rode over a nail."

"I guess." Zach grabbed a rag, left his work, and knelt down to take a look. "I'd better patch that. Why don't you grab an apple juice from the refrigerator over there? I have a box of chocolate doughnuts on my toolbox."

"Thanks!" Tommy dropped his books on the floor.

Zach grabbed his glue gun and a patch from his bottom drawer and went to work. Before Tommy was finished with his second doughnut, the tire was holding air.

"I'm not even gonna be late to school! Thanks, Zach." Tommy hopped on his bike and rode out of sight.

Forgetting his book bag.

That kid. Shaking his head, Zach grabbed the bag and jogged outside. Tommy biked back across the street in a wide space between a school bus going one way and a car going the other.

"I know, I know. I'm gonna be in big trouble if I forget my homework one more time." Tommy skidded to a stop and looped the book bag over his handlebar.

He pedaled into the street, looking over his shoulder to wave.

Zach saw it all in a flash. The loaded hay truck ambling down the road, the surprise on the driver's face, Tommy turning to stare at the oncoming truck and realizing he was in danger. The boy froze with fear.

The semi's brakes squealed, locking up. There was no way the driver could stop in time. Zach was already running. He grabbed Tommy by the shoulders and hurled him toward the sidewalk. The semi's grill slammed into Zach's shoulder and back, tossing him into the air.

Zach didn't feel anything—not pain or fear. He hit the asphalt but he couldn't feel that, either. It was as if it were happening to someone else. He rolled to a stop on his side, his forehead resting against the cool cement curb.

"My stars!" The Mint Mocha Special Gramma was serving slipped from her hand and clattered to the floor. "Tell me that isn't Zachary Drake."

Through the windows, Karen saw a loaded hay truck jackknifing in the middle of town, brakes squealing. A bicycle flew into the air and slammed against the brick front of John Corey's hardware store. A little boy lay sprawled on the sidewalk, then climbed to his feet.

"It isn't Zachary Drake." Marj Whitly leaned in her chair for a better look. "It's that little Clemmins boy. He's getting up. He's fine. What a close call!"

Karen left the espresso machine, coffee dripping, and raced around the counter. Sure enough, the little boy looked fine.

Then why was the fire chief racing out of his store, shouting orders at everyone in sight? He ran past the boy and knelt in the street. Karen recognized the grease-stained work boots just visible behind the motionless semi.

She was out the door before she even realized she was running. Sprinting across the street and pushing around people gathering in a knot on the sidewalk.

"Stay back, everyone, let them work." The sheriff caught Karen by the arm and held her. "You have to give them room, Karen."

She could only stare in horror at how motionless Zach looked. Broken and lifeless, as if he weren't even breathing.

"He's going to be okay," the lawman told her, not letting go of her. "Someone take her. Nora, is that you? Take her back to her grandmother. She can't do any good here."

"No." She was only vaguely aware of Nora Greenley, her grandmother's friend, taking her by the hand. Terror made her cold as she watched one of the town doctors stop his car and race across the road.

The little boy was crying as one of the town's volunteer firemen looked at his bruised arm. "Zach's gonna die and it's all my fault."

"He's not going to die," the fireman reassured him.

Karen could see Zach was breathing. His chest rose and fell, shallow and rapid. He looked ashen, and a streak of blood trickled down his face from a cut on his forehead.

He looked like he could die.

Someone had grabbed the backboard from the fire hall around the corner, and four men gingerly strapped Zach to it.

The men were busy setting up an IV, and Karen was hardly aware of her grandmother taking her hand. The medical helicopter arrived, landing in a field on the other side of the railroad tracks.

"Probable broken vertebrae," John Corey called

above the beat of the chopper's blades. "He's alert but in a lot of pain."

"He'll be okay." Gramma sounded sure of it. "What he needs are extra prayers and loved ones around him. Come, I'd better drive you to the hospital."

But he doesn't love me, Karen almost said, but watching four men lift Zach on the backboard and carry him across the street, kept her silent.

No, he hadn't said he didn't love her. He hadn't looked at her the whole time he'd been rejecting her, as if he hadn't been telling the truth.

She was afraid to believe it, but maybe Gramma was right. *Zach is as afraid of being rejected as I am.*

She didn't know if it were true or not, but it was worth finding out. Having Zach's love was worth risking her heart.

"Please take me to the hospital," she asked her grandmother. "I'm too upset to drive."

"Knew you'd see things my way. Nora promised she'd lock up, so let's get going." Gramma slipped an arm around her shoulder

The helicopter took off with an ear-ringing racket. Karen watched it. Zach was in there, on his way to the emergency room. *Please, Lord, take good care of that man. I love him.*

Chapter Thirteen

There were one hundred and six ceiling tiles on his side of the hospital room. Zach closed his eyes, and all he saw behind his lids were images of the ceiling tiles.

The surgery to fuse vertebrae in his neck had gone well, and they'd moved him out of ICU after the first day. He'd been trapped in this tiny room for three days and already he was going stir-crazy.

Strapped to the bed in traction, he couldn't turn his head to see the window. Somewhere out there the sky was blue. There were cars to fix, trails to ride and mountains to climb.

What had the doctors said? His chances of walking again were fifty-fifty.

Lord, I have to get out of this room. Please.

"Good to see you're awake." Pastor Bill appeared beside the bed, his face pale with fatigue and worry. "I sent your sister home. She stayed the night by your bed again. You should know there's someone who's been waiting for you to feel well enough for a visit. I'll be waiting outside."

"I don't want any visitors—" But Pastor Bill was gone.

"Hi, Zach." Karen appeared, carrying a vase of cheerful yellow flowers. "Let me put these where you can see them."

The harsh words he'd said to her haunted him, and he wished he could vanish. He'd done what he had to do. There was no way he was the right man for her.

She disappeared, her sneakers slightly squeaking on the floor. Zach heard a thud and a clink and the flowers appeared, propped on the windowsill.

She returned to his bedside, avoiding his gaze. He couldn't stop the shame creeping through him, leaving him feeling small. If he hadn't pushed her away, she would be reaching for his hand right now. Gazing at him with that sparkling affection in her eyes. Saying something to make him feel better.

He loved her with all the depth of his soul, whether it was right or wrong. He'd been tough on her, and here she was, a friend once more, bearing flowers and well wishes.

"Gramma sends her best. You know what she said?"

He didn't answer.

"That you'd be up and walking in no time. She'll sneak you in some of her taco cheese and macaroni casserole when she gets the chance."

Zach stared at the off-white ceiling tiles. A polite exchange—that's what she intended. He missed her smile and her gentle teasing. He wished he could take her hand and have the right to hold on to her.

She approached the bed. "Is there anything I can do for you?"

"Not a thing."

"I could read to you."

What he needed was her. Zach closed his eyes and tried to ignore the pain the medication couldn't kill. As bad as he hurt, it was nothing compared to the pain in his heart. If only he had the right to make her his.

"Is your pain worse? I'll get the nurse—"

"I don't need the nurse. Seeing you—" Makes me love you even more. He couldn't tell her. It wouldn't be right. There were some things a man couldn't have.

"Maybe I should let you rest. I'll be out in the waiting room in case you need anything."

"What do you mean? You're staying?"

"Do you think I'd leave you when you're hurt?" Karen's chin lifted, and he'd never seen this side of her. "I think you might not have been honest with me in your shop. You spent a lot of time telling me to leave and why, but I know how it felt when you kissed me."

"I don't think you should be here."

"But I love you." She crossed her arms over her chest as if she were protecting herself. "Do you know that? Couldn't you feel that, too?"

"You love me?" The medication must be messing with his mind. There was no way Karen genuinely, unconditionally loved a man like him.

He might want it more than anything, but it was impossible.

Her bottom lip trembled. "I know what you said before, about summer being over and I'm too nice for you, but I'm not sure that's what you really feel. Didn't we have something special? I thought we were falling in love, and then I'm not certain what happened."

"I thought it was obvious. I'm not the man for you."

"I think you are." Couldn't he see that she was risking her whole heart? "I don't care who your mother is or if she might come back to town one day. Do you think I do? Is that why you broke things off?"

"We can't be together. It wouldn't last."

"Why not? Don't you know I only see the good in you? There's a lot of good."

"I'm no one special, Karen."

"To me, you are. I see the hero in you, in an ordinary man with an ordinary life. I love you. I want to marry you and have a family with you. When I look at you, I see a courageous and gentle man I can trust with my heart."

"I'd give anything to be that man, but I'm not."

"You are to me. Or am I the problem? You said I was too nice for you. I thought you could see something good and special inside me. Tell me that you do, please. Even just a little."

How could he tell her that he saw more—much more? She'd awakened his heart. Her quiet beauty was more lovely to him than any in the world.

He loved her more than he thought possible. If only he could change his past and who he was....

It felt written in stone.

"I don't want you here." The words sounded harsh when he didn't mean them to be. He just wanted to spare his heart.

"You didn't answer my question. But either way, that's an answer, too." Her bottom lip trembled. "I guess this is goodbye."

She walked away, just like that, taking his heart with her.

Footsteps tapped into the room, and Zach realized he wasn't alone.

"That was some show," Pastor Bill commented. "I tried to stay out in the hall to give you two some privacy, but I couldn't help overhearing. Why did you send that woman away? The one who loves you even if you might not walk again?"

"What I had with Karen is over."

"Why's that? Because you're strung up in this hospital room while your back heals?"

"We both know I'm not the kind of man Karen McKaslin is going to marry and I never will be." Zach was exhausted and wrung-out. Burning, grinding pain radiated up his spine. He'd lost Karen forever.

"You know what the Bible says," Pastor Bill began thoughtfully. "'...*Those who become Christians become new persons. They are not the same anymore, for the old life is gone. A new life has begun.*'"

"That doesn't mean—"

"It does. The past is erased, and it would be foolish to throw away the future because of it. God wants good things for you, Zachary Drake. Believe that."

How could he? How could it be true? It didn't feel true. Zach closed his eyes, overwhelmed, thinking about what the pastor had said.

* * *

"What are you doing back?" Gramma looked up from serving her friends a round of steaming mochas. "I told you, running this place without you isn't a burden. I've got Michelle coming in an hour to help me close up."

Karen dropped her keys on the counter. "I'll do it."

She was so angry with Zachary Drake! She'd laid her heart open and told him how she truly felt. Thinking it would make a difference. For him. For his recovery. Especially for their future.

And he hadn't done the same. He hadn't told her how he felt. He hadn't said the words that mattered. Maybe he never loved her at all. Not even a little bit.

She was still so incredibly angry with him! No one—not even Jay—had ever made her this angry. She punched through the kitchen doors and turned on the faucet. Hot water steamed into the sink and she began rinsing dishes, then stacking a load of mugs into the dishwasher.

He's all that matters to me, she realized. *He's still all I care about.*

The door whispered open behind her. "What happened at the hospital? Is Zach all right?"

"His recovery is going well, if that's what you mean." A plate slipped from her fingers and crashed into the sink. "He's looking forward to your visit."

Gramma sidled up to the counter. "I thought you were going to stay at his side until he's out of the hospital."

"He told me to go." Karen retrieved the plate and it slipped from her fingers again. "He doesn't want me to come back."

"That doesn't sound right. I don't think he's telling the truth. He's injured, and it can't be easy worrying if he'll walk again. Maybe he's saying that because he feels he has to."

"There's nothing more I can do." Karen left the plate in the sink and shut off the water. "I'm through with Zachary Drake."

She'd survived other breakups just fine. She'd get over this one, too.

Except this time it was Zach. Zach, the man who made her laugh, who made her feel unique and treasured.

It wasn't going to be easy getting over him. If she ever could.

Chapter Fourteen

"I had such a wonderful time at the symphony," Gramma mused as she wiped down the coffee shop's counter. "Willard and I had coffee and dessert afterward and talked until one in the morning."

"I'm glad you like him." Karen squeezed water from the mop. "Are you two going out again?"

"Next weekend we're taking in a Shakespearean play. Just when I'd given up finding someone like Willard, he walks into my life. Imagine that. He could be the one."

"I hope so." Karen mopped the floor, happy for her grandmother. It was only the beginning of her relationship with the professor, but maybe he would end up being the love of Gramma's life.

Karen hoped so. She wanted to think true love existed in this world and happened to women like her.

The phone rang, and Gramma was closest to it. Karen swiped the mop across the wood floor, then dunked it into the soapy bucket.

"Zachary Drake! What are you doing calling here? How's the hospital treating you? Terrible food, is that right? I did plan to visit you this week. I'll come with my casserole, promise." Gramma laughed. "Karen, it's for you."

Karen stared at the receiver her grandmother held out for her. Twice she'd risked her heart; twice she'd tried to tell Zach that she loved him.

She'd been hurt enough. She'd risked everything for him, and she wasn't about to do it again.

Gramma waggled the receiver. "Go on," she whispered. "He wants to talk to you."

"Tell him I'm busy." She went back to her mopping.

"Zach, Karen's being stubborn and she won't come to the phone. Don't worry, I have a way of convincing her to do anything—"

Gramma meant well, but she should understand. If Zach believed he wasn't the man for her. If he didn't want her, then there was nothing she could do.

Not one thing.

She marched out the door and stayed outside until Gramma hung up the phone.

"Look at all these flowers," Chief Corey commented when he walked into Zach's hospital room. "It looks like a florist shop in here. How does it feel to be the town hero?"

"I'm no hero."

"Yeah? Well, that's not what everyone's saying. You saved Tommy's life, and no one's going to forget that.

You're going to be the most popular man in town. Of course, you don't need throngs of women adoring you. You're dating Karen McKaslin."

"We're friends, that's all."

"Are you kidding? She's in love with you."

I know. Zach remembered how she'd stood where John was standing now, saying she loved him.

A knock sounded at the door. Helen and three of her friends waltzed into the room, bearing fantastic-smelling food and colorful balloons.

"How's our town hero?" Mabel Clemmins, Tommy's grandmother, asked.

"Town hero," John repeated, reaching for his hat. "Get used to it. You're going to hear it a lot."

After his visitors left and as the evening wore on, Zach caught himself missing Karen. And thinking about what Pastor Bill had said.

He could have been killed when he'd thrown himself in front of the hay truck. No doubt about it. The doctors had told him he was lucky. Already he could wiggle his toes.

It was time for him to let the past rest. He'd stopped being Sylvia Drake's son long ago. Pastor Bill was more of a parent to him than his mother ever was.

He was his own man. He raised his brother and sister, ran his own business and had many good friends in his hometown. If God had spared his life for a reason, then Zach knew why.

He'd been put on this earth to love Karen McKaslin. And a gift like that was too precious to waste.

* * *

"C'mon, Karen, he's called like every day this week." Michelle hung up the phone. "You're going to drive that hunk away."

"I don't know why he's calling me."

"I wonder. He's only the most popular guy in town. A real hero. Everyone says so. Why he wants to talk to you is a mystery, but he keeps calling. You should at least be polite and talk to him."

"I've said more than enough. If I humiliate myself one more time in front of him, I'm going to lie down and never move again." Karen rolled the dice and moved her Monopoly piece onto Vermont Avenue.

"Ooh! You owe me," Kirby announced across the kitchen table.

Whatever Zach had to say to her, it didn't matter. Karen handed play money to her sister. She was through risking her heart on Zachary Drake.

Now, if only she could stop being in love with him. Because she *was* in love with him. She knew she always would be.

Three weeks later, Zach set the walker against the garage wall. He'd had enough of that contraption. What he wanted was to see Karen, but she hadn't been in the shop. Running errands, Helen had explained. A real excuse, this time.

His homecoming had been great. Pastor Bill had insisted he stay with his family until he was stronger, and Zach had accepted. The well wishes hadn't stopped.

If Zach needed proof of what Bill had said, about being made new, then he had it. He'd been the one who let his past affect him. When he looked at himself more kindly, he might not see himself as a hero, but he did see an average guy who'd been about as dumb as they came.

He'd hurt Karen. He'd pushed her away. Truth be told, her love scared him. But true love, he was learning, wasn't something that could ever fade. She still loved him—or so Helen and Karen's sisters assured him.

How did he get her back?

He opened his toolbox and went to work. His back hurt, but it felt good to be busy. The ring he'd bought today weighed heavily on his thoughts—a sparkling solitaire on a gold band. The one he planned to give her when she agreed to marry him.

Like that would be an easy question to ask her.

The next time you see her, just take her by the hand, bend down on one knee and say the words.

He figured it sounded a lot easier than it was, but he'd find the courage. Because he loved her.

"Hey, Zach," John called from next door where he was sweeping his sidewalk. "Guess who's coming this way with her bank deposit? Just thought you'd like to know."

Zach wiped his hands on a rag. Okay, you can do it. Just give her that grin she likes and don't take no for an answer.

Armed with courage, he headed out the door.

Karen saw him immediately. Her eyes widened and

her jaw dropped. She must not have realized he was in his garage.

"Hi," he called out, but before he could say anything more, she slipped between the buildings and walked out of sight.

"Proof that she isn't over you," John commented, broom in hand. "Trust me, I'm an expert when it comes to romance."

Zach waited, watching for her to reappear farther down the street. Yep, there she was, emerging from the side street near the bank.

His heart ached at the sight of her. He wasn't afraid, not anymore, because he knew he was the only man for her. One day soon, he was going to make her believe it.

It had been a tough week, and Karen was glad she had the afternoon off. She grabbed her denim jacket from the coat tree at the front door of her shop. "Michelle, don't scare off the customers. Gramma and I are trying to actually make a profit this month."

"Ha ha. Don't lose track of time. We meet at Gramma's house at six sharp. We've got to make sure our grandmother is smartly dressed for the upcoming winter season. I was thinking she needs some of those stylish new boots."

"I can see this is going to be an ordeal," Karen teased. "I never should have invited you along."

"Face it, Gramma needs my expert fashion sense." Michelle grabbed the mop and wrung it out in the bucket. "You could use some help too, Karen."

"I can finally afford a few new things, but I'm scared to trust you. Last time I did, you turned my hair green."

"You know what I think? Leopard skin and leather. I bet we could make a whole new look for you."

"Stop teasing!" Karen balanced her dish of soft ice cream with one hand and opened the front door with the other.

The crisp air of autumn smelled earthy and rich. Dried leaves skidded down the street, and kids just released from school ran down the sidewalk screaming and laughing.

"Butterscotch sundae, just for you, Star." Karen leaned against her horse's flank, where the animal stood obediently in a parking spot off the main street.

It was too cold to eat ice cream, but it brought back the sweetest memories. Of her and Allison as little girls, always to be found on their horses. Sharing candy and snacks, laughing and carefree.

There were more memories to make in her life, and Karen wondered what they would be.

A car slid into the parking space beside her—a polished red convertible. A classically dressed, handsome older woman emerged from the vehicle. "Why, if it isn't my beautiful granddaughter."

"Hi, Gramma. You're looking radiant."

"Being in love will do that to a woman. Willard took me out to lunch and a movie. I haven't had so much fun in ages. He's coming to church on Sunday, so help me prepare your mother. She's not likely to approve of me dating."

"She's bound to like him." Karen gave her grandmother a hug. "He's a nice man. I think he's perfect for you."

"Me, too. I'll see you this evening. I can't wait to go shopping. I need the right dress to wear on my date Saturday night."

"We'll find something to make you look gorgeous," Karen promised.

Gramma hurried up the stairs and out of the wind, her step had never been so lively—ever since she'd been dating her distinguished English professor.

And here I thought true love didn't happen to women like us.

But she'd been wrong. While she was happy for her grandmother, Karen wouldn't mind finding that for herself. No—she wasn't going to even think about Zach.

Star nudged her hand, eager for more ice cream, and she gave the horse a big spoonful.

A yellow car slipped into the parking spot on the other side of Star. The door opened and a man emerged, dressed in a T-shirt and jeans. Karen recognized the cut of his handsome profile and the dark shock of untamed hair tumbling over his forehead.

"Zach." She couldn't believe it was him. How had he sneaked up on her?

"Hi, Karen." Zach closed the car door and leaned against it, slipping his hands in his pockets. "You're looking good."

"You look better than I saw you last." What she needed to do was leave quickly, before he could see that she still loved him. She inched away.

"They say I'll be almost as good as new, but I have to take it easy for a while."

She took two more steps back. A few more, and she could dart up the steps. Could he tell by looking at her that she was still in love with him? Embarrassed, she searched for something polite to say. "I'm glad you're walking. You gave all of us a real scare."

"God's been very good to me. I'm pretty happy to be up on my feet." He rubbed his brow, looking troubled. "I was rude to you in the hospital, and I'm sorry."

"Don't mention it. I was wrong to push myself on you like that. Especially when you were so hurt."

"Why don't you stop trying to run away, come over here and let me apologize properly? It's the least I can do after the way I behaved."

"You don't have to apologize. Really." It's not like an apology could change the truth.

"I need to tell you how sorry I am. I said things I wish I hadn't."

"And I was wrong." It hurt to think how foolish she'd been, risking her heart. She changed the subject. "I'm glad you're back to work."

"Not officially. I've been tinkering for a few hours a day to keep busy." He gestured to the Chevy gleaming like new. "See what I did to your old car."

"That can't be the rusted-out rattletrap I used to drive."

"One in the same."

She ran her fingers over the dent-free front left fender. The crack in the windshield was gone. The dings and dents and rust patches had disappeared. "The paint looks great."

"That was her original color. Look." He opened the

door so she could see the interior. "I finished the uphol-
stery this morning. It's like it was when she was new."

"How did you do this? I'd never know it was the
same vehicle."

"All it took was a little work." Zach didn't tell her
how he'd thought about what Pastor Bill had said to
him. How being made new meant his past didn't have
to influence his future. "I figured we all deserve a
second chance, even a car."

"You can make a lot of money selling her now."

"Got a buyer all lined up. A collector who's happy
to have it. He's coming for it this weekend."

"I'm glad."

Good, she'd managed to keep it impersonal. But it
was time to go. The last thing she wanted to do was
talk about Zach's future, a future they wouldn't share
together. "Good luck to you. I'll see you later—"

"Wait. I'm thinking of buying a new house in the
new subdivision here in town. What do you think?"

Why was he asking her about a house? Her foot
hesitated on the bottom step. "A house is always a
good investment."

"It's also a pretty smart way to start a marriage."

A marriage? Did she hear him right? Why was he
saying this to her? She couldn't afford to hope, not
anymore. She ran up the steps.

"Karen, wait!"

For what? For him to say she was a sensible woman
to marry, now that he'd thought about it. She pushed
through the front doors and the bell overhead jangled vio-
lently.

Customers turned in their chairs to stare at her. Michelle peered over the top of the cash register. Karen kept her head down and headed straight through the dining room.

The bell jingled behind her—it had to be Zach. Why was he doing this to her? Why couldn't he go find some other nice woman and settle for her?

Out of breath, Karen shouldered through the back door and onto the walkway behind the coffee shop. Maybe Zach would get sidetracked in the dining room and she'd be free of him.

The door squeaked open behind her. No such luck.

"Hey, Karen. Wait up. You're really making me work for this. I've got this pain shooting down my leg. I can't keep running, okay?"

"Then stop following me." She'd humiliated herself enough.

"What choice do I have?" He limped up to her, breathing heavily. "I've tried calling you. I've tried talking to you, but you won't stay around long enough for me to tell you how I feel."

"Zach, I can't—"

"I don't want to lose you."

She felt as if her heart were breaking all over again. "No, we can't be friends. Acquaintances, maybe, in time—"

Something glinting in the sun caught her eye—a diamond ring. Zach was holding a diamond ring.

"I wanted to show you this." He took her hand tenderly. "Do you like it?"

The diamond was pure white and oval shaped, ringed with emeralds. "It looks like an engagement ring."

"That's because it is."

He knelt down in front of her, still holding her hand.

What was he doing? He *couldn't* be about to propose. Not after what had happened. "I can't marry you. You know that."

"Karen, remember in the hospital room when you asked me if I could love you, an ordinary girl?"

How could she forget? "I thought you might see something more in me, but I was wrong."

"You weren't wrong. I was afraid to tell you the truth, and I'm sorry for that. When I look at you, I see the woman I love." He held up the ring.

But it was his love for her shining in his eyes, written on his face, tender in his voice that she noticed.

"I've decided that I *am* the man for you. The only one who can cherish you the way you deserve to be." He kissed her hand. "Please. Marry me."

"But I thought—" All she wanted was his love, deep and true. "I thought you didn't love me enough."

"How can that be? I love you with all I have and all I am. I told you before. A man doesn't settle for a woman like you. He gets lucky. Very lucky. I want to spend the rest of my life proving that to you. If you'll have this average, ordinary guy."

All the heartache melted away, and she saw the man before her, offering her his truest love—a once-in-a-lifetime gift. She knew better than to let it slip away.

She'd risk her heart one more time. "Yes. I've

wanted to marry you for the longest time. It's like a dream come true."

"*You're* my dream come true." He slipped the diamond on her finger.

It felt so right, his ring on her hand.

Zach pulled her into his arms and brushed her lips with his. She felt it in his kiss, in the beat of his heart and in the silence that surrounded them.

God had good things in store for them. This was only the beginning.

The back door opened and Michelle's shriek rose into the air. "Did he propose? I can't believe it! Gramma, come see Karen's diamond. Hurry!"

Helen dashed out the door, the two of them clamoring around Karen to look at her ring.

"You're going to have to get used to my sisters," Karen confided in him. "Maybe if we don't tell them which house we buy, they won't be able to find me."

"No good. They'd track you down. It looks like there's no way to escape them."

He loved the way she laughed, the way she fit into his arms, the way she smiled like a promise that said they'd be happy forever.

"My chances for a great-grandbaby are looking better." Gramma beamed. "Zach, welcome to the family."

* * * * *

Dear Reader,

His Hometown Girl is a story very dear to me because I always used to worry as an average and shy girl that I would never find true love. I began to believe it more and more through the years—and that God had forgotten to add romantic love into His plan for my life. Then my good friend began urging me to meet a man she worked with. Since I had my own idea about blind dates, I refused over and over again. Finally I relented. What a surprise. That one dinner changed my life. I learned that God hadn't forgotten me—He'd just been saving the best for last.

I wish you the best and more.

Jillian Hart

REQUEST YOUR FREE BOOKS!

2 FREE INSPIRATIONAL NOVELS
PLUS 2
FREE
MYSTERY GIFTS

Love Inspired.

YES! Please send me 2 FREE Love Inspired® novels and my 2 FREE mystery gifts (gifts are worth about $10). After receiving them, if I don't wish to receive any more books, I can return the shipping statement marked "cancel". If I don't cancel, I will receive 4 brand-new novels every month and be billed just $4.24 per book in the U.S. or $4.74 per book in Canada, plus 25¢ shipping and handling per book and applicable taxes, if any*. That's a savings of over 20% off the cover price! I understand that accepting the 2 free books and gifts places me under no obligation to buy anything. I can always return a shipment and cancel at any time. Even if I never buy another book, the two free books and gifts are mine to keep forever.

113 IDN ERXA   313 IDN ERWX

Name _____ (PLEASE PRINT)

Address _____ Apt. #

City _____ State/Prov. _____ Zip/Postal Code

Signature (if under 18, a parent or guardian must sign)

Order online at www.LoveInspiredBooks.com

Or mail to Steeple Hill Reader Service:

IN U.S.A.: P.O. Box 1867, Buffalo, NY 14240-1867
IN CANADA: P.O. Box 609, Fort Erie, Ontario L2A 5X3

Not valid to current subscribers of Love Inspired books.

Want to try two free books from another series?
Call 1-800-873-8635 or visit www.morefreebooks.com

* Terms and prices subject to change without notice. N.Y. residents add applicable sales tax. Canadian residents will be charged applicable provincial taxes and GST. This offer is limited to one order per household. All orders subject to approval. Credit or debit balances in a customer's account(s) may be offset by any other outstanding balance owed by or to the customer. Please allow 4 to 6 weeks for delivery. Offer available while quantities last.

Your Privacy: Steeple Hill Books is committed to protecting your privacy. Our Privacy Policy is available online at www.SteepleHill.com or upon request from the Reader Service. From time to time we make our lists of customers available to reputable third parties who may have a product or service of interest to you. If you would prefer we not share your name and address, please check here. ☐

LIREG08

Love Inspired.
HISTORICAL
INSPIRATIONAL HISTORICAL ROMANCE

The Long Way Home

In the depths of the Depression, young widow Kate Bradshaw was struggling to hold on to the family farm and raise two small children. She had only her faith to sustain her—until the day drifter Hatcher Jones came walking up that long, lonely road. She longed to make him see that all his wandering had brought him home at last.

Look for

The Road to Love

by

LINDA FORD

Available May wherever books are sold.

Steeple
Hill®

www.SteepleHill.com

LIH82787

Love Inspired SUSPENSE
RIVETING INSPIRATIONAL ROMANCE

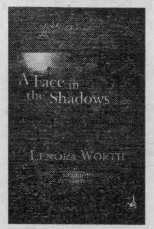

DID HE KILL JOSIE SKERRITT?

Everyone—including the police—suspected Parker Buchanan of murder. But Kate Brooks knew the brooding loner couldn't have done it. And she knew proving his innocence would take all their faith—and fast thinking—combined. Because the real killer was setting them up for a double murder...their own.

REUNION REVELATIONS

Secrets surface when old friends— and foes—get together.

Look for
A Face in the Shadows
by LENORA WORTH

Available May wherever books are sold.

Steeple Hill®

Independent bachelor no more...

Three foster kids fell into businessman Noah Maxwell's lap and shattered his orderly life. He hired single mom Cara Winters to help care for his new brood, but she sensed that his confident facade hid old wounds. Perhaps her love could inspire Noah to relinquish his independence, and give Cara and the children the fairy-tale ending they all deserved.

Fostered by Love:
A family guided them to faith, but only love could heal their hearts.

Look for

Family Ever After

by

Margaret Daley

*Available May
wherever books are sold.*

www.SteepleHill.com

Steeple
Hill®

LI87480